SPARTACUS: REBELLION

Also by Ben Kane

Spartacus: The Gladiator

Hannibal: Enemy of Rome

The Forgotten Legion Trilogy
The Forgotten Legion
The Silver Eagle
The Road to Rome

Spartacus: Rebellion

BEN KANE

preface

Published by Preface 2012

10 9 8 7 6 5 4 3 2 1

Copyright © Ben Kane 2012

Ben Kane has asserted his right to be identified as the author of this work under the
Copyright, Designs and Patents Act 1988

First published in Great Britain in 2012 by Preface Publishing

20 Vauxhall Bridge Road
London, SW1V 2SA

An imprint of The Random House Group Limited

www.randomhouse.co.uk
www.prefacepublishing.co.uk

Addresses for companies within The Random House Group Limited
can be found at www.randomhouse.co.uk

The Random House Group Limited Reg. No. 954009

A CIP catalogue record for this book is available from the British Library

ISBN Hardback 978 1 84809 231 0
ISBN Trade Paperback 978 1 84809 233 4

The Random House Group Limited supports The Forest Stewardship Council (FSC®), the
leading international forest certification organisation. Our books carrying the FSC label are
printed on FSC® certified paper. FSC is the only forest certification scheme endorsed by the
leading environmental organisations, including Greenpeace. Our paper procurement policy can
be found at www.randomhouse.co.uk/environment

MIX
Paper from
responsible sources
FSC
www.fsc.org   FSC® C016897

Typeset in Fournier MT by Palimpsest Book Production Limited
Falkirk, Stirlingshire

Printed and bound in Great Britain by Clays Ltd, St Ives plc

For Colm and Shane, oldest of friends, and the two
finest products of 'de town, hey!'

Republican Italy in the first century BC

ALPS

CISALPINE GAUL

Placentia

R. Padus

Mutina

ITALIA

Via Aemilia

Ariminum

ILLYRIA

Pisae

ETRURIA

Apennines

PICENUM

Adriatic Sea

CORSICA

Rome

LATIUM

SAMNIUM

Via Appia

Capua

Venusia

Via Appia

APULIA

Brundisium

CAMPANIA

Pompeii

LUCANIA

Metapontum

SARDINIA

Thurii

Tyrrhenian Sea

Via Annia

BRUTTIUM

Ionian Sea

Messana

Rhegium

MARE

SICILY

INTERNUM

AFRICA

0	50	100	150	200 miles
0	100		200	300 km

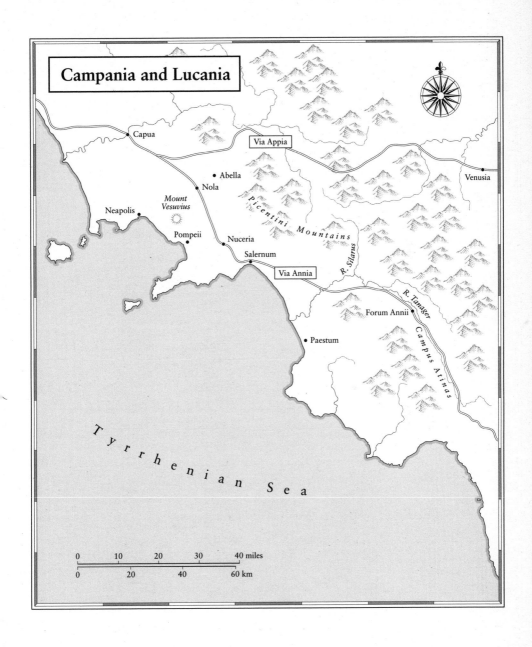

Campania and Lucania

Prologue

Mount Garganus, east coast of Italy, spring 72 BC

The furious thrumming of blood in his ears dimmed the cacophony of battlefield noises: the screams of the wounded and maimed, the shouts of his bravest followers and the moans of his most fearful. Despite the awful clamour and his ravening anger – against the Romans, against the gods, against what had happened thus far that morning – the big man's attention was all on the enemy lines, some hundred paces distant. Every fibre of his being wanted to charge up the rocky slope again, and hack as many of the massed legionaries into bloody chunks as he could. *Calm down. If we're to have any chance of succeeding, the men need time to recover their strength. They need to be rallied.*

The blaring of *bucinae* shredded the air, and he scowled. The trumpets were ordering consul Gellius' two legions to regroup. He breathed deeply, focusing on the metallic clatter of the enemy soldiers' swords off their shields as they taunted his men, trying to provoke them into another fruitless attack uphill. The pathetic response of the few warriors left with voice enough to shout was infuriating.

It was no wonder their throats were raw. He was parched with thirst himself. The fighting had begun two hours after dawn, and had only stopped as each of their three previous assaults was repulsed. There had been no chance of relocating the water bag that he'd left on the ground by his initial position. He didn't begrudge the man who'd found it. As a consequence, he was in the same situation as most of his followers. A quick glance at the sun's position in the blue sky told him that it was close to midday. *Three hours' combat with no water. It's as well that it is not summer, or half the army would have collapsed by now.* Another sour smile creased his broad face.

I

Much of his army lay dead or wounded on the crimson-coated ground before him. *What need have they of water?*

The area between the two hosts – a slope free of the peak's covering of holm oak, turpentine trees and buckthorn bushes – was festooned with the dead. The thousands of mutilated corpses would provide weeks' worth of pickings for the sharp-eyed vultures that already hung far overhead. Most of the fallen lay near the Roman lines. They lay so deeply in some spots that his men had been forced in subsequent attacks to clamber over the bodies, making them easy targets for the volleys of Roman javelins. Those who had not been cut down by the sky-blackening showers of *pila* had been halted by the legionaries' *gladii*. The deadly double-edged swords had thrust out from the impregnable wall of shields, slicing men's guts to ribbons, hacking off their legs or arms, running deep into their unprotected chests. He'd even seen some of his followers lose their heads.

In spite of their horrific casualties, they had broken through in a few places during the first frenzied attack. His memory of that small success soured in a heartbeat. All but one of their breaches – his – had quickly been repaired. His men's lack of armour and shields, and the legionaries' discipline and height advantage, had made the slaves easy targets. Seeing his men being butchered like sheep in a slaughterhouse, he had ordered the retreat. Had given up his own brutal assault which had so nearly smashed through the first Roman line.

For all the good it would have done. One breach of the enemy ranks doesn't win a battle. What does is holding one's position. Remaining disciplined. It was a harsh lesson for a Gaul. Although he had been born a slave, he'd grown up listening to tales of the terror-inducing charges by his forebears, men who had defeated Roman legions on numerous occasions, whose bravery had carried so many enemies before them. That tactic had failed miserably today.

He caught sight of a rider in a burnished helmet and scarlet cloak moving to and fro behind the centre of the Roman lines. He spat a bitter curse. *Gellius might be old for a consul, but he picked his ground well. It was foolish to let him steal a march on us and take the high ground. Foolish to rely on the fact that my forces outnumbered his by more than two to one.* The first feelings of despair stole into his mind, but he shoved them away with another oath. If he gathered the best of his men together, perhaps they could break through. If they slew the consul, the Romans would surely turn and run. The tide of battle could yet be changed.

'Come on, lads! There are still more of us than them,' he roared. 'One last effort! Let's make one final charge. If we kill that whoreson Gellius, the day will be ours. Who's with me?'

Only a score or so of voices answered him.

He ripped his bronze-bowl helmet from his head and threw it to the ground. 'Piece of Roman shit.' Striding forward some thirty paces from the disorganised mass of men, still some ten to twelve thousand strong, he turned so that they could all see his face. He was now within range of a long javelin throw. His mail shirt would probably turn away the point, he thought, but he didn't really care if it did or not. The pain would be welcome, would help him to focus his rage. 'HEY! I'm talking to you!'

Hundreds of desperate, blood-stained faces fixed him with their stares. In their eyes, he saw defeat. He didn't feel afraid. Even if they failed now, the Romans couldn't take his end from him. Dying in battle was all that he'd ever wanted. Granted, it would have been better to do it knowing that his men had beaten Gellius, but he was still a free man, and he would die that way, taking plenty of Romans with him.

Clash, clash, clash went his sword off the metal rim of his *scutum*. Men who were standing out of earshot edged closer. 'Now you listen to me,' he shouted. 'Three times we've charged them, and three times we've failed. Thousands of our comrades lie up there, dead or dying. Their bravery, their blood and their lives demand revenge. REVENGE!' *Clash, clash, clash* on the shield. 'REVENGE!'

There was a whirring noise in the air behind him. Despite his courage, his skin crawled. *Someone's thrown a pilum.* He didn't budge. 'REVENGE!' *Thump.* He glanced to his right, taking in the javelin that had buried itself in the earth not five paces from his foot. He threw back his head and howled like a wolf. 'Is that the best they can do? The stinking Roman bastards couldn't hit a pile of wheat in a grain shed!'

His men – at least those nearest him – looked more heartened.

Good. They're not done yet. 'I'm going up there, and I'm going to tear those bastards into little pieces. I'm going to hew Gellius' head from his scrawny fucking neck, and then I'm going to laugh as his army runs away.' His badly scarred nose and the Roman blood covering him from head to foot reduced his encouraging stare to a monster's ravening leer, but the passion in his voice couldn't be mistaken. 'Who's with me? Who's with Crixus?'

'I am!' cried a Gaul with long braids of hair.

'And me!' bellowed a bull-necked man in a torn tunic.

More and more voices joined in. 'CRIX-US! CRIX-US!' they cried and, grinning, he clattered his longsword off his scutum in reply. The fearful mood that had hung over the slaves vanished. But their new-found bravery wouldn't last. Crixus knew that. If they were going to succeed, they had to move at once. Turning to face the Romans, he screamed, 'Come on then, boys! Let's show them what courage means!' Without looking back, he tore up the hill like a man possessed.

Roaring like maddened bulls, hundreds and hundreds of slaves followed.

Many more did not, however. They stayed put, mutely watching their comrades charge at the Roman lines. Preparing to run for the dense cover formed by the bushes and trees on the slopes below.

Crixus sensed the presence of his men at his back. He could tell that not everyone had joined in, but a warm glow filled him nonetheless. *At least we'll die well. There will be places in the warrior's paradise for us all.* One last thought struck before the battle madness took hold and reason left him.

Maybe Spartacus was right. Maybe I should have stayed.

Chapter I

A month later . . .
The Apennine Mountains, north-east of Pisae

S partacus looked out over the flat ground at Gellius' legions, and then back at his own. Even though he was some hundred paces from the centre of his front ranks, he could feel his men's confidence. It oozed from their very stance and the way their lines were swaying back and forth. Their weapons smacked off their shields, challenging the Romans to fight. They were eager, even desperate to begin the combat. *It is a remarkable change.* Until recently, his followers – the vast majority of them former slaves – had never fought a full-scale battle. Yes, they had defeated the forces of three praetors, but those clashes had been won in the main by subterfuge. They had never faced a large Roman army on open terrain, let alone a consular one of two legions. Two months previously, all that had changed when they had ambushed the consul Lentulus in a defile to the south of their present position.

Thanks to their succession of victories, the majority of his men were now as well equipped as the heavily armed legionaries. Pride filled him. *How far they have come.* He pictured the day a year and a half before when he'd been betrayed in his own village in Thrace and sold into slavery, his fate to die in an Italian gladiatorial arena. *How far I have come. A Thracian warrior who fought for Rome, but who now leads an army of former slaves against it.* It was ironic.

Striding closer to his soldiers, Spartacus caught the eye of a broad-shouldered man whose pleasant face was marred by a purple scar on his left cheek. *One of the very first slaves to join us after we escaped from the ludus.* 'I see you, Aventianus! What hope have the Romans today, d'you think?'

Aventianus grinned. 'Not a snowflake's chance in Hades, sir.'

'That's what I want to hear.' Spartacus had long since given up telling his men not to address him so. It made no difference. He scanned the faces of those nearest him. 'Is Aventianus right, lads? Or will Gellius chase us home with our tails between our legs?'

'We have no homes!' roared Pulcher, Spartacus' main armourer and one of his senior officers. A burst of ribald laughter met his comment. He waited until the noise died down. 'But we have something far better than roofs over our heads. Something that no one can ever take away. Our freedom!'

'Free-dom! Free-dom! Free-dom!' the men yelled, stamping their feet and hammering their weapons off their shields again. It made a deafening, stirring rhythm. The clamour began to spread through Spartacus' host. Most soldiers were too far away to know the reason for the uproar, but they didn't care. Soon the din made speech impossible. 'Free-dom! Free-dom! Free-dom!'

Relishing the cries of nearly fifty thousand men, and the fact that he was their leader, Spartacus encouraged them with great waves of his arms. The uproar would raise their morale even higher, and create unease in plenty of Roman bellies. He did not doubt that it would send a tickle of fear up the skin of Gellius' wrinkled back. The consul was sixty-two years old, and reportedly had little experience of war.

'We'll smash the bastards into little pieces,' cried Pulcher when the cheering had abated. 'The same way we sent Lentulus and his lot packing!' Right on cue, the men holding the pair of silver eagles raised their wooden poles aloft. More shouting erupted.

Spartacus raised his hands, and a hush fell. 'There are two more of those to be had today!' He drew his *sica*, a wickedly curved Thracian sword, and stabbed it at the places in Gellius' forces where bright sunlight flashed off his legions' metal standards. 'Who wants to help me take them? Who wants the glory of saying that he took a Roman eagle in battle and, by doing so, shamed an entire legion?'

'Me!' roared Aventianus and a multitude of other voices.

'Are you sure?'

'YESSS!' they bellowed at him.

'You'd better be. Look at that lot.' Spartacus swept his blade first to the left, and then to the right. On both fringes of his army, hundreds of men on shaggy mountain horses could be seen. 'You'd better be sure,' he repeated. 'If we're not careful, the cavalry might get there before us.' Part of Spartacus longed to be with them. He had been a cavalryman from the age of sixteen; he had also helped to train the horsemen, but he knew that his presence in the centre of his host was vital. If his foot soldiers broke, complete defeat beckoned. Although his riders' task was huge, they outnumbered the Roman horse at least four to one. Even if – by some misfortune – they failed to rout the enemy cavalry, his infantry could still win the battle. 'Are you going to let that happen?'

'Never!' roared Pulcher, the veins standing out in his neck.

'Not if I have anything to do with it!' shouted Aventianus, jabbing his pilum back and forth.

'And me!' Carbo, who was Roman, was still surprised by the passion he felt when the Thracian spoke. About a year before, he had entered the gladiator school in Capua in a madcap attempt to pay off his family's huge debts. In his desperation, he'd first tried to join the army, but had been turned down due to his youth. To Carbo's surprise, he'd been accepted by the *lanista* as an *auctoratus*, a citizen who contracted to fight as a gladiator, but only after his courage had been tested by fighting Spartacus in a contest with wooden weapons.

Life in the ludus had been unbelievably tough, and not just because of the training. One man alone, especially a rookie, had little hope of surviving on his own. If Spartacus hadn't taken him under his wing, Carbo's career in the ludus would have been short indeed. When the chance came to escape soon afterwards, he had followed his protector. Subsequently given the unthinkable choice between leaving the motley group of slaves and gladiators or staying to fight his own countrymen, Carbo had opted for the latter. He hadn't known what else to do.

In the ensuing months, Spartacus' actions had earned Carbo's loyalty – and even love. The Thracian looked out for him. Cared for him. That was more than his own people had been prepared to do. This bitter pill had made it easier to fight against his own kind, but deep down, Carbo still felt some guilt at doing so. He regarded Gellius' lines with a clenched jaw. It's just another army to be swept aside, he told himself. Beyond them lie the Alps. Spartacus' plan was to lead them over the mountains, away from the Republic's influence. There any enemies they encountered would be foreign to him. And, if he had to admit it, easier to kill.

Before that, they had Gellius to defeat. He thought of Crassus, the man who had ruined his family and shattered his life. Hate surged through Carbo, made all the stronger by the knowledge that he'd never be revenged on the richest man in Rome. Instead he tried imagining that all the men opposite were related to the crafty politician. It helped.

His gaze was drawn back to the compact figure of Spartacus, clad in a polished mail shirt, gilded baldric and magnificent Phrygian helmet. To Carbo's surprise, the Thracian's piercing grey eyes caught his. Spartacus gave him a tiny nod, as if to say, 'I'm glad that you're here.' Carbo's shoulders went back. *I'll do what I have to today.*

Spartacus was making an appraisal of his men's mood. What he saw was pleasing. Organised into centuries and cohorts, trained and armed like the Romans, they were ready. He was ready. Here was another chance to shed Roman blood. To seize more vengeance for Maron, his brother who had died fighting the legions. The legions that had laid waste to their homeland, Thrace. *I might yet see it again. Gellius and his men are about all that stand in the way.* He half smiled. Kotys, the malevolent king of Spartacus' tribe, the Maedi, and the reason for his enslavement, would get the shock of his life when he returned. *I can't wait.* Spartacus placed the brass whistle that hung from a thong around his neck to his lips. When he blew, signalling the advance, the trumpeters would let the entire army know.

His plan was simple. He had arrayed his soldiers in two deep lines about thirty paces apart. Castus was in charge of the left wing: a Gaulish gladiator who had aided Spartacus in their escape; short, stubborn and with a temperament as fiery as his red hair. Gannicus, another Gaul from the ludus, commanded the right; he was as strong-willed as Castus, but more even-tempered, and Spartacus had more in common with him. At his signal, they would all move forward in one great bloc and, after throwing volleys of javelins, engage the Romans head on. If things went well, their superior numbers and high morale would quickly allow them to envelop Gellius' legions. This while their cavalry swept away the enemy horse and then took the legionaries in the rear. The Romans' defeat would be total, their casualties far higher than in any of the previous encounters.

By sunset, Rome will have learned another lesson. Great Rider, grant that it be so. Watch over us all in the hours to come, Spartacus prayed. Dionysus, lend us the strength of your maenads. While the Thracian hero god was his main guide in life, he had also learned to revere the deity associated with wine, intoxication and religious mania, whom his wife Ariadne worshipped. His remarkable dream, in which a venomous snake had wrapped itself around his neck, had marked him out as one of Dionysus' own. *May it always be thus.*

He filled his lungs and prepared to blow.

Tan-tara-tara-tara went the Roman bucinae.

Spartacus held his breath, waiting for the legions to advance.

The enemy trumpets sounded again, but nothing else happened.

What the hell is Gellius playing at?

To his surprise, a horseman emerged from a gap in the centre of the Roman line. Not a legionary stirred as he guided his mount straight at Spartacus.

Spartacus' men were so keen to begin the fight that few noticed.

'Let's be having them!' shouted Pulcher to a roar of approval.

'Stay where you are!' ordered Spartacus. 'Gellius has something to say. A messenger comes.'

'What do we care?' cried a voice from the ranks. 'It's time to kill!'

'You won't lose that opportunity. But I want to hear the rider's message.' Spartacus gave his men a granite-hard stare. 'The first fool who moves a muscle or throws a javelin will answer to me. Clear?'

'Yes,' came the muted reply.

'I can't hear you!'

'YES!'

Spartacus watched the approaching horseman. *I don't like it.* Fortunately, he didn't have time to brood. Less than a quarter of a mile separated the two armies. As the Roman drew near, he slowed his horse, a fine chestnut, to a walk. He appeared unarmed. Spartacus noted his polished bronze cuirass, scarlet crested helmet and confident posture. This was a senior officer, probably a tribune, one of the six experienced men who assisted

9

the consul in commanding each legion. 'That's close enough,' he called out when the envoy was twenty paces away.

Raising his right hand in a peaceful gesture, the Roman walked his mount several steps closer.

'Don't trust the bastard!' shouted Aventianus.

The Roman smiled.

Spartacus lifted his sica menacingly. 'Come any nearer and I'll send you to Hades.'

There was no acknowledgement, but at last the Roman tugged hard on his reins. 'I am Sextus Baculus, tribune of the Third Legion. And you are?' His tone couldn't have been more patronising.

'You know who I am. If you don't, you're a bigger sack of shit than you look.'

Spartacus' men jeered with delight.

Baculus' face went bright red, and he bit back an angry response. 'I have been sent by Lucius Gellius, consul of Rome. I—'

'We met his colleague Lentulus a few weeks back,' Spartacus interrupted. 'Did you hear about that little encounter?'

More gleeful cheers erupted. Baculus' mount's ears went back, and it skittered from side to side. The tribune regained control of it with a muttered curse. 'You and this rabble of yours will pay dearly for that day,' he snapped.

'Will we indeed?'

'I am not here to bandy words with slaves—'

'Slaves?' Spartacus twisted his head around. 'I see no slaves here. Only free men.'

The roar that went up this time was three times as loud as before.

'Listen to me, you Thracian savage,' hissed Baculus. He lifted his left hand, which had been held down by his side. Drawing back his arm, he tossed a leather bag at Spartacus. 'A present from Lucius Gellius and Quintus Arrius, his propraetor,' he cried as it flew through the air.

Spartacus didn't like the meaty *thump* that the sack made as it landed by his feet, or the faint stench that reached his nostrils. He made no move to pick it up. He had an idea of what might be inside. A number of his scouts had gone missing over the previous weeks; he'd assumed that they had been captured by the Romans. *Which one is this, I wonder? Poor bastard. He won't have had an easy death.*

'Go on, take a look,' Baculus sneered. 'We've kept them packed in salt especially for you.'

Not a scout then. I know who it is. 'Have you anything else to say?'

'It can wait.'

'You arrogant prick.' The bag wasn't tied shut, so Spartacus upended it. He wasn't surprised that the first thing to fall out was a severed head, but didn't expect the man's hand that followed. Spartacus took in the blood-spattered blond hair, and his guts wrenched. He rolled over the head, which was partly putrefied. Granules of salt stuck to the eyeballs, the slack grey lips and the reddened stump of the neck. The once-handsome features were barely recognisable, but it was Crixus. There could be no doubt. The massive scar on the man's nose was sufficient proof. Spartacus had inflicted the wound on the Gaul himself. Their fight had been inevitable from the first time they'd met – and disliked – each other. Yet he was still sorry to see Crixus dead.

After they had fought, and Spartacus had defeated Crixus, the Gaul and his followers had joined him. They had played a big part in their escape from the ludus. A dangerous and aggressive fighter, Crixus had been a thorn in Spartacus' side, questioning his leadership and constantly trying to gain Castus' and Gannicus' support. Crixus had broken away from the main army after a battle at Thurii in which they had vanquished the praetor Publius Varinius. Between twenty and thirty thousand men had gone with him. Spartacus had heard rumours since of their progress through central Italy, but had had no further contact. Until now. This grisly trophy didn't bode well for the fate of the men who had followed Crixus, but Spartacus kept his face impassive. 'He didn't deserve to be treated like this.'

'Did he not?' cried Baculus. 'Crixus' – he smiled at the shocked reactions of Spartacus' men – 'yes, that's who it is. Crixus was nothing but a murdering slave who maimed brave Roman soldiers for no good reason. He deserved everything that was done to him and more.'

Spartacus remembered how Crixus had ordered the hands of more than twenty legionaries at Thurii to be amputated. He had been disgusted but unsurprised by the Gaul's act. *The Romans wouldn't forgive – or forget – such a deed.* 'You did this to his corpse! Crixus would never have been taken alive,' he shouted. His inclination was to slay Baculus on the spot, to prevent him from delivering his message, but the man was an envoy, and brave too. It had taken balls to ride up to his army, alone and unarmed.

'Crixus went to Hades knowing that more than two-thirds of the scum who trailed in his wake had died with him,' announced Baculus. He raised his voice. 'Do you hear me, you whoresons? Crixus is dead! DEAD! So are more than fifteen thousand of his followers! One in ten of the prisoners that we took had their right hands chopped off. Be certain that one of those fates awaits you all here today!'

After hearing the name 'Crixus', Carbo was deaf to the rest of Baculus' threats. His world had just closed in around him. *Crixus is dead? Jupiter be thanked. Dionysus be thanked!* This had been one of his most fervent prayers; one that he had thought would never be answered. At the sack of a town called Forum Annii some months before, Crixus and two of his cronies had raped Chloris, Carbo's woman. Spartacus had helped to save her, but she had died of her injuries a few hours later. Incandescent with grief, Carbo had been set on killing Crixus, but Spartacus had asked him to swear that he would not. At the time the Gaul had still been a vital leader of part of the slave army. It was a request that Carbo had reluctantly agreed to.

Yet when Crixus had announced that he was leaving, thereby releasing Carbo from his promise, he had done nothing – because the Gaul would have carved him into little pieces. Telling himself that Chloris would have wanted him to live had worked thus far, but staring at Crixus' rotting head, Carbo knew that he'd simply been scared of dying. The immense satisfaction that he now felt, however, outweighed any concerns that he had about being slain in the impending battle. *The whoreson died aware that he failed – that's what matters.*

Spartacus could tell without looking the level of dismay that Crixus' head and Baculus' news had caused among his men. He raised his sica and moved towards the tribune. 'Fuck off. Tell Gellius that I'm coming for him! And you.'

'We'll be ready. So will our legions,' Baculus replied stoutly. He cupped a hand to his mouth. 'My men are hungry for battle! They will slaughter you in your thousands, *slaves!*'

Spartacus darted in and dealt Baculus' steed a great slap across its rump with the flat of his blade. It leaped forward so suddenly that the tribune almost lost his seat. Cursing, he sawed on the reins and managed to bring it under control again. Spartacus jabbed his sica at him. With a glare, Baculus turned his mount's head towards his own lines.

'Count yourself lucky that I honour your status,' Spartacus shouted.

Stiff-backed, Baculus rode silently away. He did not look back.

Spartacus spat after him. *I hope they're not all as brave as he.* Putting Baculus from his mind, he turned to his men. Fear was written large on many faces. Most looked less confident. An uneasy silence had replaced the raucous cheering and weapon clashing. It was changes in mood like this that could lose a battle: Spartacus had seen it before. *I have to act fast.* Stooping, he picked up Crixus' mangled head and brandished it at his soldiers. 'Everyone knows that Crixus and I didn't get on.'

'That's putting it mildly,' shouted Pulcher.

This raised a laugh.

Good. 'While we weren't friends, I respected Crixus' courage and his leadership. I respected the men who chose to leave with him. Seeing this' – he held Crixus' head high – 'and knowing what happened to our comrades makes me angry. Very angry!'

A rumbling, inarticulate roar met his words.

'Do you want vengeance for Crixus? Vengeance for our dead brothers-in-arms?'

'YES!' they bellowed back at him.

'VENGE-ANCE!' Spartacus twisted to point his sica at the legions. 'VENGE-ANCE!'

'VENGE-ANCE!'

He let them roar their fury for the space of twenty heartbeats. Happy then that their courage had steadied, he blew his whistle with all of his might. The sound didn't carry that far, but the well-trained trumpeters were watching him. A series of blasts from their instruments put an abrupt end to the shouting.

Spartacus shoved Crixus' head and hand back into the bag. If he left the remains where they were, he'd never find them again. Crixus – or at least these parts of him – deserved a decent burial. He tied the heavy sack to his belt and asked the Great Rider not to let it hinder him in the fight to come. With that, he resumed his place in the front rank. Smiling grimly, Aventianus handed him his scutum and pilum. Carbo, together with Navio, the Roman veteran he'd recruited to their cause, nodded their readiness.

Taxacis, one of two Scythians who, unasked, had become his bodyguards, bared his teeth in a silent snarl. 'Forward!' shouted Spartacus. 'Keep in line with your comrades. Maintain the gaps between ranks.'

They moved forward in unison, thousands of feet tramping down the short spring grass. On the wings, Spartacus' cavalry whooped and cheered, urging their horses from a walk into a trot. 'Gellius' riders will be pissing their pants at the sight of that lot,' cried Spartacus. His nearest men cheered, but then the Roman bucinae sounded. The legionaries were advancing.

'Steady, lads. Ready javelins. We throw at thirty paces, no more.' Spartacus' stomach twisted in an old and familiar way. He'd felt the same mix of emotions before every battle that he'd ever fought. A snaking trace of fear that he wouldn't survive. The uplifting thrill of marching side by side with his comrades. Pride that they were men who would die for him in an instant – as he'd do for them. He gloried in the smells of sweat and oiled leather, the muttered prayers and requests of the gods, the clash of javelins off shields. He gave thanks to the Great Rider for another opportunity to wreak havoc on the forces of Rome, which had repeatedly sent its armies to Thrace, where they had defeated most of the tribes, laid waste to innumerable villages and killed his people in their thousands.

Before he'd been betrayed and sold into slavery, Spartacus' plan had been to unite the disparate groupings of Thracians and throw the legions off their land for ever. In the ludus, such ideas had been nothing more than fantasy, but life had changed the day he and seventy-two others had smashed their way to freedom. Spartacus' heart pounded with anticipation. He had proved that almost anything was possible. After Gellius' soldiers had been defeated, the road to the Alps lay open.

He squinted at the line of approaching legionaries, now making out individual men's features. 'Fifty paces! Do not loose! Wait until I give the order.'

Several javelins were hurled from the Roman ranks. Scores more followed. The enraged shouts of centurions ordering their soldiers to cease throwing could be heard as the pila thwacked harmlessly into the earth between the two armies. Spartacus laughed. Only a handful of his men had responded by launching their own missiles. 'See that? The Roman dogs are nervous!'

Cheers rose from his troops.

Tramp, tramp, tramp.

Sweat slicked down Carbo's forehead and into his eyes. He blinked it away, focusing his gaze on a legionary directly opposite him. The soldier was young – similar in age to him in fact – and his smooth-cheeked face bore an expression of unbridled fear. Carbo hardened his heart. *He chose his side. I chose mine. The gods will decide which of us survives.* Carbo steadied his right arm, making sure that his javelin was balanced. He took aim at the legionary.

'Forty paces,' Spartacus called out. 'Hold steady!' He selected his target, the nearest centurion in the Roman front rank. If by some good fortune the officer went down, resistance in that section of the line would falter or even crumble. He frowned. Why hadn't the legionaries thrown their pila yet? *Gellius must have ordered his soldiers not to act until the last moment. A risky tactic.*

Thirty-five paces. With increasing excitement, Spartacus counted down the last five steps and then roared, 'Front three ranks, loose!' Drawing back his right arm, he heaved his javelin up into the blue sky. Hundreds of pila joined it, forming a dense, fast-moving shoal that briefly darkened the air between the armies before it descended in a lethal rain of sharp metal. The Roman officers roared at their men, ordering them to raise their shields. Spartacus' lips peeled up with satisfaction as he watched. Slow. They were too slow. His men's javelins hammered down, rendering scores of *scuta* unusable, but also plunging deep into the flesh of legionaries who hadn't obeyed orders fast enough. It was rare for javelin volleys to be so effective. *Seize the chance.* 'Throw your second pilum,' he yelled. The instant that those missiles had been thrown, 'Front three ranks, drop to one knee.' He glanced to either side, and was pleased to see that the nearest officers were copying his command. The trumpeters quickly relayed the order along the line. 'Ranks four, five and six, ready javelins. On my order – RELEASE!'

A third shower of pila went soaring up in a low, curving arc. To his left and right, countless more missiles joined them. Spartacus could not see any Roman javelins being thrown in response. The legionaries were in considerable disarray. With luck, his cavalry were causing mayhem on the flanks. Burning hope filled him, and he ordered a fourth volley. 'On your feet! Draw swords. Close order!'

Smoothly, his men in the front ranks moved to stand shoulder to shoulder. They slammed their shields off one another while the soldiers in the subsequent rows ran in right behind, using their scuta to strengthen the line.

The instant that they were ready, Spartacus roared, 'CHARGE!'

In a screaming mass, they thundered towards the Romans. An occasional javelin scudded at them, but there was no concerted response. Spartacus had seen his pilum strike the centurion in the chest, punching him backwards on to the shield of the man behind. He had no idea where his second javelin had gone, but that didn't matter. What mattered was hitting the Romans as hard as was humanly possible. They covered the last few steps in a blur. Time lost all meaning for Spartacus. He stuck close to the soldiers on either side of him; tried not to lose his footing; killed or disabled his opponents in the swiftest ways he could. At times the swinging bag containing Crixus' head and hand threatened to unbalance him, but Spartacus learned to anticipate its movements. His burden fed his rage, his hatred of Rome. *Crixus and his men must be avenged.*

He fought on. Punch with the shield boss; watch his enemy pull his head back in reflex. Stab him in the throat. Lift the shield to avoid the hot wash of blood that jetted as he withdrew his sica. Check left and right to make sure his comrades were all right. Search for a new target. Thrust him through the belly. Watch him crumple in agony. Brace with the scutum. Rip the sword free. Step over the shrieking mess that had been a man. Scream like a maniac. Parry a legionary's frantic hack with his shield. Slide his blade over the top of the other's scutum, taking him straight in the mouth. Hear the choking scream of agony cut short. Feel the iron catch in the Roman's neck bones. Watch the light in his eyes go out like a snuffed lamp. Push forward. Kill another soldier. Tread on his corpse. Look for another enemy to slay. And another.

On and on it went.

Suddenly, there were no more legionaries facing him.

Spartacus scowled. His bloodlust was not even close to sated. He became aware of someone shouting in his ear. Bemused, he turned his head and recognised Taxacis' squashed nose. 'Eh?'

'Romans . . . run.'

The red mist coating Spartacus' vision began to recede. 'They're running?'

Taxacis laughed. 'Yes. Look!'

This time what Spartacus saw made sense. The entire centre of Gellius' line had given way, and was fleeing the field. Hundreds of legionaries lay all around them, dead, dying or screaming from the agony of their wounds. Discarded weapons and shields littered the area. The consul had vanished. Here and there, however, small pockets of his men fought on. Often they were defending a standard, but their heroic efforts made little difference to the yelling hordes of Spartacus' soldiers who surrounded them. To either side, the legions were holding, but that wouldn't be the case for long, he saw. Already his horsemen were in sight to the rear of the Roman position, which meant that the enemy cavalry had been driven off. Gellius' flanks would not withstand a charge from behind. No troops in the world could do that. 'We've won,' he said slowly. 'Again.'

'Thanks to you!' Taxacis clouted him on the back. Spartacus could see the awe in his eyes. 'You not just . . . good general. You also fine . . . warrior. Romans thought . . . a demon had come.' Grinning fiercely, he raised a fist in the air. 'SPAR-TA-CUS!'

Every man within earshot took up the refrain.

'SPAR-TA-CUS! SPAR-TA-CUS! SPAR-TA-CUS!'

Spartacus' euphoria faded a little as he remembered those who had died to bring them to this point. Seuthes and Getas, his Thracian brothers-in-arms. Oenomaus, the charismatic German who had been first to lend his support when Spartacus had come up with the idea of escaping the ludus. Hundreds upon hundreds of men whose names he didn't even know. *I shall always honour you.* He looked down at the bag suspended from his waist. *Even you.* 'We must not forget Crixus, and all of his followers who died.'

'Crixus was . . . bastard,' growled Taxacis, 'but he was . . . brave bastard.'

'He was,' agreed Spartacus. He glanced at the nearest group of legionaries, who had thrown down their arms and were trying to surrender. Few were succeeding. Normally he wouldn't have cared, but inspiration struck. 'Spare their lives,' he shouted. 'Gather the men who wish to yield, and bring them to our camp.'

Taxacis threw him a confused look.

'You'll see later.' Spartacus did not elaborate. The plan was still taking shape in his mind.

From the moment that Spartacus had led his army out of the vast camp that morning, Ariadne had kept herself busy. First she had sacrificed a cock to Dionysus, promising the god the further offering of a fine bull if her husband emerged unscathed – and victorious – from the impending battle. Ariadne had made no attempt to enter the trance-like state that sometimes allowed her to commune with Dionysus. Years as a priestess had taught her never to expect insight or a vision when it really mattered. The god whom she followed was even more fickle than his fellow deities. Her best policy once she had made her requests of him was to occupy her mind with other matters.

There was no chance of watching the battle. Unsurprisingly, Spartacus had forbidden it, and the constant presence of Atheas, the second of his Scythians, meant that any attempt to disobey him would meet with swift failure. Yet she couldn't just wait around, worrying and lamenting, as some of the other women did. *I might be pregnant, but that doesn't mean I can't be useful.* Being busy helped her to ignore the occasional faint sound of trumpet calls that carried through the air.

She was only four months gone. Ariadne had thus far managed to conceal her rounded belly and larger breasts by wearing loose dresses and bathing out of the sight of others. From the recent glances that she'd been getting, though, Ariadne knew that it wouldn't be long before word got out that she was expecting Spartacus' child. That was if her glossy black hair and the bloom on her creamy skin granted her by her pregnancy had not already given the game away. There were other signs too. She had noticed in her bronze mirror that her heart-shaped face had grown softer and more attractive. Enjoy it while it lasts, she thought.

A thrill of joy shot through her as she pictured herself holding a strong baby boy while her smiling husband looked on. It was instantly followed by a familiar, snaking dread. What if her interpretation of Spartacus' dream was incorrect? What if he was destined to die in battle against the Romans? Today? *Stop thinking like that. He will win. We will cross the Alps while it's still summer. Get out of Italy altogether.* She felt happier at that thought.

Few tribes would dare to hinder the passage of his army – even if it was depleted – and they would make their way to Thrace. I cannot wait to see Kotys' face, she thought vengefully. He will pay for what he did to us. So will Polles, the king's champion.

'Enough daydreaming,' she said to herself. 'Do not tempt fate.'

Atheas, who was stacking a pile of bandages, looked up. 'What?'

'Nothing.' *Gods willing, my hopes will come to pass.* Ariadne counted the heaped rolls of linen by his feet. They would serve to dress the hideous wounds they'd soon be seeing. 'Five hundred. Not nearly enough.' Her eyes moved to the score of women who were ripping up sheets, tunics and dresses into dressings of various sizes. To her relief, the heaps of garments by their feet were still sizeable. 'Faster. We may well need all of those.' Ariadne wasn't surprised when the women ducked their heads and their conversation petered away to an occasional whisper. As Spartacus' wife, she was respected, but the fact that she was also a priestess of Dionysus elevated her status close to his. Slaves held the god in especial esteem. I am part of the reason that Spartacus has so many followers, she thought with pride. Long may that continue.

Putting everything other than preparations to receive the injured from her mind, Ariadne embarked on a patrol of the hospital area, which had been positioned on the edge of the camp nearest the battlefield. She checked that the surgeons and stretcher-bearers were ready, that supplies of wine for the wounded were plentiful and ordered that another fifty makeshift beds be made up. The whole process didn't take nearly as long as she would have wished. When it was done, her worries returned with a vengeance. She glanced at the sun, which had reached its zenith. 'They've been gone for four hours.'

'That not . . . long time,' pronounced Atheas, making an attempt to sound reassuring, which failed utterly.

Ariadne groaned. 'It feels like an eternity.'

'Battle could . . . last . . . whole day.'

She racked her brains for something to do, a task that would prevent her from agonising over the worst possible outcomes for Spartacus and his men.

Tan-tara-tara. Ariadne jumped. The trumpet sound was near. No more than a quarter of a mile away. Fear coursed through her veins. 'Is that the—'

Atheas finished her question. 'Romans?'

'Yes.'

'Not . . . sure.' Atheas cocked his head and listened.

Tan-tara-tara. Tan-tara-tara. The trumpets were a little closer now, allowing Ariadne to discern the irregular blasts and off-tone notes. Her heart leaped with exhilaration, and she barely heard Atheas say 'Roman trumpeters . . . play better.' *Then they have won! Let him be alive, Dionysus. Please.* Ariadne didn't run to meet the returning soldiers as she had after the battle against Lentulus. Instead she walked as calmly as she could to the start of the track that Spartacus and his men had used that morning. Atheas trailed her, shadowlike. The pair were followed by almost everyone – a crowd made up of women. Loud prayers for the safe return of their menfolk filled the air.

Ariadne's only concession to her inner turmoil was to clench her fists, unseen, by her sides. Atheas' tattooed face, as ever, was impassive.

When the cheering mob of soldiers rounded the bend and she saw Spartacus, uninjured, among them, Ariadne's knees buckled with relief. She was grateful for Atheas' hand, which gripped her arm until she regained her strength. 'They've done it again.'

'He is . . . great leader.'

Ariadne let the women stream past towards their men, waiting until Spartacus reached her. Taxacis, who was with him, called out happily to Atheas in his guttural tongue. Carbo nodded at Ariadne, who was so pleased that she almost forgot to respond.

Without being told, Spartacus' men moved away from her, allowing them some privacy. They chanted his name as they went, and Ariadne could see their fierce love for him in their eyes. Spartacus was carrying his helmet under one arm and, like his soldiers, he was spattered from head to toe in gore. It gave him an aura of invincibility, she thought: that somehow, amid the madness and destruction of battle, he had not only killed his enemies but led his men to victory, and survived. Amid the crimson coating his face, his grey eyes were still striking. There was a glowing rage in them, however, that held Ariadne back from doing what she wanted, which was to throw herself into his arms. 'You won.'

'We did, thank the Rider. Our volleys of javelins caught them unawares, and they never recovered from our initial charge. Their centre broke. Our cavalry swept their horse away, and then took their flanks in the rear. It was a complete rout.'

'You don't seem that happy. Did Gellius get away?'

'Of course. He ran like a rat escaping a sinking ship. But I don't really care about him.' Spartacus tapped the bag hanging from his waist. 'It's this, and what it means.'

Ariadne caught the whiff of decaying flesh, and her stomach turned. 'What is it?'

'All that's left of Crixus,' Spartacus grated. 'His head and his right hand.'

Horror engulfed Ariadne. 'How—'

'Before the battle began, a conceited bastard of a tribune rode up and tossed them down in front of me. Gellius wanted it to panic our men, and it did. I rallied them, though. Fired their anger. Offered them revenge for those who had fallen.'

'Was it many?'

'More than half of Crixus' army.' Spartacus' eyes lost focus. 'So many lives lost unnecessarily.'

Ariadne just felt grateful that Spartacus was alive. 'They left of their own free will.'

It was as if he hadn't heard her. 'I intend to hold a funeral in their remembrance tonight. There will be an enormous fire, and before it, we shall watch our own *munus*.' He saw her enquiring look. 'But the men who'll take part won't be slaves or gladiators. Instead, they'll be free men. Roman citizens. I think Crixus would like that. My soldiers certainly will. An offering of this magnitude will please the rider god and Dionysus. It should ensure that our path to the north remains open.'

'They'll fight to the death?'

He barked an angry laugh. 'Yes! I thought four hundred would be a good number. They can fight each other in pairs. The two hundred who survive the first bouts will face one another; then the one hundred, and so on, until a single man is left standing. He can carry the news to Rome.'

Ariadne was a little shocked. She had never seen Spartacus so ruthless. 'You're sure about this?'

'I have never been surer. It will show those whoresons in Rome that we *slaves* can do as we wish. That we are in every way equal to them.'

'They won't think that. They'll just think that we are savages.'

'Let them think what they will,' he responded sharply. Spartacus' battle rage had been replaced by a cold, merciless fury. It was a feeling that descended upon him occasionally. When Maron, his brother, had died in screaming agony, his body racked with the poison from a gut wound. When Getas, one of his oldest friends, had run on to a blade meant for him. And most recently, just before the battle against the consul Lentulus. He took a deep breath, savouring his icy anger. At that very moment, Spartacus would have slain every Roman who existed. That is the only way they would learn to respect me, he thought. To fear me. The munus will be a start.

'The humiliation will enrage the Romans. They will gather their legions and come after you again.'

'We'll be long gone,' he asserted.

Thank all the gods. Ariadne had been worried that this latest success would change his decision to leave Italy. *With luck, my son will be born in Gaul, or even Illyria.* She clung to that hope for dear life.

Chapter II

By the time darkness fell, Spartacus' orders had been carried out. Using fallen wood, captured Roman wagons and unwanted equipment, a huge bonfire had been lit at the edge of the army's encampment. Its flames climbed high into the night sky, radiating a massive heat that kept the chilly mountain air at bay. Scores of sheep and cattle seized from Gellius' abandoned camp had been slaughtered and butchered. Javelins were being used as makeshift roasting forks to cook bloody hunks of meat over the fire. The necks had been smashed off amphorae, allowing easy access to the wine within. Everywhere men were drinking, laughing, toasting each other. Some danced drunkenly to tunes from drums, whistles and lyres. The sounds of the different instruments clashed in a jangling cacophony but no one cared. It was time to celebrate. They had lived through another battle, and defeated the second Roman consul, setting his army to flight. Spartacus' soldiers felt like the conquering heroes of legend, and their leader was the greatest of them all. Spontaneous chants of 'SPAR-TA-CUS!' kept bursting out. Whenever he was seen, men offered him drinks, clapped him on the back, and swore to him their undying loyalty.

Carbo had heard the rumours too. He didn't quite believe them. Filled with unease, he stood with Navio, a stocky man with high cheekbones and two different coloured eyes. It's odd, thought Carbo, watching the thousands of former slaves. They're my comrades, yet I'm standing with another Roman. Made up half a dozen races, the men were every size and shape under the sun. Hard-faced gladiators, wiry shepherds and sunburned herdsmen. Long-haired Gauls, burly Germans and tattooed Thracians. They were still carrying their weapons, bloodied from the battle against Gellius' army. Clad in Roman mail shirts and breastplates, in simple tunics, or even bare-chested, they made a fearsome, threatening spectacle. 'Is he really going to do it?'

'Be sure of it.'

'It's barbaric.'

Navio threw him a shrewd look. 'Brutal or not, this is justice to Spartacus and his men.'

'Does he have to sacrifice so many?'

'It's common practice for dozens of gladiators to fight at a munus commemorating the death of one person. You know that. Tonight Spartacus is remembering thousands of his comrades. It's no surprise that he picked this number of legionaries.'

'Don't you care?' hissed Carbo, jerking his head at the four hundred prisoners who were roped together nearby. Scores of Spartacus' men ringed them on three sides, drawn swords in their hands. The fourth side lay open towards the fire. There a pile of gladii had been stacked up. 'They're our people.'

'Whom you fought today. Whom you killed.'

'That was different. It was a battle. This—'

'I hate everything that the Republic stands for, remember?' Navio interrupted. 'My father and younger brother died fighting men like those over there. As far as I'm concerned, they can all go to Hades.'

Carbo fell silent before his ire. Navio and his family had followed Quintus Sertorius, a Marian supporter. After Marius' death, the Senate had proscribed Sertorius. Betrayed, Navio had fought with Sertorius against the Republic for several years, but eventually their fortunes in Iberia had ebbed. But, Carbo thought, it was one thing taking on your own kind in a battle, when it was kill or be killed. It was quite another making prisoners fight each other to the death. The idea revolted him. He resolved to say something to Spartacus.

It wasn't long before their leader appeared, accompanied by Ariadne, Castus and Gannicus. Behind him walked soldiers carrying four silver eagles and a large number of cohort standards. There were even several sets of fasces, the ceremonial bundles of rods carried by magistrates' bodyguards and the symbols of Roman justice. An enormous cheer went up as the Thracian strode to stand by the heap of weapons. Despite his anger, Carbo was filled with awe at the sight of his leader with the battle trophies.

Unsurprisingly, the prisoners' terrified eyes also focused on Spartacus. They knew who he was, even if they didn't recognise him. The Thracian was renowned and vilified throughout the Republic as a monster, a man without morals, who defied all societal norms. Here he was, a crop-haired figure in Roman armour, his muscular arms and sword blade covered in their comrades' blood. Unremarkable in many ways. Yet everything about him, from his emotionless expression to his bunched fists, inspired fear, and threatened death.

'SPAR-TA-CUS! SPAR-TA-CUS! SPAR-TA-CUS!' the slaves chanted.

Spartacus raised his arms in recognition of his men's acclaim.

Castus threw Gannicus a sour look, which was reciprocated. No one noticed.

Ignoring Navio's cry of 'Wait!', Carbo trotted over to Spartacus. 'Can I have a word?'

'Now?' Spartacus' voice was harsh. Cold.

'Yes.'

'Make it quick.'

'Is it true that these men but one are to die fighting each other?'

Spartacus' gaze pinned him to the spot. 'Yes.'

'Damn right it is!' said Gannicus.

'You got a problem with that?' growled Castus, fingering the hilt of his sword.

Carbo stayed where he was. 'They deserve better than this.'

'Do they? Why?' Suddenly, Spartacus' face was right in his. 'It is how gladiators up and down the length of Italy die every day of the year, for the amusement of your *citizens*. Many, if not most of those men, have committed no crime.' Spartacus was aware of the Gauls' rumbling agreement here. 'What we're about to see is just a turning of the tables.'

It was hard to deny the logic, but Carbo still felt disgusted. 'I—'

'Enough,' Spartacus barked and Carbo bent his head. To say any more would threaten his friendship with the Thracian, never mind risk an attack from either one of the Gauls. He watched unhappily as Spartacus raised his hands again and a silence fell.

'I have not called you here to congratulate you for your actions in the battle against Gellius today. You all know how much I admire your courage and loyalty.' Spartacus let his followers cheer before continuing: 'We are here for a different reason. A sad reason. Word has reached us of the death of Crixus, and two-thirds of his men. They were lost in a bitter fight against Gellius at Mount Garganus, about a month ago.'

A great, gusty sigh went up from the watching soldiers.

They chose their own fate, thought Carbo. They went with Crixus, the whoreson.

'As well as our own dead, we must honour Crixus and his fallen men. Ask the gods not to forget them, and to allow every last one entrance to Elysium. What better way of doing that than by celebrating our own munus?' As an animal growl rose from his followers, Spartacus indicated the pile of gladii. 'Each prisoner is to pick up a sword. Pair yourself off with another, and walk around the fire until you are told to stop. At my command, you will fight in pairs to the death. The survivors will face each other and so on, until only one man remains.'

The deafening cheers that met Spartacus' orders drowned out the Romans' shocked cries. A dozen men moved among them, cutting the ropes that bound them together. None of the prisoners moved a step. Spartacus jerked his head and the guards began jabbing the legionaries with their swords. More than one drew blood, which drew jeers and catcalls down on the captives' heads. This was better than the former slaves could have dreamed of.

Still no Roman moved to pick up a *gladius*.

Carbo felt a perverse pride in what he saw. *Not all of their courage is gone.*

'Arm yourselves!' shouted Spartacus. 'I shall count to three.'

An officer wearing the transverse-crested helmet of a centurion shoved his way to the front of the mob of prisoners. His silver hair, grizzled appearance and the multiple ornate decorations strapped to his chest revealed the length of his career – and his bravery. 'And if we refuse?'

'You will be crucified one by one.' Spartacus raised his voice for all to hear. 'Right here, for the others to see.'

'Citizens cannot be—' The centurion's face purpled, and his voice tailed away as he realised that Spartacus' alternative had been carefully picked. Their choice was an ignoble yet redeeming death by the sword, or the most degrading fate possible for a Roman. The centurion thought for a moment, and then stepped forward to pick up a gladius. Straightening, he glared at Spartacus. Perhaps ten paces and half a dozen armed men separated them.

The Thracian grinned and his knuckles whitened on the hilt of his sica. 'Should you choose it, there is a third option. While I would end your life quickly, I can't guarantee the same of my men.'

'Give me half a chance and I'll cut his balls off and feed them to him,' snarled Castus. 'And that's just to get me started.'

Other men shouted what they'd like to do to the centurion, and all of his comrades. Carbo tried to harden his heart to the prisoners' suggested fates, but failed. These soldiers were his enemies, but they did not deserve to be forced to slay one another, let alone to be tortured to death. He could not say a word, however. Spartacus' patience had been worn too thin.

Spartacus was still eyeballing the centurion. 'Well?'

The officer's head bowed, and he shuffled to one side.

'Next,' called Spartacus.

Intimidated even further by the cowing of the centurion, the legionaries began miserably filing forward to pick up a sword.

Spartacus offered up a plea to Dionysus and to the Great Rider. *Let the blood of these Romans be a suitable offering to you both, O Great Ones. May it ensure that Crixus and his men have a swift passage to the warrior's paradise.* It was nothing less than the Gaul deserved. Despite his faults, Crixus had been a mighty warrior.

Ariadne did not relish the idea of what was about to happen, but it was impossible to deny the magnitude of this offer to the gods. Few deities would remain unmoved by such a gift. And if that helped her and Spartacus to leave Italy for ever, she was prepared to live with it.

Soon two hundred pairs of legionaries stood facing each other around the fire. Some, like the centurion, stood proudly with their shoulders thrown back, but the majority were pleading to their gods. Some were even weeping.

Awestruck by the role reversal, Spartacus' soldiers had again fallen silent.

Spartacus gave a short eulogy about Crixus. They would remember him for his leadership, his plain speaking, and his bravery. His men would also be remembered for their valiant efforts. Huge cheers met his words. Next, he addressed the Romans.

'You have been taught today on the field of battle that every man here is your equal, or better! Now you are to learn it in another way. All of you will have witnessed gladiators fighting and dying to commemorate the dead. You have probably never considered that those men were forced to act as they did. Tonight you have that chance, because we *slaves* will watch you do the same.' Spartacus scanned the terrified faces near him, his gaze lingering on the centurion. 'It is a honourable death to choose and far worthier than crucifixion. For that I salute you. May you die well!' He raised his sica high and held it there for a heartbeat, before letting it drop. 'Begin!'

As the prisoners prepared to set upon each other, a baying cry rose from the watching crowd. It was the same bloodthirsty sound Spartacus had heard when fighting in the arena. He wished that every man in the Senate was about to battle one another before him instead of four hundred legionaries.

Carbo did not want to watch the slaughter, but his position beside Spartacus meant that he had to. If he closed his eyes, he risked being accused of at best squeamishness, or at worst, cowardice. Despite his misgivings, he soon found himself engrossed. The clash of metal upon metal, the grunts of effort and inevitable cries of pain were mesmerising. Many of the legionaries chose to die quickly, letting their opponents thrust them through or hew their heads from their necks. Carbo wasn't surprised. Why bother trying to win a fight when victory meant a second combat, and yet more after that? What took him by surprise was the level of ferocity with which some of the prisoners went at one another. Their desire to live was great enough for them to slay a comrade without hesitation. Covered in blood, they stood with heaving chests, waiting for the other fights to end.

Carbo noted that the centurion who had addressed Spartacus was one of the two hundred 'winners'. Perhaps because of his kindly face, the senior officer reminded him of his father, Jovian. That thought tore at his heart. Carbo hadn't seen his family for more than a year, since he'd run away from home. A home that had been repossessed by Crassus, the man to whom his father had owed a fortune. Soon after he'd left, Jovian and his mother had travelled to Rome, there to throw themselves on the mercy of a rich relative. Carbo's pride had not let him accompany his parents. For all he knew, they could both be dead. *As the centurion will be soon.*

When the initial fights were over, Spartacus ordered his men to drag away the bodies of the losers. 'Any men still breathing are to have their throats cut. Pile them in a heap over there. Meanwhile, the rest of you dogs can get on with it!' A huge cheer met this announcement. Carbo felt sick. He was glad that Spartacus was ignoring him.

A short while later, five score more corpses lay sprawled amidst pools of blood. A hundred Romans remained, the centurion among them. Soon their number had been reduced to fifty, and after that twenty-five.

'You fight well,' Spartacus shouted at the centurion. 'Stand aside while the remaining two dozen fight each other.'

Stony-faced, the officer did as he was told.

The twelve men who came through the fifth combat looked exhausted.

Six legionaries survived the next brutal set of clashes. They were so tired that they could barely hold up their gladii, but there was no time allowed to rest. 'Keep fighting!' shouted Spartacus. Anyone who faltered was threatened and shoved by the guards.

Spartacus ordered the centurion to take part again when there were a trio of legionaries remaining. Given that he'd had to fight three men fewer than his opponent, it wasn't surprising that the experienced officer dispatched him with ease – nor that he won the final bout either. He stood with bowed head over the body of his last victim, his lips moving in silent prayer.

The raucous cheering that had accompanied the bloody combats died away. A strange quiet fell over the thousands of gathered men. Carbo felt his skin crawl. He glanced into the gathering darkness, almost expecting to see Charon, the ferryman, or even Hades himself, the god of the underworld, appearing to claim the great pile of dead legionaries.

'What's your name?' asked Spartacus.

The centurion lifted eyes that were bleak with horror. 'Gnaeus Servilius Caepio.'

'You're a veteran.'

'Thirty years I've served. My first campaigns were with Marius, against the Teutones and the Cimbri. I don't expect you know of them.'

'Indeed I do. You look surprised, but I fought for Rome for many a year. I must have heard about every campaign since the Caudine Forks.'

Caepio's eyebrows rose. 'It's commonly said that you served in the legions. I dismissed it as rumour.'

'It's true.'

'Rome is your enemy. Why did you do it?'

'To learn your ways, so that I could defeat you. It seems so far that I was an apt pupil.'

His men roared with approval. Pride filled Ariadne.

Caepio glowered and muttered something.

'What was that?' demanded Spartacus.

'I said that you haven't yet faced the veteran legions from Asia Minor or Iberia. They'd soon sort you out.'

'Is that so?' Spartacus' tone was silky. Deadly. The icy rage gripped him again, in part because the centurion's words had an element of truth to them. Many of the soldiers whom they had faced had been newly recruited.

'Damn right it is.' Caepio spat on the ground. Spartacus' troops jeered and he made an obscene gesture in their direction. Their response, a simmering cry of rage, shattered the silence. Dozens of men drew their weapons and moved towards him.

'Hold!' Spartacus barked. He stared at Caepio. 'My soldiers would slay you.'

'That's no surprise! Scum do not honour their promises.' Caepio threw down his sword and raised his hands in the air. 'Let them do what they will. It matters not. I'm damned for what I have done here tonight.'

'Maybe you are, and maybe you're not. Before you die, however, I have a task for you. A message to take to your masters in the Senate.'

'You want me to carry word of this so-called munus.'

'That's right.'

'I'll do it.'

'I thought you would,' sneered Castus.

'Not because of your threats. I do not fear death,' said Caepio, the pride returning to his voice. 'I accept because it is my duty to tell Rome of the depths to which you savages have sunk. Of the barbarity which you forced me and my comrades to inflict on each other.'

A furious roar met his words.

'We're no savages!' cried Gannicus. 'What happened here is no different to the way you treat slaves.'

'Slaves,' Caepio repeated. 'Not free men.'

'Rome lives by double standards,' said Spartacus harshly. 'During the war against Hannibal, when its need was great, it liberated enough slaves to raise two new legions. They were freed in return for fighting for the Republic. Those men proved that they were the equal of any citizen.'

'I cannot deny what you say, but I also know how my people's leaders will respond when they hear about this munus. This is not really about the rights and wrongs of who is made a slave and who is not, about who fights and who does not. It is about humiliating Rome, and that you have done, by defeating both consuls, by taking four silver eagles and, last of all, by putting on this display. Am I not right?' Caepio met Spartacus' stare and held it.

'You are,' Spartacus admitted, as his men howled with glee.

'It will not be forgotten, I can promise you.'

Spartacus raised a hand, halting Castus, who looked as if he was about to attack Caepio. 'Good. Because that was my intent! Tell them that Spartacus the Thracian and his men can fight as well as any of your legionaries, and by defeating the consular armies we have proved it twice.' This time, Spartacus caught the sour look that Castus gave Gannicus. 'Tell the Senate that I am not the only general here. These men, Gannicus and Castus' – he indicated them – 'played pivotal roles in the defeats of Lentulus and Gellius. Rome had best look to its security! The next army it sends our way will suffer an even greater defeat. More eagles will be lost.' Spartacus was pleased to see broad grins spread across the Gauls' faces. He had lied – neither of them were tacticians as he was – but thousands of men looked to them as leaders. He had to keep them on board.

'I shall tell the Senate everything you said. Am I free to go?'

'You are. Give him enough food to last him to Rome! He is to have no weapons,' Spartacus ordered.

'And the bodies of my comrades?'

'You expect me to say that they will be left in the open air for the carrion birds to pick on, don't you?'

'Yes.'

'They died the deaths of brave men, so they will be buried with honour. You have my word on that. I cannot say the same of the soldiers who were slain on the field, however. Many of them were cowards.'

Caepio's face hardened, but he did not argue. 'I pray to the gods that this is not the last time we meet.'

'I shall not be merciful the next time.'

'Nor shall I.'

'Then we understand each other.' Spartacus watched Caepio walk away. Another brave man, he thought. He spoke the truth too. Rome would not let this humiliation go unanswered. It made sense, therefore, to cross the Alps and go beyond the legions' reach. A sneaking doubt crept into his mind. *What if the Senate sends armies after us? It is not as if they don't know where Thrace is.* He shoved the disquieting idea away. *That will never happen.* Deep in his guts, though, Spartacus knew that the possibility, even the likelihood, was there. Rome would not forgive, or as Caepio had said, forget, this many defeats.

Little did he know that Ariadne was thinking similar thoughts. *When Hannibal Barca was forced to leave Carthage, he was pursued for the rest of his life by Roman agents.* She clenched her fists. *Stop it. Dionysus, let us escape Italy, I beg you. Watch over us always and keep us safe.*

Carbo too was watching the centurion; then, almost before he'd realised what he'd done, he had set off after Caepio. Hearing his tread, the centurion spun around.

'It's all right. I'm not going to stab you in the back.'

Caepio looked even more suspicious. 'What do you want?'

Carbo suddenly felt embarrassed. This close, Caepio did not resemble his father in any way. 'I—I just wanted to say that you're a brave man.'

'You're Roman?' Complete disbelief filled Caepio's voice.

'Yes.'

'What in the name of sacred Jupiter are you doing with this rabble? Have you no pride?'

'Of course I have.' Carbo was furious to feel his cheeks going red.

'You make me sick.' Caepio began to walk away.

'Hey! I would not have made you fight each other that way.'

Caepio turned again. The contempt on his face was writ large. 'Really? Yet you've chosen to ally yourself with a host of murdering, raping slaves. Scum who have ravaged towns and cities the length and breadth of Italy, who have massacred thousands of innocent citizens and brave legionaries. In my mind, that makes you a *latro* of the worst type.' He hawked and spat at Carbo's feet. 'That's for being a traitor to your own kind.'

Anger flared in Carbo's belly. 'Piss off, before I gut you!'

Caepio didn't bother replying. He stalked off, muttering insults.

So that's how it is. There can be no going back now. Ever. Why did I even think it was possible? It had been naïve to approach Caepio, but he had wanted to express his kinship with him. He had been unprepared for the level of the centurion's scorn. Yet an odd feeling — was it satisfaction? — filled him. *I am a latro after all. The slaves have become my family. And Spartacus is my leader.* Despite the fact that he would never see his parents again, the emotion was oddly comforting.

Gannicus took a long pull from the small amphora. He smacked his thick lips with satisfaction. 'That's a good vintage, or I'm no judge.'

Castus lifted an arse cheek and let loose a thundering fart. 'You're no judge! It's only entered your thick skull that it's quality wine because we took it from Gellius' tent.' He ducked, chuckling, as the clay vessel flew at his head. It landed a few steps beyond his position by the fire. He leaned over and picked it up before its entire contents leaked out. 'You know I'm right. Ten denarii says that you grew up on vinegar-flavoured, watered-down piss. Like me, like every farm slave that ever was. The best we could hope for every year was the dregs of the master's *mulsum* at the Vinalia Rustica. How would we know what tastes good and what doesn't?'

Gannicus cracked a sour smile by way of agreement; his moon face was less jovial that usual.

'I couldn't tell a Falernian from donkey piss most of the time, but if one thing's certain, every bloody drop taken from the Romans tastes like nectar!' Castus swigged from the amphora and tossed it back. 'To be fair, that does have good flavour.'

Gannicus' irritated expression eased. 'I told you so.'

'Look at us! We who were slaves, gladiators, the lowest of the low, living like kings!' Castus' wave incorporated the grand Roman tent that he'd insisted his men take from Gellius' camp, and the glittering gilt standards that had been stabbed into the earth before it. 'If that prick Gellius wasn't so scrawny, I'd be wearing his armour too!'

Gannicus laughed. 'It's quite something to own the breastplate of a Roman consul, eh? Even if it doesn't fit!'

'I wish I'd taken it from his corpse,' growled Castus. 'Next time the dog won't be so lucky.'

'If he has the balls to come back for another bout.'

They sat and savoured the memories of their victory, which had come in no small part from their own personal bravery.

'That was a fine spectacle that Spartacus put on earlier,' said Castus in a grudging voice.

'True. The men loved it.'

'He's got such a way with them, damn his eyes.' Castus didn't try to hide his jealousy. Gannicus knew how he felt about the Thracian. So too did the few warriors, Gauls all, who lounged nearby. 'Time was that being courageous in battle and able to drink any other man under the table was good enough, eh?'

'That and being able to hump a woman all night long,' agreed Gannicus. 'That's why you and I have got to where we are. And we've done well! Thousands of men are loyal to each of us.'

'Not nearly as many as are devoted to Spartacus,' Castus retorted. 'Did you see him fight today? He's fearless, and skilled with it. The prick is a good general too. Tricking Lentulus into leading his army through the defile was a masterstroke. It's no surprise that they fucking love him.' His reddened face twisted with the bitterness of the man who knows he is lesser.

'What I don't like is the way he expects us to do what he wants. He used to ask our opinion. Now he just does whatever he pleases,' said Gannicus, brooding.

'That might be good enough for arselickers like Egbeo and Pulcher, but not for us. Gauls have pride!'

Resentment held them silent for a while. The logs in the fire crackled and spat as the resin within poured out. The noise of the celebrating soldiers rose into the starry night sky, where their challenge vanished into the immense silence.

'I don't know that you're right,' said Gannicus, tugging on his moustache.

'Eh? About what?'

'About how much the men love Spartacus. They adore him while he leads them to victory after victory, and when he lets them plunder farms and *latifundia* with abandon. But when they're faced with crossing a huge range of mountains, out of Italy, I think that the majority of them will suddenly have a change of heart.'

'They know that that's where we're heading. Spartacus told them at Thurii.'

'There's a big difference between "knowing" something and under-standing it, Castus. All the men have had to think about since then is marching, raping, and pillaging whatever homestead they happen upon. Fighting the consular armies – and beating them – will have kept their minds off much else too. I'd wager that until recently, not one man in ten has given serious thought to leaving Italy. The grumbling that's been going on is very real.'

Castus' beady eyes filled with hope. He leaned forward conspiratorially. 'We've talked about this before. Will the majority really refuse to do as he asks?'

'That's exactly what I think.'

'I hope you're right, by Taranis! I would love to see that come to pass.'

'So would I, because the day that he announces the army is to march into the Alps is the day we act. In the meantime, we wait, watch and listen.'

In a flash, Castus' mood turned. 'We've been sitting on our hands about this since we broke out of the stinking ludus! I've a good mind just to head off on my own. Plenty of men will follow me!'

'Do what you want,' said Gannicus dismissively. 'You are your own master. But before you act, think of the prize on offer. Imagine leading forty, even fifty thousand men into battle. We'd be like the Gaulish chieftains of old. Like Brennus, who sacked Rome. They say that the ground trembled when his men were going into battle. Imagine that! The Romans would shit themselves.' He sat back and let Castus suck on the bones of that idea.

'All right, all right. We'll wait a little longer; use the time to talk more men around, eh?'

'Exactly.' Gannicus kept his expression neutral, but inside, he was delighted. If he could induce Castus to act with him, they stood a far greater chance at the Alps of persuading the majority of the army to reject Spartacus' demands. And when that happened, he would be the driving force of the pair. Castus was no fool, but his hot-headedness often led him into trouble. It also made him relatively easy to manipulate, which suited Gannicus down to the ground. He cracked the seal off another amphora. 'In the meantime, let's get pissed!'

Castus belched. 'Good idea.'

'We'll drink to Spartacus losing control of the army.'

'Even better – that he ends up on the wrong end of a Roman blade!'

'Aye,' agreed Gannicus. 'He did the job well enough at the start, but the power has gone to his head.'

They eyed one another with new intensity, both realising that the other was thinking the same thing.

A moment went by. Castus looked around, checking that no one was in earshot. 'Do you think it's possible? Those Scythians are like a pair of mad hunting dogs. And then there's the man himself. He's lethal with a blade. Or his bare hands. Remember how he all but killed Crixus, and he was as strong as an ox.'

'He's not so dangerous when he's asleep. Or when he's taking a shit,' murmured Gannicus slyly. 'Where there's a will, there's a way, eh? We just have to wait for the right opportunity .' He gave Castus a hard stare. 'You with me?'

'Damn right I am!'

'Not a word about it to anyone. This has to be between you and me.'

'Do you think I'm stupid? My lips are sealed – where that's concerned, anyway.' He reached out a hand for the amphora. 'Now, are you going to let me die of thirst?'

Grinning with satisfaction, Gannicus handed over the wine. Spartacus, he thought, your star has begun to wane. About bloody time.

Marcion had grown up on an estate in Bruttium. He was of Greek extraction, medium height, and had his father's sallow skin and black hair. Given that his parents were household slaves, it had been natural for Marcion's master to have him trained as a scribe when he was old enough. He had shown a natural proficiency for the job, and had enjoyed it too. Sadly, his whole life had been turned upside down a year previously, when his master had died, leaving as his only heir a dissolute youth with no sense of culture.

One of this boor's first acts had been to force many of the domestic slaves to work in the estate's fields, where they 'would be more productive'. Marcion had known about the harsh life and brutal discipline meted out to agricultural slaves, but until then he had never experienced it first-hand. After a few weeks, he had had enough. Spartacus' army had been camped near Thurii for some months. Rumours about how easy it was to join had been rife among the discontented farm slaves. In the dark of an autumn night, Marcion had stolen away into the hills. It had taken him only three days to reach the rebel army. A tough-looking officer had studied his farmer's tan and the calluses on his hands, and accepted him as a recruit.

Marcion had completed his initial training long since. He had fought in the battles against Lentulus and Gellius, which made him a veteran. In the eyes of the original gladiators who had escaped from the ludus with Spartacus, however, or the men who had fought in the initial battles against the likes of Publius Varinius at Thurii, Marcion and his comrades were nothing but wet-behind-the-ears rookies. He'd grown sick of their jibes, which filled his ears any time their hard-nosed centurion made them train. The old-timers liked nothing better than to stand by and make sarcastic comments. Marching was hard on Marcion's legs, but at least he was surrounded by his own, more recently recruited cohort. Zeuxis' grumbling started up again from the rank in front, reminding him that it wasn't all roses here either. The bald-headed man was older than him, and had joined a week before Marcion had. Zeuxis had the loudest voice in their *contubernium*, which he thought gave him the right to dictate to everyone. Mostly, the other soldiers in the eight-man tent group let him get on with it. Marcion found that hard.

'We do nothing but fucking march!'

'Shut it,' said Gaius, a broad-shouldered man who lived to fight. He was marching beside Marcion. 'Try not to think about it. You'll get there sooner that way.'

Zeuxis ignored him. 'How many hundred miles is it from Thurii?'

'I heard it was close to four,' said Arphocras, Marcion's favourite member of the contubernium.

'Is that all? It feels as if we're halfway to Hades.'

Arphocras winked at Marcion. 'Don't worry, Zeuxis, it's not much further to the Alps.'

'The Alps! How hard will it be to cross them?'

'It will be summer by the time we get there. The journey won't be any different to what we've experienced in the Apennines,' said Marcion, repeating what he'd overheard his centurion saying.

'As if you'd know, Greek boy,' growled Zeuxis. 'You're like the rest of us. Never set foot outside Bruttium until Spartacus led us away from there.'

The others laughed, and Marcion flushed with anger. 'That's according to Spartacus, not me!'

'Been talking to him recently, have you?'

More laughter. Marcion buttoned his lip. He would try to get Zeuxis back later.

'Spartacus – the great man. Huh! If we're lucky, he might ride by our position every day or two, but that's it,' complained Zeuxis. 'The rest of the time, we're stuck in the column, without a damn clue about what's going on. Just following the men in front like shitting ants. No wonder it takes three hours for us even to leave the camp each morning – which means we're always the last damn soldiers to reach the new one every day.' Encouraged by the others' nods and mutters, he went on, 'Getting our grain ration takes an age, never mind about the wine. And as for spare equipment—'

Marcion gave up his intention of keeping silent. Everything Zeuxis said was true, but it was part of life when one served in such a vast army. They could no more change it than force the sun to rise in the west and set in the east. 'Give it a rest, will you?'

'I'll talk if I want to. Men are interested in what I've got to say,' retorted Zeuxis over his shoulder.

'No, they're not. They just can't compete with your bloody monotone.'

Hoots of laughter rang out, and Zeuxis scowled. He swung around, nearly braining Gaius with the pole carrying his gear. 'You cheeky bastard!'

Gaius gave him an almighty shove back into his rank. 'Why don't you do as Marcion asked, eh? Give us all a break. Enjoy the scenery. Look up the blue sky. Sing us a song, even. Anything but more of your grumbling!'

Marcion grinned as everyone within earshot loudly agreed.

Frowning, Zeuxis subsided.

'Thanks,' muttered Marcion to Gaius.

'S'all right. It won't keep him quiet for long.'

'Nothing ever does,' said Marcion, rolling his eyes. 'Better just enjoy the moment.'

Taking a deep breath, Gaius began to sing.

Recognising the bawdy tune, Marcion and the rest joined in with gusto.

The miles went by far faster when thinking about wine, women and song.

Ten days later . . .
Rome

Marcus Licinius Crassus was tired and hungry. Seeing his house in the distance, he sighed with relief. Soon he'd be home. He had spent a long day in the Senate, listening to, and taking part in, the most interminable debate about building new sewers on the Aventine Hill. The fools spout enough shit as it is without literally having to talk about it, he thought, smiling at his own joke. It was incredible. Despite the recent defeat of both consuls by the renegade Spartacus, the sewerage needs of the plebs were being addressed as a matter of urgency.

Yet there was no doubt in Crassus' mind which was the more pressing matter. Spartacus. The man and his slave rabble had become a festering sore in the Republic's side. Lentulus, the first consul to be disgraced, had presented himself to the senators some weeks before. His attempt to explain his actions had not gone down well, but after a severe reprimand he had been left in command of what remained of his army. Gellius, his colleague, had appeared in the capital just a few days prior. Like Lentulus, he was a self-made man, and lacked the support of a major faction in the Senate. Like Lentulus, he had suffered considerable casualties at Spartacus' hands; he had also lost both his legions' eagles. What had brought the senators' opprobrium raining down on him, however, had not been these factors. It had been the presence of Caepio, the only surviving witness to the humiliation and killing of four hundred Roman prisoners.

Crassus' lips pinched at the memory of Caepio's testimony. Few men in the Republic could demand more respect than he, a centurion with thirty years of loyal service under his gilded belt. Everyone in the Curia had been riveted as he'd spoken. The wave of sheer outrage that had swept through the hallowed building when he'd finished had been greater than any Crassus had ever seen. He had been no less affected. The idea of slaves holding a munus, forcing Roman legionaries – citizens – to fight to the death was outrageous. Unforgivable. Vengeance *had* to be obtained, and fast. Crassus' fury and frustration mounted even further. At that moment, revenge seemed unlikely. If the rumours were to be believed, Spartacus was leading his men north, to the Alps. Only Gaius Cassius Longinus, the proconsul of Cisalpine Gaul, who commanded two legions, stood in his way, and it was hard to see how he would succeed where his superiors had failed. If Longinus were defeated, they would discover if Spartacus really was thinking the unthinkable: would he leave Italy?

Even if Lentulus or Gellius *were* granted the opportunity of fighting Spartacus again, Crassus didn't think that either consul was capable of crushing the slave army. Both of them, especially Gellius, had seemed cowed by the senators' furious reaction. *That was just three hundred angry politicians – not fifty thousand armed slaves.* Although the pair had now joined forces, in Crassus' mind they lacked the initiative – and the balls – to bring the insurrection to a swift and successful conclusion. He had brought some of his fellow senators around to his point of view that change was needed. Getting them to agree to anything further was another matter, however. The traditions surrounding high office that had evolved over half a millennium were set in stone. For the twelve months of their office, the two consuls were the most senior magistrates in the Republic, and its effective rulers. Understandably, their positions were revered. To unseat them or to force them to allow another to lead their armies during their tenure was unheard of. Undeterred, Crassus had mooted such ideas twice now. On both occasions, his suggestions had been shouted down.

Fools. They will come to regret their decision. Longinus will fail. If they are sent after him, Lentulus and Gellius will fail. Crassus knew it in his bones. Of all the politicians in Rome, he alone had met Spartacus, and gauged his mettle. He had encountered the Thracian gladiator by chance, on a visit to Capua a year before. Crassus had paid for a mortal combat in the ludus there. Despite being wounded early on, Spartacus had overcome his skilled opponent. Intrigued by the Thracian, Crassus had struck up a conversation with him afterwards. At the time, he'd taken Spartacus' confident manner as pure arrogance. Since then, in the aftermath of repeated Roman defeats, he had realised his mistake. The man wasn't just a brave and skilful fighter. He possessed charisma, ability and generalship in plenty. *Not since Hannibal has anyone posed such a real threat to the Republic,* Crassus brooded. *And the two fools who are supposed to bring him to heel are Lentulus and Gellius, whose best plan is hunt Spartacus down and confront him in battle once more. Why am I the only one to see that they'll be unsuccessful?*

I have to do something.

And he knew exactly what. It might take months, but he would win the Senate around. Scores of politicians owed him favours, money or both. He just needed some more influential allies. With their support, he could achieve a majority in the Senate. The consuls would be forced to relinquish command of their legions to someone else. *To me,* he thought happily. *I, Crassus, will lead the legions in pursuit of Spartacus, wherever he may be. I will save the Republic. How the plebs will love me!*

His litter creaked to a halt and his slaves set it down gently. Crassus waited as one of them hammered on the front door, demanding entry for their master. Rather than the hulking doorman he expected, the portal was opened by Saenius, his effeminate major domo. Alighting, Crassus lifted his eyebrows. 'You're back. I hadn't expected you so soon.'

'My business in the south took less time than I thought.' Saenius stepped on to the street, deferentially ushering his master inside.

'I'm glad to hear it.' Crassus was careful to place his right foot over the threshold first. His belly grumbled as the smell of frying garlic reached his nostrils from the kitchen. He could eat later, however. Weeks before, he had sent Saenius on a mission. 'Tell me what you discovered.'

Saenius looked up and down the corridor. Two household slaves were approaching.

Crassus had no wish for anyone else to hear either. 'Later.'

Saenius relaxed. 'I am not the only surprise for you today. You have a visitor.'

'Who?'

'The Pontifex Maximus.'

Crassus blinked in surprise. 'Gaius Julius Caesar?'

'The same.'

'What in the name of all the gods does the "Queen of Bithynia" want with me?'

'He wouldn't say.' Saenius snickered. Everyone in Rome knew the rumours. Since Caesar's sojourn a few years before at the court of Nicomedes, the elderly ruler of Bithynia, he had been dogged by the rumour that he had been intimate with his host. 'He's not dressed in fine purple robes. Nor is he reclining on a golden couch as he waits for you.'

The image made Crassus smile. 'Caesar might have done that for Nicomedes, but I think he knows better than to try it on with me.'

Caesar was the highest-ranking priest in Rome. While his post had real importance, membership of the priesthood was also a stepping-stone for those young nobles with a promising career in politics. Caesar was already one of the rising stars on that scene. *This won't just be a social visit, that's for sure.*

They entered the atrium, the grand, airy room that led off the entrance hall. Beautifully painted scenes decorated the stucco walls: the exposure of the infants Romulus and Remus on the banks of the River Tiber, the consecration of Rhea Silvia as Vestal Virgin and the founding of the ancient city of Alba Longa. The death masks of Crassus' ancestors adorned the rear wall, which also contained the *lararium*, an alcove set aside as a shrine to the household gods. Crassus bent his head in respect as he passed.

'Where is he then?'

'Don't you wish to change, or to eat something first?'

'Come now, Saenius,' chuckled Crassus. 'I ought to see him at once.' He brushed a speck of imaginary dirt from the front of his own still immaculate toga. 'Caesar may be a dandy, but my appearance will suffice.'

'Of course. He's waiting in the reception room off the courtyard.'

It was his most imposing office, decorated only the week before. It could not fail to impress. Pleased by Saenius' shrewdness, Crassus followed his major domo through the *tablinum*, the large chamber that led on to the colonnaded garden beyond. Staying under the portico, they skirted the rows of vines and lemon trees, and the carefully placed colourful Greek statues. Saenius tapped on the open door of the first room they reached. 'Marcus Licinius Crassus.'

Crassus glided past, smiling a welcome at the clean-shaven, thin man seated within. 'Pontifex! I am honoured by your presence.' He made a shallow obeisance, enough to show respect, but not enough to indicate any real inferiority.

'Crassus,' said Caesar, standing and returning the bow. As ever, his well-cut dark red robe had barely a crease. 'How wonderful to see you.'

Crassus hid his delight at the deference just shown him. Family connections might have won Caesar the position of Pontifex, but there was still no need for him to rise for Crassus. The fact that he had done so showed that he recognised Crassus' importance. It wasn't that surprising. *I am, after all, richer, more powerful and better connected.* What Crassus did not like to admit was that he possessed little of Caesar's élan.

Few other men – apart from Pompey – could win the love of the public as Caesar had. Winning a *corona civica*, Rome's highest award for bravery, at nineteen. Choosing to become an advocate in the courts and robustly prosecuting Dolabella, a former consul, at twenty-three. Gaining notoriety as a lover of numerous men's wives. However, the plebs' favourite story about Caesar – if Crassus had heard it being told on a street corner once,

42

he'd heard it a hundred times – involved his capture by pirates and imprisonment on the island of Pharmacussa off the coast of Asia Minor. Crassus hated the tale. Not only had Caesar laughed at the pirates' ransom demand of twenty talents of silver, telling them that they should ask instead for fifty, but he had repeatedly told them that when he was freed, he would crucify them all. Some weeks later, when the larger amount had been paid, Caesar had indeed been released. Despite the fact that he was a civilian, he had persuaded the provincials who had paid his ransom to give him the command of several warships. True to his word, he had captured the pirates and, soon afterwards, crucified every single one of them. This display of Roman *virtus*, or manliness, had given Caesar an enduring appeal with the Roman public. Crassus longed for such recognition. He smiled at his guest. *Prick.* 'Some wine?'

'Thank you, that would be welcome.'

'My throat's dry too.' Crassus glanced at Saenius, but the Latin was already on his way out of the door.

'A long day in the Senate?'

'Yes. Hours of talking about shit.'

Caesar's eyebrows arched.

'New sewers are planned for the Aventine Hill.'

'I see. It sounds a reasonable suggestion.'

'So you'd think. It's never that easy in the Senate, though, is it? But you didn't come here to talk about sanitation.'

'No.' Caesar paused as Saenius returned with a flask of wine.

'You may speak freely. My major domo has been with me for more than twenty years. I trust him as I do my own son.'

'Very well,' said Caesar with obvious reluctance. 'As I'm sure you're aware, the costs of living in the capital, of maintaining appearances when in high office, can be prohibitive.'

I knew it, Crassus gloated silently. He's here for a loan. Aren't they all? 'They can be. Public entertainment of any kind can be expensive.'

'A number of my friends have mentioned that you can be most accommodating when it comes to securing more . . . funds.'

'I have been known to lend money on occasion.' Crassus paused, savouring his power. 'Is that why you are here?'

Caesar hesitated for a heartbeat. 'In a word, yes.'

'I see.' Crassus rolled some wine around his mouth, enjoying the taste, and the awkward expression on Caesar's face. 'How much money do you need?'

'Three million denarii.'

Saenius let out a tiny gasp, which he quickly converted to a cough.

The pup has balls, thought Crassus. No mincing around when it comes to it. 'That's quite a sum.'

Caesar's shoulders rose and fell in an eloquent shrug. 'I want to hold a munus in the next few months. That alone will cost me five hundred thousand at least. Then there are the costs of running a household—'

'You don't have to justify your spending to me. How precisely would you pay me back?'

'From the booty I will take on campaign.'

'Campaign?' asked Crassus, frowning. 'Where? Pontus?'

'Perhaps. Or somewhere else,' replied Caesar with his typical confidence.

Crassus thought for a moment. Rome was perennially at war. Caesar could be sure of finding a conflict to fight in if he wished, but there was no guarantee that he would return with such huge wealth. *That's not why I lend men money, though, is it? It's to have them in my power. So that when I need a favour, I know that I will receive it.* He smiled. Caesar was already popular with many senators. Having him as a debtor would be advantageous. 'Fine.'

Caesar's composure slipped, reducing him to the young man he really was. 'You'll lend it to me?' he asked eagerly.

'Of course,' said Crassus in an expansive tone. 'As you may have heard, my interest rate is reasonable. Five denarii in every hundred, charged yearly. Saenius can have my scribe draw up the paperwork at once. The parchment guaranteeing you the money will be delivered to your house in the morning.'

'Thank you.' Caesar grinned. 'I will offer a bull to Jupiter in gratitude later.'

'There is one small condition.'

'I see.'

'Will you agree to it?'

'Do I have to?'

'If you want the money, yes.'

Caesar's smile slipped a little. 'As long as you don't ask me to kill my mother, I imagine that I will be able to help.'

Crassus hid his delight. *He's swallowed the hook!* 'You've probably been aware in recent days of my impatience with our consuls, Lentulus and Gellius.'

'Yes,' replied Caesar cagily.

'I say impatient? That's being kind. To put it simply, Lentulus is a fool. He walked into an ambush that a blind man would have seen. Marching his army into a narrow defile without checking the heights first? I ask you!'

Caesar rubbed his long, aquiline nose, wondering whether to mention the fact that the 'all clear' signal had apparently been given. In retrospect, it was clear Lentulus' scouts must have been killed, allowing one of Spartacus' men to give the signal that lulled the consul into a false sense of security. He decided not to mention it. 'A rash decision.'

'And Gellius? He's nothing but an old man who thought that winning a battle against a disorganised mob of slaves led by a savage would guarantee him a victory over Spartacus.'

'Strong words.'

'Maybe so, but they're true.' Crassus stuck out his jaw belligerently.

'Thus far I have not said so in public, but I agree with you,' admitted Caesar.

Encouraged, Crassus continued: 'The praetors who went before the consuls were no better. Glaber, Varinius and Cossinius were supposed to be high-ranking magistrates. Pah! The legate Furius was another idiot!'

'You could have done better yourself.'

Crassus paused, eyeing Caesar with suspicion. 'Eh?'

'As the man whose victory in a desperate battle at the Colline Gate won the day for Sulla, you would have undoubtedly cleared up the whole affair by now.'

'With the gods' help, perhaps,' said Crassus modestly. He wasn't going to admit that such thoughts had occupied his every waking moment. In reality, however, things were not quite so black and white. The mistake made by Glaber of not having enough sentries could have happened to anyone. Who in their right mind could have imagined that seventy-odd gladiators would make a bold night-time attack on three thousand men? If Furius' account of what had happened to him was to be believed, he too had been cleverly ambushed. So had Cossinius, caught naked as he bathed in a swimming pool. It was Varinius alone who had made repeated poor judgements, the last of which had culminated in his complete defeat by Spartacus at the city of Thurii. Crassus remembered how upon Varinius' return to Rome, the disgraced praetor had pleaded with him to help. Naturally, he had refused. Varinius had brought his destruction upon his own head, he thought harshly. To have allied himself with such an abject failure would have been tantamount to political suicide. He'd been decent enough to Varinius – hadn't he offered to lend the praetor's family money at lower than normal rates after Varinius was dead? 'But I was not chosen by the Senate,' he added.

'You did not put yourself forward as a candidate.'

'Why would I ask to lead soldiers against a raggle-taggle of runaway gladiators?' Crassus couldn't keep his irritation from showing. 'Besides, Glaber would suffer the job to no other.'

'That's true,' replied Caesar mildly. 'But now it has become something far more. We're talking about a full-scale rebellion.'

'Indeed we are! And the two consuls have failed us. Failed the Republic. Can you imagine what they are saying about Rome in Pontus? In Iberia? We must be the laughing stock of the Mediterranean. An army of slaves marches up and down Italy, thrashing every force of troops sent against it? It's an absolute scandal! Now we are depending on the proconsul of Cisalpine Gaul, to succeed where no one else has been able to. With but two legions, I do not envy Gaius Cassius Longinus. It's an insurmountable task.'

'Quite so.'

'I therefore intend to gain the support of the majority of the senators in the Curia. When I have done that, I will force the consuls to resign or, more likely, to surrender the command of their legions to me.'

Despite the magnitude of what he was hearing, Caesar's eyebrows rose only a fraction. 'Pompey Magnus will not be pleased if you do that.' A thin smile traced his lips. 'But that's a good thing. He loves power too much as it is.'

'The windbag has his hands full in Iberia anyway. He might have defeated Perperna, but there are plenty of tribes who still fancy a fight with Rome.'

'As always. Assuming that you succeed, what will you do next?'

'I will raise more legions in addition to the four consular ones, before taking the war to Spartacus. Aggressively. If he is still in Italy, so much the better. If he has left it, I will pursue him by land or by sea. I will not rest until he and his rabble have been trampled into the mud, and the stain on the Republic's honour has been washed away for ever.' Crassus fixed his eyes on Caesar. 'Will you join me?'

Caesar did not answer immediately, which angered Crassus. 'If you do not, there can be no question of lending you the money,' he reiterated curtly.

'I would be honoured to help.'

'Excellent. Saenius, tell the scribe to draw up the usual credit agreement. For three million denarii.' Crassus poured more wine for them himself. 'To a long-lasting friendship.'

Caesar echoed the toast, and they both drank.

'I have another request to make,' said Caesar a moment later.

What else can he want? 'Really?'

'When you are in charge of the legions, I would very much like to be one of your tribunes.'

Crassus' ego swelled. 'It would be a good opportunity for you to gain military experience.'

'Will you have me?'

'Any man who has won the corona civica would be welcome on my staff.' Crassus raised his glass in salute.

A more companionable silence fell. Outside in the courtyard, the scratch of the scribe's stylus mixed with the sound of Saenius' voice dictating the terms of the loan.

Crassus reflected on the day's end with some satisfaction. He had barely come up with his plan to gain control of the legions in Italy when Caesar had fallen into his lap. In gaining the Pontifex's support, he had also recruited a valuable staff officer. And he hadn't even heard Saenius' news yet.

Chapter III

Two weeks later . . .
Cisalpine Gaul, near the town of Mutina

The sun had just risen, and Spartacus was standing a short distance from the perimeter of his camp. Apart from the sentries on the earthen rampart, he was the only figure in sight. It was a good time to be alone, and one that he often took advantage of to collect his thoughts. He breathed in deeply, enjoying the cool air. Summer was around the corner, and each day it was growing hotter. By midday, marching would have become an unpleasant slog. It wasn't surprising that the army's progress since defeating Gellius had been even slower than usual. Buoyed up by their incredible successes, his men had spent much of the time drunk, or ransacking local farms for food, women and, of course, more wine. He hadn't tried to stop them. After what they'd achieved, they deserved to celebrate. A leader who prevented his men from doing such things became unpopular, and he couldn't risk that, not with the Alps drawing near. Spartacus knew he'd done well to get the army on the move a week or so previously. It had travelled at a snail's pace of five miles a day since, however, which was immensely frustrating.

Yet at the best of times it was hard to organise fifty thousand soldiers and the straggling baggage train that accompanied them. He had long since given up trying to control the thousands of hangers-on – women, children, the wounded, whores, traders – who swelled the host's size to ridiculous proportions. The damn column stretched for more than twenty miles. When journeying from the south, he had kept his followers in the mountains, where it was easy to avoid confrontation. Just the day before, they had left the protection of the Apennines and marched out on to the river plain of the mighty Padus. They were now permanently in the open, and vulnerable to attack. They may have driven off both consuls but Spartacus had learned over the years never to let his guard down. Squadrons of his cavalry rode at regular intervals along the column's flanks. Other units had also ranged far afield, locating enemy troops. So far it appeared that the garrison of Mutina was staying firmly behind the town's walls.

Spartacus climbed on to a nearby rock and peered north. Cloud cover meant that he couldn't see the Alps this morning, but his memory of seeing them on the far horizon as they had descended from the Apennines was crystal clear. Less than seventy miles away, the influence of the Roman Republic came to an abrupt end. The sight had made Ariadne happier than he'd ever seen; it had had a similar effect on Atheas, Taxacis and the surviving Thracians. Everyone else's reaction had been more muted, however. Gannicus had smiled and said he was looking forward to screwing a free Gaulish woman, but Castus had barely said a word. Concerned by the first real hints of resentment, Spartacus had taken to wandering through the army's camp each night, his face obscured by the throw of a cloak. Many of the conversations he had eavesdropped on were not what he would have wished to hear. Yes, there was some talk of leaving Italy behind for ever, but there was also a great deal of grumbling and complaining.

'Why does he want to leave? Everything we want is here. Undefended towns. Grain. Wine. Women. Money. All ours for the taking!'

'We've defeated every damn force sent against us. What is there to fear by staying?'

'Both consuls had to flee for their lives after we thrashed their legions. The Romans have learned their lesson. They won't come near us again in a hurry.'

Biting his tongue, Spartacus hadn't challenged this dissent. He couldn't talk to every tent group in the army. *They don't understand the Romans. They are uneducated slaves. What do they know of history?* Talk of Pyrrhus, who had defeated Rome more than once, and Hannibal, who had massacred almost their entire army in one day, and the Gaulish tribes who had threatened Italy on occasions, would mean nothing to the vast majority. Yet part of him couldn't help exulting at the level of their confidence. *Why would they want to leave? What might we do if we were a hundred thousand strong? Two hundred thousand strong? The Romans would truly fear us then.*

He dragged his thoughts back to Thrace, and how he wanted to rid it of the legions for ever. The men will listen to me when the time is right, he told himself. They love and trust in me. Not all will follow me north, but most will. He glanced at the sky. *Let it be so, Great Rider. Let their reverence for you and Ariadne, your faithful servant, remain, O Dionysus.*

But deep in his gut, Spartacus suspected that the Romans would not leave him be if he left Italy. They would want revenge for the humiliations he had heaped upon them. And if they followed him – what then?

Hearing someone approach, he turned his head. 'Carbo. Navio. I thought it would be you.' *My trusty Romans.* He'd watched their faces closely during the munus for Crixus. Navio had enjoyed watching the legionaries die, which in Spartacus' mind proved his loyalty. Carbo had protested to him about it, and had even spoken to Caepio when it was over. Spartacus had seen the centurion's contempt from fifty paces away, had seen him spit at Carbo's feet. He'd felt sorry for the young Roman, but he had also rejoiced, because Caepio's rejection would have bonded Carbo to him for ever. There were few men whom Spartacus would trust to protect Ariadne and their as yet unborn son in the event of his death. Atheas and Taxacis were two, and Carbo was another. It was a relief to know that his allegiance remained strong.

'Looking north?' Carbo was wondering why their leader had summoned them so early.

'Where else would I look? The Alps are close. We'll reach them in a week to ten days.' He was pleased that neither man looked unhappy. 'Before that we have to pass Mutina, don't we?'

'It's about ten miles away,' said Navio.

'Tell me about it,' ordered Spartacus.

'It's a Roman colony on the Via Aemilia, which runs from Ariminum on the east coast to Placentia, some sixty miles distant. Mutina is also the main base for the provincial governor and his two legions.'

'Proconsul Gaius Cassius Longinus,' said Carbo. 'He comes from an old and illustrious family.' *Like Crassus, the shitbag.*

'Longinus was consul last year, when Glaber and the other fools were sent to destroy us,' mused Spartacus. 'By now he will have heard what happened to Lentulus and Gellius.'

'At this moment, I would say he's hiding behind Mutina's walls, shitting himself,' said Navio with a laugh. 'Wishing that he had more than two legions.'

'Beware the cornered snake,' advised Spartacus. 'And to underestimate a Roman army is to invite your own destruction.'

'True,' murmured Navio. 'But we'll hammer them into little pieces regardless.'

'The scouts have found no sign so far of Longinus or his troops. That probably means that he's kept them in camp, but the easiest route to the Alps will take us right by Mutina. Who knows what the proconsul might have planned for us?' He pinned them with his eyes. 'I want you to see what you can find out.'

'What, go to Mutina?' asked Carbo in surprise.

'Yes. You're the only two who can get away with it. You're Roman. You're educated. No one will even challenge you.'

We could sleep in beds, thought Carbo. He hadn't done that for many months. 'All right.'

'Count me in,' said Navio.

'I want you back within a day. If you value your skins, remember to keep your mouths shut,' warned Spartacus. 'I'll let the army rest until you return. Then we're moving north.'

'A day,' mused Carbo, feverishly wondering if he might have time to compose a letter of farewell to his parents. The idea had occurred to him before, but their situation had made it impossible. He had no ink, no stylus or parchment, and no way of sending the message. Now, with the Alps so near at hand, their departure from Italy suddenly seemed real. Permanent. In the forum of a town such as Mutina, he would find scribes who for a few coins would write him a note.

'It's plenty of time,' asserted Navio.

'Find some clothes that are well worn and dirty. Do not wear your belts, obviously, or any weapons apart from a knife,' ordered Spartacus. 'Take only a small amount of money.'

'If anyone asks our business, what shall we say?'

'You're both farmers. That will explain your tans, and the calluses on your hands. You come from thirty miles to the south of here, in the foothills of the Apennines. Like so many others, your farms were laid waste by Spartacus' men, and your families killed. You've come to Mutina to find work, and protection from the rebels.'

It seemed a plausible story. Carbo and Navio glanced at each other and nodded.

'Go on with you! The sooner you leave, the sooner you'll be back.'

To avoid being run over by an official messenger who showed no sign of slowing his cantering horse, Carbo stepped off the paved surface of the road. He glanced sidelong at the rider as he pounded past, heading for Placentia. *No prizes for guessing what his message is. Something along the lines of 'Send me every available soldier you have! Spartacus is at the gates.'* It was a pleasing thought.

He and Navio had skirted through the deserted countryside to join the busy Via Aemilia some miles to the west of Mutina, so that when they arrived, it didn't look as if they had come from the south. Unsurprisingly, most of the heavy traffic was heading away from the threat of the slave army. There were enough travellers moving eastwards for them not to appear unusual, however. Carbo unslung his water bag with a sigh. 'Gods, but it's hot.' Taking a long swig, he threw the leather carrier at Navio.

His friend winked. 'Just as well we're not wearing our mail shirts and carrying our swords and shields, eh?'

'In Hades' name! Keep your mouth shut.' Carbo was grateful for the deafening racket made by the creaking of a passing cart's wheels.

'No one can hear me.'

'Maybe now. But in Mutina, things will be different, especially if we go to a tavern.'

'*If*?' screeched Navio. 'When!'

Carbo glowered at Navio, but he only half meant it. They'd spent the entire journey talking about finding an inn where they could drink some decent wine, and order good food instead of the burned offerings they'd grown used to. There might even be some half-decent-looking whores, Carbo thought hopefully. He hadn't had sex since Chloris, his lover, had died. There had been plenty of opportunities, but unlike most of Spartacus' men, he wasn't prepared to rape defenceless women. By now he was desperate. 'All right, all right. But we do it my way. Quietly. Carefully.

There'll be no talk of anything other than farming, our poor dead families, and what bastards Spartacus and his lot are.'

'Fair enough,' replied Navio. 'But that's as much as you're telling me what to do. You're not choosing which whore I screw.' He hurled the water bag at Carbo's head with a laugh and made a ring with the thumb and forefinger of his right hand. With a suggestive leer, he thrust his left forefinger in and out of the opening. 'That's what I want. With the best-looking woman I can find,' he growled.

Carbo chuckled. For just a moment, life felt normal.

His wariness returned fast. There was a long queue waiting to enter Mutina's main gate, which was guarded by a large group of legionaries. 'Look how many of the whoresons there are. Twenty at least,' he muttered as they shuffled along behind an ox cart laden down with freshly sawn planks. 'They've heard how we took Thurii.'

'Looks like it.'

Carbo could remember every moment of the battle at Thurii in southern Italy. In order to spring a surprise attack on Varinius, Spartacus had had his men seize the poorly defended city by subterfuge. The next day, leaving a portion of his army outside, apparently besieging Thurii, he had drawn Varinius and his soldiers into a deadly trap. Since that day, Carbo's respect for Spartacus had been unassailable. The Romans' defeat had been total, their humiliation immense.

Clearly, Longinus wasn't going to let the same happen to Mutina, or to him.

'We'll just have to brazen our way in.' Carbo was relieved to see some of the nervousness he was feeling reflected in Navio's face.

'If they ask, let's lay it on thick about our families being slaughtered. We're loyal Roman citizens, who pay our taxes and ask little in return. Where were the legionaries to protect us when Spartacus and his savages descended on our farms? And so on.'

'Fine.' However, Carbo's tension grew as they edged closer to the walls, which were heavily manned. There were ballistae at regular intervals along the stone battlements as well. He indicated them with tight nods of his head. 'See those?'

'Yes. They're prepared for a siege. Maybe Longinus is scared to march outside and fight!' joked Navio.

'Maybe. But he'll do it anyway.'

'He'll have to,' agreed Navio grimly. 'Or for the rest of his life he'll be known as the general who let Spartacus escape. He'd never command more than a squad of men on latrine duty.'

It was a pleasing to imagine a Roman general supervising the cleaning up of shit and piss, but Carbo forced himself to concentrate on what was going on ahead. The skinny man with the cart in front was having a furious argument with the legionaries manning the gate. 'You're not coming in with that damn wagon,' reiterated the *optio* in charge, a pug-nosed, officious individual. 'For the foreseeable future, no trade goods are to be allowed in unless by the direct order of the proconsul.' He scanned the list in his right hand. 'I can't see anything here about planks.'

'These have been ordered by no less than Purpurius!'

'Purpurius?' The optio yawned.

'He is an important merchant who lives by the forum.'

'Never heard of him.'

'Let me tell you that Purpurius is a friend of the proconsul!'

'I'm sure he is,' said the optio in a disbelieving tone. 'His goods aren't on my list, however.'

'It's taken me two days to get here,' pleaded the carter.

'Not my problem,' came the bored reply. 'Now back your cart up and turn around. You're blocking the entrance.'

'I—'

The optio lifted his metal-tipped staff. 'Are you deaf?'

Throwing filthy looks at the soldiers and complaining about what Purpurius would do when he heard what had happened, the unfortunate carter began the laborious procedure of reversing the oxen. Carbo, Navio and the people behind them scrambled out of the way as he manoeuvred away from the walls and, still grumbling, headed back the way he had come.

'Get a move on!' bellowed a voice.

The optio was beckoning them forward. 'Names,' he called out.

They had already decided that using their real names wouldn't matter, and it would mean that they didn't have to remember an alias. 'Paullus Carbo.'

'Marcus Navio.'

'Occupations?'

'We're farmers, sir,' said Carbo.

He looked them up and down. 'No cart, no sacks of vegetables. What's your business here?'

'We've been driven off our land,' replied Carbo bitterly.

'Ah. By Spartacus and his lot?'

'Yes, sir.' Navio's face twitched. 'The bastards killed our families. Took all of our livestock. Trampled the young wheat in the fields.'

'Left us with nothing,' added Carbo.

The optio grimaced in sympathy. 'You're not alone. The same's happened to thousands of others. Why have you come to Mutina?'

'To look for work, sir,' replied Navio.

'Work? You'll be lucky. The place is bursting at the seams with refugees.'

'We'll do anything, sir,' Carbo pleaded. 'Please.'

The optio rubbed his battered nose. 'There'll be work soon enough, I suppose. When Spartacus arrives, we'll need men who can carry rocks to the catapults on the walls. Think you can do that all day without complaining?'

'Of course, sir.'

'You look fit enough. No weapons apart from those knives?'

'No, sir.'

He gave them an abrupt wave. 'Go on then. Inside with both of you.'

Muttering their thanks, the friends hurried under the stone arch.

'Paullus Carbo? You kept that one quiet,' said Navio with a chuckle.

Carbo felt his face flame. 'I don't like the name, so I never use it.'

'Paullus, my son! Dinner is served.' Navio's tone was falsetto high, mimicking a woman's voice.

'Piss off!' He thumped Navio on the arm.

'Paullus! Time for your lessons!'

Navio's mimicry reminded Carbo of his old tutor and, despite himself, he snorted with amusement.

Navio put a finger to his lips. 'We're supposed to be grieving for our families – Paullus!'

They were so busy trying not to laugh out loud that neither saw one of the optio's men sloping after them.

A short distance into the town, the friends' attention was drawn by the delicious smell of frying food. Following their noses, they found an open-fronted restaurant on one of the first side streets off the main thoroughfare. Seeing that the place was packed with off-duty soldiers, they decided to eat there. Eavesdropping in such a place might prove fruitful. They found an empty table against the back wall and sat down. A blowsy-looking woman who reeked of cheap perfume came and took their orders. Three *asses* bought them two bowls of hearty stew, served with fresh bread, and a jug of watered-down wine. In between mouthfuls, they talked in lowered voices, all the while listening in to the conversations around them.

At length, Navio pushed his empty plate away with a belch. 'Gods, but I needed a feed like that.'

'It was good,' agreed Carbo absently.

'Longinus doesn't mind that we're outnumbered five to one!' announced a gnarled soldier at the next table. 'The motherless cur needs—'

'Shut it, Felix,' warned his companion. 'Never mind Longinus. If an officer hears you talking like that, you'll end up on a charge.'

'What do I care?' Felix slurped sourly at his wine. 'We're about to be slaughtered anyway. I might as well have a last night in clink before the end. The mattresses in there don't have as many bedbugs as mine.'

His friend snorted with laughter. 'That's as may be, but twenty lashes for insubordination will hurt a lot more than a few stinking bites. It won't get you out of fighting either. Every man who can hold a shield and spear has to report for duty. The surgeons have been ordered to empty the hospital of all but the most severe cases.'

'I know. I heard the announcement too,' grumbled Felix. 'It's just that—'

'Close your trap,' ordered his friend, pouring more wine. 'Enjoy another drink, for it might be one of your last.'

The two legionaries fell into a rambling chat about where they should go next.

'Did you hear that?' whispered Carbo. 'It sounds as if Longinus *is* going to fight.'

'Neither of them said that exactly.'

Navio was right. What they'd heard wasn't enough. Hiding his scowl, Carbo took another drink and casually cast his eyes around the nearest tables. To his left, four soldiers were devouring a roasted leg of pork.

Beyond them, a couple of what looked like merchants were talking business. On his right were the pair that they'd heard moaning and then a table of three legionaries who were swilling down wine and arguing over a game of knucklebones. Behind Navio, a junior officer and a trumpeter were amusing themselves by seeing how high a scrawny mongrel would jump to catch their leftovers. The conversations of those who were further away were impossible to make out.

Carbo told himself to be patient.

By the time that they'd finished their jug of wine, however, they had heard nothing more of interest. 'Time to move on,' he muttered. The afternoon was passing. It wouldn't be that long until it got dark.

Navio's answering grin was huge. He leaned towards Felix. 'Hey, friend! Where might two thirsty men find a decent watering hole? Preferably one that has whores who aren't riddled with pox.'

'That's easy. Try the inn two streets up, on the right. Vulcan's Anvil, they call it. You can't miss it. Full of soldiers, night and day.'

'It's a good place to get hammered,' added his comrade with a wink.

'The pussy there is top notch. Expensive, though.' Felix's red-rimmed eyes regarded them closely. 'I doubt you've got the brass to pay for one whore between you.'

'You're right, friend,' said Navio, getting to his feet. 'But there's nothing to stop us admiring the flesh on display as we drink, eh?'

'True enough. That's what most of us do in there, unless it's payday. We might join you later.'

'We'd be honoured to buy you a drink,' said Carbo, thinking the exact opposite. He nodded an amiable farewell. As soon as they were out of earshot, he muttered to Navio, 'Let's find somewhere else.'

Navio pursed his lips regretfully. 'It would be a little dangerous, eh?'

'He said it would be full of soldiers! Another inn would be far safer.'

'Think about the whores, though.' Navio's tone was wistful.

'The ones we can't afford?'

'Can't we?'

'No,' snapped Carbo.

With a sly look, Navio pulled on the leather thong that held his purse around his neck. 'I found two *aurei* in one of the farmhouses we sacked a while ago. There hasn't been anything to spend them on until now.'

'Spartacus said not to take much money,' protested Carbo.

'I know, I know. But a man's got his needs, hasn't he?'

'What do you think an *aureus* will buy?'

'What won't it buy? You'll get the fuck of your life or my name's not Marcus Navio!'

Lustful thoughts filled Carbo's head. Then he pulled himself together. 'Not in Vulcan's Anvil,' he said firmly. 'Somewhere else.'

'There'll be more than one good brothel in town,' said Navio with a shrug. 'Let's try another inn, see what we can hear. There are bound to be more off-duty soldiers complaining about Longinus.'

They began pushing their way through the crowds.

Neither saw the figure slip from the shadows opposite the restaurant to dog their trail.

Despite the warm glow from the wine, Carbo couldn't fail to notice the pinched faces and ragged appearance of the town's inhabitants. Squads of legionaries tramped to and fro, driven on by the shouts and vine canes of their officers. No one looked happy, especially the shopkeepers, who stood in the doorways of their empty establishments, regarding the passers-by with sour expressions. There were beggars everywhere, squatting on the rutted mud at the side of the street or working their way through the throng, dirty hands outstretched. Spartacus is responsible for this, Carbo thought, shocked yet proud. We all are.

Their quest to eavesdrop on conversations proved more difficult than the pair had supposed. Wandering the thoroughfares, they found numerous inns of one kind or another. There were soldiers in all of them, but the confined spaces meant that it was difficult to secure a table near enough to have any chance of listening in. The friends had to be discreet about what they were doing and, more than once, they had to content themselves with standing at the bar, or sitting on the other side of the room to the men whose banter and complaints they wanted to hear. On the one occasion that they managed to settle down next to a party of legionaries, all they gathered was that no one wanted to be serving under Longinus, two of the men had the pox and that it was three months until the next payday. When Carbo let his gaze linger for too long on the group, he was told in no uncertain terms to mind his own business unless he wanted to be picking his teeth from the back of his throat. The pair quickly moved on.

Although they only drank watered-down wine, they visited enough establishments in the subsequent hours for their senses to become dulled and their
levels of frustration and anger to grow. The fifth tavern was the worst of
the lot, a dingy hole down a side alley. It had rickety furniture, a couple of
ancient whores and the foulest wine Carbo had ever tasted. He spat out the
first mouthful, and just sat, furiously studying the contents of his clay cup
as a soothsayer would. But he found no inspiration. When a drunk spilled
his wine over him, the young Roman struggled not to beat the fool into a
bloody pulp. Glad that he had mastered his temper, he then had to stop Navio
from eyeballing a couple of legionaries who were challenging the other
customers to a wrestling match. 'Leave it. Don't go looking for trouble.'

Navio tore his eyes away from the soldiers, who had stripped to the
waist and were parading around in circles, flexing their biceps and threatening to cripple all comers. 'I could beat both of them,' he said truculently.
'At the same time.'

'I'm sure you could,' Carbo soothed. 'But now is not the time. Remember
why we're here.'

Navio shot him a sour glance. 'Not having much luck, though, are we?
That old bitch Fortuna must be in a really bad mood.'

'Our luck will turn. Let's find another drinking hole. That'll be the one
where we hear something useful,' said Carbo with all the enthusiasm he
could muster. 'And simmer down. Remember where we are.'

Navio grumbled but followed Carbo outside without further argument.

Seeing a temple dedicated to Fortuna, the goddess of luck, Carbo led
his friend over. He saw Navio's incredulous look. 'She might need placating.
Wait here. Do not cause any trouble.' Buying a small offering of a votive
lamp from a wizened old man, he went inside, where he asked the goddess's
forgiveness for Navio's words, and asked for her help with their mission.
Carbo felt better after he'd made his offering, and he led his friend in search
of another inn with renewed enthusiasm.

They heard nothing of interest in the next place, however, nor at the
busy restaurant where they each ate a plate of fried pork. Carbo's spirits
sank to match Navio's. They sat miserably, watching yet another file of
troops march past. 'We could follow them,' Carbo suggested.

Navio's withering look told him what he knew already. 'Stupid idea.'

Nothing was said for a while.

'I don't want to go back without any information,' said Carbo at last.

'Me neither, but what else can we do?'

Carbo thought of the soldiers they'd spoken to earlier. His stomach clenched at the idea of actively seeking the company of two men who, if alerted to their identities, would kill them without even blinking. But if they were very drunk, they wouldn't find out – and they might reveal something. It was a long shot, but Carbo couldn't think of anything else. 'There's always Vulcan's Anvil.'

'I thought we'd decided it was too dangerous?'

'Can you think of anything better?'

Navio sucked in air between his teeth. 'Other than walking up to an officer and asking what Longinus has planned, no,' he admitted.

'Well, then.' Now that he'd thought of a possible solution, Carbo wanted to go for it. 'Anything's better than trudging around every low-class watering hole in Mutina. We'll end up with gut rot if this keeps on.'

'True.' Navio's expression grew sly. 'Remember the whores they told us about? They're supposed to be the best in town.'

'Forget that. Let's see if our luck has turned, see if we can overhear anything.'

'And after that, a good screw!'

The idea was appealing. Carbo's unfulfilled lust plagued him night and day. Telling himself that buying a whore would be just reward for finding out what Spartacus wanted to know, he headed in search of Vulcan's Anvil.

It wasn't hard to find. A three-storey detached brick building with a large courtyard surrounded by stables, it was a grander enterprise than most. The ground-floor frontage was covered in stucco, which had been painted imaginatively with Greek columns covered in vines. Over the front door, which was manned by a pair of hulking doormen, hung a sign depicting the god of fire crouched over his anvil, hammer in hand.

They swaggered up to the entrance. The noise emanating from the window openings – laughter, singing and the noise of women's voices – was deafening. 'Sounds promising, eh?' said Navio, leering.

Even as Carbo's imagination ran riot, his skin crawled. They were about to walk into the lion's den. He gritted his teeth. The shame of telling Spartacus that he'd failed would be worse than risking his neck. And if they were careful, things would go according to plan.

The larger of the doormen, a colossus with a gaping socket where one of his eyes should have been, moved to block the doorway. 'Can I help you?' His tone didn't imply that he wanted to be of any help whatsoever.

'We were in search of a drink,' said Carbo politely.

The doorman sniffed. 'Really?'

'Yes. And perhaps a chat with some of your young ladies,' added Navio.

Now the giant laughed. 'You two haven't got the cash to afford one of our girls. Now why don't you piss off before me and my mate break your arms?'

'And legs,' rumbled his companion.

Carbo's nerves jangled an alarm. He began to back away.

'Where are you going?' Navio's tone was jaunty.

'To an inn where they're less picky about their customers.'

'There's no need for that.' Navio's hand dipped into his purse. Carbo had no time to react. Gold flashed in his friend's fingers as he stepped right up to the doorman. 'Is this good enough for you?'

The colossus' face cracked into a gap-toothed smile. 'Forgive my poor manners, sir. You are both most welcome to Vulcan's Anvil. As everyone knows, we have the finest wines and women in Mutina.' He stood aside and with a flourish of his meaty arm, bid them enter.

'Come on.'

Reluctantly, Carbo joined his friend.

'This is more like it,' said Navio as they stepped inside.

The richly decorated interior was lit by half a dozen bronze candelabras suspended from the ceiling. The solid tables and benches were carved from hardwood, and the sawdust on the concrete and tiled floor was clean. The customers were mostly soldiers, a number of whom were officers.

Navio's smile faded before Carbo's scowl. 'What?'

'You know how damn rare *aurei* are! Those doormen will be talking about us all night.'

'Relax,' said Navio in a confident tone. 'What do they care how we came by our money? I'll be sure to tip them on the way out, tell them to forget they ever saw us. We don't want our wives to find out we've been here. You know the type of line.' He winked.

Carbo still wasn't happy, but then he saw the quartet of women standing on a plinth behind the bar and all reason, all thought of their mission, left him. The four were more beautiful than his wildest dreams. His groin tightened as he realised that under their diaphanous robes, they were naked.

'I thought you'd change your mind.' Navio thumped him on the chest, bringing him back to reality. He handed over a gold coin. 'Here. Spend it wisely. I'll see you later for a drink. We can compare notes.'

Carbo clutched the aureus tightly. 'Where are you going?'

'Where do you think?' Navio replied, nodding at the prostitutes. 'We've got all night to find out what we need.'

With a pounding heart, Carbo watched his friend work his way to the bar, catch the eye of a stunning brunette and gesture to her. When she approached, their heads bent together for a moment. Long enough for the beauty to see the aureus, thought Carbo. The next time he looked, Navio was heading up the stairs with his arm around her. He didn't look back.

A man carrying two jugs of wine collided with Carbo, taking his attention away from the whores. For some reason, he thought of his parents. The letter! If there was ever a good time to have it written, it was now. He'd be back within the blink of an eye. Navio wouldn't even know that he had gone. Once it was done, he could have a drink and listen in to the loud chatter around him. With so many soldiers in the inn, it would be impossible not to hear some useful information. Then he could decide which one of the women he wanted. Excited by the prospect of completing Spartacus' mission as well as his own, Carbo slipped outside again. In the failing light, the doormen were talking to a block-headed soldier.

Sensing Carbo's presence, the colossus turned with an obsequious smile. 'Leaving so soon, sir?'

'I have a quick errand to run. Before I drink too much and forget, you see. Where's the forum?'

'That way.' The colossus pointed northwards. 'All the streets heading in that direction reach it.'

'How far is it?'

'No more than a quarter of a mile.'

Nodding his thanks, Carbo walked off.

The legionary waited until he had gone some distance up the alley before sidling after him.

The doorman proved to be correct. Carbo found the forum with ease. Although he'd never visited the town before, the large rectangular space felt familiar. Like most Roman centres of population, the forum was the beating heart of Mutina. Stalls packed the area, selling everything from tools, clothing, pots and pans to bread, meat, vegetables and love charms. It was bordered by a large number of temples – to Jupiter, Minerva, Juno and the Dioscuri, the twins Castor and Pollux – in addition to government buildings such as the court and the tax office. There were also *basilicae*, covered markets where lawyers, scribes, surgeons and pharmacists plied their trades.

Carbo headed straight for these. His eagerness waned as he crossed the threshold, however. What he was about to do was even more risky than entering Vulcan's Anvil. If the scribe got even the slightest inkling that Carbo was one of Spartacus' men, he would be arrested on the spot. He sauntered up and down the stalls, ignoring offers of a bargain price to read his fortune, to have his teeth examined and to write his will that very instant, in case the gods suddenly struck him down. His gaze settled on a portly figure sitting under a sign that read: LETTERS COMPOSED. NEAT SCRIPT. REASONABLE PRICES. Catching Carbo's eye, the scribe gave him an amiable nod. Pleased that the man hadn't verbally assaulted him as his neighbours had, Carbo nodded back. 'I need a letter written,' he blurted, feeling his resolve weaken.

'That's my job.'

'It won't be long. No more than a few lines.'

'Four asses.'

'Fine. Can you have it sent as well?'

'That will cost more. Where does it need to go?'

'Rome.'

There was a frown. 'The road south isn't safe at the moment, as you know.'

'Because of Spartacus and his men?'

A tight, angry nod. 'They say that he's advancing on the town. The proconsul is sure to act within the next day or so. His two legions are ready for a fight. With the blessings of Jupiter, Greatest and Best, we will soon rid be of the Thracian murderer and the scum who follow in his wake.'

'Let us hope so,' Carbo replied blithely. 'Can you have it sent anyway?'

'I should be able to find someone. It will cost you, mind.'

'How much?'

'Call it an even denarius.'

Carbo made a rueful face, but he would have paid far more if he'd had to. He fumbled in his purse and handed over a silver coin.

Selecting a small piece of parchment, the scribe placed it on his stained desk and weighed its corners down with pieces of lead. Dipping his stylus into a pot of ink, he looked enquiringly at Carbo.

'"Honoured Father and Mother, I live in hope that this reaches you both healthy and well."'

The scribe pursed his lips with concentration as he finished the line. 'Yes?'

'"I can only apologise for the lack of communication since I left home. I departed because I wished to" . . .' Carbo paused, wondering what he should say. '. . . "help the family's financial problems in my own way, rather than doing as Father wished. I know that this makes me an undutiful son, but I could not bear the thought of becoming a lawyer."'

'I don't blame you,' said the scribe, scowling at the stallholder opposite, a tall man with oiled hair and an imperious manner. 'Liars and thieves, the lot of them.'

Even more aware of the need to choose his words with care, Carbo smiled. 'Continue.'

'"I still hope to help with regard to Father's *obligations* in the future. For the moment, however, that will have to wait. I am about to embark on a long and dangerous journey, one from which I may never return."' *May? Will.* But he couldn't say that, in case the scribe got too curious. His letter was surely odd enough as it was. '"Before my departure, I wished to let you know that I pray for you both daily. May the gods watch over and protect you. Your loving son, Carbo."'

The scribe signed off the letter with a flourish. 'Thinking of seeking your fortune abroad?'

'Yes.' *You cannot even imagine.*

'With a merchant?'

'That's right.'

'Gaul, or somewhere even further afield?'

'I have to meet a man in Placentia who is heading for Gaul and then Britannia,' lied Carbo.

'You're a braver man than me,' said the scribe with a shudder. 'They say that the seas around Britannia are full of terrible monsters. Its natives live under the malign influence of the druids. Their warriors fight naked, eat the flesh of their enemies, and make drinking cups out of their skulls.' He took Carbo's feigned horror at face value. 'Of course I didn't mean that you would come to any harm. No doubt you'll be home within the year, a wealthy man.'

'No doubt.' Real grief gripped Carbo. Despite the lie about his intentions, his imminent departure was no less final. If only he could turn up on his uncle's doorstep and say goodbye to his parents in person, instead of sending them a coded letter. *Be content. It's the best you can do.*

'To whom should the letter be sent?' asked the scribe, folding the parchment into a little square.

Carbo's mouth opened and closed. He wanted to say, 'Jovian Carbo, at the house of the lawyer Alfenus Varus, who lives on the Esquiline Hill in Rome,' but his tongue had stuck to the roof of his mouth. *What am I doing? This is insane.*

'Well?'

Still Carbo said nothing.

'The letter's no good without a name and address.'

'Leave it. I've changed my mind.'

'Change of heart?'

'Yes,' Carbo muttered. 'My prayers will have to suffice.'

'Family are always hard to deal with.' The scribe's tone was sympathetic.

'Yes,' replied Carbo gruffly. 'I want my denarius.'

'Give me four asses, and it's yours. I have to be paid for my time,' said the scribe with a frown.

Carbo rummaged in his purse and handed over the small coins. In return, the scribe tossed him the denarius. Carbo nodded his thanks and left. He had to concentrate on his real mission and find out what he could about Longinus' plans. After that, he could drown his sorrows. In the morning, they'd return to their camp, where Spartacus would be waiting. He walked past a druggist's stall, vaguely noticing a legionary who was engrossed by the bottles and lotions on display without discerning it was the same individual who had been talking to the doormen outside the inn. He also missed the man hurrying over to the scribe.

By the time he'd reached Vulcan's Anvil again, it was nearly dark. He was ushered inside with more greasy smiles. Carbo scanned the room, but there was no sign of Navio. His eyes were drawn to the women behind the bar. A raven-haired temptress now stood where the brunette had been. She was even more gorgeous than the others, and Carbo knew that she was the one he'd pick. But before that, he had work to do. Ordering a jug of Campanian, he found a space on a long bench that ran along one wall, which fortuitously afforded a good view of the door as well as the stairs to the floor above.

Casual glances revealed that his neighbours were soldiers. Carbo's guts churned, but he slurped at his wine, eager for the confidence that its effects would bring, and listened to every word he could.

To his left, three junior officers were bitching about their centurion. 'All he cares about is spit and polish,' moaned one, a fresh-faced *tesserarius*.

'I know,' agreed the *signifer*, who was a decade or so older. 'That bullshit has its time and place, but when we're facing the fight of our lives, you'd think he could concentrate on other things.'

'I hear what you're saying, lads.' The optio was a tall man with jug ears. 'But Bassus has been around the block more times than you and I can imagine. Focusing the men's minds on boring duties like keeping their kit sparkling clean helps them not to think about more worrying things.'

'Like Spartacus and his fucking army, you mean,' said the tesserarius heavily.

'Precisely.'

'I hope to Hades that Longinus knows what he's at,' muttered the signifer. 'If he doesn't, we're all buggered.'

Carbo pricked his ears.

'Shut your trap,' growled the optio. 'You know we're not supposed to talk about it.' He glanced to either side, and Carbo busily filled his cup again. Fortuna, please let me hear something, he prayed.

To his disappointment, the officers then began talking about the whores on display. Carbo turned his attention to the group of legionaries on his right, but they were arguing furiously about whose turn it was to order the next round. It appeared to be the turn of a slight soldier with mousy brown hair, although he was denying it, meeting his comrades' protests and insults with a small, amused smile. The men's racket was so great that Carbo couldn't hear what anyone else in the vicinity was saying. He wanted to find another spot where he might be more successful in eavesdropping, but he knew that would look odd. He'd chosen his spot and he had to stick to it.

Catching the eye of a passing serving boy, he ordered more wine and a plate of bread and cheese. The food would line his stomach, and stop him getting too pissed.

'Well, well. If it isn't our friend from the restaurant!'

Carbo's heart sank as he looked up. He managed to pull a grin. 'You found your way here then?'

'Seems like it,' said Felix with a belch, throwing himself down beside Carbo.

'Where's your friend?'

'Gaius? He's getting the drinks in. It was my job to find a seat. Gods — this place is bloody heaving!' He leaned towards Carbo, filling the air with wine fumes. 'Is your mate giving one of the whores a seeing-to?'

'Yes.' Carbo's gaze flickered to the stairs, which were empty. *Hurry up, Navio!*

'Where'd he get the money?'

Carbo thought frantically. 'We pooled what we had and drew lots. Navio won. It wasn't a huge amount, but he managed to talk one of the women around. The man has a golden tongue,' he lied, cursing silently because he'd just blown any chance of sex, at least while Felix was around. He now had to act as if he had very little money.

'Lucky bastard. I'd love to do the same, but that kind of cash only comes my way on payday. Not that I'm likely to be here the next time that comes around!' He gave Carbo a knowing grimace. 'There's a big fight coming.'

'I know. Here, have some of my wine while you're waiting.' He emptied the dregs from a used cup on the table and filled it to the brim.

'I don't mind if I do.' Felix took a long swallow and smacked his lips with satisfaction. 'It's not bad. Better than the vinegar they were serving in the restaurant, eh?'

'That wouldn't be hard.'

'Too true! Felix is the name, lad. What's yours?'

'Carbo.'

They nodded at each other in a friendly way. This is weird, thought Carbo. I might have to kill this man in the next few days. Or he me.

'You look a likely sort. Why aren't you in the legions?'

He shrugged. 'I come from a farm. Working the land is all I've ever known.'

'Farming? You can keep it. Too damn boring if you ask me! There's far more adventure serving in the army.' Felix's face darkened. 'Until the likes of Spartacus come along of course.'

'Longinus will get the better of him, surely?'

'The proconsul is not a worker of magic! He only has two legions. The Thracian has upwards of fifty thousand men. That's poor odds by anyone's standards.'

Carbo let his face go sour. 'Is that it then? Longinus will be defeated, as the consuls were?'

It was as if Felix couldn't help himself. 'Despite what I said earlier, Longinus is a crafty old bird. He's got a plan. One that should catch the son of a whore unawares.'

'Oh?' said Carbo offhandedly. Inside, his heart had begun to race.

Felix tapped the side of his nose. 'It's on a need-to-know basis.'

'Of course.' Hiding his fury, he poured more wine.

'You're a good man, Carbo, like me. To your health, and mine. To the death of Spartacus and every last one of his shitbag followers!'

'I'll drink to that,' Carbo muttered.

Raised voices at the door diverted their attention. A group of legionaries in full battle dress had entered. Directed by an optio, they were splitting into pairs and moving through the room, studying the men at every table.

Carbo's stomach did a nauseating somersault. *What in the name of Hades do they want?*

'It's the fucking watch,' growled Felix.

'Why are they here?'

'The usual reason. They'll be looking for soldiers who are out without a pass.' He saw Carbo's blank look and pulled a small wooden tablet from his purse. 'We all have to have these to leave barracks. If you're caught without one, it's ten days in the clink.'

'Ah.' But Carbo's disquiet returned the instant he saw a block-headed legionary talking to the colossus at the door. It was the same soldier who had been outside when he'd gone to the forum. This could be no coincidence. Carbo's eyes slid to the stairs. Still no sign of Navio. *Damn it!*

A figure loomed over them.

'Gaius! I thought you'd got lost.' Felix jerked a thumb at Carbo. 'This is the lad we met earlier. Carbo's his name.'

Gaius let out a suspicious grunt as he took a seat beside Felix.

'Hey, come on. He's been sharing his wine with me.'

'Hmmm. Where's his friend?'

'Screwing one of the whores.'

From the corner of his eye, Carbo could see a pair of legionaries drawing nearer. What made his heart nearly leap out of his chest, however, was the sight of the block-headed soldier weaving his way between the packed tables, studying each man's face. It would only be moments before he reached them. *He's looking for me.* Carbo knew it in his gut. He was about to stand when a full cup of wine was shoved in his face. 'Get that down your gullet.'

'Thanks.' Carbo threw it back in one swallow.

'Jupiter's cock, you've got a thirst on you! Sure you don't want to join the legions? You'd fit right in.' Grinning, Felix poured him another.

Again Carbo made to leave, but his plate of bread and cheese arrived. He kept the serving boy as long as he could, fumbling around for the right coins and asking him where the toilets were. It was a waste of effort, because the moment the servant moved on, his place was taken by the block-headed legionary.

'You're looking in the wrong place, pal,' said Felix, truculently waving his pass. 'We've all got one of these. Why don't you piss off back to the guardhouse and leave us in peace?'

'Shut your mouth, soldier.' The gimlet eyes did not waver from their path along the faces lining the bench.

Carbo buried his nose in his cup of wine, hoping against hope that he wouldn't be noticed.

'You. Look at me.'

Shit.

'I'm talking to you, sewer rat!'

'Back off, you prick,' said Felix. 'He's a civvie.'

'I want a word with him.'

'Why don't you pick on someone your own size?' demanded Felix, getting to his feet.

'Keep your damn nose out of this.'

'He's a friend of mine, cocksucker. Leave him alone.'

Carbo sensed Felix step forward and shove the block-headed man in the chest. What should *he* do?

'You stupid bastard! I've been watching him all day. He and his mate are loaded down with gold coins. What are two pieces of shit doing with money like that? This one has also had a scribe write a letter to his parents, telling them he's going on a long journey.'

'Eh?' said Felix stupidly, looking down at Carbo, whose throat had closed with fear. *The prick must have seen Navio pull out his aureus and then followed me from here.* He had no time to think further.

'They're damn spies. Spartacus' spies!'

Carbo leaped up. He dashed the contents of his cup into the block-headed legionary's face, and followed that by upending the table between them. The cursing soldier went down with crockery clattering all around. Throwing the bewildered Felix an apologetic look, Carbo sprinted towards the stairs. There was no chance of getting out of the front door, and he couldn't abandon Navio.

'Stop him! He's a spy!'

A pair of legionaries moved into his path. Carbo jumped on to the nearest table, scattering cups of wine everywhere. As the men around it bawled in surprise and anger, he bounded on to the one beyond that, and then back to the floor. Four more steps, and he'd be at the foot of the staircase. A hand tugged at the back of his tunic. Carbo drew his dagger, spun and slashed the soldier who had grabbed him across the arm. Blood sprayed into the air and his assailant fell away, screaming.

Carbo went up the steep flight two steps at a time. He risked a glance at the room below, and his heart raced even faster. Led by the block-headed legionary, more than a dozen soldiers were heading his way. He'd be able to check one room for Navio – no more.

Carbo shot up the last few stairs like a slingshot. Ahead of him, a corridor led left and right. *Which way? Left.* He darted into the passage, which was dimly lit by a single hanging oil lamp. Erotic scenes had been painted on the walls, but Carbo paid them no heed. There were doors to both sides, at least four of them. Gods, which should he choose? He could hear studded sandals thundering up after him. He squeezed his eyes shut. *Fortuna, help me!* The first door Carbo saw when he looked again was the second on the left. He shoulder-charged it, smashing it open with a splintering of wood.

For once, the goddess of good luck had answered his prayers.

'What the—' bellowed Navio, whose bare arse was sticking up from between the open legs of the brunette.

'Up! Get up! They know who we are!'

'I—' Navio's protest died in his throat as he heard the men on the stairs. He scrambled off the now screaming whore and grabbed his *licium*.

Carbo's gaze shot around the little room and halted on the small window opening. 'Come on!' He tore over and threw open the shutters, which cracked off the outside wall. Sticking his head out, he saw a tiled roof — part of the ground floor — a short drop below. He shoved his bloodied dagger back into his sheath. Heaving a leg out into space, Carbo gripped the wooden frame as he pulled his other leg out. Instantly, he dropped to the tiles. He looked up and was relieved to see Navio's bare legs following him a heartbeat later. With a thud, his friend landed beside him, bollock naked but clutching his undergarment. Carbo stifled his urge to laugh.

'Which way?'

Angry shouts reached them from the room above.

Carbo tried to get his bearings. There was more light to his left, which meant it was more likely to be the front of the inn. Not the best route to take. 'This way!' Taking as much care as he could on an uneven, angled surface in the pitch black, he worked his way across the tiles. There was a muttered curse behind him as Navio stubbed a toe.

'Where are they?' shouted a voice. 'Get a torch!'

Carbo stumbled and almost fell off the edge of the roof. There was just enough light for him to make out the paved surface of a yard, a cart and a water butt. *It's the inn's stable yard.* Taking a deep breath, he jumped, landing hard on the cobbles below. Half winded, he glanced up, seeing no one. *Thank the gods.* Navio thumped down beside him.

'What in Hades shall we do?'

'Lose those bastards who are right behind us!' whispered Carbo. 'We're dead meat otherwise.' Seeing a gap between two of the stable buildings, he tore towards it. He had no idea where it led.

As it happened, it was the dungheap, which was enclosed on three sides by a wall.

A series of heavy thuds from the yard announced the legionaries' arrival.

There was nothing for it. Trying not to breathe, Carbo began to clamber up the pile of shit. Soon he was ankle-, and then knee-deep in the stinking ordure. Driven by sheer desperation and the panting breaths of Navio behind him, he floundered up until the top of the wall was within reach. Pulling himself atop the bricks, he took a swift look at what was on the other side before letting himself fall. Fortunately, it wasn't far to the ground of the narrow alleyway.

'Where are you?'

'Here, on the other side,' answered Carbo. 'If you want to live, climb!'

Navio's head appeared, followed by his torso and a leg. 'I'm covered in shit.'

'That's the least of our worries.' Navio lowered himself and they crouched down for a moment, listening hard. Confused cries from the inn's yard revealed that their escape route had not immediately been found. It wouldn't be long, however. As soon as someone brought light, the legionaries would see their trail up the dungheap. They had to move, and fast. The alley they were in was formed by the walls of two large buildings. Blocks of flats or large houses, thought Carbo.

'What the fuck are we going to do?' asked Navio. 'They'll have men on all the streets around the inn. The first one who spots me will know who I am.'

Carbo caught the edge of desperation in his friend's voice, and tried not to let it infect him. He trotted down to the strip of light that formed the alleyway's exit on to the street. Peering to the left and right, he let out a stifled groan. A group of legionaries was already combing the thoroughfare from either end. Every second man held a flaming torch aloft, providing light for their companions to poke their heads into every nook and cranny.

Navio saw his face. 'Not good?'

Carbo explained what he'd seen.

'What have we done to deserve this?'

'We thought with our pricks instead of our heads,' snapped Carbo.

'You're right. I'm sorry,' muttered Navio.

'It's not just your fault. I went along with you.'

'Hey! Over here! I think they climbed up this way,' shouted a voice on the other side of the wall.

'Let's kill the first man over,' said Carbo. 'Take his sword, and hopefully get another from the next one. At least we can die like men.'

Navio nodded in savage agreement.

They trotted back up the alley.

What a stupid way to die, thought Carbo.

Then, to his utter amazement, a door in the wall to his left opened. A boy in a threadbare tunic that was far too big for him emerged, clutching a bucket full of kitchen slops.

Hope flared in Carbo's breast. Even as the slave saw them, and opened his mouth to scream, Carbo had placed a hand over his mouth. 'Don't make a sound. We're Spartacus' men. Legionaries are after us. Can you help?'

'Give me a damn hand up!' bellowed the voice that Carbo had heard a moment before. 'Quickly!'

The boy's eyes flickered to the wall and back again.

'We're dead men if you don't,' hissed Carbo.

The boy pulled his hand away. 'Come inside.' He melted back into the darkness.

Carbo didn't think; he just followed. He felt Navio pushing in after him. The boy brushed past and pulled the door silently to. There was a *snick* as he slid the bolt home, and then they all stood there in the pitch black, panting. Listening.

Thud. 'I'm over.'

'Can you see anything?' called a second voice.

'There's no sign of the bastards, no.' A metallic *shhhh* as a sword was pulled from its scabbard.

'I'm nearly waist deep in the shit!'

'I don't care! Get your arse over here.'

Muffled curses, and another *thud.*

The jingle of mail. The pad of two men moving with great care.

'They're long gone.'

'You don't know that,' said the soldier who'd been first over the wall. 'Here's a door, look.'

Carbo's grip on his dagger tightened.

'Which is locked from the inside,' said the second legionary acidly. 'They've headed on to the street, no doubt. One of the patrols will pick them up soon enough.'

'Let's hope so.'

'What are you worried about? They won't have discovered a thing.'

'All the same, we don't want Spartacus hearing about our hidden catapults.'

Carbo froze.

The soldier's companion sniggered. 'He won't have a clue. The slave scum will march along the road north, cocky as you like, following our decoy force. They'll get the shock of their lives, though, when they get pulverised by the ballistae.'

'Ha! And even if some of them get away over the Alps, they won't find much of a welcome should they head for Thrace,' said the first man with a laugh. 'Someone told me that Marcus Lucullus has recently smashed the Thracian troops who were fighting with Mithridates. By all accounts, he's now laying waste to half of that damn area.'

The legionaries' voices died away as they walked down the alleyway.

'Did you hear that?' whispered Carbo.

'Yes. Incredible.'

They weren't yet out of danger, but Carbo couldn't believe the luck that had befallen them.

Navio chuckled softly.

'What are you laughing at?'

'A few moments ago, I was ploughing the most beautiful whore I've ever seen. Now I'm naked, covered in shit and standing in a pitch-black larder, freezing my arse off. But it doesn't matter, because of what we just heard.'

Carbo had to bite the inside of his cheek to stop himself laughing.

Despite the disquieting news about Thrace, it felt good to be alive.

Chapter IV

The friends' luck continued to hold. After it was clear that the legionaries had gone for good, the friends had allowed Arnax, the sallow-skinned boy who had saved them, to light an oil lamp. The flickering flame had revealed a dingy room full of brushes, cleaning rags, buckets and a sink full of dirty crockery. It was a perfect hiding place. Few people – even slaves – chose to enter a scullery unless they had to. While Carbo had questioned Arnax, Navio had been able to clean off the worst of the manure and finally don his licium.

They had soon established that Arnax belonged to an old man who lived on his own with a handful of slaves. As long as he kept the floors, the kitchen and the courtyard clean, Arnax was left to his own devices. This discovery had permitted the pair to relax a little. Their spirits had risen soon after when the boy had reappeared with a tunic and a pair of sandals for Navio, as well as some food, and water from the house's well.

They had readied themselves to leave around midnight. It hadn't taken much persuasion to get Arnax to join them. 'When the soldiers haven't found us by daybreak,' Carbo had warned, 'they'll retrace their steps. It will be easy to see where we jumped over the wall. Two big shitty sets of footprints will lead to this door. When they arrive to talk to your master, there will be one person to blame. You.'

At that, Arnax's thin face had paled.

'Come with us,' Carbo had urged him. 'You'll be free, like everyone else in the army. We can always use a clever lad like you.'

'I'm only eleven.'

'That's of no matter. The cooks, the blacksmiths and the grooms who look after the cavalry's horses always need help.' Carbo had seen the disappointment in Arnax's dark eyes and relented. 'Or you could keep our gear clean and cook for us.'

'I'll do it!'

And that had been that.

Taking a piece of rope from the scullery, the trio had stolen through the city, grateful for the total cloud cover that had reduced the light at street level to almost complete darkness. The friends had then been even more thankful for Arnax's presence. He had a keen sense of direction, and had guided them to the south wall, avoiding a number of patrols. Once they had spotted the sentries pacing the battlements and timed the frequency of their passing, it had been a simple enough affair to climb up, fix their rope to a pillar on the ramparts and scramble down to the ditch at the foot of the wall.

From there, it had been a long but satisfying walk to their encampment, which they had reached just after dawn. Arnax's eyes had grown to the size of small plates at the sheer number of men and tents, and Carbo had clapped him on the arm. 'See now why there's a feeling of panic in Mutina?'

Showing the awestruck Arnax to their tent, the pair had left him with instructions to cook them breakfast. They had gone in search of Spartacus at once. Wary of being punished, both were reluctant to confess the full story of what had happened. If asked to explain the ripe smell still emanating from Navio, they had decided to say he'd drunk too much and fallen into a dungheap as they'd walked through the dark streets. Carbo had had to fish him out.

They found Spartacus seated at his campfire, talking to Castus and Gannicus. Atheas and Taxacis stood nearby as always, like two guardian wolves.

Castus grimaced as they approached. 'Phoah! Someone stinks of horse shit.'

Gannicus smiled at Navio's embarrassment. Even Spartacus grinned. 'What in the Rider's name happened to you?'

'Where have you been?' demanded Castus.

They didn't know about our mission, thought Carbo. Spartacus wants to show them how smart he is.

'Mutina,' said Navio.

Suspicion flashed across Castus' face, and he shot a glance at Gannicus, who didn't look happy either. 'What in Hades were our two *Romans* doing there, Spartacus?'

'Falling into dungheaps. What else?'

Castus' face grew red. 'Don't try to be funny with me.'

'Why were we not told of this?' growled Gannicus.

'Do I have to tell you everything?'

'You used to share with us what you were planning—'

'You are here now,' interrupted Spartacus curtly. 'They were gathering information. You can both hear their report first-hand. Is that not enough?'

Castus made to say more, but Gannicus, who looked angrier than Carbo had ever seen him, laid a hand on his arm. Glowering, Castus subsided into silence.

'Your mission didn't all go according to plan, I take it? I don't recall telling you to fling yourselves into horse shit.'

'We had some problems, sir,' replied Navio awkwardly.

Spartacus' eyebrows made a neat arch.

'We, err . . .' Navio hesitated. 'We had a few drinks. I ended up in a dungheap. Carbo pulled me out.'

The Gauls chortled.

He hasn't had to lie. Carbo felt a trace of relief, but it didn't last. *Yet.*

'Nothing wrong with that, as long as you also did what I asked to.' Spartacus' voice had lost its amused tone. 'Did you discover anything?'

'We did,' said Carbo, eager to move on. 'Longinus is planning a surprise attack as we advance past the town. Apparently, there's an area of hidden ground within range of the road north. That's where his ballistae will be.' He wasn't sure why, but Carbo did not mention what the legionaries had said about the recent Roman victory over the Thracians. He was grateful that Navio didn't either.

'Fucking Roman bastards,' Castus ground out. Gannicus agreed loudly.

'Do you know where the spot is?' asked Spartacus.

'No.'

'Or how many catapults he has?'

Carbo shook his head in apology.

Spartacus rubbed a finger along his lips, thinking. 'It's a clever move.

Longinus could have twenty ballistae – or more, if he thought of this a while ago. A good workshop can turn out one piece every few days. Naturally, the artillerymen will have ranged them in beforehand.' He turned to the Gauls. 'Imagine the carnage, say, two dozen catapults would cause. They could release six volleys before our soldiers had a chance to respond.'

'And that's when the legions would attack,' said Gannicus.

'It is. Was there any more, Carbo?'

'No,' he said uneasily.

'It's of little matter. That will be Longinus' plan for sure. But now we can do our best to make sure that he fails.' Spartacus' gaze grew distant.

Castus wasn't happy, however. 'Why didn't you find out more?'

You're not the one who risked his life to find this out, thought Carbo furiously. Instead, he said, 'Because the soldiers who mentioned it walked away.'

'Then why didn't you follow them?' came the instant retort.

'We couldn't,' replied Navio with an irritated look.

'Were you too pissed? Is that when you fell in the dungheap?' sneered Castus.

'Does it matter?' interjected Spartacus. 'They were never going to be able to do much more than eavesdrop on conversations anyway. If they'd made themselves obvious, they wouldn't be here now. Returning safely with news of Longinus' plan is sufficient.'

'So you say,' snapped Castus. 'I don't, though. There's far more to this than meets the eye. Eh, Gannicus?'

'Aye. The pair of them are as shifty as a cuckold when the husband arrives home.'

'You don't trust them?'

'No,' Castus snapped. 'They're Romans.'

Spartacus' expression hardened. 'We've had this before. Both of these men have proved their loyalty many times!'

'They say that blood is thicker than water. I've always agreed with that myself,' said Castus.

Which is why I wouldn't trust you as far as I could throw you, you Gaulish dog.

'I say we beat it out of them,' suggested Castus belligerently.

Rather than defend his men, Spartacus eyed Gannicus. 'Do you think the same?'

'They're holding back something. That's as clear as the nose on the end of my face. As the *leaders*' – Gannicus laid especial emphasis on the last word – 'of this army, we're entitled to know everything – and to find out by whatever means necessary.'

Now is not the time for a quarrel. There is a battle to fight. Spartacus rounded on the friends. 'What the fuck happened?'

They didn't say a word.

'By all the gods! Unless you want Castus and Gannicus and their men to teach you both a lesson you'll never forget, speak!'

Shocked now, Carbo glanced at Navio, who gave a resigned shrug. 'There were soldiers everywhere in the town, but none of them were saying much. It was obvious that they'd been ordered to keep their mouths shut. We'd had little luck at a restaurant, so we moved on to a number of taverns. We heard nothing, so decided to try out an inn favoured by soldiers' – Carbo felt his cheeks flame – 'that was supposed to have good whores.'

Spartacus' brows rose, but he hid his amusement. Atheas and Taxacis chortled at Carbo's embarrassment, but the two Gauls were far less happy. 'You got sent to Mutina on an intelligence mission, but you were more interested in emptying your ball sacks. It's unbelievable!' barked Castus.

'And then?' said Spartacus.

'Navio went upstairs with a whore.'

'How did you pay for her services?' The question was voiced softly, but there was no missing Spartacus' threat.

'I had a couple of aurei with me,' replied Navio unhappily.

'Despite the fact that I told you to take only a little money.'

'Yes.'

Spartacus' lips thinned to a white line. 'You've got a nerve. Go on,' he directed Carbo.

It was time to admit *his* foolishness. Carbo felt sick. 'I went to the forum.'

'What for?'

'To find a scribe.'

'A scribe?' Spartacus' eyes bulged.

'Yes. I dictated a letter to my parents in Rome.'

Both the Gauls let out disbelieving laughs.

'Are you a complete fucking idiot?' cried Spartacus.

'If anyone had seen you, they had only to read the note to know who you were,' roared Castus. 'You need your stinking Roman head cut off!'

'I didn't send it,' said Carbo quickly. Quailing before Spartacus' ferocious expression, he went on, 'but someone must have seen me, because soon after I returned to the inn, a party of soldiers searched the place. I was recognised, but I managed to run upstairs. Fortuna guided me to the right door.'

'You would have deserved it if they had caught you,' muttered Castus.

But you wouldn't know about the hidden catapults, thought Carbo furiously. He had the sense to keep this retort to himself. 'We jumped out of the window, and scrambled down to the inn's yard. I ran into a gap between two buildings, but it led to the stable dungheap. There was no option other than to climb up it, and over the wall. Navio didn't have any clothes on' – here he ignored the Gauls' mocking laughter – 'and he fell over as he was trying to climb up.'

'You must have burst in when he was in mid-thrust,' said Castus with a leer.

'Err, I was quite busy, yes,' said Navio, looking angry and very uncomfortable.

Castus and Gannicus sniggered. The Scythians guffawed. Even Spartacus laughed.

'You managed to escape, though,' Gannicus' tone was a touch more friendly than before, which encouraged Carbo. A little humiliation was better than more accusations of treachery.

'Yes. We jumped over into an alleyway. I checked out the exit, but the street beyond was full of soldiers. We thought that was it, but the gods intervened again. A door in the wall of a house opened and a slave boy came out. I told him who we were, and asked him to help. He did. We simply walked inside and he shut the door.' Carbo grinned at the memory. 'A moment later, a couple of legionaries landed in the alley, and passed right by us.'

'That was when we heard about Longinus' ambush,' added Navio.

'Our job was done. We waited until it was very late, and then, guided by the boy, we made our way to the defences where we scaled the walls. It was easy to get back here,' said Carbo.

'You're a pair of fools,' Spartacus snapped. The Gauls loudly echoed his words.

Knowing that they were by no means out of danger, the friends looked at the ground.

'But . . . if they hadn't done what they did, we wouldn't know that juicy bit of gossip. Eh, Castus? Gannicus?'

'The gods move in strange ways,' admitted Gannicus.

'Happy, Castus?'

'No. Always trying to cover your men's arses, aren't you, eh? Why bother? It's a wonder that the fools managed to come back alive.'

'Yet they did, and with useful information,' said Spartacus.

'I suppose,' said Castus grudgingly.

'Next time you have a secret mission in mind,' said Gannicus, 'I want to know about it beforehand, eh? Either we're all leading this fucking army, or we're not.'

'Agreed,' lied Spartacus. He had no intention of telling the Gauls of everything he did, but he needed their support in the forthcoming battle. 'Next time, I'll be sure to fill you in.'

Castus' grunt conveyed every shade of suspicion under the sun. Gannicus looked a little happier, but that was as good as he'd get.

Spartacus' eyes moved to Carbo and Navio. 'The next time I give you an order, I want it obeyed to the letter. No taking gold coins instead of small change. No deciding to write letters to your parents.' He gave Carbo a particularly stony look. 'I've never heard of such stupidity in my life. The only reason I'm not letting the Scythians loose on you is because of your previous record. If anything like that *ever* happens again, you'll both end up as pickings for the vultures. DO YOU UNDERSTAND?'

'Yes,' they muttered in unison.

'Be certain that you do.'

They shuffled their feet, all too aware of the Scythians' predatory eyes on their backs and of the Gauls' glowering anger.

Spartacus' attention moved on. 'Some cavalry must be sent to reconnoitre the road past Mutina,' he announced. 'If they see anything suspicious, they'll mark its position, but ignore it. Let the Romans think that their little secret is safe. We can send out more scouts under the cover of darkness.'

'Once the spot has been found, we destroy the catapults!' Castus' face was fiercely eager.

'Damn right we will,' snarled Gannicus. 'And Castus and I will be in charge.'

Spartacus saw the level of their anger, and wondered if he should have told them about Carbo and Navio's mission. Would it have mattered if he had? 'That's just what I was going to suggest.'

'Good, because we're going to do it anyway,' snapped Gannicus, grimacing as Castus growled in approval. 'A thousand men with buckets of oil and some torches is all we need to turn Longinus' artillery into little piles of ash.'

'Fine.' Spartacus pulled an encouraging grin. *Keep them sweet for the moment.* 'Once the ballistae are out of the way, we'll only have two legions to think about. The ground to either side of the road is flat. It won't matter where we face them.'

'I can't wait,' snarled Castus. 'We'll slaughter the cocksuckers.'

'With the help of the Great Rider, that's exactly what we'll do,' said Spartacus with satisfaction. He didn't say a word about the Alps. Such a controversial topic would set Castus and Gannicus off again. He shoved that problem to one side. 'We can talk about the exact details when the cavalry return.'

'Fine,' said Castus. He eyed Carbo. 'What was the name of the boy who saved you?'

'Arnax.' *What do you care?*

Castus grunted. Then, talking animatedly with Gannicus about how they would destroy Longinus' forces, he left.

Deep in thought, Spartacus began poking a stick into the fire. It was a clear sign of dismissal.

'I need a wash,' said Navio quietly. 'And breakfast is waiting. Coming?'

'Not yet,' replied Carbo. He framed the word 'Lucullus' with his lips and Navio nodded in understanding.

'See you.'

Carbo found Spartacus regarding him quizzically when he turned. 'Was there something else?'

'There was, actually.'

Spartacus scowled. 'How else did you disobey my orders? Atheas! Taxacis!'

'It's nothing like that,' said Carbo, his heart racing.

Spartacus let the Scythians come right up to Carbo's back before he lifted a hand. 'What then?'

Carbo wiped away the sweat that had sprung out on his brow. *Gods, why didn't we do just as he said?* 'The Romans suspect that you're going to leave Italy.'

'That's not surprising given the route we've taken so far,' said Spartacus dryly. 'Why do you mention it?'

Carbo checked that that the Gauls were well out of earshot. The Scythians had Spartacus' trust, so their presence didn't matter. 'They also said that Marcus Lucullus has inflicted a recent heavy defeat on Thracian troops who'd been fighting for Mithridates. He's now continuing his campaign into Thrace.'

Spartacus spat an oath. 'You overheard exactly that?'

'Yes.'

'What else did they say?'

'Nothing. I'm sorry.'

Spartacus' eyes probed his for a long moment. 'I'm grateful to you. You did well not to reveal that to the Gauls. Why did you not?'

'I'm not sure,' replied Carbo truthfully. He remembered how quarrelsome the Gauls had been. 'Maybe it was because I suspected that they would use it as an excuse not to leave Italy.'

'You are shrewd. I sometimes wonder if they have ever intended to do so, but news like that would set their minds in stone.'

'Will you leave still?'

'Of course. With every man who'll follow me,' said Spartacus with a confidence he was not sure he truly felt. 'It makes sense to do so. Three large-scale defeats mean nothing to the Romans. They have a bottomless pool of men to replenish their legions. At least in Thrace I would be on my own territory, among my own people. It won't take much to unite them and start another uprising.' *Let that be true, Great Rider.*

Carbo nodded, feeling reassured. Despite the roasting he'd just been given, his memories of how Spartacus had saved him in the ludus, and of how he'd intervened to save Chloris, were always in his mind. He'd follow the Thracian anywhere. To hell. To Thrace. It didn't matter.

'Go on, be off with you. Get some food in your belly and have a rest. You've earned it.'

Carbo grinned at the change in Spartacus' tone. 'If I'm not to take part in the attack on the ballistae, I might go hunting this afternoon.'

'Fine. One more thing.'

'Yes?'

'Not a word to a soul about Lucullus. Tell Navio to keep his mouth shut too,' Spartacus warned. 'On pain of death.'

'Of course,' said Carbo, his heart thudding again. He walked off, unaware that he had added a mountain to Spartacus' concerns.

Sending Atheas to fetch his cavalry commanders, Spartacus sat for a while in silence. Ariadne was not in their tent. For that, he was grateful. He wanted to think about the shocking news before having to talk it over with her. There was no way of knowing if the report of Lucullus' victory was true, but he had to assume that it was. Why would a legionary make up something like that? It wasn't as if the Thracians hadn't been beaten by Rome before. It's only a setback; we Thracians have inflicted plenty of humiliating defeats on the bastards too, he thought, remembering with satisfaction his own tribe's stunning victory over Appius Claudius Pulcher, the proconsul of Macedonia, five years earlier. Deep down, however, Spartacus knew that the task he had set himself once they reached Thrace had just been made much harder. Was it even possible? *Don't think like that!*

'You're in a different world. I can never usually get this close without you noticing.'

Ariadne's voice dragged him back to reality. He smiled, burying the news of Lucullus. 'It was a good idea to send Carbo and Navio to Mutina.'

Ariadne stiffened. 'They're back?'

'Yes. Longinus has set a trap on the road north. His ballistae are hidden away, but ranged in so that they could rain down volleys on the army as it marched past. A perfect ambush.'

'Damn Romans,' said Ariadne angrily. 'What will you do?'

'Pinpoint the artillery's exact location. Then the Gauls will destroy it tonight.' He saw Ariadne's surprise. 'They were outraged that I had sent spies to Mutina without telling them. Letting them have this mission was a gesture to bring them around, but they'll do a good job. Gannicus in particular is like a hound on a tight leash. We'll march in the morning. Catch Longinus before he has had a chance to react.'

'He only has two legions.' Ariadne wanted to hear the small figure again. 'We have more than fifty thousand men.'

'That's right, my love. We will win, have no fear.'

'I know.' Unconsciously, she placed a hand on her belly. 'Our son will be born outside Italy.'

He put his arms around her to shove away the uncertainty that had flared up again in his mind. 'I cannot wait to hold him.'

She gave him a fond glance, and saw something in his expression. 'What are you not telling me?'

He didn't answer.

'Spartacus? What is it?'

His eyes regarded her steadily. 'I'm not going to say right now. I need to think about it.'

A knot of fear clenched in her stomach. 'Is there Roman another army nearby?'

'It's nothing like that.'

She searched his face for a clue.

'Leave it, Ariadne. You will find out in due course.'

She didn't like the fact that he wasn't being open with her, but she did not probe further. This was no time to sow discord. There were ballistae to destroy and after that, another Roman army to defeat. She cast a longing look to the north, towards the Alps. *When we stand at their foot, everything will seem much clearer. We will head eastwards.* She did not want to entertain any other possibility. This hope was what had sustained her in the months since their breakout from the ludus. Yet Spartacus' reticence had planted a seed of doubt in her mind.

Ariadne decided to seek Dionysus' aid. It was not in the nature of any deity to answer requests directly, but it did happen on occasion. Her spirits rallied at the memory of the time they had been trapped at the top of Vesuvius by three thousand legionaries. In their hour of greatest need, Dionysus had shown Spartacus the wild vines that could be used to make ropes. Maybe he would help again now? While their situation was nowhere near as desperate as before, Ariadne felt in need of the peace of mind that divine guidance would grant. A welcome calm descended over her.

It lasted for a few heartbeats. Then, like a sting in the tail, Ariadne thought of the munus that Spartacus had held. Had it been too bloody? As if that wasn't enough to be worried about, she agonised over the occasion at Thurii when she had lied about the god's will. She had told the entire army that Dionysus had sent her a dream in which they were to travel to the east under his protection, to lands that were unconquered by Rome. Ariadne had admitted her falsehood to no one, not even her husband. I did it for good reasons, she thought. To prevent Crixus trying to kill Spartacus. To win the troops over, and to stop them from splintering into many factions. Her inner demon answered at once. *It doesn't matter why you did it. To suit your own purpose, you pretended to speak with a divine voice. That shows a deep disrespect for the god.*

Her guilt swelled immeasurably. 'I must go and pray,' she said in a tight voice.

'A good idea.' Troubled, Spartacus watched her go.

By early afternoon, the cavalry he had sent out had returned. They had located the most likely spot for the Roman ballistae to be hidden. Some five miles from their camp was a hollow behind a slight incline that was bounded on two sides by a dense arrangement of trees. His horsemen had seen figures moving in the copse, but as instructed, they had not investigated further. To maintain as much secrecy as possible, Spartacus ordered them to say nothing to their comrades.

Gannicus and Castus had picked a thousand of their best men for the mission. As well as barrels of olive oil and torches, they had armed their troops with every axe that could be found. The two Gauls, Spartacus and the cavalry officer who'd led the patrol conferred as the sun fell in the sky. There were hours to go before the chosen soldiers left. To prevent them being seen by Roman scouts, the force would not move out until it was dark.

Spartacus was pleased. Things augured well. On the spur of the moment, he decided to join Carbo. Hunting was something that he had always enjoyed, but there had been precious little time for it of recent months. He ignored the host of tasks that needed doing, and that it was a little rash to leave the camp without guards. It would do him good, he decided, to forget Longinus, Castus and Gannicus, and the damn Alps for a few hours. *Nothing will happen. The Rider will look after me, as he always does.*

'Put your back into it!' roared Julius, his face a handsbreadth from Marcion's. 'Just because we're nearly done for the day, just because we've hammered the Romans both times that you've fought them, doesn't mean you can start slacking. Training is training, and it goes on until I say so!'

Marcion's mouth set into a scowl of concentration. He raised his shield and advanced towards Gaius, his tent mate. He wished that Julius would piss off and annoy one of the other soldiers in their unit, but there was little chance of that. Their centurion never moved on until he was satisfied.

He glanced to either side. Beyond his century, the rest of his cohort was also busy. Further on, many hundreds of men were being forced by their officers to run, to fight, as he was, with covered weapons, or to attack other groups in formation. Shouts and commands mixed with the *clack, clack* sound of swords hitting scuta and the deeper *thump* of shield bosses making contact with each other. In the distance, he could see the cavalry charging en masse, wheeling and turning in graceful but deadly arcs. It was the same as always, he thought wearily. If we aren't marching or fighting, we're bloody training.

'Move it!' yelled Julius.

Marcion peered over the rim of his scutum as he shuffled forward. Gaius was about ten paces away. Marcion could only see his friend's eyes, and his feet. The shield Gaius carried protected almost his entire body, as Marcion's did his. It left precious little to attack. He still knew what to do.

He darted forward, hoping to catch Gaius off guard. Marcion used all of his force, smashing his shield boss into Gaius' scutum. Although Gaius had braced himself, the impact rocked him back on his heels, and he wasn't able to dodge Marcion's blade as it came sliding over the shield's iron rim. 'Damn you!' he spat.

'You're dead,' said Marcion with a smile.

'You won't get me like that again,' Gaius swore.

'Glad to hear it,' came Julius' sarcastic voice. 'If this was real life, you'd be choking out your last breath by now. Do it again.'

The words had barely left the centurion's lips when Gaius threw himself across the space that separated him from Marcion. This time, it was Marcion who went over, landing on his arse with his shield on top of him. Winded by the fall, he could do nothing to prevent Gaius ripping aside his scutum and pretend to skewer him through the neck.

Gaius leered. 'That'll teach you, you pup!' He backed off, allowing Marcion to get to his feet.

'Better, Gaius,' declared Julius. He threw a hard glance at Marcion. 'Not as good as you think, are you?'

Stung, Marcion had the sense not to answer.

'Right, that'll do you for the day.' Julius raised his voice. 'DISMISSED! Same time tomorrow, you sacks of shit!'

With a relieved sigh, Marcion stripped the leather cover from his gladius and slid it back into its scabbard. He made sure that the centurion was out of earshot. 'Julius is fucking annoying, but he's right. We have to keep sharp, eh?'

Gaius hawked and spat. 'Aye, true enough. A man needs Fortuna on his side every time he goes into battle. Even the best soldier can end up staring at a string of his own guts, or worse. Remember Hirtius?'

'Of course.' Marcion winced. Hirtius had been one of their tent mates. A short barrel of a man, he'd been prodigiously strong. That hadn't stopped him taking a stray pilum in the eye during the fight against Gellius' legions. His deafening screams had gone on until Zeuxis had done him a mercy by cutting his throat.

'Who's cooking tonight?' asked a familiar deep voice.

'It's your bloody turn, Zeuxis!' Gaius cried indignantly.

'Is it?' Zeuxis wiped the sheen of sweat from his pate and flicked it at Gaius, who dodged, cursing.

'You know damn well it is!'

'Don't look at me!' said Marcion as Zeuxis' head turned. 'I'd much rather have your tasteless offering than have to cook.'

'Me too,' declared Arphocras, who had been Zeuxis' sparring mate. 'You're such a chancer! Every eight days, it's the same.'

Zeuxis shrugged. 'I can't help it if my memory's not what it was.'

'Just as well that we remember for you, eh?' jibed Marcion.

Despite Gaius besting him, Marcion's mood was lifting. This was his favourite part of the day. Training was over. The hottest hours had passed, but it was still a good while until sunset. After he'd cleaned the dust off his equipment, there was time perhaps to fill a bucket from the river and to have a wash. Most of his tent mates weren't bothered, but the love of small luxuries that Marcion had grown up with died hard. After a hard training session, he liked nothing better than to get clean. It was best to slope off on his own, however. If Zeuxis realised, he'd never hear the end of it. A desire to bathe regularly did not mean that he liked other men, he thought angrily, just that he had possessed some culture. It was Zeuxis who was the primitive, not him. He smiled.

His dreadful cooking proved it.

Carbo had been busy all day. After a hearty bowl of barley porridge and honey prepared by Arnax, he had slept for several hours. Then, as he would have done normally, Carbo had sought out the cohort of which he was second-in-command. His senior officer was Egbeo, a huge Thracian who was one of Spartacus' most devoted followers, and whom Carbo had grown to trust implicitly. He'd found Egbeo training the men. 'You might think that the Roman dogs are scared of us now, but they're not! You can never take them for granted,' the Thracian had roared over and over. 'You still need to drill with each other. You have to know in your gut that when the order comes, every man around you will do exactly as you do. That he will advance. Form close order. Throw his javelins. Charge the enemy. Help to form a wedge. Even to retreat!' Carbo had smiled at the guffaws this produced and, invigorated by Egbeo's speech, had set to with a will. However, once the practice was over and he'd spent a little time chatting with his men, he found himself at a loose end. He remembered his idea of going hunting and when Navio had returned from training his own cohort, he suggested they went together.

'Come on. It'll be better than having to look at Gannicus' men preening themselves before they leave.'

'True enough,' said Navio with a grimace. Although they were supposed to be keeping quiet about what they were to do, Gannicus' troops were doing a poor job of it. 'What do you fancy going after?'

'I'll take whatever we can find. Boar. Deer. A bird for the pot.'

'Can I tag along?'

Arnax's eager face made Carbo smile: he was becoming fond of the boy. 'All right. We're not likely to meet any Roman patrols.'

Arnax's face fell. 'How can you be sure?'

There was a familiar laugh. 'Because they're too damn scared to come anywhere near my army.'

Arnax goggled. 'Oh,' he said in a small voice.

'Spartacus!' Carbo took in his leader's hunting weapons. 'Have you come to join us?'

'I haven't been on a hunt in months.'

'If you're sure,' said Carbo, thinking about what might happen if they *did* meet a Roman patrol.

'I am.' *Ariadne is worried about nothing.*

Spartacus' tone brooked no argument. Carbo shrugged. Navio grinned. 'Another bow increases our chance of success.'

Spartacus nodded a friendly greeting at Arnax, who looked even more frightened. 'So this is the lad who helped you out in Mutina?'

'That's him,' said Carbo.

'You did well to aid my men, boy. What do they call you?'

'A-Arnax, sir.'

'A strong name.'

Arnax said nothing.

'I don't bite.'

Arnax glanced at Carbo, who gave him an encouraging smile.

'Thank you, sir,' he ventured.

Spartacus cocked his head. 'What is it? You've heard terrible things about me?'

'Y-y-yes, sir.'

'What have you heard?'

No reply.

'Tell me,' Spartacus commanded.

Again Arnax looked to Carbo, who said, 'Tell him.'

'Apparently, you eat babies.'

Spartacus' mouth twitched. 'Really?'

'Y-yes.'

'Who said that?'

'My master. People in the forum,' muttered Arnax.

'He's not your master any more. You're free now.'

Arnax's fearful expression eased a little.

'I can also tell you that I am an ordinary man like Carbo or Navio. I don't eat babies, nor do I breathe fire. As I said, I am grateful that you saved my men. You are welcome here.' Arnax said nothing, and he frowned. 'Still not happy?'

To Carbo's shock, Arnax blurted, 'You killed all those legionaries. The ones who had to fight each other to the death.'

'Arnax!' hissed Carbo.

Spartacus' eyebrows rose. 'Spirited, isn't he?'

Arnax's momentary courage fled him, and his eyes lowered.

'Do you know why *munera* have historically been held?'

'To commemorate the death of someone rich or famous,' Arnax replied.

'That's right,' said Spartacus. 'Nowadays, of course, they're held any time some high-and-mighty or up-and-coming noble wants to impress the masses. Men fight and sometimes die in those munera, don't they? Slaves, who have no choice in the matter.'

Arnax nodded.

'My munus was to mark the death of thousands of my former comrades in battle. In my mind, that makes it far more valid than the *entertainment* that is laid on for the populations of towns the length and breadth of Italy every month or two. I had every damn right to do what I did.' He pinned Arnax with a hard stare. 'Understand?'

In the silence that followed, Carbo was surprised to find himself in agreement with Spartacus. The munus had upset him badly at the time, but for months now, he had trained and fought alongside former slaves. They were his trusted comrades. If it was acceptable to force men such as they to fight as gladiators, then it was permissible to do the same to Roman prisoners. He watched Arnax, pleased, surprised and a little worried by the way he'd stood up to Spartacus. *Agree with him.*

'Yes,' the boy said at last.

'A real fighter you've got there, Carbo. I think I can understand now why a slip of a lad like him saved your lives at the risk of his own. He'll make a good soldier one day – as long as he learns to watch his tongue.'

'He will,' replied Carbo.

'Ever been hunting?' Spartacus asked Arnax.

'No.'

'This can be your first time. We take bows and arrows for deer and birds, and these in case we meet a boar.' He handed over his heavy hunting spear. 'You can carry that.'

Arnax beamed. 'Where are we going?'

'Carbo?' asked Spartacus.

'There are plenty of tracks in the woods to the north of the camp. I thought that would be a good place to start.'

'If we want to have a chance of killing anything, we'd best get moving, eh?' Navio slapped his mail shirt. 'Help me take this off,' he said to Arnax.

Aided by Spartacus, Carbo also removed his. Although it made sense to leave the heavy shirt behind, he felt naked without it. Talk of the meat that they'd be roasting over their fire that night soon put his concerns to rest, however.

The four wended their way through lines of tents to the edge of the vast encampment. Despite the fact that Spartacus kept his head down, his men hailed him at every step. It took a mile or more before the sights and sounds of the huge army were left behind, but eventually they found themselves alone, a world away from the hustle-bustle of the camp. It was a fine spring day, and the warm temperature was most welcome after the long winter months. Carbo felt glad just to be wearing a tunic.

He led the little party fast across the open ground that sloped downwards to the north. It was covered in short grass and clumps of aromatic sage and juniper. His eyes scanned the dirt for signs of deer or boar, but all he saw were the tracks of small creatures such as the startled hare that had bounded off between a dark green myrtle shrub and a mass of prickly buckthorn. There was plenty of birdlife. Several large black birds with red markings around their eyes and impressive fantails darted off into the undergrowth as they passed. They looked good enough to eat, but a swift glance at Navio and Spartacus told Carbo that they too wanted bigger quarry.

He ignored the pair of hooded crows that chattered angrily at them from a cork oak tree. In the distance, Carbo heard the distinctive hammering of a woodpecker, a bird sacred to Mars, the god of war. He quickly offered up a prayer. *Give us a good hunt, O Great One.* They walked on, entering the shelter of the woods. Motes of dust floated lazily on the sunlight that filtered through the branches of laurels, stone pines and strawberry trees. It was peaceful – eerily so. Carbo thought of the copse a short distance away that contained hundreds of Roman soldiers and their ballistae, and his skin crawled. He began to see a legionary behind every tree, and wished that he had not taken off his mail shirt. Navio's hiss startled him. 'Pssst!'

Carbo looked. Ten paces off to his left, Spartacus was pointing at the ground. He padded over. At the Thracian's feet were two large hoof imprints with a characteristic pair of indents behind them. 'Red deer. A big one.'

'It's a stag,' said Navio excitedly.

'Looks like it,' agreed Spartacus.

At once Carbo's gaze moved to the trees in front of them. Of course he saw nothing. The marks were fresh, but the stag would be some distance away.

When they had followed the prints for a little way, their suspicions were proved correct. 'See this?' Carbo showed Arnax. 'We know it's a male deer because the rear tracks fall to the inside of the front ones. That happens because his chest is a lot larger than his hindquarters.'

'Where is he?' Arnax's eyes were alive with interest and delight.

Spartacus stooped and pressed his fingers into the nearest print. 'Nowhere that close. But the earth is still a little damp. He passed by here today. Probably sometime in the morning.'

Arnax hefted the spear in his right hand. 'Will we find him?'

Carbo grinned at the boy's enthusiasm. 'Who knows? We shall have to follow his tracks and see. Now is the time to pray to Diana for her help.' Using a loop of leather made for the purpose, he slung his spear across his back. Then he slipped an arrow with a narrow head from his quiver and nocked it to his bowstring.

'That won't take down a deer,' joked Navio.

'We might see another hare, or one of those black birds,' answered Carbo a trifle defensively.

'It always pays to be ready,' said Spartacus, selecting a shaft of his own. 'For whatever – or whoever – we might meet.'

Carbo felt gratified. During the time the slave army had travelled from deep in the south, he'd spent a lot of time scouting with Atheas. The Scythian never moved without a weapon in his hands.

Some time later, however, his vague unease had been replaced by frustration. He had seen no phantom legionaries, and there had been no game worth bringing down either. Irritatingly, the stag's tracks had petered out on a bare rocky slope that led to the bank of a fast-flowing stream. The trio had cast about, searching for signs of where the animal might have left the hard ground and forded the watercourse, but had had no luck.

'The damn creature must have sprouted wings and flown away,' said Navio, frowning.

Arnax glanced briefly at the sky before looking down again, embarrassed.

Carbo hid his grin. He'd forgotten how innocent children could be. 'Let's not give up.'

'I want to keep going,' agreed Spartacus, who was revelling in the sensation of being with comrades, tracking nothing more than a deer. There were no men asking him for equipment, no new recruits who needed instruction, no horses to be broken or officers asking him for guidance. He hadn't felt this relaxed in an age.

'Look!'

The excitement in Arnax's voice caught everyone's attention. Spartacus' gaze followed the boy's pointing arm down the slope, through the gap in the trees to the flat ground that lay beyond. 'That's no deer.' He studied the three figures who were running at full pelt towards the woods.

'They're being pursued,' hissed Carbo. Some distance behind the fugitives rose a tell-tale dust cloud. His stomach clenched. 'Riders.' They were too far away to estimate their number, but the spiral of dust was large. It was also closing in fast on the running men.

'Roman deserters?' suggested Navio.

'They're more likely to be escaped slaves,' said Spartacus.

Carbo and Navio exchanged glances, wondering what to do. The safest thing would be to return to the camp. Surely, their leader would think the same thing.

'Those men could be coming to join us,' grated Spartacus.

'The riders who are after them outnumber us,' warned Navio.

Everyone in the camp — Ariadne, the Scythians, Pulcher and Egbeo — would want me to melt away into the trees. Even Castus and Gannicus would advise walking away from this situation. But who are they to tell me what to do? I decide what risks I take — crazy or not. A wicked grin split Spartacus' face. 'It's been a while since I faced long odds. I'm going down there. You in?'

Chapter V

'Of course.' Carbo wondered why his leader was being so foolhardy, but he didn't say so. Instead he returned his narrow-headed arrow to his quiver and pulled out a barbed shaft.

'Fine,' said Navio with a crooked smile and did the same.

'W-what are you going to do?' Arnax's voice was quavering.

'Slip down to the edge of the trees and see what's going on.' Spartacus pointed a finger at the ground. 'You're going to stay here, where it's safe.'

'But—'

'But nothing. You're too young to fight, yet the Romans – if that's who the riders are – would cut you down in the blink of an eye.'

'You're to do as Spartacus says,' ordered Carbo loudly, trying to calm his own nerves. 'You can hide easily here, and see what happens. If the worst comes to the worst, return to the camp. Can you retrace your steps to find it?'

'Yes, I think so.'

'Good. When you get there, find Pulcher or Egbeo and tell them what happened,' Spartacus directed.

'Pulcher. Egbeo. Yes.'

'If I have been killed, they are to lead the army.' Or however many of the men will follow them rather than Castus or Gannicus, he thought cynically. 'Atheas and Taxacis are to look after Ariadne. Let's go.' Taking his spear from Arnax, Spartacus trotted off with Navio on his heels.

Carbo paused long enough to clap the boy on the arm. What had he got Arnax into? he wondered. He glanced at the dust cloud, which had grown larger. Now he could see the shapes of individual riders, at least fifteen of them. What the hell was he getting himself into? His pulse raced as he began to descend the slope.

Reaching the bottom first, Spartacus moved at once along the edge of the trees, searching for the best spot to observe what was going on. He was careful to keep far enough back to prevent his being seen. He soon spotted the fugitives. They were definitely slaves, he decided. All three were thin, barefoot and dressed in ragged tunics. The men had almost reached the shelter of the woods, but they looked more terrified than ever. That was because the front riders – three Roman cavalrymen in mail shirts and bronze helmets, carrying long, slashing swords – were nearly upon them. Behind thundered many more.

'Quickly!' he hissed at Carbo and Navio. Darting to the shelter of a holm oak at the very limit of the trees, he dropped his spear and stabbed a row of shafts into the earth in front of him. Nocking an arrow to the string, Spartacus drew a bead on the first rider, an unshaven man with long hair. He glanced to either side. A few steps away, Carbo and Navio were also ready. 'How far?' he muttered.

'Eighty to a hundred paces, give or take,' replied Carbo. Navio growled in agreement.

Spartacus pulled back to full draw. 'On my count. One. Two. Three!'

Their arrows shot through the air. Two punched the first rider off his horse's back, and Spartacus swore under his breath. He should have named his target. The last shaft, Carbo's, struck a man behind the leader straight through the throat. He was dead before he even hit the ground. The men's companions roared with anger, but they did not slow down. Leaning forward across his mount's neck, one swung down with all his might at the last of the three fugitives. An excruciating scream shredded the air. A sheet of blood sprayed from the man's back, and he fell to the ground like a puppet with cut strings.

'In here! In here!' shouted Spartacus. He took aim and let another arrow fly. 'Loose as fast as you can,' he roared. 'We have to make the scumbags think that there are plenty of us.'

Hiss! Hiss! Hiss! The trio released shafts as fast as they could.

Two more horsemen went down. A steed that had been struck in the chest reared up in agony, unseating its rider. The man immediately behind could not react fast enough, and with a massive *thump*, the horses collided. Carbo's delight at this faded as a yelling cavalryman closed in on the second fugitive, delivering an almighty blow to his right side. The slave stumbled and cried out, but incredibly he kept running. Carbo took a little satisfaction as his next arrow took the Roman rider in the groin, below the bottom of his mail shirt. *Hiss! Hiss!* Two more shafts scudded out, striking another pair of riders.

The wounded slave's gaze scanned the trees. He'd seen their arrows. He shouted something at his companion, and they changed direction slightly, aiming for where Spartacus and the others were standing. Carbo stared at the man's face, twisted with effort. 'Paccius?' he whispered. Disbelief filled him. It couldn't be the Samnite who had been his family's best slave, and who had trained him to use a sword and shield. Could it? Then the man staggered and almost fell, and one of the nearest Romans whooped with triumph. Before Carbo knew what he was doing, he was sprinting out of the cover of the trees. Into the open.

'What are you doing, you fool?' Spartacus yelled.

'Come back!' Navio roared. 'You'll be killed.'

The taste of Carbo's fear was acid in his throat, but he kept running. He nocked an arrow to his string. 'I'm coming, Paccius. Hold on!'

A cavalryman closed in on the injured fugitive and Carbo swore. There was no way that he could loose accurately as he ran. *Zip!* Something flashed past him, striking the Roman in the chest. The shaft punched through his mail shirt, throwing him backwards off his mount. Another arrow shot by, hitting a horse and causing it to stumble. Its rider did well not to be unseated, but he was still out of the fight. Carbo felt a surge of gratitude towards Spartacus and Navio.

The first slave was now only twenty paces or so away. His mouth gaped open with the impossible effort of trying to outrun horses.

'We've got to help your friend,' Carbo yelled, gesturing madly. 'Go back and help him.'

The slave looked at him as if he were mad, but he obeyed.

Things were not good. The Romans had split up. Three were coming at him from the left, and four from the right. The remainder were aiming for the injured slave and his comrade. Carbo felt nauseous. What had he done? There was no way that he could release enough arrows to kill, or even injure, all his opponents. Even if he took down a few of them, the rest would slice him up with ease. *I'm a dead man.* His conscience spat back at once. *At least you tried to save Paccius.*

That was when the wounded slave looked straight at him. Carbo realised with horror that while he bore more than a passing resemblance to the Samnite, he was a different man. *I'm going to die for nothing.* Carbo sucked in a ragged breath. He prepared to sell his life dearly. The cavalrymen on the left were nearest. He tugged out an arrow, put it to the string and loosed in one smooth movement. Instantly, a horse was riderless. His next shot missed, however, and his third glanced off a rider's helmet. Nonetheless, the Romans' charge checked a little. The injured man, helped by his companion, limped past Carbo towards the trees. He risked a glance to his right, and his gorge rose. Four riders were thundering down on him. *Maybe the slaves will reach cover before I'm dead.* It was a faint hope, but it was all Carbo had as he aimed at the lead horse.

Hiss! Hiss!

Two arrows flew by him. The front rider was struck in the leg, and he pulled up, screaming blue murder. The other shaft missed. Nonetheless, Carbo's spirits rallied. He let fly, hitting the first Roman himself, this time in the arm.

'You fucking idiot!' Spartacus came hammering in on his right side, bow at the ready. 'If you want to live, run! In twenty paces, stop, turn and shoot one shaft. Then run and do the same again.'

Filled with awe, and the screaming hope that he might survive, Carbo obeyed. Ten paces on, he saw Navio. The Roman's face was twisted into a terrible rictus of concentration. He had arrows gripped in the same fist that held his bow, and was drawing and loosing with incredible speed. 'Run!' he shouted. 'Run!'

The next few moments passed by in a blur. Carbo ran and shot, shot and ran. He had no time to see if any of his arrows hit their targets. All he knew was that there were still enemies attacking them and that he was nearest cover, while Spartacus and Navio were the most exposed. When he'd reached the relative safety of the tree line, he looked around. Dismay tore at him. 'Spartacus, look out!'

Fifty paces out, Spartacus knew that he'd made a grave mistake in deciding to try and rescue Carbo. It had been an unconscious choice, spurred partly by his regard for the young Roman and partly by the devilment that had made him intervene against the horsemen in the first place. A small part of him wanted to prove that he was even braver than

Carbo. But now, with an enemy charging in from both left and right, he knew that the Rider had deserted him at last. Good cavalrymen worked in unison, and he did not have time to release two arrows. By the time he'd loosed at one, the other would be cutting him in half. Navio was busy with his own opponent, and Carbo's aim left something to be desired.

This is not the way I wanted to die.

But he wouldn't go without a struggle. He made an immediate decision which rider to shoot. The nearest one. Closing his ears to the hammering of hooves and the Romans' war cries, Spartacus took aim at the rider, who was less than fifteen paces away. At this range, he could not miss. He didn't even watch the arrow fly. The instant it left the string, he let go of his bow, and flung himself to the ground. The blade that would have decapitated him scythed overhead. There was a shouted curse, and Spartacus rolled to his right, away from where he thought his enemy's horse would go. He ripped free his sica. With it gripped in his hand, he felt a fraction better.

'Die, you whoreson!'

Spartacus flung his arm up and met the downward swing of the Roman's long sword. Sparks flew as the two lengths of iron scraped off each other. He slid away again, desperate to get to his feet. The rider guided his horse back a step and, leaning over, drove the point of his weapon at Spartacus' stomach. With a lunge to the side, Spartacus prevented it skewering him to the ground. As it was, it shredded the side of his tunic and cut a flesh wound in his side. Pain flared, and he groaned. *Great Rider, help me!* His opponent's comrades would soon be on them.

'Hades is waiting for you!' cried the Roman.

With the strength of sheer desperation, Spartacus came up on to his knees. He met another blow with a savage overhand parry that caught the rider off guard. Before the man could bring down his blade again, Spartacus leaped up and grabbed his nearest foot with his left hand. With a great heave, he wrenched the Roman's leg upwards, unbalancing him. Arms flailing at the air, the man toppled off the other side of his horse.

Spartacus had no chance to savour this tiny victory. Three more riders had nearly reached him. It was pointless running. The trees were still too far. 'Gently,' he muttered, gripping the horse's mane with one hand and balancing his right fist and sica on its haunches. He threw himself up on its back just in time to see the closest cavalryman take an arrow in the belly. That left two men who were about forty paces from him. Spartacus tensed as they rode forward, but to his delight, another shaft almost struck one of their horses. Cursing, they reined in.

Spartacus didn't wait to see what happened next. He aimed a hefty kick at the Roman he'd unhorsed, sending him sprawling to the dirt again. Then he dragged his steed's head around and, drumming his heels into its sides, aimed it at the trees. Navio gave him a fierce grin as he rode up. 'Grip the mane,' Spartacus ordered.

Navio had never run with a horse before, but he knew of the Iberian skirmishers who'd fought for Hannibal. They often went into battle in such a manner. Coming in close, he grabbed a handful of the thick hair and as the beast trotted off, let its momentum give him extra speed.

As they reached the tree line unharmed, Carbo loosed an arrow. He shouted with pleasure as it sank into a horse's rear. The rider lost his seat as his steed bucked and kicked with the pain of it.

Spartacus threw himself to the ground. 'Quick! Get under cover.'

Throwing glances over their shoulders, they ran into the trees. The horse trotted off aimlessly.

'Stop. Ready an arrow.'

Chests heaving, they stared out at the Romans, of whom five or so remained uninjured. The cavalrymen made no attempt to dismount or to enter the woods.

'If they come in here, they'll lose all their superiority. The whoresons have had enough!' said Spartacus with savage delight. He was still alive! Never had he survived such insane odds.

Carbo and Navio began howling like wolves. Was there anything Spartacus couldn't do? Following his example, they loosed more shafts until the horsemen had retreated further. 'Keep an eye on them,' Spartacus ordered Navio. 'Best check on the men whom we nearly died for, eh?' he barked at Carbo. They trotted to the two fugitives, who were a little further under the canopy. The man who'd been injured was lying on his back, moaning.

Carbo winced as he drew near. The Roman's sword had sliced in above the hipbone, opening his abdomen like a ripe fruit. Blood was oozing, pouring, jetting from the scarlet-lipped edges of the massive wound. Numerous loops of bowel were exposed. Everything was coated in a layer of grit and dirt from where the man had rolled on the ground. Carbo's nostrils twisted in distaste. 'I can smell shit.'

'Me too,' came Spartacus' grim reply.

That was it, thought Carbo bleakly. Even if he lived until they got him back to the camp, even if the surgeons could close the horrific cut, the man would die. No one survived when his guts had been pierced. No one.

They stooped over the third fugitive, who was trying to comfort his companion. 'You made it, Kineas. Well done.'

Kineas groaned. 'Water.'

'Here.' Spartacus pulled the stopper from his leather carrier and handed it over.

Kineas' comrade helped him to take a tiny mouthful. Rather than swallow the water, he inhaled it, which sent him into a paroxysm of coughing that set off a fresh wave of bleeding from his wound.

'What are they doing?' Spartacus called.

'Still sitting on their horses, waiting,' shouted Navio.

The hairs on Spartacus' neck prickled. 'Go back and see what's happening. I want no more stupid risks today,' he said to Carbo. He knelt down. 'What's your name?'

'Publipor,' replied the third man, who was perhaps thirty. His thin face was pinched by hunger and suffering, and now sorrow.

'We can do nothing for your friend. He's dying,' whispered Spartacus.

'I know,' said Publipor bitterly.

Carbo reached Navio, who was watching the group of horsemen. They had withdrawn perhaps a hundred paces, beyond accurate bow range. 'I don't like it,' said Navio. 'Why haven't they either dismounted and come in here after us, or just pissed off? There could be other troops in the area.'

Carbo squinted into the dust cloud that yet hung in the air behind the Romans. He could see nothing. Navio was right, however. Something didn't feel right. 'Spartacus?'

'What?'

'They look as if they're expecting reinforcements.'

Spartacus caught the tone of Carbo's voice. 'Time to go.'

Kineas' eyes opened. For a moment, they wandered, unfocused, before settling on Publipor. His forehead creased. 'Why——?'

'Easy,' murmured Publipor. 'Don't try to talk.'

Kineas finally took in Spartacus. His frown deepened, and he pointed a finger at Publipor. 'He——' A fresh bout of coughing took him. More blood gouted from his wound and what colour was left in his hollow cheeks vanished. He sagged down on the earth and his eyelids fluttered closed.

Publipor let out a deep sigh.

'It's hard when a comrade dies,' said Spartacus quietly. *I have seen it too many times.*

Publipor's lips twisted with an unreadable emotion.

'We have to leave him.'

Kineas' eyes jerked open and he tried to sit up. 'I should never have——'

The effort was too much for him, and he slumped back down on to the crimson-soaked ground. He drew one more shuddering breath, and let it out with a loud rattle. Publipor bent over him, catching the last gasp. Then he gently closed Kineas' staring eyes.

Spartacus only let him grieve for a heartbeat. 'We must go.'

Publipor got to his feet and eyed them awkwardly. 'I do not like to ask anyone for money, but I have none. Kineas needs a coin for the ferryman.'

Spartacus fumbled in the little purse that hung around his neck and produced a denarius. 'Here.'

Publipor accepted it with mumbled thanks. He bent, opened Kineas' mouth and slipped the coin on to his tongue. 'Rest in peace,' he said heavily.

Carbo and Navio came trotting in. 'There's another dust cloud coming,' said Carbo.

'Is that so?' snapped Spartacus.

Carbo didn't see the fist that cracked into the side of his head. Stars burst across his vision, and he dropped to the ground. A kick in the belly made him retch. Dazed and nauseous, he looked up at Spartacus.

'What in the name of all the gods were you thinking? Did you want to die?'

Navio glowered at him, adding to the pressure.

Carbo spat out a gob of phlegm. 'No.'

'What then?' Spartacus' voice cracked like a whip.

'I-I thought one of the men was a slave belonging to my family. A man who was dear to me. I couldn't stand by and watch him be butchered like a pig.'

'Were you right? Was it he?'

'No,' replied Carbo miserably.

'Even if you had been correct, charging out like that was the wrong decision to make. You answer to me! Unless I tell you, you do not run off like a fucking maniac trying to commit suicide.' Another mighty kick was delivered.

Carbo rolled into a ball, trying to protect himself. No more blows landed.

'Look at me!'

He dragged his eyes up to meet Spartacus' flinty stare.

'If you ever do such a damn stupid thing again,' and he bent over, ramming a forefinger into Carbo's chest for emphasis, 'I will shoot you in the back myself. I only risk my life for a soldier once. Do. You. Understand?'

Carbo had never seen Spartacus so angry. 'Yes.'

'LOUDER!'

'YES!'

Without another word, Spartacus led the way up the slope.

Carbo stumbled to his feet. Navio didn't help him, and he knew that if he couldn't keep up, they would leave him behind. I deserve no less, he thought miserably. His stupidity had nearly got them all killed. He was fortunate that Spartacus hadn't slain him.

Spartacus' pace was brutal but no one complained. Apart from picking up Arnax, he didn't stop running until they had gone a couple of miles. Even then, it was but a brief pause to listen for sounds of pursuit. *I have tested the Rider's regard for me enough for one day.* He only let up when the army's tents came into view.

Publipor's jaw dropped at the sight. 'You must be some of Spartacus' men.'

Carbo was able to raise a grin at that. 'You're not far off.'

'What do you mean?'

'You're looking at the man himself.' He indicated his leader.

'Y-you are Spartacus?'

'I am.'

'The gods be praised!' Publipor clutched at Spartacus' hands like a supplicant to a king. 'I owe you and your men my life. Thank you.'

'It's Carbo you should be grateful to.' Spartacus' smile did not reach his eyes.

Publipor's attention moved to Carbo. 'How can I ever repay you?'

'Join our army. Swear allegiance to Spartacus,' replied Carbo awkwardly. He knew that this gesture would not restore him to the Thracian's favour, but he wanted to show that he was still loyal.

'Of course. That is all I want to do.'

'You were trying to reach my army?' asked Spartacus.

'Yes. We had been on the run for four days.'

'You did well to evade the riders for that long.'

Publipor shuddered. 'No, they only happened upon our trail today, about three miles back. We hid as best we could, but they kept finding our tracks. When they flushed us out, the woods were the best cover we could see. We had no chance, but then the gods intervened to bring you here with your men.' Awe filled his eyes. 'I've never seen anything like that mad charge that you did to save me and Kineas.'

'The gods were definitely on hand,' agreed Spartacus. *Acting in combat as I did today wouldn't just get me killed. It would get scores of men slain, perhaps even lose the battle. I am eternally in your debt, Great Rider. I will not make the same mistake again.* 'You want to become a soldier?'

'Yes.' He bobbed his head. 'I'd be honoured to serve you.'

'Good. Have you come far?'

'I detect a southern accent in your words,' added Carbo.

'You do.' Publipor sounded surprised. 'I'm from Apulia.'

'You've travelled as far as we have, or further,' said Spartacus. 'Did your master bring you up here?'

'No. I was with Publius, my master, on business when I heard news of Crixus' army in the area. I ran away and joined them, to be free. That's where I met Kineas and the other man. Things went well for a while, until Gellius arrived.'

'By the Rider! You were at Mount Garganus?'

'Yes.'

'No other survivors have reached us thus far. I'm glad to have you.' Spartacus gripped Publipor's shoulder, which elicited a small smile. 'It must have been a black day.'

Publipor's eyes clouded over again. 'It was terrible.'

'But you survived. You did not run?'

'No,' replied Publipor steadily. 'I did not run. At least not until Crixus had been killed, and it was clear that all was lost.'

'I want to hear the full story,' Spartacus announced. 'But not here.'

He was keen to understand how, despite his superior numbers, Crixus had lost the battle. Maybe Gellius had outmanoeuvred him? Just because Spartacus' own forces had had the better of him didn't mean that the consul had not directed his forces skilfully. Roman generals were famous for their resourcefulness. *I must be careful with Longinus. The smallest error and we could lose tomorrow. Even this close to complete freedom, we could fail.*

The thrill of saving Publipor, of surviving when he shouldn't have, vanished.

Spartacus began brooding again about the Alps. He had been trying to avoid the question, although it swirled around in the back of his mind like a repetitive bad dream. Going on the hunt had been a way to forget his troubles, albeit briefly. *Don't try to deny it*, he thought. *When it comes down to it, it's not certain if the army will follow me out of Italy. And if they won't leave, I'm not sure I want to either.*

The answer will come to me. The Rider will show me the way.

For once, his staple prayer rang very hollow.

Some days later . . .
Rome

Crassus pursed his lips in disapproval as Longinus' lictores filed through the Curia's massive bronze doors. 'The man has some nerve allowing them to precede him in here,' he hissed.

A nearby senator heard. 'As a proconsul, Longinus is entitled to eleven bodyguards.'

'I'm fully aware of how many lictores a proconsul merits,' Crassus shot back. 'My point is that he is showing an indecent amount of cheek to show up in this fashion. If the stories are to be believed, Longinus didn't just lose to Spartacus, he was thrashed! His legions were almost wiped out, losing yet more eagles in the process, and the man was fortunate to escape with his life. It would be more appropriate if Longinus came in with no pomp, no ceremony. Humbly, seeking our forgiveness for his failures.'

The senator considered replying, but Crassus' fury made him think better of it. He turned his back.

'It *is* unbecoming that he's making such an entrance,' commented Caesar, who was standing close by.

Crassus smiled. Thus far, he was pleased with his decision to lend Caesar the three million denarii. His new ally had brought scores of the younger senators into his camp, and was being proactive in recruiting more. His attention returned to the lictores. His face went a shade of purple. 'The arrogant bastard hasn't even had them remove the axes from their fasces!'

His words sent a ripple of shock through the six hundred senators. Within Rome's sacred boundary, only a dictator's lictores were allowed to carry the axes in the fasces that signified the right to execute wrongdoers. To break this rule was sacrilege of the most serious kind.

'A bad time to seek out such bad luck,' said Caesar loudly.

Gnaeus Cornelius Lentulus Clodianus and Lucius Gellius, the two consuls, strained their ears to hear the scandalised whispers, but their rosewood chairs at the end of the rectangular room were placed too far from their senatorial colleagues.

Longinus' lead lictor rapped his fasces on the marble floor.

A disapproving silence fell.

'I announce the proconsul of Cisalpine Gaul, Gaius Cassius Longinus.'

'Savour your position, because you won't be in it for much longer,' said Crassus, making no effort to be quiet.

His supporters, who now numbered more than 150, tittered.

'Silence!' said the lictor, but his bark lacked its customary authority.

Crassus' pleasure grew. He didn't yet have enough senators to command a majority, but Longinus' defeat would only lend fuel to his fire and, by all the gods, he would make the most of this situation. Since the news of Spartacus' latest victory had reached Rome a day and a half before, Crassus had spent every waking moment considering what he would say.

A couple more derogatory comments were made about Longinus. Crassus was pleased to note that they came from the other side of the floor, traditionally the area where Pompey's faction stood. He heard the words 'A disgrace to his office' and 'Another stain to the Republic's honour' and exulted. *I will gain control of the legions – I know it,* he thought. *Be careful,* warned his cautious side. *Let Longinus place his own head on the block.*

Lentulus, who was an unremarkable-looking man with receding brown hair, spoke to his chief lictor, who rapped out an order. At once his fellows hammered their fasces off the floor.

A hush fell. When the consuls – even those who had been defeated – demanded silence, they got it.

'Let the proconsul approach,' cried Lentulus' lictor.

The bodyguards' formation parted, and Longinus stepped smartly forward. He was a man of medium height and build, with a hard-bitten look. As a general who had been on campaign, he was wearing a red tunic. A sash of the same colour was tied around the lower part of his gleaming bronze cuirass. Layered linen pteryges covered his groin, and he wore a magnificent crested helmet. Even his calf-high boots were polished. He very much looked the part, and under normal circumstances, his appearance would have garnered approving comments from the senators. Not so today, Crassus observed with delight. In a clear sign that his peers were unhappy with his conduct, Longinus walked the length of the Curia in complete silence. He halted at the low dais upon which the two consuls sat, and saluted.

'Proconsul,' said Lentulus.

Gellius inclined his head. 'You have returned.'

'Yes, consuls,' replied Longinus stiffly. 'I have come to make my report about recent events in the north.'

Crassus held in his explosive reaction. *He mustn't move too soon.*

Someone else did it for him. '"Recent events"?' cried a senator off to his right. 'Is that what you call your humiliation by a rabble of slaves?'

A loud growl of agreement met these words, and Longinus scowled.

'Order! I will have order!' shouted Lentulus. Twin spots of scarlet marked his cheeks. Crassus revelled in the consul's anger. Lentulus had had precisely the same experience at Spartacus' hands just a short time prior. The taunt could as well have been aimed at him or Gellius as Longinus, and there was nothing that Lentulus could do to deny it.

A resentful silence fell once more.

'Why are your lictores' fasces still decorated with axes, Longinus?' Caesar shouted. 'Are you trying to anger the gods even further than they already are?'

Longinus was stunned by the intervention of the Pontifex Maximus. 'I—'

Lentulus' eyes bulged as he took in the lictores standing by the entrance. He exchanged a look of outrage with Gellius. 'What is the meaning of this, proconsul?'

'It was an oversight, nothing more. We had been riding all night to get here. Of course I did not wish to upset the gods!' He called to his lictores: 'Remove the axes at once! Sacrifices of atonement are to be made at the major temples. See that it is done!' His bodyguards hurried from the building, and Longinus regarded the consuls again. 'I will perform my own penitence to the gods as soon as I may,' he said humbly. 'It will never happen again.'

'Damn right it won't,' snapped Crassus.

Other comments – angry and concerned – filled the air.

'Let us have your report,' ordered Gellius.

'As every senator here knows, I have command of two legions. The slave Spartacus leads in excess of fifty thousand men. Knowing that these men had come fresh from their victories' – Longinus cleared his throat while pointedly ignoring the consuls – 'over other Roman forces, I decided that my best option was to mount a surprise attack on his army as it marched towards the Alps. To this end, I located a suitable position a short distance from the road near Mutina. Upwards of thirty ballistae were built and transported there in secret. My plan was for the catapults to rain down an intense bombardment on the unsuspecting slaves, creating havoc, before my legions advanced on them from the north.'

'Something tells me that it didn't quite happen that way,' said Crassus quietly.

Beside him, Caesar's lips twitched.

'A good plan,' admitted Gellius. 'What went wrong?'

'Somehow Spartacus got wind of what I was up to. A strong force of slaves attacked the soldiers guarding the ballistae at night. They caught my men off guard. The cunning dogs were armed with axes, and they brought barrels of oil. The catapults that weren't incinerated were chopped into kindling.' Longinus sighed. 'Spartacus' army marched north the following morning. I could not just let the whoreson pass by Mutina without a fight, so I led my men out and confronted him.'

A few senators made sympathetic noises. 'He doesn't lack courage,' said one.

Crassus was pleased to note, however, that the faces he could see were still registering disapproval.

'Go on,' directed Lentulus.

'I had my legions deploy in the classic *triplex acies* formation. We had trees on our left, which prevented any use of cavalry, so I deployed all of my horse on my right. The enemy came to meet us in much the same fashion. Spartacus has learned to fight as we Romans do. His troops are, for the most part, well armed and well disciplined.'

Shocked cries rang out.

I told you months ago that Spartacus was not to be underestimated, thought Crassus. But you didn't listen. Secretly, he had been amazed by the degree of the Thracian's successes, but he would not admit that to a soul.

Longinus waited until there was silence again. 'His horsemen have been well trained too. They outnumbered my six hundred Gauls by at least five to one. As the armies engaged, my cavalry was driven back, allowing the enemy riders to sweep around to my legions' rear. After that, the fighting grew very heavy. Despite this, my soldiers held their ground for a long time. In the end, however, the fierce attacks from both front and behind were too much.' Longinus paused to compose himself. 'My men broke and ran.'

'Your eagles?' asked Gellius.

A shadow passed across Longinus' face. 'Lost.'

'Both of them?'

'Yes. I stayed until the bitter end, trying to retrieve one. I would have died on the field if it hadn't been for one of my centurions, who, with his men, forcibly removed me. I wish that I had been slain, but it is also my duty to report my failings to the Senate. This I have done. I now await the sentence of my peers – whatever that may be.' Longinus bowed his head.

Despite himself, Crassus was impressed by the proconsul's performance. *He is courageous, both in battle and here on the treacherous ground that is the Senate.* Crassus soon hardened his heart. *He is just another general who failed. His failure will gain me more support. Perhaps today I can make my move.* He glanced around the room and was annoyed to see that Longinus' words appeared to have aroused sympathy in a good number of senators.

The consuls conferred with each other before Lentulus raised a hand for quiet. 'Our thanks for doing your duty by reporting what happened. While the news of your defeat and the loss of your eagles is calamitous, it is not without precedent.' He glanced at Gellius. 'My colleague and I have both failed against Spartacus.'

'Damn right you have,' shouted Crassus. 'Along with all the fools that you sent before that. You bring shame on the Republic!' His heart raced in the brief pause that followed. Had he gone too far?

'Shame! Shame on you both!' cried Caesar.

'Shame!' yelled another senator.

The call took on a life of its own, growing in size and volume until the very walls of the Curia rang with it. 'Shame! Shame! Shame!'

Crassus' glee knew no bounds. The news of their armies' previous defeats had produced nothing like this level of discontent. It would surely provide him with more supporters.

The uproar took some time to subside. When it did, Longinus was still in his position before the consuls, straight-backed, head bent in composed acceptance of his fate.

Perhaps because he had defeated Crixus, thereby retaining some honour, Gellius was the first to speak. 'Longinus must be made to pay for his failure. What punishment would you hand down, senators of Rome?'

A pregnant silence fell.

Crassus was surprised to find himself undecided. Others who had failed, among them the miserable Varinius, had been ordered to commit suicide, although naturally enough, the two consuls had escaped such sentences.

Yet neither of them were men of Longinus' stature. Here was a man from an illustrious family, who had served the Republic as master of the state mint, praetor and, only the previous year, as consul. Why should he have to suffer the ultimate punishment – death – when his inferiors did not? Was exile a better alternative? Crassus regarded Longinus. *He's an able man. It would be pointless to have him fall on his sword.* 'After he has made amends with the gods, let him be stripped of his office, and pay a large fine to the treasury.'

A short pause.

'I think that would be a fitting punishment,' said Caesar loudly.

'Agreed,' called one of Crassus' supporters.

Loud murmurs of concurrence rose from his faction. No one else spoke.

Crassus seized the moment. 'There's no need for Longinus to die. Not when others who've failed also have escaped such a fate.'

'Too true!' Caesar's tone was acid.

Crassus smiled beatifically at the consuls' futile glares. *This is only the start, you fools.*

'Longinus must stand down,' cried a senator who followed Pompey.

'Stand down! Stand down! Stand down!' went the chant.

Irritated, Gellius waved his hand. 'All right. It seems, Longinus, that your fellows wish you to resign as proconsul. And to pay a fine?' He glanced out over the floor.

'YES!'

'You are to pay a fine to the state treasury of . . .' He conferred with Lentulus. '. . . five hundred thousand denarii.'

'Don't forget his penance before the gods,' said a voice.

Longinus lifted his head. 'It will be the first thing I do when I leave the Curia. I thank my fellow senators for their clemency. I will continue to serve the Republic in every way that I can.' Undoing the red belt that signified his status as a general, he let it fall at the consuls' feet. He saluted them, and then, without looking to either side, walked proudly from the room.

An audible sigh rose up from the gathered politicians.

'And so to the real issue of the day,' whispered Crassus to Caesar.

'What to do about Spartacus.'

'Precisely. The consuls must also be made to pay for Longinus' failure. The poor choices that he made reflect upon them as leaders of the Republic.'

'Do you think that this is the time to make our move?'

Our move, thought Crassus with some satisfaction. *Caesar is definitely with me.* He glanced around, trying to gauge the mood. 'I'm not sure. Let's hound them for a little bit and see what happens.'

Fasces clattered on the floor, interrupting their conversation.

'Longinus' news may have been catastrophic, but it only firms our resolve. Rome does not take defeat lying down,' Lentulus announced in a confident voice.

'The slave Spartacus and his followers must be brought to bay and defeated once and for all,' added Gellius.

'Defeated!' yelled a voice. 'Rome must be victorious!'

'Victorious! Victorious!' shouted the senators.

The consuls gave each other a pleased look. The tide of anger against them seemed to be turning.

'And who precisely will lead the Republic's legions to victory?' Crassus' loud question cut through the clamour like a hot knife through cheese. Silence descended. He cast a scornful glance at the consuls. 'You are the elected consuls, the most senior magistrates in the land. I honour your positions, but I am no longer inclined to support you in this war.' He looked around, smiling at the senators' shock. 'Yes, this *is* now a war. Should we support two men who have already been convincingly beaten by Spartacus? Who have lost no fewer than four silver eagles between them? Who have made Rome the laughing stock of the Mediterranean? I say that to do so would be to imperil our very Republic.'

'What are you suggesting, Crassus?' bellowed Lentulus. 'Are you wishing to seize power, as Sulla did?'

Suddenly, Crassus felt the weight of hundreds of pairs of eyes upon him. He cursed inside. Had he misjudged the senators' mood? 'I—'

Lentulus gave him no time to finish. 'Didn't you do well enough out of Sulla's proscriptions?'

Laughter broke out at once. Crassus glared, but he had lost the initiative.

'Are you not rich and greedy enough already? Let us not forget how you preyed like a vulture on those who fell foul of "the Butcher". As a consequence, your riches are immense, but they are also stained with blood,' said Lentulus loudly.

'Any purchases that I may have made were entirely legal,' Crassus declared. But it was too late. Everywhere he looked now, he saw revulsion on his peers' faces. Even Caesar had moved a step away. 'They were all legal, I say!'

'Maybe they were,' retorted Gellius, 'but you didn't see us queuing up to buy those properties!'

Utterly furious, but now powerless, Crassus bit his lip.

In a clever move, the consuls did not address the floor for a few moments. They let the senators' outrage at Crassus dominate the mood. Then Gellius, who was the better speaker, rose from his chair. He took two steps forward, to the edge of the dais, and waited.

The hubbub abated.

'Lentulus and I have made our mistakes, but we are still the elected consuls of Rome. Is that not true?'

A low rumble of agreement.

'And, until recently, we have performed our duties to the satisfaction of the majority, have we not?'

'You have,' called out a voice.

No one said another word.

'For all our faults, we are both possessed of Roman *virtus*. It is indeed a scandal that Spartacus has defeated so many of our armies. It will *not* happen again! Lentulus and I have brought our legions together. Reinforcements made necessary by our *problems* have been recruited. The remnants of Longinus' command is to be brought south to join with ours, making a combined force of more than four legions. Auxiliaries are being sought out in Cisalpine Gaul as I speak. Word has been sent to Gaul and Iberia that we need horsemen. In a matter of six to eight weeks, we will have an army that numbers more than thirty thousand men.'

Crassus wasn't beaten yet. 'What if Spartacus seeks battle again before that time?'

'We will meet him on ground of our choosing, and wipe him from the face of the earth. This I swear to Jupiter, Minerva and Mars,' declared Gellius to loud shouts of approbation.

'And if, as some suspect, he leaves Italy?'

'Lentulus will remain here, to raise more legions and to safeguard the Republic. I shall track the slave rabble by land or sea with our armies. He won't get far. When I find them, I shall destroy them completely. If by some small chance Spartacus reaches Thrace, I can unite with Lucullus' forces there. Between us, we shall smash him into pieces. Either way, we shall have victory!'

'Victory!' cried the senators. 'Victory!'

In that moment, Crassus knew that his opportunity had been lost. He wasn't above laying one more baited trap, however. 'Very well. You will defeat Spartacus together?'

'We will,' the consuls declared.

'May Jupiter be your witness,' said Caesar, giving them a pointed stare.

Gellius' blood was up. 'May he strike me down if we fail!'

Lentulus looked less than pleased with his colleague's fervour, but he couldn't back down either. 'I make a vow to Jupiter Optimus Maximus that we shall succeed.'

'Excellent,' said Crassus with false enthusiasm. 'The Republic will be triumphant once more!'

The unsuspecting senators were delighted. They cheered and whistled like an excited crowd watching a gladiatorial contest.

Crassus moved closer to Caesar. 'Thank you for speaking when you did,' he said from the side of his mouth. 'Gellius fell into your snare without even noticing.'

Caesar inclined his head in recognition. 'But Lentulus knows he's been manoeuvred into a corner. He looks as if he's swallowed a bowl of hemlock.'

'What do I care?' whispered Crassus. 'If by some miracle the fools succeed, the problem of Spartacus will have been dealt with. If they fail, they will not have a leg to stand on. No general can be defeated twice and stay in office, especially when he has taken a sacred oath in front of six hundred of his fellows.'

'It was a clever move. You turned the situation around nicely.'

Crassus demurred politely, but inside he was exultant. If anything, what had transpired was better than if he'd achieved his aims that day. The legions in Italy were shrunken, battered and demoralised. Taking charge of them and attempting to defeat Spartacus would be to risk disaster.

This way, he had all eventualities covered and now he would have time to continue planning his best course of action. One thing was certain, thought Crassus. The Republic needed more soldiers than it currently had on its home territory. Pompey had a good number of legions in Iberia. So too did Lucullus, in Pontus. If either man were recalled to defend the Republic, they would not hand over the command of their troops to anyone. They would want all the glory. *The glory that should be mine.* Crassus decided at once to talk to Caepio, the sole survivor of Spartacus' munus. He would provide a strong rallying point for any legions Crassus might raise. Men would flock to serve under him.

Crassus' mind tracked back to the time he had fought for Sulla. Many of the soldiers who had fought for the Butcher in the civil war would still be alive, tending the little plots of land that had been granted to them upon their discharge. Sulla had known well that nothing made a veteran of twenty years' service happier than to receive exactly what he'd been promised on the day of his enlistment. Crassus thought of Pompey, and scowled. *That prick is good at honouring his soldiers' discharge, just as Sulla was.* If the truth be known, he hadn't done as well by his legionaries in the past, but fortunately there hadn't been that many of them. Sulla's, on the other hand, numbered in their thousands. *They will remember me, the man who won the battle of the Colline Gate, the man who was Sulla's loyal captain.* A popular saying came to mind, making him smile. 'Everyone who has a soldier's heart remains a soldier, even if his body has grown old,' Crassus said softly. 'Nor will they refuse the handsome wages I offer.'

It was time to set Saenius another task. His major domo had done much already to try and recruit spies within the slave army, but the day's developments meant that there was plenty more to be done. Raising new legions took time, and although he didn't yet have the jurisdiction to do so, Crassus was sure that he could implement the first steps of the lengthy process. With a decent number of veterans, he would have a nucleus around which he could build an army when the time came.

Crassus knew in his bones that the consuls would soon meet Spartacus in battle. Nothing that he had seen today told him anything other than Lentulus and Gellius would lose. When they did, he would seize his chance.

We will meet again, Spartacus, thought Crassus. This time, you will learn the lesson that I should have taught you the first time we met. We Romans have no equals, and you are nothing but a savage. A talented, intelligent savage, perhaps, but a savage nonetheless. When your army has finally been ground into dust and you are choking out your last breath, you will understand that.

How I look forward to that day. I will take the credit for saving the Republic, and the masses will love me – for saving their lives and their livelihoods. That upstart Pompey can forget being the most popular man in Rome. In taverns and shops, on every street corner, the citizens will talk of no one but Crassus. My fame assured, I will be held in the same regard as men such as Sulla and Marius – for ever.

Chapter VI

Near the foot of the Alps, Cisalpine Gaul

Ariadne woke with a headache. Stretching, she felt a crick in her neck as well. She sighed. Her poor sleep hadn't just been because of the baby's activity. Her rest had not been helped by a never-ending, hideous nightmare, in which she could not find Spartacus on a road that had been decorated with a crucified man every forty paces. It was a huge relief to see him breathing heavily alongside her. She studied his features in a concerted effort to forget the gory images of the dream. It worked. With the tip of a finger, she traced the faint scar that ran off his straight nose on to his left cheek. She touched his square, determined jaw and his brown hair, close-cropped in the Roman military fashion. Ariadne was admiring his well-muscled, wiry torso when he gave a violent twitch and muttered something. At once her enjoyment soured.

Judging by the way he'd moved about all night, he had not slept well either. She wondered what had caused his unease. *I'll ask him when he wakes.* She herself had long since given up trying to rest. Despite her weariness, she was determined to be cheerful. This was the day that she had longed for since their remarkable escape from the ludus in Capua. Back then, it had been an impossible hope. Yet against all likelihood, her husband's soldiers had defeated every Roman army that had been sent against them since. Now Mutina lay some twenty miles to their rear, the legions that had garrisoned it broken and scattered to the four winds. No battle-ready enemy troops remained in the area. The previous day, their army had crossed the bridge over the River Padus. Their path lay wide open.

Ariadne had to feast her eyes on the wondrous sight again. She unlaced the tent flap and looked out. At last a smile crept on to her face. She hadn't imagined it. Towering before her, from west to east in an immense, unbroken stony wall, were the Alps. All we have to do, she thought, is cross those peaks, and we'll be free. For ever. Why, then, did she have a knot of worry clenched in her gut? An old saying came to her: Many's the slip between the cup and the lip. *I won't be happy until we have actually reached the other side of the mountains.*

'Checking they're still there?' Spartacus' voice came from behind her.

She pulled her head inside the tent. 'You're awake.'

'Yes. Well, have they vanished?'

She punched him lightly on the arm. 'You're making fun of me.'

'Just a little. I want to see them too.' He threw off his blankets and crawled to the entrance. He was quiet for a moment. Then, 'Thank the Rider. I didn't dream them up. We really are beyond the reach of any legionaries in Italy.' In Italy, he thought darkly. What about Thrace? A wild land that most of my soldiers have only heard of in tales. Will they want to go there — to face more legions? Or will they refuse? If that happened, Spartacus was aware that he did not want to be a general without an army.

'You're going ahead with your plan to talk to the men.'

'Of course. This is an immense step that we're taking. I have to check that they're all of the same opinion.'

There it was, she thought. The festering worry that both of them had been feeling for some time, but neither had mentioned. She couldn't have been alone in hearing the discontented talk around the campfires. 'You think some of them won't?'

He didn't answer.

'Who? Castus or Gannicus?'

Spartacus sighed.

'What is it?'

Despite his wish to avoid confrontation with Ariadne, he'd always known that he would have to tell her. It had to be before he addressed his soldiers too. He owed her that much. 'A lot of men aren't happy with the idea. There has been grumbling about it for a while, but over the last couple of nights, it has grown worse. You might not have noticed it, but I hear it all as I move through the camp.'

'But—'

'It's not surprising, Ariadne. The bulk of them were born here in captivity. They weren't freeborn, like you and I. They don't know what it's like to live in their own homeland, with no one to call master. As far as they're concerned, Italy is a land rich for the plunder. It's fertile, with countless farms and latifundia to prey upon. Why would they want to leave it? A lot of those who weren't born into slavery think that too.'

'They should leave because they would get away from the damn Romans!' she said, feeling her cheeks redden with anger.

'Yet the majority think that they can beat any army that they face. Why wouldn't they?' His lips twisted in a wry grimace. 'Look at what they've done. I've told them over and over that the Romans never give up, but words mean little when they've never known anything except victory.'

'There must be a way to convince them.'

'At the end of the day, I can't make the army follow me. It's not as if there aren't other leaders who will be reluctant to cross the Alps, men who want to stay in this land that has given them so much.'

'You mean Castus and Gannicus.' This time, she spat their names.

'Yes. They stayed with me when Crixus left, but you know how unpredictable they are, especially that piece of dirt Castus. He has never liked following my lead. This is when he'll make his move, and I wager Gannicus will go with him. A good chunk of the army will follow them.' *And the pricks don't even know about Lucullus. If they did, and told the men, most would leave.*

'If that happens, what will you do?'

They stared at each other without speaking.

'The Thracians would come with me. Carbo, Navio, the Scythians, obviously. I'd say that maybe ten to fifteen thousand other men would do as I ask. But the rest I'm not sure about—'

'Leave them then!' cried Ariadne. 'They can choose their own fates! To be slaughtered in a month, or a year, by another Roman army.' She saw the pain in his eyes. 'I know that they're your men, but you don't have to act as they do.'

'I know,' he said stiffly. 'But there's more to it than that.'

She gave him a searching look. 'Is this what have you been holding back from me?'

He didn't answer her question. 'When Carbo and Navio were in Mutina, they heard word of Marcus Lucullus, the Roman general who has been fighting in Asia Minor. He has defeated the Thracians who were in Mithridates' pay and moved into Thrace itself. Large areas have been laid waste.'

'The Romans have campaigned against Thracian tribes on and off for more than thirty years. Hitherto they've never bothered to mount a full-scale invasion. Why would things have changed?'

'I don't know, but his campaign is continuing.'

Dionysus, no! How can you have let this happen? Ariadne wanted to scream at the heavens, but she held in her rage and fear. 'Surely it's even more reason to leave? You could lead the fight there.'

'That might appeal to you and me, maybe, but not to the majority. What do Castus and Gannicus care about Thrace? Or the rest of them?'

'Do the Gauls know?' She couldn't take her eyes off his face.

'No, thank the Rider. I'm not planning on telling them either. Carbo and Navio know not to say a word to a soul.'

That was some consolation, she thought bitterly. 'Why didn't you tell me this before?'

'I didn't want to worry you. Besides, there was little point until Longinus had been defeated.'

'I see.' Although she was angry, Ariadne was partly glad that she hadn't known until now. She had enjoyed her fantasy – which had just been replaced by a tide of acid disappointment. Her gaze moved to the bright sunlight entering the tent, and outside, the towering spectacle of the Alps. They seemed far larger than they had a few moments prior. 'Even if we cross the mountains, the Romans will find us in Thrace.'

He scowled in agreement. 'It wouldn't take long for news of our arrival to reach Lucullus' ears. He'd want to take us on – and that's assuming that the Senate doesn't send an army after us as well.'

'Have you forgotten the other tribes? You planned to unite them under one banner. To lead the fight against Rome. Surely they would come together when they saw how many men followed you?'

'I thought about this long and hard. You know how quarrelsome our people are. They like to call no man leader. It's as likely that they would attack us as join us. It would be an enormous task to bring together more than two or three tribes. Only one man has ever ruled all of the Thracians, and he did not do so for long.' He let out a long, weary breath. 'Father was wrong. Thrace is not a land that can be united.'

'You could do it,' she urged.

'Maybe. And maybe not. It's probable, however, that I'd have to fight to control at least some of the tribes, handing the advantage to Lucullus. That's if someone didn't assassinate me first. Here, on the other hand, I already have an army in excess of fifty thousand soldiers. Men who do not need convincing to follow me. In Italy, there is also an endless source of recruits to our cause. If I stay, even the troublemakers such as Castus will continue to follow my lead. For the moment at least.'

'I can't believe you're saying this!'

In that instant, Spartacus silently voiced the truth that had come to him during the long dark of the previous night. The rumblings of discontent in his forces were all too real. It was by no means certain whether the men would follow through on their threats, but he had a bad feeling about it. *I will not leave the majority of my soldiers behind. Not to end up where I began – in Thrace, with every man's hand turned against me and the Romans plundering the land at will.*

'You don't want to give up command of your army, that's what it is.' She glared at him.

He met her stare. 'No, I don't.'

'I knew it!' she screamed. 'You're too damn proud.'

'If the men will leave, I shall go. If the vast majority will not, then I am staying,' he replied, jutting out his chin.

'And if I decide to cross the Alps without you?'

'I would be saddened to see you go. Naturally, I would send men to protect you.'

'You would choose your troops over me?' Tears – of sadness, of rage – sprang from her eyes. 'Your wife, who is bearing your son?'

'First and foremost, I am a soldier, Ariadne,' he growled. 'Not a husband. You've known that from the moment we met.'

Ariadne's joy at seeing the Alps vanished. She felt as if Dionysus and every other deity in the pantheon had just withdrawn their goodwill. Somehow, she rallied herself. 'You're talking as if it's certain that the men will refuse to follow you over the mountains. You could be wrong.'

'Perhaps.'

Ariadne felt her shoulders sag. 'So we have marched the length of the land for nothing?'

'It wasn't for nothing. When we left Thurii, I fully intended to cross the Alps. And I still will—'

'If the army follows you,' she interjected furiously.

'Yes.'

Her eyes filled anew.

Spartacus reached out a hand to comfort her, but she recoiled as if his touch was poisonous. He let her be. 'I am a leader. A general. I have come to my position through merit. I will not just give it all up and hand my power to a sewer rat like Castus or a schemer like Gannicus.' *Even if it hurts you.*

'You've said before that Rome's legions were like the monster Hydra. For every one head that is destroyed, two more grow in its place. If you stay here in Italy, they will raise ever more legions against you.'

'Maybe they will. But Hercules bested the Hydra. Perhaps I can too,' he replied, the pride she had accused him of filling his voice.

'But in Thrace you would have a better chance—'

'In Thrace?' Spartacus laughed, angry now. 'For what I have done, the Romans will never leave me alone. They will send their legions after me even if I travel to the ends of the earth.'

In her heart, Ariadne knew he was right. If her husband left his soldiers secretly, and found with her some remote place to live in, they would have a life untroubled by Rome. But he would no more do that than the sun would dance in the sky. *Warfare is his destiny. It always has been.* She could not change that, any more than she could his nature. Nor did she want to, she realised sadly. She loved him as he was. Brave. Fierce. Charismatic. Clever. Reckless at times. And, above all, proud.

What did it mean for him, though? she wondered. And for her?

He began to get dressed. 'I told Egbeo and Pulcher that I wanted the men assembled after they had eaten. Will you come to hear me speak?'

'Yes,' she heard herself say.

'Will you stay or go?'

'That depends on what you do.'

They stared at each other.

'Your answer is ambiguous. Will you follow me?'

'I haven't decided yet,' she replied, lifting her chin.

I'm not the only one with pride, thought Spartacus. 'I see.'

Neither spoke again as he prepared himself.

Ariadne remembered her hideous dream. Was that the fate that the gods held in store for him?

Spartacus would do his best to win the men over. That way, he and Ariadne would definitely stay together. His gut told him a different story about his soldiers, however. That didn't weaken his resolve. His troops needed a leader. And he was that man — whatever the path they chose.

Spartacus had ordered the construction of a raised platform at the edge of the camp the night before. Ten men from every century in the army were to gather in front of it where they could easily hear what he said. The senior officers of each cohort were also to present themselves there. The rest of the host was to stand as if on parade, behind and to either side of the chosen soldiers. Spartacus' plan was to speak slowly and to pause regularly, allowing runners from the central group to carry his exact words to their comrades. If he could win over the gathered men, he stood a chance of doing so for the whole host. But a chance was all it was. The waiting faces he saw on his way to the dais were not happy.

He threw back his shoulders. This was the most important address that he would ever make. It was good that the Roman battle standards they'd seized had been put on display. The evidence of his successes, six silver eagles, the wooden staffs bearing the insignia of more than thirty cohorts and two dozen sets of fasces were arrayed behind the platform. It was an incredible haul, he thought proudly. Even a general such as Hannibal would have been impressed. It could not fail to make an impact on his men. Would it be enough, though? He climbed the steps, past the trumpeters who stood ready to attract everyone's attention. His mood soured further. 'Castus and Gannicus are already here,' he muttered to Ariadne, who was a pace to his rear. 'Look.'

The Gauls were moving among the soldiers in front of the stage, chatting genially and slapping men on the shoulders. *Treacherous bastards.*

'They're trying to pre-empt me.' Whatever chance he'd had of convincing the men was slipping away before his eyes. Spartacus told himself that it was his imagination, but the roar that met his appearance was more muted than usual. 'SPAR-TA-CUS!'

He raised his arms in acknowledgement. 'I see you, my brave soldiers!'

The assembled men liked that. So too did the troops within earshot. There was no need for what had been said to be passed on. The chant was taken up with huge enthusiasm. 'SPAR-TA-CUS! SPAR-TA-CUS! SPAR-TA-CUS!' Weapons were hammered off shields, adding to the din. The wall of sound rose up into the clear blue sky.

Spartacus saw the Gauls' annoyance and was inwardly pleased. *They love me more than you two arrogant pricks.* He beckoned them up on to the platform. As they did, he walked up and down, indicating the standards. Then he barked an order to the trumpeters, who blew a short but piercing series of notes. A silence quickly fell. The men were eager to hear his message, whatever it was.

'Do you see these?' Spartacus shouted. 'We have six silver eagles. That's six legions we have beaten! And that's not taking into account all the Roman troops that we sent packing! You are brave and valiant soldiers, who have stood toe to toe with legionaries and come out as winners!' He let the nearest men roar themselves hoarse before he went on. 'Three praetors. One legate. One proconsul. Two consuls. Those are the generals you have faced and bettered. It's an incredible achievement. Be proud of yourselves – very proud!' He could see the surprise on Castus' and Gannicus' faces. *They're wondering why I'm boosting their egos.* Soldiers from the central grouping sprinted off, bearing word of what he'd said. Their messages were greeted with unbridled delight by the rest of the army.

It took a long time for the cheering to die down, but Spartacus waited patiently, ignoring the glowering presence of Castus and Gannicus nearby. Finally, it was time to speak again.

'For all of our successes, we have not won the war. Unfortunately, the Republic can take far more of a battering than we have given it and still remain standing. Hannibal annihilated four legions at the Trebia. Three legions at Trasimene. Eight legions at Cannae. Yet in the end he was still beaten. Why? Because Rome never gives up. Its people are more stubborn than you can ever understand. They will *not* accept defeat. The manpower available to them is inexhaustible. Even now, new legions are being recruited to replace the ones we massacred. Give it six months or a year, and they will have an army, stronger than any we've yet fought, ready to confront us.' Spartacus saw disgruntled looks being exchanged, mutters passing from man to man. *They don't like hearing that.*

Ariadne didn't like his words either. *O gods above, please let them agree. Let us leave this cursed land behind for ever.*

'You know why I have asked you here this morning. Many months ago, I said to you that I would lead you out of Italy. Away from Rome and its damn legions!' He pointed at the Alps. 'When we cross those, which at this time of year is not difficult, we shall be totally free. Not just at liberty to do as we have here, but free in the truest sense of the word!' Spartacus cast a glance at the two Gauls. Castus had a sneer spread across his ruddy face, and Gannicus looked downright angry. In that moment, Spartacus sensed that they knew about Lucullus. How, he wasn't sure, but they knew. The cold realisation of what they had been telling the men as he arrived slid into his mind.

A scan of the nearest soldiers told him that his encouraging words had only had a partial effect. Many men were still unhappy: scowling, frowning or listening as a comrade whispered in their ear. Even the threat of more legions did not compare with the idea of leaving Italy and entering unknown lands. Lands where other legions waited for them. That was it. He had to tell his troops about the Roman threat to Thrace, or Castus' and Gannicus' underhand tactic would work. The soldiers would know him for a liar, and might not follow him anywhere. Spartacus felt bitter at being forced to reveal his secret, but the gods had taken matters into their own hands – as they so often did. He just had to accept what had happened, and make the best of it. He had to seize back the initiative.

He held up a hand. 'At least that is what I would have wished. News came to me near Mutina, however, that troubled me deeply. That caused me to reconsider my plans. We will stay in Italy!'

A loud cheer rose from the nearest men, and Ariadne let out a hiss of dismay and anger.

Spartacus ignored her, instead rejoicing in the dismay coating both Gauls' faces.

'What made you change your mind?' shouted a soldier with a horsehair-crested helmet.

'Apparently, Lucullus, the Roman general, has attacked Thrace. His campaign continues even as we speak.'

'Attacked Thrace? Why in the gods' names would we leave here then?' shouted the soldier, aiming his question at those all around him. They roared with laughter.

Spartacus did not answer. He watched as the news spread through his army like the ripple of wind through a field of wheat. It moved faster than any of his words about glory, victory or freedom. Castus' face had now gone purple. Gannicus looked stunned. Their reactions were proof that his hunch had been right. He felt a grim satisfaction at having stolen their thunder. Of course they might still break away, but the advantage was with him. He cast his eyes over the army, and listened to the swelling roar of approval.

'Where would you lead us instead, Spartacus?' cried the soldier in the horsehair helmet.

The men around him quietened.

From the corner of his eye, Spartacus saw Castus moving forward, but he half turned and made a chopping gesture at the trumpeters.

Tan-tara-tara-tara. The noise drowned out all sound on the platform. Castus went puce with fury, but there was nothing he could do until the instruments fell silent. The instant that they did, however, Spartacus leaped in. 'Do you want to know where I would go now, my soldiers?'

'YES!' To his delight, Pulcher began the cry: 'SPAR-TA-CUS!'

At once the reply was shouted back. 'SPAR-TA-CUS! SPAR-TA-CUS!'

Castus tried to speak again, but no one was paying him any attention. The chant was already spreading through the assembled troops. Spartacus found himself grinning. *How could I ever leave them?* He signalled at the musicians once more. The men's clamour abated before the trumpets' crescendo. Castus' mouth opened as their sound died away, but Spartacus was having none of it. 'I would take you south again. To our old stamping grounds around Thurii, where the land is rich and fertile.'

'And there are plenty of farms to plunder!' roared the soldier.

'And women to screw!' shouted another voice.

'That's right.' Spartacus didn't like the way his men sometimes behaved, but he didn't try to control every breach of discipline. Indiscriminate killing and rape had been part of warfare since time began. The troops regarded such things as part of their pay, and in a way he did too. If he tried too hard to stop them, they would turn on him. 'In the south, we will continue to recruit men. To train. To arm ourselves. To prepare ourselves for the legions that will come after us.'

'And we'll thrash them, just as we've done the previous ones!'

'Yes,' said Spartacus confidently. Inside, he felt less certain. But he had chosen his path. All he could do now was tread upon it, to the best of his ability. With as many men as would follow him. Already part of him had begun to exult at the thought of defeating more Roman armies. 'Will you march with me to Thurii, and to victory?'

'YES!' The soldier in the horsehair helmet punched the air with a fist. 'SOUTH! SOUTH!' yelled the closest men.

This time, the runners were not needed. Everyone who heard the cry repeated it, and the two words spread like wildfire through the host. 'SOUTH! SOUTH!' the soldiers roared, stamping their feet and clashing their weapons off their shields.

Despite his concerns for the future, pride filled Spartacus at the sound.

'You sly Thracian bastard. You always try to get one up on us, don't you?'

He turned at the sound of Castus' voice. 'Try? I think I just did.'

Castus' lips peeled back into a snarl and he took a step forward. 'You—'

'Not in front of the army,' snapped Gannicus. 'Not now.'

Breathing heavily, Castus stopped.

'Who told you about Lucullus?' demanded Spartacus coldly.

'Fuck that!' shouted Castus. 'You were supposed to tell the men that you were going to Thrace.'

'I changed my mind.' *I had to.*

In a flash, Spartacus' motives became clear to Ariadne. *He saw that they knew.* The realisation did nothing to ease her disappointment.

'The clever bastard did it because he knew that the men wouldn't follow him, and he didn't want to relinquish command to us,' said Gannicus, his eyes bright with malice.

'My reasons are my own,' growled Spartacus. 'Are you coming south with me? Or are you going to leave now, as you planned?'

'Damn you to Hades, Spartacus!' Castus' right hand dropped to his sword.

Spartacus' fingers caressed the wooden grip of his sica. It would be a bad idea to fight in front of his men, but his anger at the Gaul had overflowed. 'Try it. Go on!'

Castus let his hand fall to his side. 'Now's not the time, you Thracian goat-humper.'

'I'd rather screw goats than corpses, like you do.'

Castus ground his teeth, but he kept his hand off his sword. 'I think we'll keep you company for a little longer, eh, Gannicus?'

'Breaking the army up now would only make the Romans' task easier. When they hear that we have turned around and marched south, the consuls might join forces. I wouldn't like to be facing that army with anything less than our full strength.'

Always the shrewd one, thought Spartacus. 'And after that?'

'We'll find a suitable time,' replied Gannicus in a sly tone. He held up a warning finger. 'But pull any more tricks like the one about Lucullus again, and I'm leaving with every man who will follow me.'

'And me!' added Castus.

'You can do what you like,' growled Spartacus. *You're more trouble than you're worth.* 'But until that point we'll continue to fight as one army?'

The Gauls exchanged a look, and then a nod. 'Yes,' said Gannicus. 'But we decide on any strategy together.'

'Fine.' *You both know that I am the best tactician.* Spartacus' mind was filled again with one burning question. 'Who told you?'

'It's annoying you not knowing, eh?' asked Castus, gloating. He glanced at Gannicus. 'Shall we tell him?'

'I don't see why not. He'll work it out soon enough.'

'Arnax,' revealed Castus.

'Arnax?' *Of course.* 'He was also there in Mutina.'

'That's right. He heard every word that your Roman lapdogs did. It didn't take much for him to tell me. A bit of friendship, a couple of hot meals. A coin or two. He sang like a songbird. A good lad, he is.'

'I see,' said Spartacus in an offhand tone. Inside, he was raging. What a stupid mistake! When he'd told Carbo not to speak to anyone, he hadn't even thought of the boy. With an effort, he reined in his bubbling fury.

'I would watch your back from now on,' said Castus.

Gannicus snickered.

'Are you threatening me?'

'Me? Threaten you?' Castus' tone was mocking.

'Piss off,' said Spartacus. 'Unless you want a fight right now.'

Castus hawked and spat. 'Come on, Gannicus. Something around here stinks.' Stiff-legged, like male dogs walking away from a rival, the Gauls stomped off the platform.

Spartacus watched them go. As when Crixus had finally made plain his intentions, he was relieved to know that the pair would leave. Yet he hoped that they could maintain some kind of working relationship. Keep the army together for at least another couple of months. That would give him enough time to find new recruits to replace the men who would leave.

He realised, that, having reached safety, he had just decided to walk back into the lion's den. Remaining in Italy was provocation of the most severe kind, greater even than the munus he had celebrated. The Romans would never leave them in peace. As far as Spartacus knew, the Senate had not sued for peace in its own land since it had lost a war to the Samnites more than two centuries before. It certainly wasn't going to do so with a slave.

He glanced at Ariadne, still wondering what her response would be. 'I had little choice – I saw that Castus and Gannicus knew about Lucullus. Fucking Arnax! It's all his fault. He'll soon be sorry.'

'What are you going to do to him?'

'Crucify the little bastard. It's no less than he deserves.'

Horror filled her eyes. 'You can't do that.'

'If it hadn't been for him, the army might well have done what I asked! That was what you wanted, wasn't it?'

'Maybe so, but that doesn't mean I would kill a child over it. Especially one who didn't know any better. It wasn't as if he'd been told not to say anything!'

'That's of no matter,' he grated. 'Men – or boys – are either with me, or against me.'

Ariadne thought of the baby in her belly, and of Arnax's youth. No more than a decade in the difference, she thought. Outrage filled her. 'Do it, and you risk bringing down the wrath of the gods upon yourself and your army. I can see this.'

He stared at her for a moment. She glared back, daring him to challenge her. 'Very well. I'll just give him a good thrashing.'

Ariadne let out a sigh of relief. He had not become totally unreasonable.

'If I hadn't spoken when I did, they would have accused me of lying,' he said in a conciliatory tone.

'I know.'

'This is my army, not theirs. I'm damned if I'll hand it over to them.'

'I know that too.'

Spartacus thought that her voice sounded less angry than before, but he wasn't sure. 'The war is only beginning. It will be more bitter and more bloody than anything that has happened thus far.' He wanted to ask her to stay, but his pride wouldn't let him. 'What will you do?'

If I remain, our son will be born in Italy. What will happen to us, great Dionysus? The silence that met her question was resounding, but Ariadne firmed her resolve. She had chosen to accept Spartacus as he was. She would make the best of this situation, even if it was not what she wanted to do. 'You are my husband.' She moved to his side. 'I would not be separated from you. We will face the future together, as we have always done.'

'I am glad.' Drawing her closer, Spartacus surveyed his army. Pride filled him once more. Rome's pool of manpower might be immense. Its determination might be never-ending. The tasks before him might be comparable to those faced by Hercules. Yet he had more than fifty thousand brave soldiers who would follow him to the doors of Hades. The Gauls would leave, but the losses in his ranks could be replaced. More slaves came to join them every day.

Give me time, Great Rider, and I could raise an army of one hundred thousand men, or even more. That will make the senators tremble in their beds.

Especially if one day we arrive at the gates of Rome.

Chapter VII

Picenum, near the coast of north-eastern Italy, summer 72 BC

Marcion stamped his feet up and down, hoping that nobody would notice his anxiety.

An instant later, Gaius nudged him. 'Feeling nervous?'

'Aren't you?' hissed Marcion.

'No. Today's not the day I'm going to die.'

'How can you know that?' demanded Marcion. 'Our damn cohort is near the centre of our line, where the heaviest casualties will be.'

'Gaius is too stupid to know if Hades is coming for him,' said Arphocras with a snicker.

Gaius scowled as the rest of them winked and smiled. They might not be admitting it, but apart from Gaius, there was a nervous tinge to everyone's expression, Marcion noted. His gaze was drawn again to the massed ranks of legionaries on the slope high above. 'I can't believe that we're going to charge up there!'

All eyes followed his. The enemy's position – at the top of a ridge – was daunting to say the least. A rocky peak prevented any chance of outflanking to the left, and the Roman right flank was protected by a large section of catapults.

'Our cavalry are useless here. It's a frontal assault by us – or nothing,' said Arphocras sourly.

'Good!' exclaimed Gaius. 'The quicker we get to grips with the stinking Romans, the better.' He looked around for support, but all he got was filthy stares.

'Spartacus has gone bloody mad,' grumbled Zeuxis. 'His victories have gone to his head. I told you this would happen.'

'We're going to die.' Arphocras sounded resigned. 'Even if the Romans lose, we'll never know about it.'

Zeuxis rubbed the double-ended phallic amulet that hung from a thong around his neck and mouthed a prayer. Several of the others did the same.

They're really scared. Somehow, Marcion rallied his courage. 'Spartacus knows what he's doing.'

'Does he?' Zeuxis sounded even more dubious than ever.

'He's never made a mistake yet, has he?'

'That means nothing. No one's perfect,' replied Zeuxis angrily. 'And what's his secret plan here? Any fool can see that charging up a slope is tantamount to suicide, yet that's what we're about to do.'

'There are only two legions on the ridge,' growled Gaius. 'We outnumber the bastards by six to one.'

'But we can't all engage at the same time: their front is too narrow. Besides, the odds aren't as great as you say. The other consul's legions won't be far away,' snapped Zeuxis. 'They'll fall on our rear at the first opportunity.'

Gaius glowered, and Marcion intervened. 'Spartacus is no fool. Remember how he set the trap for Lentulus? How he had Longinus' hidden catapults destroyed the night before we marched?'

Zeuxis' lip curled. 'I don't know. This attack seems like a very good way to get a lot of men killed.'

Trumpets blared from some distance to their right, and they craned their necks to see what was going on.

'It's Spartacus!' Marcion pointed at the horseman who had emerged from the ranks some two hundred paces away. He began riding up and down, addressing the troops nearest him.

'SPAR-TA-CUS!' The usual chant began.

Marcion was delighted. The closest soldiers also seemed pleased, and the news rippled through the cohort.

'Bloody typical,' said Zeuxis. 'We can't hear a damn word.'

Marcion glared, but the older man ignored him.

'How are we supposed to feel encouraged by this? We might as well just pray to the gods. Or talk among ourselves. That'd be as much use as standing here pretending that we have a clue what's going on.'

Marcion's anger overflowed. 'Stop your moaning, will you? Either that, or piss off!'

Zeuxis gave him a startled look.

'Like it or not, we're going to fight this cursed battle soon. Some of us might get killed, but at least we're free men. We're here of our own choice! I don't know about you, but I'd rather be here than back on the shitty *latifundium* where I grew up. I was treated like an animal.'

'Damn right!' shouted Gaius. 'There's no going back.'

'Well said,' Arphocras elbowed Marcion. 'We're Spartacus' men, whatever happens.'

The rest of their comrades gave each other sheepish grins while Zeuxis glowered in resentful silence.

Marcion's attention returned to Spartacus. He drew his sword, and Marcion's breath caught in his chest. The sica was stabbed repeatedly at the Roman lines, and the soldiers near Spartacus roared in appreciation. 'This is it. We're going to attack.'

To his surprise, the command was not given. Instead Spartacus rode along the front of the army, towards them. He came to a halt not twenty paces from where they stood. The soldiers went crazy, cheering and banging their weapons and shields together. Marcion and his comrades joined in. Even Zeuxis.

Spartacus raised his arms for calm. 'You know that there are only two legions facing us. That the other two are in the area, waiting for their chance to strike at us. Most likely, you're worried, even a little scared. I'd wager that Lentulus is banking on your fear. The toga-wearing man-humping piece of filth is also relying on his colleague Gellius to arrive and fall upon the rear of our army.' He smiled at the unhappy murmurs which followed.

Zeuxis glared at Marcion.

Marcion held his breath. This wasn't all that Spartacus had come to say – was it?

Spartacus watched them, let them stew in their uncertainty for several moments before he spoke again. 'Our scouts have done us proud. Yesterday they brought me news of Gellius' position. More than twenty thousand of your comrades are about to march out under Castus and Gannicus and confront him. Rest assured, your backs are safe! We have plenty of time to demolish Lentulus' spineless rabble.'

The mood changed, as a spring gale clears out the last traces of winter. Men laughed and cheered and thanked the gods.

'Will you help me to go and do that?' shouted Spartacus.

The roar that followed proclaimed his soldiers' enthusiasm in no uncertain terms.

Inevitably, the cry began again. 'SPAR-TA-CUS!'

The Thracian rode up and down, acknowledging the acclaim.

Marcion gave Zeuxis a not entirely friendly nudge. 'Happy now?'

'I'll follow him up there.'

Marcion grinned. From Zeuxis, that was an endorsement of the highest kind.

Some weeks later...
The Apennines, south-central Italy

Carbo got up and adjusted the large rock that served as his backrest. He sat down again with a contented sigh, pulling the blanket around his shoulders and moving his feet closer to the burning logs. The days were still hot, but at night the altitude meant that temperatures fell fast. Thankfully, sitting by a fire was enough to keep a man's bones warm.

'I'll be glad to see Thurii,' said Navio.

'It isn't far now, thank Jupiter,' said Publipor.

'I can't wait for some flat ground. I'm sick of going down one hill only to climb another,' Arnax piped up.

They all chuckled. The bruises from Spartacus' beating had faded within days, but it had taken weeks for Arnax to get over the shame of having talked to Castus. He had recently started coming out of his shell.

'It's practically your home territory, Publipor, eh? Brundisium isn't that far from where we will overwinter,' said Carbo with a wink. After his arrival, the Apulian had joined a century in his cohort. In the time since they had left the Alps behind, he had become a constant companion and friend.

'You're not wrong.' A shadow passed across Publipor's face.

Carbo took it to be worry. 'Have you got a woman there you left behind? A family?'

The shadow became sorrow. 'I did. A wife. Three children.'

Silence fell. Navio busied himself by loading more logs on to the fire. Arnax, who was scouring Carbo's sword with a piece of wire, found a rust spot to concentrate on above all else. Carbo let his gaze follow a stream of sparks upwards into the brilliant night sky. It wasn't surprising that he hadn't discovered this about Publipor before. Few men in the slave army bothered to tell their comrades of their past – himself included. 'What happened to them?'

Publipor cleared his throat. 'They were carried off last year. Cholera.'

'I'm sorry,' said Carbo.

'That is a hard burden for anyone to bear,' added Navio with some feeling. 'War is one thing, but sickness . . .'

'Aye, well. What can a man do? The gods give, and the gods take away. I should be grateful that I am still here. Still breathing.'

Publipor didn't look grateful at all, thought Carbo. He'd found it hard thinking that he would never see his own parents again, but at least they were alive. It wasn't completely mad to think that they might meet again one day. They weren't that far away: Rome lay perhaps two hundred miles to the north-west. The army had been even closer to it a week or two before. Carbo had considered deserting for a short period, or even asking Spartacus if he could visit his parents, but he had discounted the idea as foolish. He'd made a fool of himself twice over with the Thracian, and he wasn't about to do it again.

'We are lucky yet to be alive, and that won't change in the months to come,' said Navio darkly. 'Just because we defeated the consuls at Picenum doesn't mean that another army won't come looking for us. It will be a lot bigger than the ones we've seen so far too. As my father used to say, make the most of every day that dawns . . .'

'For it might be your last,' finished Arnax in a solemn tone.

Navio laughed. 'You've been listening to me carefully, eh?'

Even in the dim light, it was possible to see Arnax blush.

Navio reached over and ruffled his hair. 'You're making a good fist of Carbo's gladius. Take a look at mine when you're finished, will you?'

'Of course.' Delighted, the boy glanced at Publipor. 'Shall I clean yours as well?'

'When it needs doing, I'll do it myself,' the Apulian snapped. 'Understand?'

'Sorry.' Arnax dropped his eyes.

'I'm tired,' Publipor growled. 'I think I'll turn in. Good night.'

Carbo and Navio muttered their replies. Arnax watched him go in silence.

'Don't worry about it, lad. He wasn't having a go at you. He's troubled about his family,' said Carbo.

'It takes at least a year before the pain eases in any way,' pronounced Navio with a sigh.

'What pain would that be?'

They turned in surprise. 'Spartacus!' said Carbo with a grin.

Navio also smiled. 'Welcome.'

The Thracian inclined his head in greeting and then threw a hard look at Arnax, who looked as if he wanted the ground to open up and swallow him.

Spartacus sat down by the fire. 'What pain were you talking about, Navio?'

'The pain of losing those that one loves.'

'I see.' *The Rider watch over you, Father. Maron, my brother. Getas and Seuthes, my comrades.* 'We must all have lost people. It's one of life's trials. A man must deal with it as best he can.'

'Wise words,' said Navio.

They sat in silence for a short time, Carbo and Navio wondering what had brought their leader unannounced to their fire.

'We'll reach Thurii in the next month,' announced Spartacus. 'It will be good to stop marching, eh?'

They murmured in agreement.

Spartacus chuckled. 'You want to know why I'm here, eh?'

'You haven't just come for an idle chat,' said Carbo in a dry tone.

Spartacus regarded him steadily. 'No.'

Publipor emerged from his tent, a twig protruding from his lips. He had begun brushing his teeth when he became aware of their visitor. He spat quickly. 'Spartacus! It's an honour to see you.'

'Publipor. You're keeping well?'

'Yes, sir. Thank you sir.' Publipor raised his twig by way of apology. 'I was about to turn in. I'll come back out, though.'

'No need to do that on my account. Get some rest. It will be another long day tomorrow.' Spartacus' tone was friendly but commanding.

Publipor looked relieved. 'All right then. Good night, sir.'

'Sleep well.' Spartacus turned back to Carbo and Navio. 'A good man,' he said quietly.

'He is,' agreed Carbo. 'He's a great tracker. Thanks to him, we bring back a deer or a boar most times we go out.'

'It's natural that he's good with a bow. How's his sword craft coming along?'

'Quite well,' replied Navio. 'Give it a couple more months and he'll be up to scratch with the rest of the men.'

'Good. We should have the time at Thurii to train unhindered. It's unlikely that the Romans will attack us in the winter. But they'll be on the move.' Spartacus' face darkened. 'You know that, don't you? There is no way under the sun that we will be left alone.'

'Yes,' they both answered. Arnax's eyes grew wide.

'At the moment, we have no idea what the dogs are planning. They, on the other hand, get word of our passage from every citizen farmer whose land we pass through.'

'Not much we can do about that,' said Navio. 'And good intelligence on what the Romans are up to is hard to come by. The deserters who've joined us can't risk going back to their units. They'd be crucified.'

'I know. I have heard one interesting thing, however. Yesterday, one of the patrols stopped a trader who'd come from Rome. He had some news.'

They leaned forward, agog with interest.

'Crassus has been given charge of the campaign against us.'

Carbo felt the blood drain from his face. 'The same man who——'

'Yes. The same prick who ruined your family. The one whom I fought in front of at Capua. Strange how the strands of fate twist, eh?'

'Yes,' whispered Carbo, clenching his fists.

'Apparently, Crassus is to speak to the Senate soon. I was thinking that it would be good to hear what he has to say. Maybe even slip a blade between his ribs if the opportunity arose. That would knock the bastards back on their arses for a while.' The idea had seemed daring – even rash – from the outset, but now that he'd spoken it out loud, Spartacus revelled in the thrill of it. He was going to go, and no one would stop him.

Navio's eyebrows rose. 'Would you trust me and Carbo again?'

'Not you and Carbo, no.'

Carbo sat forward with a start. 'What, you mean——?'

'You and me, yes. We'll go to Rome. Straight to the viper's nest! See what we can find out.'

'Are you serious?' An image of his parents flashed unbidden into Carbo's mind. Guiltily, he shoved it away.

'Never more so.' He could still hear Ariadne's voice warning him not to go; see the disbelief on Pulcher's and Egbeo's faces. 'I'm the leader of this army. I decide what happens.'

Carbo nodded. 'Just you and me?'

'Yes. You can play the big farmer's son. I'll be your slave.'

'That could work,' muttered Carbo, bemused.

'What about the army?' hissed Navio. 'You can't leave Castus and Gannicus unchecked. Those pieces of shit will ruin everything!'

'No, they won't. They want to find a good overwintering spot as much as I do. Once they've got to Thurii, all they will want to do is to drink wine and fornicate.' Spartacus knew this for a lie. The Gauls would redouble their efforts to recruit men to their cause in his absence. His mind was made up, however. He would reassert his leadership when he returned. 'I've spoken to Pulcher and Egbeo about what to do should any Roman forces appear. They can intervene if the Gauls decide to do something crazy.'

Navio looked dubious, but he didn't argue.

'What about Ariadne? Isn't she due any day now?' Like every other soldier, Carbo held Spartacus' wife in high esteem. Despite her advanced pregnancy, she still walked like everyone else. 'It's good for the baby,' she said daily with a bright smile. Yet Carbo had seen the strain on her face that very afternoon. Spartacus had to be aware of that. 'Don't you want to be here for the birth of your son?'

Spartacus gave him a hard look. 'Ariadne informs me that she won't go into labour for another three weeks. I believe her. Women know about these things.'

'I understand,' muttered Carbo.

'We'll leave tomorrow, and reach Rome in little over a week and a half. If we can buy horses, it will be even quicker. Two or three days there should be sufficient. The horses will make the return journey faster too.' He glanced at Navio. 'You will have had just enough time at Thurii to erect a hut for Ariadne before we arrive.'

'It'll be the first thing we do.'

'If you're sure . . .' said Carbo doubtfully. He hadn't ever ridden that much.

'I am.' Spartacus said nothing of the fierce argument he'd had with Ariadne over it. She had totally opposed his going, not, she said, because he might miss the birth, but because of the dangers that he would face. 'What if you are recognised in Rome?' she had uttered repeatedly. Spartacus had laughed. 'Who will recognise me? The likelihood of seeing someone who knows me are less than a icicle surviving the midday sun.' Then he'd taken her hand. 'I have to find out what the cursed Romans are planning. This chance to kill Crassus will only be there once.'

'And if you get caught?'

He'd laughed. 'That won't happen. I'm going to take Carbo with me. He's a native. I'll act as his slave. We'll be on a short business trip to Rome, just two men in a crowd of thousands. What could go wrong with that?' Ariadne had finally acquiesced, because she'd seen that he would not be swayed, but there was now a further tension between them. It can be resolved when I return, thought Spartacus.

'So, will you come?'

As with the first time Spartacus had made such a request of him, man to man rather than from leader to a follower, Carbo was touched. He was also secretly pleased, because in Rome, the opportunity to meet his parents might arise. 'Of course.'

'Good.' Spartacus got to his feet.

'Won't you have some warmed wine?' Carbo made a gesture that sent Arnax scrambling for the amphora in their tent.

'No. I want a clear head in the morning. We'll need to cover more than twenty miles a day.'

'I understand. Arnax, leave it.'

'Heat some up anyway,' ordered Navio. 'I'll have a cup even if Carbo's not going to. I'll raise a toast to your success, and more importantly, safe return.'

'Thank you.' Spartacus cast them a warning glance. 'It goes without saying that no one is to speak of this. To anyone.'

Carbo and Navio nodded.

'I wouldn't, I wouldn't, I—' blurted Arnax, looking mortified.

'It's all right. I know you won't talk.' With a curt nod, Spartacus disappeared into the darkness.

Navio jerked his head after the Thracian. 'Gods, I'd wager you didn't see that coming.'

'I still can't believe it.'

'Neither can I. Didn't your parents end up in Rome?'

Carbo had told Navio his whole story after the fuss over his letter. 'Yes.'

'Tempted to see them?'

'I don't know. I might not have the chance.'

'When will a better opportunity come your way?'

'Leave it,' muttered Carbo.

Navio raised his hands, palm outwards. 'Fair enough.'

Carbo stared into the flames, brooding. If the truth be known, he was wary of meeting his parents again. What would he say to them about where he'd been for the last year and more? He would have to lie about absolutely everything. Despite this, his heart ached at the thought of them.

Carbo woke long before dawn. Moving carefully so he didn't disturb Navio and Arnax, he threw off his blankets. He rolled them up, placing them in his pack, which was lying ready by his side. He had gone to bed fully dressed, so all he had to do was slip on his sandals, grab his dagger and creep outside. Although Carbo half expected to see Spartacus, he gave a start at the figure which loomed out of the semi-darkness. 'Been here long?' he whispered.

'A little while.'

'Couldn't sleep?'

'Something like that.' *I was tired of the disapproval radiating from Ariadne.* Spartacus regretted not saying goodbye, but the cool between them had hardened overnight to a thick frost.

It was strange seeing his leader without his sword, helmet and mail shirt, thought Carbo. Spartacus was dressed in a simple wool tunic and sandals. He was carrying a pack and a stout cudgel. A sheathed knife hung from a leather strap over one shoulder. He looked like any agricultural slave.

'I'm ready,' said Carbo.

'Give me your bag.'

'Eh?'

'If you're the master and I'm the slave, then I have to carry both our packs. From the start. Only the gods know whom we'll meet on the road. No point arousing suspicions, is there?'

'But—'

'Hand it over.'

Feeling awkward, Carbo did as he was told.

'You've got no weapons?'

'Just this.' He tapped his dagger.

'Fine. Let's go. It's a long way to Rome.'

Carbo cast a last glance at his tent. His guts lurched at the thought of never seeing Navio and Arnax again. I'll be back before they know it, he told himself. Pushing back his shoulders, he set off, with Spartacus a step behind.

'May the gods go with you!' called a low voice.

Turning, Carbo saw Navio's head sticking out of their tent. He grinned. 'Thank you.'

Nodding farewell, the two men strode off between the lines of tents. It took a long time to work their way to the edge of the huge camp, which was situated in a flat area between two forested peaks. Nearing the perimeter, they passed several sentries, who smiled and waved them on. 'They think we're just going on a reconnaissance of the local area,' muttered Spartacus. 'I had Pulcher send out the word last night.'

'What will they say when we don't come back?'

'If anyone asks, Pulcher is to say that we may have gone south ahead of the army, to check the lie of the land. It doesn't matter too much if the men don't believe the story. All anyone is thinking of now is reaching Thurii. We'll return before there's any serious problem.' Spartacus pictured Castus, who had been delighted when he'd told him about his planned mission. Gannicus had seemed pleased too, but the chance of some decent intelligence and of killing Crassus had to take priority. They won't win that many men over, he told himself.

Leaving the encampment behind, they walked up a steep slope covered in beech trees and worked their way down the other side. The eastern sky was paling fast now, but it no longer mattered. Only the sentries and Publipor had seen them go.

At least that was what they thought.

Nine days later, the pair had nearly reached Rome. Annoyingly, finding suitable mounts had proved to be overly time-consuming. They had therefore walked, covering more than twenty miles every day, still considerably faster than the slow pace of the slave army. It had been tough going, but Carbo hadn't complained. Spartacus was bearing both their packs while he got to walk with only his water bag to weigh him down.

They had come down from the mountains at the first opportunity and taken the fastest route to the capital: the Via Appia, which ran from Brundisium to Rome. Paved with blocks of black basalt, it was the Republic's main artery, carrying wagons full of trade goods, soldiers, travellers and civil servants of all types. Carbo and Spartacus had been swallowed up in the tide of humanity that flowed towards the capital, just another master and servant going about their business.

As they had arranged, the pair only spoke on the road when there was no one else in sight. At the roadside inns where they had stayed each night, Carbo had taken a small room while the Thracian slept in the stables or even outdoors. It was customary for agricultural slaves to be treated rather poorly, and Spartacus had wanted them to look no different. Everything had to go without hitch, because time was of the essence. If he stayed away too long, the Gauls might actually do some real harm. And he might miss the birth of his son.

'We must be close now,' said Carbo, pointing at a particularly grand brick-built tomb. 'They're getting larger.' The mausoleums had lined both sides of the road for miles, memorials to the wealthy and powerful.

'You're right. There are fewer *latrones* and cheap whores on view too.'

It was true, thought Carbo. The skulking shapes who lurked by the whispering cypress trees and crypts with their statues of the dead had all but vanished. 'The city guard probably doesn't tolerate them close to the city.'

'There it is,' said Spartacus softly. 'Up ahead. Look.'

Above the heads of the people in front and framed by the trees on either side, Carbo made out a high stone wall. 'It's bloody enormous!'

Spartacus grunted irritably. Rome's defences were intimidating to say the least. As tall as five men standing on each other's shoulders, the wall was faced with large slabs of yellow tufa. He could see soldiers patrolling to and fro on a rampart that ran along the top. A fortified tower perched on either side of the iron-studded gates that led into the capital. Both had a couple of light catapults. Spartacus had only ever had a vague notion of taking Rome, but now it vanished entirely. *I would need engineers who could build me hundreds of huge ballistae. Even then, it would take months to pound enough holes in the defences to storm the place successfully. Months during which other legions would have been raised elsewhere in Italy.* He forced away his bad humour. 'How old is it?'

'More than three hundred years,' replied Carbo proudly. 'It was erected in the aftermath of the sacking of the city by the Gauls.'

'Impressive, but it's a damn shame that it was ever built. Things with Hannibal might have been very different otherwise. And for me too.'

Carbo's pride vanished.

'How long is it?'

'Five miles. It encompasses all seven hills. There's a deep defensive ditch too. We'll see that as we get closer.'

'I can't wait,' said Spartacus dryly.

Embarrassed by his enthusiasm, Carbo fell silent.

'Where does your uncle live?'

'On the Esquiline Hill.'

It had been inevitable that Carbo would tell Spartacus his family's full story. The Thracian had already known of Crassus' part in their downfall. 'Do you want to see them?' Spartacus had asked. 'Yes.' Carbo had studied the fire as he'd replied, his rashness in dictating the letter in Mutina vivid in his mind. 'I think you should go,' Spartacus had said, stunning him.

'Do you still think it's a good idea to make contact with my parents?'

'If there's an opportunity, yes. You could be killed any time.'

Carbo's skin crawled. 'I don't think that the Esquiline is far from the Capena, the gate we're heading for. It won't be hard to find out.'

'Steady on,' Spartacus warned. 'Let's find a place to stay first. Check out the lie of the land. See what's going on.'

Carbo flushed. 'I'm sorry.'

'You'll get your chance.'

Contenting himself with that, Carbo strode on, determined to appreciate the sights of the city he'd heard so much about but never seen. He had grown up on tales of the capital and the Forum Romanum, the open space where citizens met to socialise, do business and to petition senators, and which was overlooked by the Capitoline Hill with its massive temple complex and immense statue of Jupiter. There wouldn't be time, but he also longed to see the Circus Maximus, a natural stadium formed by the steep sides of the Aventine and Palatine Hills.

His wonder soon turned to surprise. After they had passed under the mighty Servian wall, only the basalt road maintained its grandeur. It was still broad enough for two carts to pass abreast. On either side, however, the streets that led off up the hills were narrow and unpaved, and no different to Capua's. The buildings towered higher than Carbo or Spartacus had ever seen – three, four and even five storeys tall, but for the most part, they looked poorly built. The air was thick with the smell of decaying rubbish, human waste and the acrid tang of urine from the fullers' workshops that were clustered round the Capena Gate. And the people. There were more people than either man had imagined could be gathered in one place. They pushed and jostled, so intent on their business that they didn't even look at the other passers-by.

The crush was added to by the queues of wagons which filled the roadway. Loaded with vegetables, sides of pork, steeply piled terracotta vessels and every other merchant good imaginable, they were drawn by pairs or larger teams of oxen. Their drivers roared curses at one another and at the pedestrians, blaming everyone but themselves for the throng that slowed all traffic to a snail's pace. Carbo made for the edge of the street, hoping to make better progress, but the open-fronted shops, restaurants and taverns there filled the ground before their premises with stalls, tables and items for sale. Any available space between was occupied by toothless beggars – a combination of lepers, amputees and scrawny children – or jugglers, snake charmers and other performers.

'It's no good,' he said in frustration. 'It will take us all day to get anywhere if we stay on the Via Appia. I don't know any of the side streets, though.'

'That's easy to sort out.' Spartacus clicked his fingers at a snot-nosed girl in a threadbare tunic. 'Want to earn an *as*?'

The urchin was by Spartacus' side in a heartbeat 'Yes, sir.'

'No need to call me "sir". I'm a slave.'

'Fair enough,' said the girl with an uncaring shrug. 'New to the city?'

'Yes. My master here is looking for lodgings for a few nights. Central if possible. Nothing too flash, but not a dive either. Somewhere that the beds are clean and the food won't poison you. And where the wine is actually drinkable.'

'Do you need whores?'

'Unless you can guarantee that they haven't got the pox, no,' said Carbo.

This produced a smile and a mouthful of rotting teeth. 'I know just the place. The Elysian Fields. It's between the Esquiline and the Quirinal.'

'Is that far?' asked Spartacus.

'Not the way I'm going to take you. Follow me!' The urchin darted off up an alleyway.

Carbo eyed Spartacus uncertainly.

'What are you waiting for?'

'Do you trust her?'

'She's seen my cudgel, and the fact that we've both got knives. The child'll know it would be foolish to betray us. My money says that she will take us straight to a decent enough inn.'

Carbo wasn't so sure, but he wasn't in charge – even if it looked as if he was. 'All right.' He sped after the girl. Spartacus followed.

Not long after, they had arrived at The Elysian Fields, a nondescript premises just off the Vicus Patricius. A brief investigation by Carbo revealed that the girl had done as she was asked. The tavern was small but clean and well appointed, and the proprietor, a genial ex-soldier, seemed honest. Having paid the urchin, Carbo took a room on the first floor. Spartacus found the ostler and secured a spot on the floor of the stables. A short and casual conversation determined that the city was awash with the news of Crassus' appointment to lead the Republic's armies. 'The consuls couldn't argue with him any longer, could they?' the ostler commented sourly. 'Between them, the stupid fools had been whipped three times by Spartacus. Enough's enough, eh?'

'Indeed,' muttered Spartacus, hiding his smile. 'So Crassus is going to finish off the slaves, is he?'

'So he promises. He's in the process of raising six new legions. Using his own money too. Now that's what I call devotion to the Republic.'

Spartacus had expected to hear bad news but not quite so soon. He cursed savagely inside. Crassus was more of an organiser and leader than he looked then. When six new legions were added to the survivors of the consuls' armies, he would have almost ten legions. *Great Rider, I will need your help even more than ever.* 'That's impressive. So it's true that he is the richest man in Rome?'

'Damn right it is! Made most of it during Sulla's proscriptions, he did. Bought up the properties of those who'd been executed hand over fist.' The ostler spat. 'Another way he makes his money is to turn up wherever there's a fire. He offers the owners of any burning buildings a tiny fee for the deeds. Nearly all accept. It's either that or they get nothing. Crassus has his own private fire brigade. When he's done the deal, they put out the blaze. Afterwards, he's got the ground to erect a new building on – and for a steal.'

'He sounds unpleasant.'

'Yet they say that he's as polite a man as you can meet. He contributes regularly to the plebs' grain dole. Crassus is a real bull with hay on his horns.' The ostler winked. 'Tell your master that he could see him address the citizens this very afternoon if he wished.'

'Really?' asked Spartacus casually. 'Where would that be?'

The ostler's eyebrows rose. 'I forgot that you're not from the city. In the Forum.'

'My thanks. I'll tell him.' Chewing on a strand of hay, Spartacus sauntered off in search of Carbo.

Carbo was dozing on the most comfortable bed of their journey yet when a loud knock shattered his reverie.

'Master?'

He sat up with a start. 'Yes?'

Spartacus was already halfway inside the low-ceilinged room. 'They are indeed serving food downstairs, master. Roast pork or grilled fresh fish. Shall I order some for you?' He closed the door. 'You'll never guess what's happening this very afternoon.'

'What?'

'Fucking Crassus is to address the people in the Forum.'

Suddenly, Carbo was fully awake. 'Who told you?'

'The ostler. Six legions he's raising, in addition to the remnants of Longinus' and the consuls' forces. In total, he will be leading close to ten legions.'

Carbo felt sick. 'That's a lot of legionaries.'

Spartacus' grin was savage. 'I told you it would get harder.'

'Are we going to try and kill him?' whispered Carbo.

'That's what we came here for, isn't it?'

Now adrenalin surged through Carbo. 'Yes.'

'Gods, you look as if you want to kill him more than me!' said Spartacus with a laugh.

'He ruined my family, dragged my father's good name into the mud, took the roof from over our heads. And for what? Three months' missed payments on his stinking loan!' Carbo's dagger jumped into his hand. 'It would give me the most incredible pleasure to slit his scrawny throat.'

'Steady on.'

Spartacus' hard stare unnerved him. 'I'm sorry.'

'There's no need to be sorry. You have good reason to hate the prick.

But a situation like this demands a cool head. Who knows what protection the man will have? Rest assured that after his recent elevation in the world, he won't be walking around with no one looking out for him. If we go rushing in like a pair of fools, the only person laughing afterwards will be Crassus – at our bloody corpses. You don't want that, do you?'

'No,' muttered Carbo.

'We'll make a judgement once we've seen what's going on, and who's around. Not before.' Spartacus had seen far too many men slain in battle because they had acted rashly. Now was not the time for recklessness. 'It may well be that we get no chance to assassinate Crassus. If there isn't, we will just walk away. Clear?'

Carbo swallowed his resentment. If it wasn't for the Thracian, he'd have long since been food for the worms in the ludus' cemetery. 'Yes.'

'Put that damn blade away then, and order me to follow you out for some food.'

It took an instant for Carbo to register Spartacus' meaning. Sheathing his knife, he grinned. 'I fancy a stroll around the great city,' he said loudly. 'We can find somewhere to eat as we walk.' He pulled the door wide. Although there was no reason to be suspicious, he was glad to find the corridor beyond empty. Carbo threw up as heartfelt a prayer as he'd ever made. *Mighty Jupiter, O Greatest and Best, grant us the opportunity to kill Crassus. Guide my blade – and that of Spartacus.*

In his haste, he forgot that requests of the deities needed to be phrased with meticulous accuracy.

Chapter VIII

Taking a deep breath, Ariadne crouched down and let the contraction wash over her.

'That's it,' murmured the midwife. 'Now push.'

All thought left Ariadne as she obeyed. Her jaw clenched, and beads of sweat formed on her brow. An inarticulate moan left her lips. The pain was intense, but Ariadne did not let it better her. *I will stay in control.* Finally, her abdominal muscles relaxed and she sagged down on to her knees.

'Good. I can see the head. It won't be long now.'

My son will be born soon, thought Ariadne with satisfaction. She hadn't been overly surprised when her pains started while Spartacus was still away. She had told him that their baby wouldn't be born until after his return to make it easier for him to go, but in her gut she had known it might well be sooner. In the event, her labour had begun the previous night. She was grateful that it started when it had because the army was camped, and in a good location by a mountain stream.

She resumed her posture – crouching low, her back slightly curved and her knees bent. One of the women she was friendly with stood in front of her so that Ariadne could grip her hands for support. Another contraction took her. The time since the previous one had shortened.

'Push,' murmured the midwife. 'You must push.'

Ariadne groaned.

'Is she . . . all right?' Atheas' voice, from outside the tent, was full of concern.

'Yes, yes. Go and make yourself busy somewhere else,' ordered the midwife.

As the pain eased, Ariadne remembered how when she had woken Atheas, the tattooed warrior had looked genuinely worried. Despite her discomfort, Ariadne had smiled. One of the most ferocious warriors she had ever met, reduced to an awkward, mumbling shadow of himself. *So it is with men.* She had calmly told him to fetch the midwife, an old crone who had joined them months before. Next, Atheas had carried word to Castus and Gannicus. Ariadne could still remember the Scythian's surprise when he told her what they'd said. 'They didn't argue at all. Both of them said that the army would stay put until the baby was born.'

Of course they said that, she thought. If they had insisted the day's march go ahead, it would place her at risk. A day here or there didn't matter to their progress, and while both were brave men, she doubted that either would want to face Spartacus' wrath if something went wrong.

Her muscles tightened again, and Ariadne knew that this was it. She began to push as she'd never done before. The midwife, who was behind her, gave her an encouraging slap. 'Come on, don't let up. You're nearly there.'

Ariadne felt a rush of liquid spattering her lower legs, and heard the midwife make a soft exclamation of pleasure. In the same moment, the immense pressure on her lower abdomen eased. Her strength vanished, and if it hadn't been for the woman holding her arms, Ariadne would have fallen. Anxiety gripped her.

'You have a boy,' said the midwife softly. 'He seems healthy, thank the gods.'

'A son. I knew it was a son. Show him to me.'

'Lift your leg.' As Ariadne obeyed, the midwife moved beneath her, taking care not to damage the cord.

A small, red, mucus-covered bundle of limbs was handed to her. Ariadne thought her heart would break with the beauty of it. 'Hello, my son,' she whispered, enfolding the babe in her arms. 'Welcome, oh welcome.'

'Help her to the mattress,' directed the midwife.

Ariadne felt herself being turned. Hands at her back lightly supported her as she took the few steps to the blankets. She lay down, clasping the newborn to her. A specially prepared wool blanket appeared, her son's swaddling cloth. It was laid over her chest. Ariadne stroked the tiny head, which was covered in downy black hair. 'You're a handsome boy, just like your father. All the girls will want to chase you.'

'What are you going to call him?' asked the midwife.

'Maron. After Spartacus' brother, who was killed fighting the Romans.'

There was a nod of approval. 'It's a powerful name.'

Ariadne heard her friend protesting, and then there was someone else in the tent. She looked up to see Atheas crouched over her, a reverent expression on his normally hard face.

'He is . . . boy?'

Ariadne smiled. 'Yes.'

'Healthy?'

She shook her head in assent. 'Maron is his name.'

'It is . . . well.' Atheas' teeth glinted white in the gloom. 'The gods must be . . . thanked. The Great Rider . . . especially. I . . . see . . . it done.'

'Thank you,' said Ariadne. Offering her own gratitude to Dionysus could wait until later.

Grinning like a fool, Atheas retreated.

Ariadne closed her eyes. She was more tired than she had ever been.

The midwife prodded her. 'Drink this. It's a tonic. There's a herb in there to help you pass the afterbirth, and others to help you sleep and replenish your energy. And the baby must feed. You can rest when he's on the breast.'

With the old woman's help, Ariadne coaxed Maron on to one of her nipples. He sucked at it with gusto, bringing a smile to her lips. 'He likes his food.'

'That is good,' pronounced the midwife, peering at him with satisfaction. 'He'll thrive.'

He will do even better when Spartacus returns, thought Ariadne, trying to ignore the pangs of worry that she had been feeling ever since his departure. Nor had she had any messages from the god about her husband. At least there had been no repeat of the dreadful nightmare in which she could not find his body among hundreds of crucified men.

I will see him again. I must, because he has to meet his son.

She glanced down at Maron, and a smile traced its way across her lips. 'Your father will be so proud when he sees you.'

The baby sucked even harder, as if in reply.

Within a few moments, sleep took her.

When they emerged from the inn, Carbo was surprised to see the urchin lounging against the wall of a building opposite. Irritated, he pretended not to notice her, but that didn't stop the girl from darting over.

'Going somewhere?'

'What's it to you?' Carbo snapped.

'Thought you might need a guide.'

'Well I don't. Clear off.' Carbo headed down the Vicus Patricius, pretending he knew where he was going.

The urchin skipped alongside, whistling tunelessly.

Carbo could sense Spartacus smiling behind him. 'I thought I told you to beat it!'

'I'm a free citizen,' replied the girl. 'You can't stop me from goin' this way too.'

'Can't I?' Carbo's tone was acid.

'No,' came the bold reply.

Carbo increased his pace, leaving the girl trailing in his wake. His speed made little difference. A couple of hundred paces later, the Vicus Patricius was joined from the left by the Via Labicana, and the press grew as just as great as before. Carbo came to an abrupt halt. The junction was packed with carts, litters and people on foot.

'Get a move on, boys!' A group of soldiers led by an optio shoved their way out of the crowd, and marched in the direction of the Elysian Fields. Behind them shuffled a file of slaves led by a hard-faced man carrying a whip. Hollow-cheeked, clad in rags, chained to each other by the neck, the slaves were clearly bound for the market. There was a funeral procession, the corpse wrapped in fine linen sheets borne aloft on a couch by male relations. Following ancient tradition, slaves carried burning torches. In front, a party of musicians played a dirge over and over, as if that would part the crowds. Carbo glanced around, helpless and frustrated.

'Sure you don't want a guide?' piped a familiar voice.

Carbo half turned, as if to look at the urchin, but also throwing a silent enquiry at Spartacus. Catching the Thracian's almost imperceptible nod, he barked, 'What's your name?'

'Tertulla. Tulla for short.'

'How many summers have you seen?'

'Seven or eight. I think.'

'You think?'

'Don't know for sure. I've been on my own since I can remember.'

'You've got no family?'

Tulla gave him a defiant look. 'Don't need no sympathy, mister. I do fine by myself, all right?'

'I'm sure you do.' Despite Tulla's boldness, Carbo felt compassion for her. She was small, dirty and ill fed. 'Where do you live?'

Again the defiant stare. 'Clemens the baker lets me sleep by his oven in return for keeping watch on his shop. Look, do you want some help or not?'

'Got places to go, have you?' interjected Spartacus.

'I have, as it happens.'

'I see,' said Carbo knowingly. 'Don't let me stop you from heading off.'

At once there was a change of demeanour. 'It can wait.'

Carbo rubbed his chin, letting the girl stew for a moment. 'How far is the Forum?'

'About half a mile. Maybe less.'

That was what Carbo had thought. 'Another as to take us there then.'

'Three.'

'Eh?'

'Look at the crowd!' Tulla pointed. 'It's going to get worse from here on. Everyone wants to hear Crassus speak. Isn't that what you're going for?'

'Crassus? No, I just want to see the place for myself,' Carbo lied blithely.

Tulla excavated the contents of one nostril and flicked it away. 'You picked a bad day for sightseeing.'

'I'll give you two asses, and no more.'

Tulla's grubby paw shot out. 'I want payment up front.'

Carbo rooted in his purse and tossed a coin into the air.

It was expertly caught. 'That's only one as!'

'You'll have the other when we get there.'

Tulla didn't bat an eyelid. 'It will cost the same to get you back to the Elysian Fields. It's best to do that before dark, believe me.'

'I tell you what,' said Carbo on impulse. 'You can act as our guide for the whole of our visit. I'll pay you an even denarius for the next three days.'

'For two days.'

'Fine.' That was the figure Carbo had had in his head anyway.

'Half now,' Tulla demanded.

'You've got to be joking! You'd vanish the moment we arrive in the Forum.' Carbo handed over a second as. 'I'll give you another one tonight.'

'All right,' came the grudging reply. 'But you can buy me a sausage on the way.'

Reminded of his own grumbling stomach, Carbo grinned. 'Do you know a good place to buy some?'

Tulla was already ten paces down an alleyway. 'The best in Rome! Come on!'

Carbo glanced at Spartacus.

'Well done. She'll be useful. Especially if we have to get away in a hurry.'

'That's what I was thinking.'

'Watch what you let her hear,' warned Spartacus. 'She would sell us out in a heartbeat.'

Carbo nodded grimly.

'Let's get some food then. My belly thinks that my throat's been cut.'

'Me too.' Carbo hurried after Tulla, who was nearly out of sight.

The girl was right about the food stall. The garlic and herb sausages that Carbo bought for them were some of the best he'd ever tasted. Shoved into the middle of a freshly baked loaf of flat bread bought from the baker's next door, they were indescribably delicious.

From the sausage vendor, Tulla led them through a maze of narrow alleys. Underfoot, they trod on broken pottery, items of smashed furniture and refuse from the surrounding *cenaculae*. The air was fetid, and more than once Carbo stepped in oozing matter that gave way beneath him. 'This is shit we're walking in,' he hissed accusingly at Tulla.

'Might well be in places. Watch where you put your feet,' came the nonchalant answer. 'It's the same in all these back ways. I can take you back to the main street if you want.'

Carbo turned his head.

'No,' muttered Spartacus.

'Keep going,' ordered Carbo with a sigh.

'We're nearly there,' said Tulla by way of consolation. Sure enough, their ears soon filled with the commotion that only a huge gathering of people can make. Carbo's heart quickened as Tulla led them triumphantly out into an open space. 'Here you are.'

At once Carbo's eyes were drawn above the throng to the flat-topped steep hill that loomed over the Forum. At the edge of the summit was an immense, painted statue of Jupiter, bearded and imperious. It had been positioned to watch over the city, and was truly magnificent. So too was the great gold-roofed temple behind. Despite himself, Carbo was filled with reverence. His lips moved in silent prayer.

'Impressive, eh?' said Tulla. 'I've seen peasants fall to their knees when they see it.'

Anger filled Spartacus at the whole spectacle of the Forum, the statue, the temples, the very centre of the Republic. How he longed to tear it all down, but it was too great. He fought a rising sense of frustration and gloom. *The best I can hope for is a stalemate of some kind.*

'Where will Crassus speak?' asked Carbo. 'From the Curia steps?'

Tulla shook her head. 'More likely from the platform by the Rostra.'

Carbo could sense Spartacus' question. 'That's a pillar decorated with the prows of captured Carthaginian ships, isn't it?' he asked.

'Something like that,' came the uncertain reply.

'It was built after the first war with Carthage,' Carbo declared confidently, remembering his boyhood tutor's history lessons.

A war that was primarily fought at sea. And which the Romans won despite the fact that at its outset they didn't have a navy, thought Spartacus sourly.

'That's where the Vestal Virgins live.' Tulla pointed to a circular temple, the roof of which was visible off to the left. 'There are lots of other temples around the edges of the Forum too. There's one to Castor and Pollux, one to—'

'Yes, yes,' interrupted Carbo. He had sensed Spartacus' restlessness. 'Let's get a move on, eh? If we have to make our way through this crowd, it will take all day.'

'Weren't you listening to what I said? This is what it will be like everywhere in the Forum. Half of Rome wants to hear Crassus tell of how he will crush Spartacus. The shops in the markets will probably be shut for the duration too.'

'Oh.' Carbo pretended to be disappointed. 'Still, I suppose we could listen to Crassus while we're here.'

Tulla gave him a withering look. 'You'll have trouble hearing a word he says from this spot.'

'Can you get us closer?'

'Of course! We'll just go around the back streets.' She pushed past and headed confidently back the way they had come. 'I'll take you right to the Rostra.'

'Excellent,' said Carbo, pleased yet again by Tulla's resourcefulness.

This time the girl took them into a series of alleyways that criss-crossed the roads that fed into the Forum. It was a case of walking at speed for a few dozen paces, shoving their way across a busy street and then hurrying along another narrow passage. Eventually, they ended up at the back of a long, tall building. Inside, Carbo could hear the noise of many voices competing against each other. 'Is this a market?'

'Yes. A court too. The Basilica Aemilia. It's full of lawyers, scribes and tradesmen. Even soothsayers, if you're after a reading.'

'I've no need of that,' said Carbo, curling his lip. 'They're all liars and charlatans.'

'That's what Clemens says. He won't let them sit anywhere near his shop. He even used his broom to drive off the last one who tried! The haruspex cursed him, but Clemens just laughed. He says that the gods look after a pious man.'

'A wise man, your baker,' said Spartacus.

Tulla looked pleased. She guided them another twenty steps to where the alley opened on to a larger way. 'That's the side of the Curia,' she said, indicating the edifice opposite.

Carbo stared across at the simple brick-built wall and the line of glass windows that were visible under the edge of the tiled roof. The structure wasn't imposing in any way, but he was still filled with awe, and not a little pride. He walked over to touch the brickwork. It felt as if he was touching history. This was where the Senate had met for close to half a millennium.

Spartacus kept his face blank, but even he was somewhat impressed. *So this is where the decisions are made.*

Cheering broke out off to their left, attracting their attention.

'RO-MA! RO-MA! RO-MA!'

'Perfect timing,' said Tulla with a cheeky grin. 'That'll be Crassus.'

Carbo's heart began to thump in his chest. He glanced at Spartacus, whose expression had grown hawkish. 'Take us as close as you can,' he ordered Tulla.

The street was very busy. Everyone was heading in the same direction that they were, but Tulla had a knack for finding the smallest gaps. Carbo had to shove in after her to keep up. Inevitably, those he was pushing past grew irritated and more than one curse was hurled at him. Carbo's polite excuses kept most of the citizens sweet. For those who weren't convinced, there was Spartacus' hard face at the back. No one wanted to argue with the compactly built slave with the penetrating grey eyes.

After much use of their shoulders and elbows, they reached the front of the crowd, which was positioned all around the front of the Curia. A line of lictores with crossed fasces prevented the people from going too close to the hallowed building. Behind the bodyguards, on the Curia's steps, stood score upon score of senators, their brilliant white togas and haughty expressions marking them out as superior to the vast majority.

Yet they're as keen as the rest to hear the man of the hour speak, thought Spartacus. It's no wonder. So far, they've behaved like a gaggle of hens when a fox gets into the coop. They need a proper leader, someone who can play the general as well as the politician. Is Crassus the man they've been looking for?

'Told you I'd get you here. Happy?' whispered Tulla with an impish smile.

'Yes. Well done.' Carbo's gaze took in the Curia's great bronze doors – *they're enormous* – and to the left, a stone pillar decorated with anchors and ships' bronze prows, before stopping on a simple wooden platform that stood the height of two men above the crowd. It was occupied by a pair of soldiers in scale mail carrying standards, and a grizzled officer in a mail shirt covered in *phalerae*. A dozen legionaries stood in front of the dais, holding their shields balanced before them. Carbo frowned. It was most unusual for soldiers to be fully armed within Rome. Normally, only lictores were entitled to carry bladed weapons inside the city walls. Crassus must be putting on a show of force, he decided. He didn't think to mention it to Spartacus, who might not know the rule. Beside the troops trumpeters waited, their instruments held at the ready. 'Crassus hasn't arrived yet.'

'No,' replied Spartacus in an undertone. 'But look who has.'

'Eh?'

'That's Caepio. Remember him?'

The name tugged at Carbo's memory, and he stared again at the trio of soldiers on the podium. 'Gods above, you're right!' It was the centurion who had survived the bloody munus that had left 399 of his comrades dead. 'What's he doing here?'

'I'd wager that Crassus is going to use him to rally support for his new legions. Clever bastard.' *Maybe I should have killed him too. Sent my message to the Senate a different way.* Spartacus grimaced. *No. He's a brave soldier who deserved to survive.* 'It will work well too. Men love to hear the story of someone who survived against the odds.'

Crassus isn't just a money-grabbing bastard. He's shrewd too, thought Carbo uneasily. He glanced up at the statue on the hill. Jupiter, give me the chance to kill him today. Please.

The crowd some distance away suddenly began to chant. 'RO-MA! RO-MA! RO-MA!'

Their cry was taken up at once by the masses. The noise was deafening, and mesmeric. All it lacked was the metallic clash of swords off shields, reflected Carbo, for it to resemble an army before battle. It was most odd. He felt entirely at home, yet a complete stranger. This thought was followed by the sobering realisation that if any man in the vicinity knew who he or Spartacus was, they would help tear them both to shreds. And that if he didn't also cheer, someone might notice. He glanced at the Thracian and saw that he was miming the word 'RO-MA'.

Carbo's respect for his leader grew some more, and quickly, he did the same.

Tulla was jumping up and down, screaming at the top of her voice.

A handsome, broad-shouldered man of middle years clambered up the platform's steps and into view. The multitude's noise grew even greater, and the three soldiers snapped to attention. The newcomer acknowledged them with a salute of his own, and turned to face the Forum. He lifted one hand and waved it, as if to welcome them. The mob went wild.

Carbo stared at Crassus, his face twisting with hatred. He hadn't seen him since the day the politician had visited the ludus in Capua. Then, Carbo had been but a rookie fighter. Now, he was a veteran of many battles. *Let me get close to you, you stinking cocksucker. With your last breath, you'll hear me whisper my father's name.*

The cry changed. 'RO-MA! VIC-TOR! RO-MA! VIC-TOR!'

Crassus echoed the call, which increased the crowd's excitement even more.

He knows how to work them, Spartacus admitted. No doubt the piece of filth is a good orator too. He eyed the dozen soldiers in sight, and prayed that Crassus walked off afterwards with only a few of them in tow. *Great Rider, grant me the chance to kill him. I ask you to guide my knife.*

At length Crassus raised his arms. On cue, the trumpeters blew a fanfare. Silence fell.

'Citizens of Rome, I salute you!' shouted Crassus.

Their reply was a crescendo of whistles and cheers.

'You have come here today for one reason.'

'It's not to borrow from you, that's for sure!' cried a voice from the depths of the crowd.

His comment was met with hoots of laughter.

Crassus smiled benignly. 'Yet my riches are not what they were, good people. Am I not using my own money to raise six new legions? With every week that goes by, hundreds of thousands of denarii are being spent on men, provisions and equipment. I do not grudge a single as of it, however, because this vast expense is for the good of the Republic!'

'CRAS-SUS!' roared a man near Carbo. Those around him quickly took up the cry, and the mob responded in kind.

'They're Crassus' men,' whispered Spartacus in Carbo's ear. 'Planted in the crowd.'

Sewer rat. Carbo let his fingers caress the bone hilt of his dagger. In the press, no one could see.

Again Crassus raised his arms. The uproar died away. 'To be truthful, I am honoured to provide every assistance that I can to help the state. I would give the clothes off my back if I had to. We must do what we can! Is that not true?'

'YES!'

'We must act now, because Italy is threatened from within – as it has not been for more than a hundred years! It is not vile Pyrrhus this time, or the gugga Hannibal.' Crassus let the crowd roar their abuse for a few moments. 'No, it is someone far worse. Far more vile. We are threatened by the lowest form of life – a *slave*. A creature who goes by the name of *Spartacus*.'

The mob's scream that followed had no form. It had no words; it was pure anger. Pure loathing. Pure revulsion.

You son of a whore. I would cut your liver out and feed it to the vultures. Spartacus had been expecting this, but the insults fanned his fury to new heights. All he could do, however, was stand there and listen. He straightened his back, as if he weren't a slave. I'm standing right here, he thought proudly, and you don't even know it.

Carbo steeled himself against the crowd's fervour. *The bastards. Spartacus is a great man. He treats his followers better than Crassus his debtors, that's for sure.*

'Since his escape from the ludus in Capua, Spartacus has gathered to himself an army. It is a force made up of the dregs of humanity. In it are slaves with grudges against their masters and herdsmen who hated their *vilici*. Every lowlife who wants to rape and pillage has thrown in his lot with this Spartacus. This *gladiator*. This *Thracian*. Together they have attacked countless farms and estates the length and breadth of Italy. They have burned villages and even sacked towns. It has all been done with total disregard for human life. Thousands of citizens have been massacred! Innumerable women have been violated!'

Again Crassus paused, allowing his audience to express their vitriol. When the baying had died down, he assumed a sorrowful expression. 'Sadly, that is not the whole tale. Thus far, the men who have been sent to deal with Spartacus have failed spectacularly. These were no callow youths either. No, they were praetors or legates, men who had previously proved themselves able to do their duty to the state. Caius Claudius Glaber. Publius Varinius. Lucius Cossinius. Lucius Furius. Yet all, all came to grief at the hands of the slaves. After these setbacks, we placed our trust in our consuls. Thus it has always been in Rome. When the Republic asks, the consuls answer. They lead our legions out to victory.' Crassus acknowledged the great sigh that went rippling through the crowd. 'It was not to be, however. Although Lucius Gellius had an initial success against a small breakaway force of slaves, his colleague Gnaeus Cornelius Lentulus Clodianus suffered a humiliating defeat soon after. His men ran from the field, leaving their standards and even their eagles. The bodies of the dead from that battle had scarcely cooled when Gellius' troops were proved to be no better than those of Lentulus. Thousands more legionaries were slain; more standards and eagles were lost. To add to the indignity, four hundred of our soldiers were forced to fight to the death as part of a so-called munus to honour Spartacus' erstwhile comrades. No doubt you have heard the tale. Beside me stands the only man to survive. This valiant centurion, Caepio.' He gestured at the grizzled officer, who bent his head as the crowd cheered. 'When I heard the dreadful news,' Crassus went on, 'I thought to myself, surely Rome's shame could be made no greater?'

Oh yes it could, thought Spartacus with dark satisfaction as the mob roared their fury. Carbo studied the frenzied faces around him. He was staggered by the depth of hatred. The irony wasn't lost on him. But for a trick of fate, he could have been feeling exactly the same way. Instead he was Spartacus' man, through and through. For good or ill.

'I was wrong. Just a few weeks ago, Gellius and Lentulus faced the slave rabble in Picenum together. There, even their combined forces were not enough to overcome Spartacus. Dozens more standards, among them another two eagles, were abandoned to the enemy. A myriad of new widows were made. More of our children were left fatherless.' Crassus bowed his head for a moment before letting his gaze trail over the crowd. 'This level of disgrace, this level of humiliation could not go on. Could it?'

'NOOOO!'

'I'm glad that we are in agreement.' He cast a quick, triumphant look at the senators, knowing that Gellius and Lentulus were among their number. 'I could not ignore the Republic in its hour of need, and so I put myself forward to take charge of the war. In their wisdom, my fellow politicians saw fit to award me the power of proconsular *imperium*.'

'You're the only one for the job, Crassus!' bellowed a ruddy-faced man near Carbo.

Prolonged cheering indicated the mob's happiness with this announcement.

Crassus gave a small nod in acknowledgement. 'Do you also want me to crush the slave rabble?' He waited for a couple of heartbeats. 'Do you?'

'YES!'

'I am but an instrument of your will,' said Crassus with a humble smile. 'Once my new forces have been raised, I shall have ten legions with which to crush Spartacus. The word is that he and his scum have passed by Rome on their way south. Rats usually return to the same hole, so it's likely that the slaves will head for the area around Thurii, where they overwintered before. Wherever they go, I shall track them down. Once they have been run to ground, I shall annihilate them. This I swear as Jupiter, Greatest and Best, is my witness.' He glanced at the huge statue as if to confirm his vow.

'KILL THEM ALL!' shouted the red-faced man.

'KILL! KILL! KILL!' chanted the crowd.

Spartacus filled his lungs and let out a long, slow breath. *It will be a fight to the death then.*

Tulla roared along with the rest, but this time Carbo couldn't bring himself even to mime. He glanced around, and was reassured by Spartacus' unyielding stare. *He'll have a plan. He always does.*

At length, Crassus had the trumpets sound again. It took a while, but eventually a calm of sorts settled over the Forum. 'Citizens of Rome, I would have you listen to a more experienced man than you or I. A soldier who has served the Republic for more than thirty years, who has fought in more campaigns than he can remember. His body is covered in battle scars, all of which are to the front. The phalerae that cover his chest bear witness to his valour. I give you the embodiment of Roman courage and virtus: Gnaeus Servilius Caepio!' With a grand gesture, Crassus ushered the centurion forward.

Loud cheering broke out again, and the watching faces filled with respect.

Caepio looked neither right nor left as he advanced. He wasn't one for trying to win the crowd, Spartacus thought, remembering their short conversation after the munus. He was a soldier, plain and simple, who spoke his mind. Just what was needed right now. *Crassus has thought this through, from beginning to end.*

'I thank you, Marcus Licinius Crassus,' said Caepio. 'People of Rome: I salute you.'

They roared with delight.

'I stand here today not far shy of my sixtieth year. I'm still in my harness, mainly because it's easier to sleep in it than it is to remove it.' He smiled as they hooted and whistled at his joke. 'If the truth be known, I would rather fight a war outside Italy. That's not possible at this moment, though. Our people need help! No decent man should be able to sleep at night knowing that so many of our fellow citizens are being murdered or burned out of their properties. This cannot go on! We must not let it go on!'

'RO-MA! RO-MA!' shouted the crowd.

'Armies do not appear as if by magic, though. Crassus needs volunteers – lots of them. For every legion raised, nearly five thousand strong soldiers are needed. Citizens are flocking to the Republic's banner from all over Italy, but thousands more are still needed. Are there any men between the ages of seventeen and thirty-five years here today?'

A multitude of voices answered in assent.

'Good,' barked Caepio. 'I venture that there are not a few of Sulla's veterans also here. Men who gave loyal service and who were rewarded with money and a plot of land upon their discharge. Am I right?'

'You are!'

'We salute you, Gnaeus Servilius Caepio!'

Cries rang out all over the Forum.

'It's good that you've come here today, because you too can help the Republic in its hour of need. Your bodies might have grown old, but your hearts are still those of soldiers, eh?' Caepio smiled at the roars that met this remark. 'I'd wager that there are plenty of you who hunger for the feel of a gladius in your hand again. Who would give up your farms for a season or two just to stand in a shield wall with your comrades once more. Who would shed their blood to see Spartacus and his raggle-taggle army sent to Hades! Am I right?'

The mob off to Carbo's left swayed and then parted as a group of hard-bitten veterans shoved their way forward into the small amount of space before the platform. 'We're with you, Caepio,' cried the lead man. 'Every one of us!'

A chorus of shouts rang out – two here, another one there, three further away – pledging their support.

'Well done, lads. Sulla would be proud of you,' declared Caepio. He scanned the entire crowd. 'As you know, this is not the place to join the army. I want every man who's going to volunteer to make his way to the Campus Martius. You know where it is! The recruiting officers are already there, waiting for you to come and sign up. As a gesture of gratitude for your courage, Crassus has authorised an advance of ten denarii to every man who signs his name on the line today.'

Whoops of joy met this announcement, and there was an immediate surge towards the streets that led north out of the city.

Looking satisfied, Caepio stood back.

'Well done, centurion,' said Crassus. 'Our job – in Rome at least – is done.'

But mine is not. Spartacus watched Crassus intently. *What will he do? Speak with some of the senators? Wait until the Forum has emptied?* If his enemy didn't move soon, they would have to walk away. The crowd around them was thinning fast. Before long, they would stand out like sore thumbs.

'Where do you want to go now? The Campus Martius? That's where

I'd go if I were old enough,' said Tulla, waving her arms back and forth as if she were marching, 'and I was a boy,' she added ruefully.

'Not there,' said Carbo, who was also eyeing Crassus. He had his lie ready. 'I would join up, but I'm an only son. I have to help run the farm.'

'That's not much of an excuse,' said Tulla in an accusing tone.

Stung despite himself, Carbo gave her a smart clip behind the ear. 'Watch your mouth! My time in the army will come. Just not right now.'

With a sulky look, Tulla retreated out of range.

Quickly, Carbo bent as if to tighten one of his sandal straps. 'What do you think?' he hissed. 'Do we make a move?'

Spartacus sized up the situation. Crassus was deep in conversation with Caepio. He wasn't going anywhere fast. 'Let's go towards the Basilica Aemilia. Hang around the entrance and see what he does.'

'I'm thirsty,' said Carbo, straightening. He eyed Tulla. 'Is there any room for wine sellers among the lawyers and scribes in the basilicae?'

'There are a few,' came the sullen reply. The girl's face changed as Carbo flipped three asses into the air.

'Go and buy a cup of some decent stuff. Falernian or Campanian. We'll be waiting by the door nearest the Curia.'

'Yes, sir!' Tulla spun on her heel, the coins gripped tight in her grubby fist.

'You'd better come back,' Carbo called. 'I expect some change!'

'Don't worry. I want the rest of my denarius!' With that, Tulla vanished into the crowd.

Chapter IX

Carbo ambled towards the nearest door of the basilica; Spartacus followed. Placing his back against the wall, Carbo cast an idle eye about, in the manner of a man who has nothing particular on his mind. Crassus was still talking to Caepio, although he'd come down a couple of steps.

'I fancy a few cups of wine, not just the one,' Carbo said loudly. 'The excitement's over as well. After this, I think we'll head back to the Elysian Fields.'

'Yes, master,' replied Spartacus.

'Want to see the future, good sir?'

Carbo turned. A man of indeterminate age in a grubby robe stood before him. The blunt-peaked leather cap on his head and his obsequious manner told him what he already knew. 'You're a haruspex.'

'That's right, sir. Place a denarius on my palm and I'll endeavour to see what the gods have in store for you.'

Ten legions are coming my way. 'Piss off,' Carbo said curtly.

The haruspex began to protest, but Spartacus took a step forward. 'Are you deaf? Peddle your lies somewhere else, or I'll give you a set of bruises that you most definitely didn't foresee.'

Muttering dire imprecations, the man sidled off.

Carbo didn't really believe in soothsayers, but it was a little unnerving that after what he'd just heard, the man had picked him out from everyone else. He made the sign against evil.

Spartacus had other things on his mind. 'Pssst! He's moving. With only six men guarding him too,' he hissed with delight. 'Caepio's one of them.'

Carbo's eyes swivelled. With two legionaries in front and four behind,

Crassus was heading in their general direction. To his surprise, one of the leading soldiers was indeed the veteran centurion. 'They're aiming for the same street we came in on. What should we do?'

Spartacus knew that the odds were long indeed, but his blood was up. 'We go for it.' *Whether we'll get away afterwards is uncertain, but it's worth the risk.*

Carbo's heart was like a pounding drum in his chest. This is what he'd prayed for so hard, but two against six? The legionaries were fully armed too, and all they had were daggers. *I can't back down.* He gave Spartacus a tight nod. 'How do you want to do it?'

'Let's get ahead of him. Head into the alley that Tulla brought us down. Charge out as they come alongside. We take a soldier each – the ones nearest us – and put them down, hard. Then you go for whichever legionary gets to you first. I'll kill Crassus. You'll have to hold off the rest as they come at you. Think you can do that?'

'Yes,' said Carbo with all the confidence he could muster. *I'm a dead man. What does that matter though, if we succeed?*

'The instant I'm done with Crassus, we flee back up the alley and lose ourselves in the back streets.' His eyes drilled into Carbo. 'Clear?'

He licked dry lips. 'Yes.'

Spartacus honed in on the fractional delay in his reply. He chuckled. 'You want to kill him, don't you?'

'I do.'

'Think you can murder an unarmed man? You'd just have to hack into him, as you would with a side of pork. No thinking, no hesitating.'

Sudden doubt tore at Carbo. Could he slay Crassus in cold blood? He had always thought he could, but now the chance had fallen into his lap, he wasn't so sure. His eyes fell away from the Thracian's.

'I'll do it,' Spartacus said.

Carbo rallied himself with images of his parents having to leave the house that been in the family for generations. The familiar rage flared in his belly. 'I can do it,' he protested.

'No,' replied Spartacus in a hard voice. 'This is the only opportunity that we'll ever get. There can be no cock-ups.'

Furious with himself, Carbo acquiesced.

'Lead on then, or they'll get ahead of us. Let's pray that Tulla doesn't come back before we're out of sight. The last thing we need is her shouting after us.'

'Right. I've had enough of waiting for the brat,' said Carbo loudly, assuming his role of master once more. 'Let's head back to the inn.' He strode off, not twenty paces ahead of Crassus and his escort. It was hard not to look behind him as he walked. The jingle of the legionaries' mail was clearly audible. *I'll have to get close enough to stab my man in the throat.* His anxiety grew, and his fingers stole of their own volition to the hilt of his dagger. *Jupiter, let my aim be true.*

After they had slain two of the legionaries and while Spartacus was killing Crassus, their companions would turn on him. Carbo did not have time to dwell on what might happen after that. Crassus will die, he told himself. He reached the alleyway and quickly turned into it.

Spartacus came spilling in behind him. His knife was already in his hand. 'Ready?'

Drawing his own blade, Carbo nodded.

Spartacus padded to the corner of the building and peered around it with great caution. Then he stepped back and glanced at Carbo. 'They're fifteen paces away. You take the front legionary on this side. I'll take the next one. Move the instant your man is parallel with us. Don't wait until he or Crassus have passed by or they might realise what's going on.'

'Yes.' Spartacus was taking the harder kill, but Carbo didn't argue. He moved in front of the Thracian, as far forward as he could without actually being seen, and pressed himself against the cool brickwork.

'Ten paces they'll be now,' whispered Spartacus. 'Nine. Eight. Seven. Six.'

Carbo held his dagger with the tip pointing towards the ground, the way he'd been trained. It provided a far stronger grip, and was almost impossible to knock from his fingers. His gaze narrowed to the space before him: the gap that led to the street. He was aware of the blood rushing in his ears, the crunch of *caligae* on the uneven ground and the clink of mail. In the background, noises from the basilica – and Spartacus' voice. 'Five. Four. Three.'

Carbo tensed.

'Two. One. Now.'

The first thing Carbo saw was the edge of a scutum. Then a mailed shoulder, and a head covered by a crested bronze-bowl helmet. Carbo darted forward. Grabbing the top edge of the shield with his left hand, he ripped it downwards. The unsuspecting legionary was jerked downwards and to the side, exposing his neck. Raising his knife, Carbo hammered it into the hollow to the side of the collarbone. He was aware of Spartacus shooting forward like a wraith to his left, of the other soldiers' confused faces turning towards him, of Crassus' shocked expression. A scream of agony from his victim dragged him back. He ripped free his blade, releasing a spray of bright red blood into the air. Carbo stabbed the man again for good measure, and let him fall.

'It must be them!' roared the second man at the front – Caepio. 'Protect Crassus!'

At the time, the words didn't register with Carbo, because his attention was focused on Caepio, who was charging at him with a drawn sword.

Fortunately, Caepio tripped as he leaped forward. His scutum, which should have thumped into Carbo's chest, instead caught Crassus in the side, sending him stumbling to one side.

'Kill him, you fool!' screeched the politician, backing away towards the wall of the Curia.

Gripping his gladius, Caepio advanced.

From the corner of his eye, Carbo saw a pair of bodies on the ground and Spartacus scrambling forward at Crassus. The two last legionaries, his mind screamed. Where in Hades are they? He couldn't look around, though, because Caepio was coming at him fast. One. The centurion's shield boss was rammed at Carbo's face. Two. A throat-ripping thrust of his sword followed. He dodged the first and backed away from the second.

'I recognise you! You're the traitor I spoke to after the munus.' Snarling with pleasure, Caepio swept forward. 'Ready to choke on your own blood, you vermin?'

Carbo didn't answer. Shieldless, his only form of defence was to retreat. That took him further away from Spartacus, and the fifth and sixth soldiers, who he now saw had not made for him. Instead, they had somehow got between Crassus and the Thracian and were shielding him with their scuta. Carbo cursed. With just a dagger, there was no way that Spartacus could succeed. There was nothing he could do to help either. Every time he tried to move in the direction of the Forum, Caepio blocked his way. He shot a glance behind him. A safe distance away, a crowd of shocked citizens were watching their every move. He spat another oath. The same would be happening beyond where Spartacus was. The alarm would have been raised. Any moment, more soldiers would come to Crassus' rescue.

Spartacus knew it too. He made one last desperate attempt to reach Crassus, darting in to one side of the legionaries guarding him. He managed to strike the leftmost man in the fleshy part of his shield arm. As he did, Crassus cursed and shrank back against the wall. If I'd had more time, thought Spartacus, it might have made a difference. No one could hold the heavy weight of a scutum for long after suffering such a wound. But the soldier's companion drove at him with a flurry of blows from his shield and sword, and he had to withdraw. A quick glance towards the Forum told him that his attempt was over. A large group of legionaries, accompanied by men in civilian clothes – some of the veterans, no doubt – were sprinting up the street.

He pinned Crassus with his stare. 'It's not to be this time. But next time you won't be so lucky.'

Crassus glared at him. 'I should have ordered you killed that day.'

'That's right, you cocksucker. A stupid mistake, eh?' called Spartacus over his shoulder as he ran off.

'After him!' screamed Crassus, shoving his guards in the back and gesticulating wildly at the approaching men. 'It *is* Spartacus! A gold piece to the man who brings me his body!'

Caepio was too busy with Carbo; he didn't see Spartacus coming. *I could kill him easily enough.* Yet the dignity with which the centurion had conducted himself still lingered in his mind. Instead he shoulder-charged Caepio from behind, sending him flying to the ground. Spartacus bounded over him with a great leap. 'Fortuna is smiling on you today.'

'Curse you for a treacherous assassin!' Caepio spat. 'I won't forget this.'

'Neither will I.' What a missed opportunity, thought Spartacus grimly. Crassus should be coughing out his last breath. He locked eyes with Carbo. 'Let's move!'

They fled up the street. Neither saw the little figure in their wake, darting in and out between the pursuing soldiers. There was a cup of wine in her hand.

Spartacus led the way. He ran through the dimly lit alleyway, barging past an old man carrying a hen by the neck, to a junction with another. He turned left blindly and hared up that, followed by Carbo. Fifty paces later, the narrow way forked. He took the right. A moment later he cursed as his feet sank into a stinking pile of semi-liquid waste. 'A dung heap.' His teeth flashed in the darkness at Carbo. 'They won't want to follow us through this. If they do, at least they'll be covered in shit as well.'

Carbo peered back whence they had come. He couldn't hear any sounds of pursuit. 'I think we've lost them.'

'Maybe. They'll be searching every street by now, though. We need a place to lie low.'

'Shouldn't we get out of the city?'

'It's too late for that. The first thing Crassus will have done is to order soldiers to every single gate. Anyone trying to leave will be questioned, certainly for the rest of the day. We'll have a better chance if we can hole up somewhere until tomorrow and try then.' It will still be damn risky, thought Spartacus. Had it been worth the risk? Yes, because if their attempt had succeeded, the Romans would have been thrown into complete disarray.

'We could always hide here.'

Spartacus indicated the narrow window openings above them. 'Someone will see us, and put two and two together. It'll be dangerous to head back to the Elysian Fields, but it's our best option.'

Carbo didn't like the idea either, but he couldn't think of another. He swung his head this way and that, trying to get his bearings. 'Do you even know which direction it is?'

'No.'

'We'll try this way,' said Spartacus, taking a step forward.

'You'll get even more lost if you do.'

Carbo turned to see a small shape scurrying out of the gloom. He couldn't help but grin. It was Tulla, still clutching the dregs of a cup of wine.

'You!' spat Spartacus. 'Why have you followed us?'

'You haven't paid me.' Tulla's voice died away as Spartacus took a step towards her.

'Did you see what happened?' demanded the Thracian.

'Y-yes,' replied the girl, backing away. 'Is it true that you're Spartacus?'

Spartacus darted forward and grabbed Tulla by the front of her tunic. Carbo's breath caught in his chest.

'It is.'

'Y-you've just been pretending to be a slave? Why?'

'To find out what's going on here. To discover what Crassus is planning to do.'

'And when you saw a chance to assassinate him, you took it.'

'That's right.'

'Are you going to kill me now?' Despite Tulla's bravado, her voice quavered.

'I'm not in the habit of murdering children, but I don't want the soldiers to find us either. There's no other way, really.' Spartacus placed his knife against the side of Tulla's scrawny neck.

Carbo saw the fabric covering the girl's groin darken as she lost control of her bladder. 'Spartacus, please!'

The Thracian didn't answer, but his knife stayed where it was. Tulla's eyes flickered from Carbo up to Spartacus and back again, but she had lost the ability to speak.

'You're to become a father soon,' said Carbo.

'What has that to do with it?' Spartacus demanded harshly.

'If you have a daughter, imagine her when she's Tulla's age.'

'I am to have a son, not a daughter,' Spartacus barked. 'And he will be no gutter rat.' The tip of the dagger dug into the skin, causing Tulla to wail in terror and letting a fat drop of blood drop to the ground.

'Wait! We could make a deal with her.'

Spartacus stared at Carbo without speaking, but again his knife remained still.

'Offer her an aureus to guide us to the Elysian Fields,' said Carbo quickly. 'She will stay there with us and in the morning, we'll give her another gold coin to take us to one of the quieter gates.'

Spartacus chuckled. 'That's enough to live on for a year! Why would I do that when I can simply cut her throat and keep the money?'

'Because it would mean one less life being lost. She's an innocent child.'

'Innocent? So were the children in Thracian villages that the fucking Romans murdered a few years back!' The muscles in Spartacus' forearm tensed.

'Do it for me then,' said Carbo, wondering if he was going too far. 'Please.'

Spartacus' lips thinned. 'You dare to question me?'

'She will not play us false,' urged Carbo. 'I know it.'

Spartacus used the point of the blade to force Tulla's chin upwards. 'Hear that? Carbo trusts you. With his own life.' He shot a flinty look at Carbo, whose mouth went very dry. 'Are you worthy of that trust?'

'Y-y-yes, sir.'

He let her go and Carbo let out a ragged breath. *Thank the gods.*

The Thracian fumbled in the purse that hung unseen around his neck. 'Here.'

Tulla grabbed the coin, and turned it over and over. 'This is only a denarius!'

'That's right. And this,' said Spartacus, flicking a gold coin between his fingers, 'is one of the aurei you're going to earn. If I give it to you now, you'll probably still play us false. And I'll have to kill Carbo here.'

Tulla's eyes grew beady.

'It's more than you've ever had in your damn life,' said Carbo angrily, sure that the money was motivating the girl more than *his* life.

Tulla reached out to try and snatch the aureus, but Spartacus lifted his hand out of reach. 'You will be paid in full if you do as I've asked. But if you don't, I will hunt you down and kill you. Not nicely, like I was going to do just now. Very slowly.'

Tulla's face went pale beneath the grime. 'All right. You know that the gods will keep you to your side of the bargain?'

Carbo was relieved to hear her words. If she believed in oaths, she would not betray his trust. If she did, he had little doubt that the Thracian would kill him. Despite Spartacus' continuing trust, he'd already made two mistakes too many.

'I do,' said Spartacus solemnly.

This seemed to satisfy the girl. 'Two aurei in total then.'

'Yes. The balance payable when you take us to the gate in the morning.'

'Along with the amount we agreed for the job of guiding you around.' Tulla's jaw jutted out stubbornly.

'Can you believe this girl?' Spartacus barked a laugh. 'She'd bargain with the ferryman!'

Despite the danger he had placed himself in, Carbo grinned.

Spartacus spat on his hand and shoved it forward. 'It's a deal.'

'Deal,' agreed Tulla, gravely accepting the grip.

Some time later, they found themselves in a side alley that overlooked the Elysian Fields. Tulla made to enter the street, but Spartacus pulled her back. 'Wait. Let's not be hasty.'

Staying in the shadows, they watched the inn. Several tables outside were occupied. A balding man dozed with his head against the front wall; a bored-looking whore toyed with her bracelets; two older men argued amiably about which horse-racing team was best that season. Carbo's unease reduced a fraction. There didn't seem to be any reason for alarm. He glanced at Spartacus.

'Not yet.'

Tulla rolled her eyes, but she too stayed where she was.

A boy pushing a small cart went by, shouting about the fresh fruit juice he had for sale. A matron passed in the other direction, issuing orders to the trio of house slaves who hurried behind her, carrying her shopping. The delicious smells issuing from a baker's shop a short distance away mixed with the smell of burning charcoal, and manure from the pens behind a butcher's. The cattle held there roared their protests. *Ting. Ting. Ting.* The sound of metal hammering off metal reached them from a smithy. A cripple hobbled by on a crudely fashioned crutch.

Carbo began to relax.

Beside him, Tulla was jiggling with impatience. 'Do you think it's safe yet?'

Spartacus shook his head.

'But everything is going on as norm—'

Tramp. Tramp. Tramp.

Tulla's eyes widened. Sweat slicked down Carbo's back as Spartacus peered briefly around the corner. 'Soldiers. Eight, nine, ten of them.'

A moment later, a party of legionaries came to a halt before the inn. A burly figure emerged from within and sat down with the two old men. Focused on the soldiers, Spartacus didn't see the man give them a tiny nod. Carbo did, but put it down to nothing more than a greeting. Six entered; the remainder waited outside.

Spartacus had been right to be cautious, thought Carbo, but their predicament was only a fraction less dire than before. 'What in Hades do we do now?'

'Good question.' Spartacus racked his brains. *Great Rider, help us.*

'What about a whorehouse?' suggested Tulla. 'You could stay in one of those overnight.'

'No,' retorted Spartacus. 'Places like that live on gossip. Besides, they could be searched. Believe me, Crassus is going to have this city turned upside down to try and find us.'

'We could try going to my uncle's house and finding out where my parents live,' said Carbo slowly. 'If we clean ourselves up, it might work.' His mind raced. What would he say to Varus? To his mother and father?

'That's a damn good idea. If the worst comes to the worst, we can hold them hostage until the morning.' Spartacus eyeballed Carbo.

'Very well.' Carbo almost wished that he had said nothing. He didn't want his parents to remember their last meeting with him – for surely this would be the last – to be tainted in that manner. But they had to escape.

Spartacus gave a satisfied nod.

'Where does your uncle live?' asked Tulla.

'On the Esquiline Hill. I'm not sure where.'

'Can you find his house?' asked Spartacus.

Tulla gave a long-suffering sigh. 'Of course. I might need to ask around a little.'

'Well, what are you waiting for?'

Tulla thumbed her nose at Spartacus and headed back down the alley.

Marcion had drunk more than the rest of his comrades, and his pounding head the next morning had made it easy to turn down his comrades' suggestion of a swim in the river that lay near the camp. They hadn't been gone long, however, before his rest was disturbed again by the sound of widespread cheering. Irritably poking his head out of his tent, he discovered something that sent him fumbling for his clothes. Ignoring his hangover, he ran all the way from the camp to the broad watercourse. 'Did you hear the news?' he called excitedly as he came barrelling down the slope, dodging past other soldiers.

There were scores of men in the water, bathing, washing their clothes, filling water containers or doing as his tent mates were, sporting about in the shallows near the bank. A few looked up, but none of Marcion's comrades heard him.

'Ariadne has had her baby!' he shouted.

That got him some attention.

Arphocras, one of the nearest to Marcion, was shoving a comrade's head under the surface. The sun glinted off the droplets in his close-cropped hair. 'What did you say?'

'Tell us!' cried a soldier Marcion had never seen before.

'Ariadne has given birth to a healthy boy!'

A lop-sided grin twisted Arphocras' face. 'A son? The gods be thanked. That's wonderful news. Let's hope that Spartacus comes back soon, eh?'

'He will,' declared the soldier who'd spoken first.

Marcion nodded. Unlike many others, Zeuxis prominent among them, he still felt sure that their leader would return. He wasn't sure why this was, but the news of Maron's birth had increased this belief.

The others were still play-fighting. 'Hey!' he yelled. 'I've got big news!'

No one paid him any notice. Marcion was not surprised. During their weeks of marching under the hot summer sun, few of the mountain streams they'd encountered had been safe enough to enter. This one was, making it a huge draw to the soldiers. Despite the ragging he got for washing regularly, his comrades could not deny the sheer pleasure of being able to bathe in running water.

Marcion's gaze was drawn back to Arphocras, whose victim had just managed to struggle free. His head had been half-submerged, so he had no clue what Marcion had been saying either. With a triumphant roar, he threw his arms around Arphocras' neck and dragged him under. Water fountained into the air as the pair thrashed about.

Ten paces further out, Gaius had Zeuxis on his shoulders, and was facing up to two more of their comrades. Shouting curses, Zeuxis and the other man on top grappled fiercely, trying to throw one another into the water. It wasn't long before Zeuxis' 'steed' lost his footing and fell. Zeuxis began to topple backwards, but he seized his opponent by one arm and, shouting with glee, managed to take him down as well.

Their antics made Marcion forget his news for a moment. Keen to join in, he began to strip off. He had just pulled his tunic up over his shoulders when an immense blow sent him flying forward, his limbs flailing. A heartbeat's delay, and Marcion landed in the river. He thrashed about madly, trying to find the bottom. Heaving himself upright, he ripped off his tunic and coughed up several mouthfuls of liquid. 'Who did that?' he roared. 'Who did that?'

Laughter filled his ears, and he looked up at the bank. 'You bastard!'

'The opportunity was too good to miss,' said Antonius, another of his tent mates. 'You were standing there, shouting your head off like bloody Julius.'

Marcion grinned. Throwing their disciplinarian officer into the river was a most appealing idea.

'What were you bawling about?' asked a deep voice.

'Zeuxis. Finally!' He dodged the balding man's charge with ease, giving him a push that, to his immense satisfaction, sent his argumentative tent mate face first into the river.

'Ariadne has given birth,' Arphocras butted in.

That put a smile on most men's faces, but Zeuxis, dripping water, scowled. 'I wish the babe no harm, but that's the last thing we need.'

'It's not as if it's a surprise. She's been pregnant for nine months!' retorted Arphocras to a ripple of laughter.

'That's not what I mean,' growled Zeuxis. 'Castus and Gannicus aren't going to be too pleased about this, are they?'

'Who cares what those whoresons think?' demanded Marcion. 'Not us, that's for sure.' He was pleased when a number of men nearby voiced their agreement. It was hard to ignore, however, that some soldiers were throwing him foul looks. Even worse, they weren't Gauls. The rot is spreading, he thought unhappily.

'It might force them to act. They've been planning something since we turned around at the Alps,' said Zeuxis. 'If I've heard what they promise us in exchange for loyalty once, I've heard it a hundred times. A free rein with every farm and estate that we attack. The right to use iron and gold as trading items. We'll all be rich men soon, if Castus and Gannicus are to be believed!'

'What's your point?' snapped Marcion, tired of Zeuxis' constant complaints. 'I know you think it's lies that the Gauls are peddling.'

'They're not lies, that's the problem,' replied Zeuxis sourly. He dropped his voice a fraction. 'That's why so many men are listening to them. You mark my words, if Spartacus doesn't come back soon, there'll be trouble. Real trouble.'

The others exchanged worried looks.

'It's not that bad,' protested Marcion, but he'd heard the whispers too.

'Isn't it?' asked Zeuxis. 'An army needs its leader, and if he is absent for too long, then someone else will take the space. It won't be Egbeo or Pulcher either. They're not ruthless enough.'

'We don't want change. We're still Spartacus' men, eh?' asked Marcion, glaring at his comrades.

His reply was a muted chorus of 'Ayes', but Zeuxis' voice wasn't one of them. He glared at Marcion. 'The only reason that I joined Spartacus' army was to get away from my damn master. You might be different, but a lot of men did the same as me. It was good to learn how to fight, I suppose, and to give the Romans a taste of their own medicine. Spartacus brought us victory after victory as well, so I kept following him. You could say that I became loyal to him, yes. But now he's fucked off and doesn't look like coming back. He's left us at the mercy of a pair of Gaulish savages! So much for his loyalty to *us*. I'm damned if I'll stick around for much longer.'

'We can't just let Castus and Gannicus take control!' cried Marcion.

'How are you going to stop them?' hissed Zeuxis. 'You're an ordinary foot soldier, like me. Like all of us. What can you and I do against the likes of the Gauls? They've got thousands of followers! Thousands. If we challenged Castus and Gannicus, we'd be food for the vultures and you know it.'

Marcion looked to his comrades for support, but he found none. No one else was actively agreeing with Zeuxis' gloomy prediction, but nor were they arguing with it. Misery filled him. The laughter of a few moments before seemed a lifetime ago.

Where are you, Spartacus?

'Help me, please.'

For a moment, Ariadne could not work out where she was, or who was addressing her. She was alone on a road paved with black basalt slabs. The sun beat down from a clear sky. Above her she saw clouds of vultures. Her skin crawled. *Why are there so many?*

'Help. Water.'

Ariadne's head turned, and she took in the man who hung from a simple wooden cross before her. Horror filled her. 'Egbeo?' she asked in disbelief.

'Ariadne.' The big Thracian's voice was husky and dry. Far weaker than normal. 'Help me.'

She took a step closer. The cross was a simple affair, little more than an upright two handsbreadth in width, and a crosspiece of similar size that stretched to either side. Ariadne saw that she could hack through the rope that bound Egbeo's feet to the vertical, but the thick iron nails that had been driven through his wrists were beyond her. To prevent removal, their heads had been hammered flat on to the wood, pinning his hands in one agonising position. 'I can't help you,' she said. 'I'm sorry.'

'Thirsty. I'm so thirsty.'

Ariadne's helplessness reached new heights. She had no water bag with her. Glancing up and down the road, she could see no well, no buildings. Just a line of occupied crosses, stretching away on either side as far as she could see. 'How many men have been crucified?' she whispered in horror. 'It must be hundreds.'

'Thousands,' croaked Egbeo.

Suddenly, Ariadne knew why she was here. Terror twisted her stomach into a painful knot. 'Spartacus – where is Spartacus?'

Egbeo didn't answer.

'Where is my husband?' Desperation turned her voice shrill.

The lines on his haggard face grew even deeper. 'He—'

A hand shook her shoulder. 'Ariadne!'

Startled, she opened her eyes to find the midwife crouched over her. 'You were having a nightmare—' She was interrupted by a mewling sound from beside Ariadne. 'And you woke the baby. I think he's hungry.'

'Yes, yes, of course.' Failing to clear her mind of the graphic images, Ariadne scooped up Maron, whose cry was growing louder. *It cannot be coincidence that I've had the same hideous dream three times, can it?* She kissed her son on the forehead. 'I'm sorry for disturbing you, my darling. Come here.' Placing him on her breast with the help of the midwife, she lay down again. 'My dream was terrible.'

The old woman cackled. 'It's the herbs. They often bring bizarre and unsettling images. Things that we do not want to happen, or things that we fear.'

'Do the visions ever come true?'

'Sometimes, but it's almost impossible to know the real ones from the false. My advice is for you to forget all about it. You've got more important things to be doing than brooding over a nightmare.'

Ariadne nodded in agreement. That would be best. She busied herself by gazing at Maron, and imagining what he would look like as he grew up. Would he inherit Spartacus' piercing grey eyes or her brown ones?

Would he be compactly built, like his father, or take after her family, who were slighter framed? Soon though, her mind began to wander. Inevitably, it returned to her dream. With Spartacus in Rome, her natural reaction to it was to assume the worst for him. *How can it be the herbs when I've had the same vision before? Could Spartacus be already dead?* She took a deep breath. On the previous occasions that she had seen the lines of crosses, there had been no Egbeo, no conversation. Surely, the big Thracian's presence in the nightmare meant that it could not be taking place in the present or the near future, because Egbeo was alive and well, and here with the army. That had to mean that Spartacus was not one of the crucified men.

The old woman coughed, and Ariadne glanced at her. *Maybe none of it means anything.* Her attempt to reassure herself lasted no more than a heartbeat. A dream so dramatic didn't keep returning unless it was of some significance.

Maron stirred, and she caressed the back of his head. 'Hush, my little one. It's all right. It's all right.' *Dionysus will look after us, as he always has. Spartacus was not one of the men I saw.*

As she closed her eyes and tried to rest once more, Ariadne was haunted by one question. She could not make herself forget it.

What had Egbeo been trying to tell her?

On their way to the Esquiline, Spartacus had Tulla purchase two new tunics from a rundown clothes shop on a side street. Discarding their bloody ones on a dung heap and with their knives cleaned and sheathed, the trio were able to take to the main thoroughfares once more. There were parties of soldiers everywhere, but they were paying little heed to the passers-by. Despite this, Carbo's heart was racing, but he swaggered along as if he were walking through Capua. Spartacus was careful to look at the ground. Finding a small open-fronted restaurant at the base of the hill, Carbo stood at the counter and ordered some food while Tulla went in search of Varus' house. Both watched the passing patrols, but fortunately the soldiers seemed interested only in inns and taverns. Despite the fact that no one had challenged them, both were glad when the girl returned.

Tulla was immune to their worries. 'It's two streets up,' she announced breezily. 'We'll know it by the embroidered cushions on the benches outside.'

Carbo rolled his eyes.

'What's she talking about?' demanded Spartacus.

'There are seats outside the houses of the rich for their clients to sit on as they wait to be seen. My uncle has always been one for ostentation.'

Tulla led them up the flagged street, weaving her way through the traffic. She took a left at a fountain decorated with a central gilded statue of Neptune, and then the second right.

Carbo spotted the cushions first; he remembered his mother talking about them. 'That's it.'

They approached. Apart from the soft furnishings on the otherwise empty benches, Alfenus Varus' house could have been one of thousands in Rome. As with many others in this part of the city, it stood alone, a rectangular building with a high outer wall whose only features were a massive studded door and a line of small glass windows. This feature was rare indeed. Carbo's mother's words echoed in his head. 'He always has to have the latest fad, no matter how expensive it is.' *The fool.* Already he was not looking forward to seeing his uncle again. Yet the thought of his parents drove him on. Somehow he would make them understand what he'd done.

Tulla sat down on the bench to the left of the door. Spartacus remained standing.

Carbo realised that they were both looking at him. He straightened his tunic and ran his hands through his hair. Then he stepped up and rapped the iron elephant trunk knocker off the timbers. It made a deep, thumping noise.

He waited for a long time, and was just about to knock again when a shutter at head height opened. A pair of eyes stared out suspiciously. 'Yes?'

'Is Alfenus Varus in?'

There was an audible *Phhh* of contempt. 'Not to the likes of you.' The shutter began to close.

This reaction to his scarred appearance was second nature to Carbo. Once, it would have cowed him. Now he took a step forward. 'I think you'll find that that's not the case. I'm his nephew.'

The shutter stopped. 'You're who?'

'Paullus Carbo, his nephew.'

'The son of Julia, Alfenus' sister?'

'Yes.'

'Wait here.'

Carbo was about to ask if his parents were still living in the house, but the shutter had already slammed home. There was a faint sound of footsteps receding, and then silence.

'That wasn't exactly the warmest of welcomes,' muttered Spartacus.

'Alfenus thinks that Mother married below her station. He has always looked down on us. He's a good man really.' Carbo's protest was automatic, and echoed his father's words. For the first time in his life, however, the sentiment felt false. The few times he had met Varus, the man had been nothing but patronising and arrogant. It was as well that he'd left the family home, Carbo decided. Otherwise, his father *would* have sent him to live here under Varus' supervision, to train as a lawyer.

A moment later, he heard someone returning down the hall. There was a metallic *snick* as the bolt was drawn back, and the door opened. A shrew-faced man with grey hair looked out. 'You're to come in.' His eyes moved distastefully from Spartacus to Tulla. 'Your slave, and your . . . ?'

'Guide.' Good, thought Carbo. I didn't even need to lie to him.

'I see. They can remain outside.'

Carbo gave what he hoped was a reassuring glance to Spartacus, and crossed the threshold. The door was shut with an air of finality, making him uneasy, but he squared his shoulders. This was no time for weakness.

'Leave the knife here.' The slave indicated a recess to one side of the entrance. Inside it, a massive man sat on a stool with a club between his knees. He seemed dull-witted, but fully capable of braining someone if he was ordered to. Carbo handed over his dagger without protest.

'Follow me.' The slave walked off without looking to see if he obeyed.

They went straight into the tablinum, where a garish, painted statue of a dolphin decorated the *impluvium*. The scenes from classical myth that adorned the walls were portrayed in similarly gaudy fashion, and not to Carbo's taste. He studied the death masks of Varus' ancestors as he passed by the lararium. They had the same self-satisfied expression as he remembered his uncle wearing, a sort of 'I'm superior to you' look. He realised he'd been intimidated by it as a child. Now, he loathed it.

The large colonnaded garden beyond was just as grand as Carbo could have imagined. It was overdone: all coy nymphs peeping from behind ornamental bushes and grandiose mosaic patterns on the floor. Everything shouted wealth but not class. Varus was sitting in a chair that was shaded by a large lemon tree. A fine blue glass full of wine sat before him, on a table inlaid with gilt. Behind him, a slave used a palm leaf to fan the air. His uncle had once been handsome, thought Carbo, but years of good living had weighed down his big frame with rolls of fat, and given him a jowl worthy of a prize boar. His straight nose was the only feature in which Carbo could see a resemblance to his mother. Varus was studying a half-unrolled parchment, pursing his plump lips as he read. Although he must have heard them approach, he gave no immediate acknowledgement.

The slave waited. Carbo waited too, a well of anger bubbling within him. With an effort, he controlled his temper. *Stay polite. We need his help.*

After a little while, Varus lifted his gaze.

'Your *nephew*, master.' The slave took a few steps back.

A well-feigned expression of surprise crossed Varus' fleshy features. 'Can it be true? Are you really Paullus Carbo?'

'Yes, Uncle. It is I,' said Carbo in as humble a tone as he could manage.

'There is a certain resemblance to your mother, I suppose.' Varus' tone was dubious. 'The severe scarring from the pox makes it hard to see, however. Not the most good-looking of men, are you?'

It took a great effort for Carbo not to leap forward on to Varus, fists pummelling. 'I am honoured to meet you at last, Uncle,' he said, ignoring the question.

The jowls rose and fell in response. 'You have long since been given up for dead. After a year without so much as a word as to your whereabouts, your parents concluded that you had died, or been killed. And now you return, unannounced? What kind of son does that make you?'

'I was going to send a letter—'

'A letter? When?'

'About three months ago.'

'It never arrived.'

'I decided not to send it.'

'You don't have much of a conscience, eh? Nothing changes,' thundered Varus. 'Did you know that after you abandoned your parents without a word, they delayed leaving Capua for two weeks? They lived in a garret as they searched everywhere for you. But you had vanished, as if you had gone down to Hades itself.' He glared at Carbo.

Guilt hammered at Carbo's temples. *They didn't check the ludus. They didn't think I'd stoop so low.* 'I left the city, went to the coast. Took service with a merchant who was sailing for Asia Minor and Judaea.'

Varus' eyes bulged. '*That*, when you could have been learning to become a lawyer?'

'I did not wish to enter that profession,' replied Carbo stiffly. *I didn't want to live here, with you ordering me about like a slave.*

Varus made a contemptuous gesture. 'You should have obeyed your father's wishes and my recommendation! There would have been none of the heartache.'

It's all Crassus' fault. But for him, I wouldn't have had to run away from home, or to come here. Their failure to assassinate the politician hit Carbo even harder.

'As for your poor mother, well, she did nothing but grieve for you. I'm sure that's half the reason the fever took her so easily.' He adopted a grieving expression that screamed its falsity. 'Oh yes, she's dead.'

His uncle's face swam in and out of focus. 'W-when?'

'Let me see,' mused Varus. 'About three months ago, I think it was.'

Even if his letter had arrived, it would have been too late. Carbo's grief tore at him with renewed savagery. 'It was a fever, you say?'

'Yes, yes. Even though they have drained the swamps, the bad airs linger over the city at various times. No one is immune. I myself was lucky to survive a bout several years ago.'

You self-centred pig! thought Carbo furiously.

'Her death quite took away your father's will to live. If he had known that his only child was living, perhaps he would have taken better care of himself. As it was, well . . .'

No, Carbo screamed silently, *Great Jupiter, do not let this be happening!* 'Father is dead too?'

'Yes. Not a week since.'

'A week,' repeated Carbo like a fool. *Seven days.*

'That's right. If you had thought to make amends just a little sooner, he might have seen you.'

Carbo closed his eyes. 'Did an illness take him as well?'

'No. I had my major domo make some enquiries afterwards. It seems that he was attacked one night outside the *cenacula* where he lived. According to those who saw it happen, it was a case of simple robbery. The scum who killed him didn't know that he had little more than two asses to rub together, nor did they care. He was drunk and alone. They stabbed him, rifled him for any valuables and then left his body in the gutter like so much rubbish.'

His mother's death would have hit his father very hard, thought Carbo. Jovian would have thought himself abandoned in the world once she had gone. It was easy to see how he might have turned to drink in solace. 'You said he was living in a cenacula. I thought that my parents were staying here with you.'

'After my sister's death, tragic though it was, all obligations I had towards Jovian disappeared. He left the day after Julia's funeral.'

'He left, or you asked him to go?'

'I asked him. It was better for everyone concerned.' Varus' smile was as practised as a whore's.

Carbo could scarcely believe what he was hearing. 'So my mother was barely in her tomb when you put my father out on the street. Have you no heart?'

Varus gave him an offended look. 'It wasn't as if he had no money for rent or food. At the time, he was working for a local merchant.'

'And that made it acceptable, I suppose?'

'How dare you take that tone with me, you impudent pup!' snapped Varus. 'Where were you when your family needed you? I was the one who took them in, who gave them a roof over their heads and put food in their bellies, who listened to their tragic tale over and over. I – not you.'

A wave of shame subsumed Carbo. 'I was trying to earn the money to help with Father's debts,' he muttered. *At least that's how it started out.* Once they had broken out of the ludus, there had been no opportunities – other than theft – to make any money, and Carbo wasn't a thief. Spartacus had also banned the use of gold and silver in his army. The only metals of use, he said, were iron and bronze, for making weapons. *I was going to do so much. Yet I have done none of it, and now my parents are dead.* Tears pricked his eyes.

Varus was oblivious. 'Clearly, you haven't met with much success. Look at you, dressed like the poorest kind of pleb.' His lip curled. 'I wonder how you even managed to save the money to buy a slave.'

The sheer level of his uncle's contempt helped Carbo to swallow his grief. He would deal with it later. What mattered right now was securing a safe place to hide until the next day. Where could be better than here? he thought with black amusement. 'He's not a slave.'

'Eh?' Varus' pudgy forehead creased into a frown. 'Who is he, then?'

'He's a friend.' Carbo took the few steps that separated him from his uncle at speed. Picking up the glass by its stem, he smashed it off the edge of the table. As Varus gaped, he swept around to the rear of his chair. A great shove sent the slave with the palm leaf stumbling backwards. Carbo threw his left arm around Varus' neck in a choke hold. Gripping the jagged stump of the glass like a knife, he touched it to his uncle's throat. 'Up.'

'What are you doing?' Spittle flew from Varus' lips as he stood. 'Have you gone entirely mad?'

'Not quite. Tell your major domo to get the brute at the entrance to surrender his club. He is to open the front door and allow my companions in. My friend is to tie up the brute, and then return here with the girl.'

'You are insane,' hissed Varus.

'Maybe I am.' Carbo pushed the broken glass against his uncle's skin until it drew blood. There was a loud squawk of pain. 'I will happily shove this in all the way,' he murmured. 'Just keep answering me back.'

'Y-you heard him,' Varus wheezed at the major domo, whose complexion had gone pasty. 'Do as he says! Quickly!'

The grey-haired slave hurried off.

'C-can I sit down?' asked Varus. 'I feel faint.'

'Fine.' Carbo released his grip and let his uncle slide, shaking, back on to his chair. 'Don't move.'

'Why are you doing this?'

'Shut up.'

'Carbo—'

'I said, shut your fat mouth! It would give me extreme pleasure to see you bleed out, you overblown piece of offal.' Carbo's mind was full of images of his parents, and his heart was full of sorrow and shame. Killing his uncle might not make that pain go away, but it would help.

Varus heard the threat in his voice, and subsided.

It wasn't long before the major domo arrived with a grim-faced Spartacus and Tulla in tow. The Thracian smiled when he saw Carbo. 'I have tied up the doorman, and locked the door. No one is going anywhere without my say so.' He waved a set of keys. 'This isn't the kind of welcome I expected.'

'Nor I,' replied Carbo harshly. 'But my parents are both dead. Uncle Varus here' – he gestured with the jagged piece of glass – 'is the only family I have remaining. Not that that means he is dear to me, because he is not. After my mother died a few months ago, he put my father out on the street. In his grief, he took to drink. He was murdered a week ago.'

'I am sorry,' said Spartacus. He gave Varus a pitiless look, and returned his gaze to Carbo. 'So here is as good a place as any for us to stay.'

'Yes.'

'Good thinking.'

'You must be really rich,' said Tulla, eyeing Carbo's uncle with not a small amount of awe.

Varus glowered in response. The urchin took a step backwards.

Carbo knew that Tulla had probably been kicked out of the way by men such as his uncle all her life. He poked Varus with the glass. 'Answer the girl. Politely.'

'I suppose you could say that I am wealthy, yes,' said Varus sullenly.

'Thought so,' said Tulla in a grave tone. She wandered off, trailing a hand in a water channel that fed the plants.

Carbo grinned. Tulla had given him an idea. 'Do you keep any cash in the house?'

'A-a little, maybe. Not much.' Varus' eyes flickered as he spoke.

'You're lying.' Carbo glanced at Spartacus. 'Isn't he?'

'Definitely.'

'We could do with the money, eh?'

'Gold always comes in useful.' Spartacus was more concerned with getting out of the city unharmed, but he saw that Carbo needed to do this. He would act in much the same way if he ever saw Kotys again.

Carbo's anger towards his uncle had gone ice cold. He took hold of one of Varus' hands and pulled it down on to the table. He raised the stump of glass high. 'I'm going to count to three. If you haven't answered by then, I will stick your fat fucking hand to the wood. One.'

Varus' jowls wobbled with terror.

'Two.'

'All right, all right! There's a box under a loose tile in the lararium.'

'Tulla!'

Spartacus' explanation of what to look for sent the girl sprinting off.

Carbo released his uncle's hand, which seemed to give Varus some courage. 'So you came here to rob and murder me, is that it?'

'Weren't you listening?' asked Spartacus. 'We need somewhere to stay.'

'I-I don't understand.'

'I wanted to spend the night with my parents,' said Carbo. 'That's why I came to your miserable bloody house.'

'I see.' Varus looked awkward. 'You didn't know that they were dead.'

'How could I have known?' spat Carbo.

'Look!' Tulla's beam stretched from ear to ear. In her arms she bore a small iron box. 'It's full of gold coins and jewels!'

'We'll take that with us,' said Spartacus with a wink at Carbo.

'Have it all,' cried Varus eagerly. 'You'll be able to afford the best tavern in Rome.'

Spartacus' smile vanished. 'We'll stay here.'

Varus' mouth opened to protest, but then he thought better of it. 'Who are you?' he whispered.

'I am Spartacus.'

Varus' eyes darted to Carbo, who nodded in confirmation. 'S-Spartacus?'

'That's right.'

Varus' face went even paler. 'But you're supposed to be with your army, near Venusia.'

'Clearly, I'm not.'

'Jupiter above, you'll torture me to death!'

'Is that what they say I do to my prisoners?'

Varus nodded fearfully. 'Terrible, terrible things.'

'It happens with every army – even Roman ones,' interjected Carbo. 'Spartacus tries to stop it.'

'Don't waste your breath,' said Spartacus wearily. 'He won't believe you.'

Looking at the fear and loathing smeared all over his uncle's face, Carbo knew the Thracian's words to be true. At that moment, part of him wanted to bury the piece of glass in Varus' heart. There was something more important that he could ensure was done, however. 'Where are my parents buried?'

'Your mother lies in the Varus family tomb, and your father' – Varus licked his lips unhappily – 'is in a simple grave in the public cemetery.'

'You filth!' Carbo's rage surged out of control, and he slashed Varus across the cheek. 'Even in death you could not treat my father with honour!'

Varus collapsed howling to the ground with blood pouring from between his fingers.

'I ought to slay you right here,' Carbo shouted, pulling Varus up by the front of his tunic.

'There is another way.'

Spartacus' voice penetrated Carbo's fury. 'Eh?'

'You could make him swear to erect a fine tomb for both your parents, and to have them reinterred there.'

Carbo heard the wisdom in Spartacus' words and loved him for it. Despite his ruthlessness, the Thracian cared for him. He let the moaning Varus fall again. 'Did you hear that?'

'A tomb, yes, for your parents. It will be the finest I can have built—'

'It doesn't need to be the finest. Just make it fitting to their station.'

'I will, I swear it. If I do not, may Jupiter strike me down.'

'If you do not,' growled Spartacus, 'I will come back and feed you your own prick and balls.'

Varus' jowls wobbled again, and a fat tear actually ran down each cheek. 'I understand,' he whispered.

Carbo's rage subsided a little. At least he could now rest in the knowledge that they would lie together in a decent tomb. With luck, one day he would be afforded the opportunity to visit it.

One day.

After what they had heard earlier, it seemed a slim hope.

Chapter X

When Ariadne woke again, the position of the sunlight on the tent told her that it was late afternoon. The *churring* of the cicadas was louder than ever, but the heat of the day had begun to abate. She gazed down at Maron, who was asleep on her chest. 'My son,' she whispered.

Hearing her voice, the midwife came fussing over. 'How are you feeling?'

'Tired, but well.'

The old woman lifted the blanket and checked between her legs. 'Good. There's only been a little bleeding. In the morning, I'll get you up.' She grinned, revealing lines of brown pegs. 'Word gets around fast. Hundreds of soldiers have already been asking to see Spartacus' son. Atheas has had to post sentries to stop them approaching the tent.'

Ariadne listened. Sure enough, there were numerous muttered conversations outside. She was filled with pride at this proof of the men's love for their leader. 'How many are out there now?'

'Dozens.'

'We cannot let them wait. Take the baby, so I can sit up.'

'You need to rest,' said the midwife, alarmed.

'I can do that later. Besides, I want them to see Maron.' She handed him to the crone. 'Swaddle him, please.' Ariadne sat up carefully. She reached for the bronze mirror that sat beside the bed and used it so that she could comb and tie back her hair. She found her dark red woollen cloak and threw it over her shoulders. It would conceal her nightdress, and remind everyone that as well as being Spartacus's wife, she was also a priestess. She wondered about taking out her snake too, but decided against it. Seeing Maron would impress them enough. 'I'm ready,' she announced, reaching out for the baby.

'Are you sure? You've just been through childbirth. You mustn't overdo it,' scolded the midwife.

'I won't stay outside for long.'

There was an exasperated sigh. The old woman lifted the tent flap.

A hush fell at once.

Holding Maron to her chest, Ariadne stepped into the sunlight.

A loud *Ahhhh* rose into the air from the large crowd of men who stood before the tent. Among them, Ariadne recognised Navio, Pulcher, Egbeo, and many others. 'You have come to see Spartacus' son?' she asked.

'YES!' they shouted.

Startled, Maron woke up and began to cry.

The men gave each other embarrassed grins.

'Hush now,' Ariadne whispered, comforting Maron. 'Those are your father's soldiers, who have come to welcome you into the world.' It was as if he understood her words. He quietened, and began to nuzzle for her breast. 'In a moment, little man.' She advanced, so that everyone could see. 'Our son is healthy, and has fed well.'

Men laughed, grinned and slapped each other on the back.

'What's his name?' asked Egbeo.

'Maron.'

They cheered.

'After Spartacus' brother, who died fighting the Romans?'

'Yes.'

'It's a good Thracian name. A strong name,' declared Egbeo.

'Behold Maron, son of Spartacus,' cried Ariadne, raising him into the air.

That made them roar until they were hoarse.

Maron began to cry again and, seeing his distress, the men fell silent. Ariadne cuddled him until he was content once more.

'May he grow up to be as strong and clever as his father,' called a man with a black beard.

'As good with a sword and spear as Spartacus!'

'And as good-looking as his mother,' added a voice further back.

Ariadne joined in the laughter. Here, basking in the adoration of Spartacus' soldiers, it was easy to forget her nightmare. But she knew that when she went back inside, her fears would return. Ever since they had turned away from the Alps, she had worried about the future. They could not march around Italy for the rest of their lives. The Romans would not permit it. To think otherwise was naïve in the extreme. Yet most of the men seemed to believe just that.

'Ariadne,' said a familiar voice.

'Castus.' She could not keep her displeasure from her voice. 'And Gannicus,' she added with a trace more warmth. Inside, her stomach was churning. Neither man would wish Spartacus' son and heir well. She wouldn't put it past them to slip a blade into Maron's heart. Ariadne took some relief from the fact that Atheas and Taxacis, scowls locked in place, were right at the Gauls' backs. 'You've come to see Maron?'

'We have,' said Castus with a half-smile. He came closer and Ariadne had to force herself not to back away.

Castus peered at the baby. 'He's handsome. May he grow up healthy and strong.'

'Just like his father,' added Gannicus with real heartiness. 'And may the gods watch over him always.'

'Thank you,' said Ariadne, still wary.

Castus made to speak, but Gannicus intervened. 'We shouldn't stay. She's tired.'

'It was good of you to come.' Despite their apparent goodwill, Ariadne eyed the pair with deep suspicion. Since the showdown about where the army would go, she had avoided talking to them. As far as she was concerned, they had betrayed Spartacus. They could not be relied upon. Yet although relations had been strained, Spartacus had continued to deal with them. 'Because I have to,' he'd said to her repeatedly. 'Otherwise the split will come sooner.' *I want to know now.* She had heard enough talk about how they were cajoling men to follow them. She threw caution to the wind. They wouldn't attack her or the baby, not with the Scythians at their backs. 'When are you going to leave?'

Castus flushed. 'We're just leaving.'

'That's not what she meant,' said Gannicus, his eyes narrowing. 'Is it?'

'No.'

'What makes you so sure that we will?' asked Castus.

'Come on. A blind man could see how angry you were when Spartacus told the men that he would lead them south again. Besides, you told him that you would when the time was right.'

'I might have changed my mind,' he said with a silky smile.

'But you haven't.'

Castus didn't deny it, but he didn't answer either.

Ariadne turned to Gannicus. 'I know that you will split off eventually. Have you decided when?'

Gannicus sucked on his moustache and said nothing.

Ariadne felt safe enough to let her temper rise. 'Well?' she demanded.

'I haven't decided,' Gannicus admitted. 'We'll see how the land lies after we make camp near Thurii.'

'But you will break away?'

'Yes.' He held her gaze. 'Spartacus is a great leader, but a man can't follow another all his life.'

'Thank you for your honesty.'

He smiled, reminding her why she had always preferred him to the shifty Castus. Yet she still wouldn't trust either man. Without the Scythians' presence, she would have been scared.

'When were you planning on telling me that?' Castus' tone was accusatory.

'In my own good time.'

'The best thing would be to unite forces. Go together.'

'True. Let's not argue about it here, eh?' Gannicus glanced at Ariadne. 'Wishing the blessings of the gods upon you and your son.' He reached out and threw an arm over Castus' shoulders. Still grumbling, the red-haired Gaul let himself be led away.

Ariadne watched them go. *They'll probably go in the spring. That would make most sense, after the hard weather is over.* The knowledge sent relief, and a little sadness, flooding through her veins. After the uncertainty, it was better to know. Once she told Spartacus, he could make plans, work on the men's loyalty, seek out even more recruits. But they still needed a place to head for. Thurii was a long way from Rome, but it wasn't an impregnable fortress, or inaccessible. To reach it, all the Romans had to do was march down the Via Annia. *Where would be best?*

Maron whimpered, distracting her. Ariadne retreated into the tent, racking her brains. There had to be somewhere that they could go. She would ask the god. Dionysus had helped her previously. Perhaps he would again now.

'You prick!' hissed Castus when they were clear of the throng. 'You told her when you would leave before me?'

'I said I'd see how the land lay after we got to Thurii. I didn't say when I'd leave.'

'We hadn't even talked about that!' Castus spat.

'We had decided that we wouldn't make any definite decisions until then. By inference, that meant we would move some time after that.' Gannicus couldn't stop the sarcasm creeping into his voice.

'Don't you fucking patronise me!' shouted Castus. 'I thought we were supposed to be acting together?'

'We are.'

'Well, if you want me and my men as allies, and I'd wager my left ball that I've got a damn sight more of them than you' – here Castus shoved his face right into Gannicus' – 'there'd better be more sharing of information in future.'

Gannicus had had enough of Castus and his perpetual grievances. He shoved the redhead hard in the chest. 'Screw you! I've told you before that if you want to go it alone, you can do it anytime. See how far you get with only five or six thousand men! You'll be massacred by the first Roman legion that you come across.'

'Is that right?' Castus' sword hummed free.

'Oh, so you want to fight me now?' snapped Gannicus, beginning to draw his own weapon.

'No, I want to chop you into little fucking pieces.'

Gannicus felt his own rage beginning to rise. With an effort, he brought it under control. He wasn't scared of taking on Castus, but it was a pointless exercise that would end with one or both of them injured or dead. He let his blade slide back into the scabbard. 'This is stupid.'

Castus darted forward. 'There's nothing stupid about hewing your smart-arse head from your neck,' he cried, drawing back his right arm. 'Tell Hades I said "Hello".'

'You know I'm not a coward, Castus. You know I'm also your equal with a sword. Before you kill me, think about what you're doing. Remember our plan to seize control of the whole army? To be like Brennus, the chieftain of old?'

It was as if someone had thrown Castus into a pool of icy water. A degree of sanity returned to his eyes.

'Is that what you want still?' Gannicus continued.

'Of course.'

'Then put away your damn weapon. Let's talk about how we can make our idea a reality instead of butchering each other like a pair of drunken warriors arguing over a woman.'

Lowering his arm, Castus leaned towards him. 'We could start by going back and slitting that bitch's throat – and killing the baby too.'

'I'd do it in a heartbeat, but we would never get close enough. Did you not see how closely the Scythians were watching? Even if we managed it, the men would turn on us when they found out.'

Castus looked disappointed. 'Best to do something like that at night, I suppose. Secretly.'

'Let's stay focused on one idea.' Gannicus glanced around. 'Killing Spartacus. Once he's out of the picture, it will be a lot easier to rally the army around us. Ariadne and the brat can be dispatched then too.'

'Egbeo and Pulcher will also need to be killed.'

'Agreed.'

'What had you in mind? An ambush on him when he's coming back here?'

Gannicus winked.

Castus' answering grin was predatory. 'How will they find him?'

'It's a gamble, I know, but I'd say that he and Carbo will travel the same way they went to Rome. Straight down the Via Annia.'

'You're right. All they'll need to do is find a good spot to spy on the road some distance from here. They can do the job at night.' Castus' grin slipped. 'We can't send Gauls in case anyone sees them and points the finger at us.'

'I've got a group of mixed bloods in mind. You know the types.'

Castus nodded. On the large latifundia, it was common for slaves of different origins to have children together. Thousands of the soldiers in Spartacus' army were such. These men felt no loyalty to one race or another, as the Gauls, Thracians and Germans did.

'They're mostly farm slaves, former herders and the like. They answer to me, not Spartacus, and every one of them would slit their own mothers' throats for a purse of silver.'

Suspicion flared in Castus' eyes. 'You're not just sending your men. Not for something this big.'

'Send a few of your lot as well,' replied Gannicus, holding up his hands. 'But make sure that they're capable of getting the job done.'

'If we pick five each, that will be plenty. Even Spartacus can't kill ten men.'

'He's not alone, remember?'

'Surely you're not worried about that little sewer rat Carbo?'

'Worried? No. But he can handle himself in a fight.' Gannicus sucked in his moustache. 'Ten men should be enough, though.'

'They'd best leave tonight. Gods, but I'd love to go myself.' Castus eyed Gannicus sidelong. 'Make sure the job's done properly.'

'No.'

'Why not? Spartacus won't tell any tales afterwards.' He leered. 'Neither will his little catamite.'

'That Thracian has more lives than a cat. He might get away. Imagine that he does, and that he's seen you. What's the first thing he'd do?'

'All right, I see what you're getting at.' Castus' face soured. 'We would lose any chance of uniting the army under our command.'

'Precisely. But if we only send men whom we trust, who are not Gauls, there's far less of a trail back to us if things go wrong. And even if this doesn't work, we'll find another opportunity,' said Gannicus. 'The slyest cat uses up its lives in the end, eh?'

The next morning, Carbo and Spartacus rose early. Varus' cook served the trio a hearty breakfast of bread, honey, nuts and cheese. The rest of the domestic slaves, a dozen or more, gathered in the doorway and windows of the kitchen and stared in awe at Spartacus. Feeling sorry for them, he said nothing. They had all asked to come with him when they left, and he'd had to refuse. What he needed were hardened agricultural slaves and herdsmen, men who were used to the outdoors and, if possible, to hunting. The frustrated slaves had then wanted to turn on Varus, and he'd had to forbid that as well. 'You will only bring a sentence of death upon yourselves,' he'd warned. It wasn't uncommon for the authorities to execute every slave in a household in which the master had been murdered. For his own safety, therefore, and to ensure that he could make no attempt to escape, Varus, together with his major domo and doorman, had been locked overnight into an office.

Spartacus had resolved to confine the household slaves before they left. That way, Varus would have no real reason to punish them for not raising the alarm. What he hadn't yet decided was their best way of leaving the city. At dawn, he'd sent Tulla out to spy on the nearest gates. To Carbo's evident relief and Spartacus' amusement – he had judged the girl would honour her vow – she had soon returned. She reported that all the entrances were being heavily guarded. Many of those who sought to leave were being questioned. Not surprising, thought Spartacus.

'We should split up,' he said as they sat in the courtyard, listening to the muttered complaints issuing from Varus' prison. 'The guards will be looking for two men, not one.'

'What if you get taken?' asked Carbo.

'If I do, I do. The gods will decide my fate.' A wry shrug. 'That's why I'm giving you the gold. If I am captured, you are to find the army. As soon as the baby is strong enough to travel, you are to escort Ariadne away – as we previously discussed. The Scythians will go with you.'

The memory of the dawn before they'd fought Lentulus – and what Spartacus had asked him to do – was etched in Carbo's memory. He nodded miserably, feeling the loss of his parents even more. 'What of Navio? Egbeo? Pulcher? The rest of the men?'

'They can choose their own paths. It won't be up to me any longer. But whatever may happen to me, my family will be safe.'

'Of course. If the day should ever come, and I pray to the gods that it does not, I shall do everything in my power to save them.'

Spartacus gripped his shoulder. 'I know you will.'

'And if I am captured?' Carbo threw the words out to confront his fear. *At least my pain would end.*

'Your comrades and I will never forget you. We shall make offerings to the gods, and hold a feast in your honour. Inside the next two months, I shall send a man to check on the progress of your parents' tomb. If Varus hasn't done what he said, he'll lose a few fingers, and be warned that the next time, it will be his hands. That will hurry him along.'

A lump rose in Carbo's throat. 'Thank you.' It will not come to that, he told himself.

'Enough miserable talk,' declared Spartacus. 'Since when are soldiers good at seeing through disguises? We will both get through. If you cut down one of Varus' best togas, you can just act like a rich young noble.'

'Very well. What will you do?'

'Take the simplest option.' Spartacus' eyes let his eyes go vacant and his lower lip fall slackly. A trickle of spit dribbled down on to his chin. He made a noise halfway between a distressed animal and a man in pain. He shuffled across the courtyard, hunching his back and dragging one of his legs. All the while, he kept moaning.

Carbo stared in amazement. Tulla looked horrified.

Abruptly, Spartacus stood up. 'Convinced?' he asked with a smile.

They both shook their heads in assent.

'Good. That's settled then.' He eyed Tulla. 'I'd wager that the busiest times are the first few hours of the day, and the last hour before the gate shuts.'

'That's right.'

'There's no point waiting until sunset. We want to get as far from the city as possible today. We go now,' declared Spartacus. Inside, he wasn't quite so certain. Crassus would be sparing no effort to find him. The politician would suspect that if he was captured, the rebellion would soon be over. *How right he would be.* Castus and Gannicus were no generals. Navio was an able tactician, but because he was a Roman, many distrusted him. Egbeo and Pulcher were brave and capable enough, but they lacked the charisma necessary to hold together tens of thousands of men. *I have to get out. Great Rider, watch over me. Dionysus, help me to return to my wife, your priestess.* The prayers helped. Spartacus felt his inner calm return. 'Tulla, you will leave us before the gate. I'll pay you now.' He reached for the purse around his neck.

Dismay filled the girl's eyes. 'Now? But I might betray you!'

'I don't think you'll do that, will you?'

'No.'

'I knew it. You're a good girl.' It had been the right decision not to kill her, thought Spartacus.

Tulla's chin wobbled. 'I don't want you to go.'

'Of course you don't, but we must,' said Spartacus in a kindly tone. 'My army is waiting for me.' *And my wife and son.*

'Take me with you!'

'I cannot.'

'Why?' wailed Tulla.

'You cannot fight.'

'I can be a scout! I'll clean and polish your equipment. There must be something I can do.'

'Tulla, you have a stout heart, but you're too young.' Spartacus stooped to the girl's level. 'However, there is something you could do for me here.'

'Really?'

'Yes. I want you to hang around the Curia, the basilicae and the better classes of baths. You know, the places where senators tend to congregate. Keep your ears open and your mouth shut. See what you can find out. Any information about Crassus or their legions could be very useful.'

Tulla's eyes shone. 'I can do that!'

'I'm relying on you.' Spartacus clapped her on the arm. 'I'll send word to you at the Elysian Fields, on the ides of every month. You can tell the messenger everything that you've heard.'

'I will!'

Carbo admired Spartacus' ability to make people believe in him. The day before, he'd been on the point of killing the girl. Now she was eating out of his hand. Not only that, but he had neatly restored Tulla's pride. Now she had a purpose. As he himself did, with his oath to protect Ariadne. In the depths of his grief, that knowledge gave him strength.

Spartacus gave them both an encouraging nod. 'Let's move.'

Carbo's guts had turned to liquid by the time he came within thirty paces of the gate. The Thracian had opted to go ahead of Carbo. They had arranged to meet about a mile out of the city, by a tomb that they both remembered. Carbo and Tulla – who was still hanging around – had watched with bated breath as Spartacus had joined the queue that packed the street leading up to the gate. They had grinned at the loud exclamations of disgust and the way people had moved as far away from him as possible. Spartacus' idea of grabbing a fuller's bucket of urine and emptying it over himself had continued to pay off royally. The guards, supplemented by ten hard-faced legionaries, had begun to complain as soon as his ripe smell had hit their nostrils. When Spartacus had shuffled before them, dribbling, moaning and covered in piss, they had urged him out of the city with the butts of their pila.

It had been as easy as that, thought Carbo enviously. Great Jupiter, let it be the same for me. His prayer did little to ease his concerns, or to propel his feet forwards. Yet he couldn't hang around for much longer without starting to attract attention. Wealthy young men didn't loiter on street corners. Already he had had some strange looks.

Since the Thracian had left, Carbo had seen one man – a foreigner, maybe Greek or Dacian – accused of being Spartacus. Protesting his innocence in poor Latin, the man had been hammered to the ground in a flurry of blows, trussed up like a hen for the pot, and dragged off to be interrogated. After that, Carbo had hoped that the guards' vigilance would lapse a little, but it was not to be. They continued their aggressive questioning of all men of fighting age, as well as stabbing their pila into any carts loaded with merchandise.

Gods above, facing death in battle is easier than this.

'Good luck!' hissed Tulla from her spot against a wall a dozen paces away.

Carbo gave her a terse nod, and walked to join the line. He forced himself to take a deep breath in through his nostrils, counting his heartbeat as he exhaled. After he had done that several times, he felt calmer. A wagon drawn by two oxen pulled up behind him. Carbo half turned. One of the beasts sniffed at him, and then tried to lick his arm. Normally, he liked the way cattle did that, but now he recoiled from its long tongue and threw the carter a poisonous look. The man glared at him. 'It's what oxen do, isn't it? Won't do you no harm. Anyone who'd ever been around livestock would know that. Bloody city folk!'

Carbo sniffed haughtily and turned his back.

The man in front shuffled forward a few steps. He did the same.

And so it went for what seemed an eternity.

As he edged closer, Carbo strained his ears to pick out what the soldiers were saying. Most of the conversations were short.

'Name?'

'Julius Clodianus.'

'Trade?'

'Stonemason.'

'Where are you going?'

'To a new tomb about two miles out.'

There was a snort of laughter. 'Not your own then, I take it?'

'No,' the mason replied sourly. 'It's that of a rich lawyer. He requested that the family mausoleum be enlarged before his funeral. New brickwork, marble floor, expensive Greek statues: you name it, he wanted it. A dozen of us have been working on it fit to burst for a week now.'

'Trying to take it all with him, is he? It won't work!' The soldier jerked his head. 'On your way.'

The next man was a sailor on shore leave who was going to visit relations living in the countryside. He was ushered out with loud good wishes. The woman following was a villager who had been to Rome to seek Minerva's help at the temple on the Capitoline Hill. She called down the blessings of the goddess on the guards as they waved her through. Then there were only two more people in front of Carbo. Sweat oozed down the back of his neck. His skin prickled. Varus' toga had been cut down, but the wool was still heavy and over warm for the time of year. He shuffled forward, the barrage of shouted questions and answers merging into one.

'Next!'

Carbo blinked. The man ahead of him was already walking under the archway of the gate.

'Come on, young sir! We don't have all day.'

A second soldier leered. 'Daydreaming about your favourite whore?'

Carbo's anger made his flush grow deeper, and the legionaries, thinking he was embarrassed, roared with laughter.

'The lad must have been doing just that,' said the first man. He turned back to Carbo. 'Name?'

'Paullus Carbo,' he said proudly. He'd considered lying, but there was no need.

The soldier caught his regional accent. 'Not from Rome, are you?'

'No. I'm from Capua.'

'Been here for business or pleasure?' He winked at his companions.

Carbo scowled. 'Business.' *If only you knew what.* 'For my father.'

'Heading back to Capua?'

'Yes.'

'On foot? The likes of you normally ride or travel in a litter.'

Fortunately, Carbo had thought of the answer to this question. He looked down. 'My horse is gone.'

'Stolen from the inn's stables, was it?'

'No. I wagered it.'

'Fortuna's tits! And you lost it?'

More hoots of amusement.

'That's right.'

'So now you have to walk back to Capua?'

Carbo nodded, making his expression as sulky as when he'd been a boy.

The legionary pulled a face. 'A hundred miles is a long way to walk.'

'And don't we know it?' added his comrade, chortling. 'We have to do it while carrying half our bodyweight in equipment!'

'Can I go?' asked Carbo resentfully.

'Eh? Yes, you can go,' the soldier replied. 'Have a safe journey. There are plenty of latrones about between here and Capua.'

'If you're really unlucky, you might even meet Spartacus,' said the second man. 'That is, if he's—'

'Shut it!' barked the first legionary.

His companion turned away with a scowl.

'On your way,' ordered the legionary.

Muttering his thanks, Carbo made his way out of the gate. The soldier's words had made his mind race back to their attack on Crassus. Caepio had shouted something. What had it been? 'It is them!' To his frustration, Carbo couldn't remember the exact words. Then another misgiving surfaced. When the patrol had arrived at the Elysian Fields, a man had come out of the tavern, and nodded to the officer in charge. Had it been more than casual conversation? Carbo wasn't sure. But when he put the two instances together with the comment by the soldier at the gate, he felt very suspicious indeed. Was it possible that Crassus had known that

Spartacus was in Rome? His pace picked up. He had to tell Spartacus at once.

They had a spy in their midst.

It didn't take Carbo long to reach the tomb. He found Spartacus sitting in the shade of a cypress tree that stood beside it.

Spartacus raised a hand in greeting. 'You look hot.'

'This damn toga,' said Carbo, wiping his brow with the back of his arm. 'It's not the weather to be wearing it.'

'But it got you out of Rome, and at least you didn't have to cover yourself in piss.'

Carbo grinned. 'True.'

'Was Tulla still there when you left?'

'Yes.'

'You made a good call with her.' He clapped Carbo on the arm.

He swallowed, remembering his leader's tacit threat to kill him if Tulla should prove treacherous. 'Thanks.'

Spartacus heaved himself to his feet. 'Let's start walking. I remember a well not far down the road; we can wash there.'

'There's something you need to know first.'

Spartacus' eyes narrowed. 'What is it? Tell me as we go.'

Quickly, Carbo filled him in on his suspicions. When he had finished, Spartacus did not say anything for a long time. Carbo watched him nervously, wondering whether the Thracian thought he was crazy.

'Interesting,' said Spartacus.

A sense of relief crept over Carbo. Spartacus believed him.

'We must have been followed out of the camp. So few people knew about it that there wouldn't have been time to send word to Rome before we left.'

Carbo's mouth went dry at the thought of a new possibility. 'Do you think Castus or Gannicus would have done it?'

Spartacus frowned. 'There's no way that Gannicus would betray us like that. I doubt if even Castus would. He hates my guts, and he wouldn't cry if I were killed, but he hates Rome as much as I do.'

'Who then?'

'It could be anyone, Carbo. In an army of sixty thousand men, not all of them are going to be happy. That's without taking into account the women and hangers-on.'

'Yes, but to betray you?'

Spartacus thumped him. 'Not everyone is as loyal as you.'

'Well they should be,' muttered Carbo, blushing. 'We *have* to find out who it is.'

'That would be like trying to find a needle in a haystack.' Spartacus shrugged. 'Atheas and Taxacis will watch my back. So will you.' *It's just another enemy to add to the ones I already have.* But he didn't need to worry about being murdered for a few days. The journey south should be easy; they might as well make the most of it. 'Where's that well? I can't pitch up at the camp stinking of piss. No one would take me seriously.'

Carbo's tension eased, and he let out a chuckle. 'Between my nerves as I went through the gate and this damn toga, I've sweated out half the bloody Tiber.'

Spartacus made a show of leaning over and inhaling. 'No. I can't smell a thing except piss.'

'You reek,' said Carbo, guffawing. He'd never seen Spartacus act so light-hearted.

'Then the sooner we get there, the better, eh?'

Carbo strode out with new energy. Other than the wish to see his parents' tomb one day, he had no reason to return to the capital, or Capua, where he'd grown up. He was with Spartacus. Carbo had always been loyal to the Thracian, but the discovery of his parents' deaths had made that bond even stronger. It had also brought home to him the importance of his comrades. Men like Navio and Atheas, and even Arnax and Publipor, were his family now. The knowledge made his grief easier to bear.

Alerted by his major domo, Crassus turned from the half-circle of men around him. 'Ah, Caepio! Welcome!' he said genially. He beckoned to the veteran centurion who stood in the doorway of the tablinum, waiting to be called in.

Caepio marched in proudly. Sunlight entering from the square hole in the centre of the roof glinted off the phalerae on his chest. He came to a halt before Crassus and saluted. 'I came as soon as I got your message, sir.'

'Good. All well since yesterday?'

'Yes, thank you, sir. As you know, I wasn't hurt. I'm just sorry that I didn't get to kill Spartacus.'

'You did a fine job stopping his accomplice. If there had been two of them, things might have come to a different ending. For me at least!'

'Thank the gods that you weren't injured, sir, but I'd still be happier if I'd buried my blade in his guts.'

Crassus' lips turned upwards. 'See the mettle of this man? He is the embodiment of Roman virtus. This is what every soldier should aspire to.'

There was a polite murmur of assent.

'Caepio, meet some of the legates who will command my legions. This is Gnaeus Tremelius Scrofa.' A tall, thin man inclined his head in reply to Caepio's salute. 'Lucius Mummius Achaicus.' A stocky officer with a haughty expression met Caepio's salutation. 'Quintus Marcius Rufus.' There was a smile from a short man with spiky black hair. 'Caius Pomptinus.' This one was clearly a cavalryman, thought Caepio. He had bandier legs than an ape. 'Lucius Quinctius.' Older than the rest, he was the only one to half bow at the centurion. A commoner originally, like me, decided Caepio. 'And last but definitely not least, Gaius Julius Caesar, one of my tribunes,' said Crassus.

'Honoured to meet you, sir.' Caepio saluted for the sixth time. Like everyone, he'd heard the story about Caesar's capture and imprisonment on Pharmacussa. Here was a man with real balls. 'Ready to crucify a few slaves, as you did with those pirates, sir?'

'More than ready, centurion.'

Caepio's smile reminded Crassus of a wolf he'd seen cornered in the arena. His decision to recruit the veteran had been a good one. He wondered sometimes if Caepio fully approved of him – he wasn't a career soldier after all – but he didn't care that much. Caepio had seen how Crassus longed to destroy Spartacus, which, after his experience at the munus, was exactly what he wanted too. 'Now that the introductions are over, let's get down to business. I've called you here for a council of war. I know that you were not expecting to do more than assemble your units over the next couple of months, but yesterday's events have changed everything. Spartacus cannot be allowed to strike at me – at Rome – with such impunity. We must respond swiftly!'

Caepio growled in approval. 'Catch them unawares, that's what we want to do!'

'What are you suggesting, sir?' asked Scrofa. 'Increasing the number of troops at the gates?'

'No,' said Crassus as if to a child. 'It was a slim hope that we would catch Spartacus leaving the city. We can safely assume that the whoreson has flown the coop by now.' He gave Mummius a hard look.

'My soldiers interrogated everyone whom they thought was suspicious, sir. More than a hundred men were detained.'

Crassus glanced at Caepio, who shook his head. 'None of whom proved to be Spartacus.'

'No, sir, but—'

'Quiet, Mummius. You failed! If you had moved faster, we might be interrogating Spartacus right now, instead of planning our campaign against him.' Crassus knew he was being hard on Mummius, but the man needed to know who was in charge. He – and the others – had to be sent a clear message from the start.

Mummius lapsed into a glowering silence.

'As you know, I had intended spending the autumn and winter filling our recruitment quotas, and in arming and training the men. Now I want to bring our plans forward. Significantly.'

'The number of volunteers has been exceptional, sir,' agreed Quinctius. 'And the workshops are also turning out equipment at a great rate.'

'I should bloody hope so. I'm paying twice the market rate for every item to all the smiths for a hundred miles!' Crassus raised a hand, silencing the chuckles this produced. 'My intention is that the army is to be ready to march in a month.'

'A month?' repeated Quinctius.

'But the men won't be ready, sir,' said Scrofa. 'Basic training takes at least eight weeks.'

'I know that,' replied Crassus acidly. 'The ground to the south of Rome is flat. The recruits can train every day after we have finished marching.' Ignoring his officers' surprise, Crassus went on, 'Up until now, Rome has been humiliated by Spartacus. That time has now gone! No doubt the slaves are expecting to have an easy few months while we prepare our forces. Well, they're going to have none of that. We're going to take the war to them straightaway. Isn't that right, Caepio?'

'Damn right, sir.'

'I know that thousands of veterans have heard your call and joined up, sir, and that we have the remnants of the consuls' legions, about fourteen thousand men, but over half the army is made up of new recruits,' said Scrofa. 'Would it not be wiser to wait until they have been fully trained until we move against Spartacus?'

'Who is the commander here?' barked Crassus. 'I make the bloody decisions, not you. Or any of the rest of you! Is that clear?'

'Yes, sir,' Scrofa muttered.

'We move in four weeks. It takes more than a month to march to Thurii. That's eight weeks in total. With veterans like Caepio on our side, I would suggest that that's plenty of time to train the men.'

'That's sufficient time for my soldiers to be ready, sir,' Mummius declared eagerly.

'I should think so! Given that you and Rufus each command a legion formerly led by one of the consuls, you have the least number of raw recruits.'

Mummius coloured. Rufus also looked embarrassed.

'My troops will be prepared, so help me Jupiter,' said Scrofa.

The other officers hastily added their agreements.

Crassus studied their faces. Their resolve seemed genuine. It was a start. 'Very well.'

'What is your plan when we find Spartacus, sir?' asked Scrofa.

'It's very simple. We bring him to bay like a boar on a hunt. Ready our legions. Soften his men up with catapults. Advance, and butcher the lot of them. And that will be that.' His eyes roved challengingly over them. It was Scrofa, whom he'd already judged to be one of the most courageous, who spoke first.

'You really think it will be that simple, sir?'

'Yes, Scrofa, I do. The time has come to rid Italy of Spartacus and his filth. What better way to do it than in head-to-head battle? That has ever been the way of Rome's magnificent legions.' He glanced at Caepio, who rumbled his approval.

'But the men who have fought Spartacus before, sir, they—' Mummius hesitated.

'We all know that they have run before,' said Crassus in a silky tone.

'And if it happens again, they will be punished so severely that none of them will ever think of running again.'

In the lull that followed, the only sounds were the voices of slaves who were tending the plants in the central courtyard.

Crassus pinned them one by one with his stare. 'I am talking of decimation.'

Quinctius' mouth opened and closed like a fish out of water.

'Decimation, gentlemen. Do you understand?'

'Yes, sir,' was the unanimous, shocked response.

'That practice hasn't been used for generations, sir,' ventured Scrofa.

'All the more reason to revive it then,' said Crassus. 'Anyone else?'

No one except Caepio and Caesar met his gaze.

'Excellent.' It was good that his officers were so horrified, thought Crassus. Anger was still coursing through his veins at the thought of how nearly Spartacus had come to killing him. 'I meant every word that I said. I will do whatever it takes to defeat that Thracian son of a whore. Whatever it takes.'

I swear to you, great Jupiter, that I will not rest until he is — or I am — dead.

Chapter XI

When the time came that day to search out a suitable place to set up camp, the pair were nowhere near a village, or even an inn. Carbo was glad. It had been a week since they'd left Rome. The high temperatures had meant that even when they climbed away from the fertile plain of Campania with its dense pattern of farms and estates and into the more mountainous region of Lucania, it was pleasant to sleep outdoors. Their solitude meant they could talk without the worry of being overheard. They had provisions, wine and blankets, and the horses they'd bought four days prior meant that they could ride in search of the most secluded sites with ease.

To Carbo's chagrin, he'd had to continue wearing Varus' toga each day. As Spartacus said, it gave him a wealthy air, which would explain, should anyone comment, why his 'slave' was astride a horse rather than walking. Having to bake daily in the thick woollen garment was another reason that Carbo preferred camping. Every evening, with Spartacus watching in amusement, he would strip off the toga and jump into the nearest stream to wash off the day's accumulation of sweat. He shifted his shoulders unhappily, looking forward to doing the same again as soon as they'd stopped. After that, he could relax by the fire with a hunk of bread and cheese, and a beaker of wine.

He would try, for a while at least, to forget his sorrow over his parents. Even though Carbo had done what he'd thought was best at the time – entering the ludus to earn money – he was still racked by guilt over his decision. Guilt that he hadn't stayed with his parents, and gone to Rome with them. Guilt that he hadn't sent any money to them in the subsequent months, or tried harder to establish contact. Deep down, he knew these thoughts for fantasies, but that didn't ease his pain. To cope, he stoked his hatred for Crassus into a white-hot flame. If it wasn't for him, his parents would still be alive. Give me one more chance to kill Crassus before I die, he prayed repeatedly.

Carbo hoped that Spartacus would tell more tales of his youth in Thrace. He had been surprised and intrigued over the previous few nights as his leader had opened up more than he ever had. Carbo now knew the names of Spartacus' father, mother and brother, as well as his childhood friends. He'd listened avidly to tales of hunting boar and wolves, of raiding horses and sheep from neighbouring tribes, and to dramatic legends about the Great Rider, the deity favoured by most Thracian warriors. Carbo didn't realise it, but Spartacus' stories were partially aimed at taking his mind off his parents. The Thracian had seen him brooding as they rode.

Spartacus made little or no mention of the war waged by his tribe on Rome, or of his time with the legions. Carbo had been content with that; he wanted no reminders of the reality of their own situation. Both men were enjoying the relative freedom from worry that their journey had granted them.

Behind him, Spartacus was thinking about Ariadne, and wondering if she had yet given birth. He made a silent request of the gods that she would have a straightforward labour. Women who didn't often died, along with their infants. That grim thought made him wish that they had resolved their differences before he'd left. It would be the first thing to do upon their return, he decided. It was pointless letting arguments go on for this long, especially when danger – or death – lurked around every corner.

For the moment, though, they were still on the road. He might as well enjoy the loud *churring* of the cicadas from the oaks and chestnuts on each side. Relax to the *clop, clop, clop* of their mounts' hooves off the basalt slabs. Relish the heat of the sun, which was slowly dropping towards the jagged-tipped mountains to the west. If he ignored the fact that the road was paved, he could almost be in the Thrace of his youth, an all-too-brief time when he had been utterly carefree.

The skin on the back of Spartacus' neck prickled, and he turned his head. In the haze that shimmered over the road, he saw a small figure, approaching fast. Behind it thundered three more riders. 'Company,' he said quietly. 'Four horsemen.'

With a start, Carbo came back to the present. He twisted around to see. 'Are they messengers?'

'More likely a messenger with an escort,' said Spartacus.

'His message must be important. They normally travel alone. Where are they heading? Pompeii and Paestum are behind us.'

'Perhaps Crassus is sending word to Thurii, hoping it will reach the city before our army.'

Carbo took a mad notion. 'Two to one isn't bad odds, eh?'

'Don't go getting any ideas. They'll be armed with swords. Whatever news they're carrying isn't worth risking our lives for.'

Carbo settled back on his horse. Spartacus was right.

They rode on, glancing regularly behind them. When the riders had drawn nearer, the pair guided their mounts into the shade of the trees on one side of the road. They watched as the lead horseman approached at the gallop, followed a short distance later by his three companions.

Any doubt about the man's job vanished as he came closer. He was wearing typical military dress: a mail shirt over a padded tunic and a crested bronze-bowl helmet. A leather satchel bounced up and down off his right hip, and a long cavalry sword hung from a baldric over his left shoulder. His mount was of fine quality, and it carried an 'SPQR' brand halfway down its neck.

Perhaps it *would* be worth finding out what message he was carrying, Spartacus thought with a flash of devilment. No. I've been in enough danger recently.

The rider gave them a haughty look as he drew level, but he didn't check his steed.

'Safe journey, friend,' called Carbo.

All he got by way of reply was a grunt, and then the messenger was gone.

Carbo's pulse increased as his gaze returned to the three horsemen to the rear. If there was to be any danger, it was from this trio, whose job was a fraction less urgent than the lead rider. The first two galloped past without as much as a glance at them, and he began to relax. Carbo barely saw the small stone that was sent flying by the back hooves of the lead horse. It shot up like a slingshot to strike the last horseman in the face. He bellowed in pain and did well not to lose his seat. With a savage tug on the reins, he brought his mount to a halt in front of Spartacus' and Carbo's position. Cursing, he fingered the deep cut on his right cheek, which was already bleeding heavily.

'Are you all right?' asked Carbo.

'Eh?' He only seemed to notice them now. 'Yes, yes. It's but a flesh wound.' He dragged free a strip of cloth that was wound around his baldric and pressed it to his face.

'Men such as you must be used to far worse,' said Carbo, adopting an admiring tone.

'True. It certainly won't stop me getting to Messana.'

Spartacus pricked his ears at the last word. *Messana is on Sicily.*

The messenger gave them an appraising look. 'You risk getting hurt yourself, young master, being out on the road with no one but your slave. Don't you know about Spartacus and his rabble? They control much of southern Italy now. Come across any of them, and it's the last thing you'll ever do.'

'I know all too well, but my family has few slaves left,' said Carbo with a sigh. 'They pillaged our farm a month or so ago; most of them ran off then to join Spartacus. The local militia wouldn't do a thing about it, of course: they're too damn scared. Father sent me to Rome, to ask for help at the Senate. I was there last week to hear Crassus speak. It was wonderful! Our suffering won't last for ever, thank the gods. Ten legions he's raising!'

'That's right,' said the rider with a confident grin. 'When they march south, the ground will tremble. Spartacus' slaves will soil their pants at the sight of them.'

A shout echoed down the road, and the rider gave Carbo a friendly wink. 'I'd best be off. May you reach your door safely. Tell your father to remain steadfast and to pray to Jupiter.'

A nerve twitched in Spartacus' cheek, but the messenger didn't notice.

'How soon will Crassus march?' asked Carbo.

'That's something only he knows. But it will be sooner than you think! The bastard slaves will get the shock of their lives when the legions come down this road! Farewell.' With an evil laugh, he rode away.

'Curse Fortuna for the old bitch that she is!' Carbo spat under his breath.

He glanced at Spartacus, whose face bore a black scowl. 'How soon do you think he's talking about?'

'Who knows? It can't be any quicker than three months, I wouldn't have thought. The legions are only being raised now. The soldiers have to be trained before he can even consider fighting us. At least we heard it in advance. It gives us time to plan. Imagine if the first thing we'd heard was that Crassus' army was ten or fifteen miles from Thurii.'

Carbo didn't especially want to think about that. 'What will we do?'

'Do? We wait a while until those whoresons are gone, and we hightail it back to our camp, wherever that is.'

'I meant when Crassus gets here.' Carbo had avoided asking Spartacus about it until now.

Spartacus' lips peeled back, revealing his teeth. 'Why, then we fight. We fight!' *To the end, whatever that may be. Victory – or death!* 'Don't think that I am out of tricks,' he added. 'I'm not. By a long way.'

Carbo nodded. Rallying his courage, he swore a silent oath to himself. If – when – that fight came, he would stand in the line with everyone else. With Spartacus. To the bitter end. Even if it meant his own death. Standing shoulder to shoulder with those whom he loved was all that mattered. That, and killing Crassus. He glanced at Spartacus, who was whistling a tuneless ditty under his breath. *Gods, does nothing scare him?* Carbo felt prouder than ever to follow the Thracian.

By the time the sun had set, they were sitting by a small fire, blankets around their shoulders and skins of wine in hand. The tethered horses watched them, happy now that they had been watered and fed. As usual, their camp was close to a stream and out of sight of the Via Annia. They had tracked uphill some quarter of a mile through the woods, coming upon a little dell that was dominated by a massive fallen beech. Placing its bulk between them and the road had been a natural choice. Although they'd had no indication that there had been any pursuit from Rome, it paid to be cautious.

'That messenger mentioned that he was travelling to Messana,' said Spartacus.

'On Sicily, yes. What's that got to do with us?'

'Two slave rebellions took place there in the last hundred years, didn't they? Do you know much about them?'

'Only what my father told me when I was younger.'

'Try to remember everything you can.'

Carbo's curiosity grew. 'The first one started sixty-odd years ago near the city of Enna. It was led by a slave called Eunus, a Syrian who was reputed to be able to predict the future thanks to messages sent to him by the gods.'

Spartacus thought of Ariadne, and a half-smile tugged its way on to his lips.

'Eunus had been approached by some slaves who were being mistreated by their masters. Encouraged by his prophecies, several hundred of them fell upon the inhabitants of Enna. They slaughtered everyone, even the babies and the domestic animals.' Carbo thought with repugnance of the carnage he'd seen in Forum Annii the day that they had attacked it. Of the violent end that Chloris had suffered. Yet thanks to Spartacus, the violence had not been as severe as it had in Enna. It was something to be grateful for, he supposed bitterly.

'Go on.'

'Hearing the news, many slaves ran away to join Eunus. Soon he had more than ten thousand men under his command, and he crowned himself king. In the subsequent weeks, he and his troops fought the local Roman forces several times and overwhelmed them by sheer weight of numbers. Before long, another uprising began elsewhere on the island. It was led by a Cilician by the name of Kleon. However, instead of fighting Eunus as the Romans hoped, he united with him. The slaves inflicted numerous more defeats on the Romans over the next three years. Finally, the Senate sent Publius Rupilius, one of the consuls, to deal with the uprising.'

'I wonder if they took so long to react properly because Sicily is so far from Rome,' mused Spartacus.

'That's what people say.'

'And the second rebellion?'

'It followed much the same path. Bad treatment of slaves. A charismatic leader, who was supposed to be able to talk to the gods. Widespread massacres of the local population.'

'How long did it last for?'

'Four years, until the Senate sent a senior general to deal with it.'

'Were the leaders of either uprising trained soldiers?'

'Not as far as I know.'

Spartacus' heart leaped. *What could I do in a place like that then!* 'Why Sicily, though?'

'My father always said that it was because of the density of its farms, and the huge number of agricultural slaves.'

'They would provide us with thousands more recruits, eh?'

'Two legions are stationed there.'

'Two legions haven't posed much problem for us before, have they?'

'I suppose. But how would we get our soldiers across the straits?'

'Simple. Sicily grows much of the grain that feeds Italy, doesn't it? The ships that carry the grain are immense. I've seen them. We'd just need to get a thousand or so men over to the main merchant port, seize as many as we could, and sail them back to the mainland.' Spartacus grimaced. 'Our main worry would be the Roman navy.'

'I doubt they'd be much problem. Since the last war with Carthage, the navy has been in decline. Pirates from Cilicia and Crete all but control the Mediterranean. They frequently take ships off the southern Italian coastline.'

'Is that right?' asked Spartacus, smacking one fist into the other with delight.

'That's what I've heard. The bastards even sail up the coast as far as Ostia. The Senate makes angry noises about them, but nothing much has been done since Publius Servilius Vatia's campaign ended early three years ago. Any ships the Republic has have been busy in the war against Mithridates of Pontus.'

'That's excellent, Carbo. Maybe pirates can carry us over to attack the grain ships, eh?'

A slow smile spread across Carbo's face. Spartacus' plan sounded crazy, but they had succeeded so often before when the odds were stacked against them. Why couldn't they one more time? 'That sounds good.'

'It's time to get some rest,' said Spartacus with a yawn. 'Your turn to take first watch. Wake me in a few hours.' Arranging his blanket, he lay down by the fire. He was asleep within moments.

Carbo placed another piece of wood on the flames. Then he sat back and listened and watched. The fire crackled and spat a stream of orange sparks into the air. Fifteen paces away, the horses were two large black shapes spotlit against the beeches. A gentle breeze carried up from the valley below, making the branches of the trees creak. Fallen leaves rustled nearby as a small creature went about its night-time business. An owl called. From the stream came the reassuring murmur of moving water. Carbo relaxed. Before he had moved to Capua, he had lived for years on the family's farm outside the town. The sounds of nature were familiar, and comforting.

Soon his eyelids drooped. Carbo fought the creeping languor for a little while, but every time he roused himself, he heard and saw nothing of concern. It had been the same since they'd left Rome, he thought sleepily. What could it matter if he had a brief rest?

Some time later, he awoke with a start. He glanced around, heart pounding. A few paces away, Spartacus was sound asleep. The clearing was empty. The stream pattered down the slope, talking to itself. Far off, a wolf howled its loneliness at the sliver of moon that was just visible through the canopy. Everything was as it had been, apart from the fire, which had all but gone out. Carbo's blanket had slipped off his shoulders, and he felt chilled to the bone. *Gods, I must have been asleep for hours.* Feeling guilty, he began poking at the ashes with a stick to see if there was any chance of rekindling the blaze. He was pleased to see that there were still some hot embers.

One of the horses nickered and shifted from foot to foot.

Carbo froze. Grateful now for the night vision that the fire's absence gave him, he peered in the direction of their mounts. As before, he could only see their outline against the darker shadows of the trees.

Nothing happened for several moments, and his concern eased.

The horse nickered a second time.

Carbo tensed again. Pricking his ears, he stared at the beasts.

Nothing.

There was silence for a short while.

Then the horse stamped a hoof on the ground.

Now Carbo's stomach twisted into a painful knot. Letting the blanket slip from his shoulders, he crept over to Spartacus. He placed a hand on the Thracian's shoulder, praying that Spartacus wouldn't make a noise.

To Carbo's relief, he came awake instantly – and silently. He sat up.

Carbo placed his lips against Spartacus' ear. 'One of the horses isn't happy.'

'Anything else?'

'I heard a wolf. Far off, though. That's it.'

Spartacus nodded. He pointed with a finger around the dell and then put to a hand to his ear.

They sat side by side, waiting. Listening with all their might.

An owl hooted off to their right. The sound didn't concern Carbo, but he felt Spartacus stiffen.

When the cry was answered from the trees to their left, Carbo was nearly sick. The horse being unsettled and two owls being so close could not be a coincidence. When a third call reached their ears, any doubts in his mind vanished. *Shit.*

Spartacus moved his face close to Carbo's. His mouth framed the words 'Let's go.'

'The horses?'

'Leave them.'

Carbo saw Spartacus draw his dagger, and quickly did the same. On hands and knees, and making as little noise as possible, they crawled uphill, away from the fire. Twenty paces on, Carbo heard more owl calls to their rear. His skin crawled. They were closer this time. Expecting to feel a blade sinking into his spine with every step, he followed the Thracian.

Spartacus didn't look back. He increased his speed, aware that they had to get out of the clearing fast. Every instinct was screaming that there were men out there who had come to kill him. There were three at least, but that wouldn't be all of them. Anyone who wanted to slay Spartacus would send no less than six to eight men, perhaps more. He ripped open his knee against a protruding root, and had to bite his lip against the pain of it. He crawled on, cursing the fact that there was almost no undergrowth. Although there was little to impede their progress, it also meant that there were far fewer places to hide.

More owl calls. Spartacus counted them. One. Two. Three. Four. He thanked the Great Rider that none originated in front of their position. They hadn't been surrounded – yet.

Finally, he reached the dell's edge, and a large oak tree with a split trunk. He stood up. Carbo bundled in beside him and without speaking, they both looked back towards their fire, which was discernible by the faint orange light of the last glowing embers.

Show yourselves, you bastards, thought Spartacus.

Carbo felt as if he were in a nightmare. It was his fault for falling asleep. Who in the name of Hades was hunting them?

Nothing happened for the space of thirty heartbeats. 'They're making sure that we're asleep before they move,' Spartacus hissed.

First one horse, then the other whinnied.

All at once, four shadows emerged into sight, three spilling over the fallen beech and one rushing in from its far end. They could just make out the spears gripped in each figure's right fist. The men ran straight at the piles of discarded bedding. A brief, frenzied flurry of blows rained down on the blankets, but the assassins soon realised that their quarry had vanished. Muttered curses filled the air, and one man growled, 'The bastards have gone!'

A hefty cuff round the head from one of his companions silenced him. Another owl call rang out, more urgent this time. The men spread out, moving on the balls of their feet across the clearing. Towards Spartacus and Carbo.

'Time to go,' whispered Spartacus.

'Which way?' asked Carbo, desperation tearing at him.

'Up. We'll go slowly at first, but when I say, we run like the wind. That is, if you want to live!' Spartacus' teeth glinted in the moonlight, and Carbo wished again that he had his leader's courage. Jamming his knife back into its sheath – he didn't want to drop it – he nodded grimly.

'I'm ready.'

'Good lad.' Spartacus turned and padded away as silently as a wolf.

Carbo's memories of that night would stay with him for ever. He had never had the need to travel in the mountains at night before, and hoped that he never had to again. At least not when he was being pursued by an unknown number of armed men, when all he had was a measly dagger. At first, the going was easy enough, but soon Spartacus began loping up the slope with long, ground-covering strides. *How the hell can he see where he's going?* Carbo wondered, following as fast as he could. His heart hammered in his chest, not from the effort of running, but from fear. He felt as if he were a deer being pursued by a group of hunters. Behind every tree and bush lurked a potential enemy, and with each step he risked breaking his ankle on a jutting root or a piece of deadwood. He had previously thought that he had a good sense of direction, but their journey changed his opinion. The dense canopy overhead afforded only the occasional glance at the night sky, which confused him even more. Spartacus, on the other hand, sped onwards and upwards as if Hermes, the messenger of the gods, was guiding his every step.

Every so often, they halted to listen out for sounds of pursuit. On the first occasion, they could discern the faint noise of men moving below them, but these had receded by the time they paused a second time. After that, to Spartacus' satisfaction and Carbo's immense relief, they heard nothing else. Carbo hoped that the Thracian might slow down after this, but he was sadly disappointed. Spartacus began to move even faster, his feet flying over the ground as if they had wings. It was hard for Carbo to keep up, and to avoid having his eyes taken out by the whipping recoil of the branches that Spartacus pushed aside.

Perhaps an hour had elapsed when they reached the crest of a ridge. Moving along it for a short distance, they came to a clearing. For the first time, they had a good view of the sky, which was illuminated by a myriad of glittering stars. The moon's position overhead told them that there were still many hours until daybreak. Spartacus peered into the open space for a moment before he entered it, cat soft on his feet. Carbo followed, casting frequent uneasy glances to their rear. He heard nothing. For the first time, his unease settled a fraction.

'If there was any light, we'd have a good view from here.' Spartacus pointed out into the blackness.

'Where in Hades are we?'

'I've no idea,' replied Spartacus with a grin. 'But I think this ridge is the same one that flanks the Via Appia, which means it runs roughly in a north–south direction. We'll just follow it.'

'We could end up miles off course.' Carbo instantly felt like a fool. 'But we don't really have an alternative, eh?'

'No,' replied Spartacus grimly. 'Those whoresons will be on our trail the moment it gets light, so we have to travel as far as we can before then. Gods, but I'd love to stay behind, though. Lay an ambush for them, maybe take a prisoner.'

'Find out who they are?'

'Yes!'

'I don't think they were Roman.'

'Nor do I. If we'd been followed from Rome, they would have already attacked us. It's nothing to do with the messenger whom we spoke with either. He wasn't interested in us.'

'It's not just that. The man who spoke had a strong accent. There's no way that he was a native Latin speaker.'

'It's as I thought. Only someone who knew that we'd gone to Rome could be responsible.'

Alarm filled Carbo. 'You mean Castus or Gannicus?'

'Yes, or someone else with a grudge against me.' *The bastards. How dare they, after all I've done for them?* If the pair had appeared at that moment, Spartacus would have torn them apart limb from limb.

'Damn traitors!'

'It's to be expected. Many men don't like following one leader. If it had been in Thrace, it could have happened before now,' said Spartacus, glad that he'd stayed.

'Maybe we could grab one,' Carbo began.

'No! We saw four of them, and I'd wager that was less than half their number.'

'Then we'll have no way of finding out who sent the treacherous bastards,' protested Carbo.

'Sometimes you have to live with uncertainty.' Spartacus nudged him. 'It keeps a man on his toes!'

Carbo pulled a smile, but it felt more like a grimace.

'We'll find out more when we get back,' Spartacus declared. 'You did well to wake me when you did. I don't think it's too much to say that I owe you my life. Thank you.'

Pride filled Carbo. Then, remembering how he'd only woken from his nap by chance, his throat closed with guilt. He could never admit to it. 'A-any time,' he managed to mumble. 'It's no more than you've done for me.'

Spartacus flashed him a confident grin. 'Come on. It's a long way until we reach safety.' He didn't voice the worry that had been gnawing at him since he'd had time to consider who might have sent out the killers. *Great Rider, I ask you to keep Ariadne – and our baby – safe.* He turned and sped towards the far side of the clearing.

Dusk was falling the next day when they reached the army's camp. Carbo was footsore, thirsty and more hungry than he ever could remember being, but he was alive. He wanted to cheer. 'We've made it.'

'Not yet, we haven't.'

He stared at Spartacus in shock. 'But that's our army. It won't take long to go down the slope.'

'We've been gone more than two weeks. Who knows what's happened in that time?' If Castus and Gannicus were capable of sending assassins after him, what else might they have done?

'What shall we do then? Do you want to' – Carbo swallowed the word *hide* – 'stay here while I check things out?'

Spartacus chuckled. 'I'm not scared – I'm just being cautious. We'll aim for the larger tents in the middle. That's where Ariadne and the Scythians will be.'

'What are your plans after that? Are we going to round up a few cohorts and kill the Gauls?'

'There's nothing I'd like to do more if it's they who are responsible,' snarled Spartacus. 'But they've been hard at work ensuring the loyalty of their followers. If they were killed, upwards of ten thousand men might desert. That's a loss I can't afford right now.'

'So you're going to let them get away with it?'

'That's not what I said at all,' replied Spartacus with a small smile. 'Let's go. Keep your head down as you walk. Most men won't even notice us.'

'If you say so.' Carbo nervously touched the hilt of his dagger for reassurance.

'I do. You go first. I'll follow.'

Praying that Spartacus was right, Carbo led the way. It wasn't long before they started meeting soldiers: men who were returning from an afternoon hunting, a tryst with a woman in the privacy of the woods, or simply those who needed a place to void their bowels. Carbo ignored everyone he met. If a greeting was thrown in his direction, he grunted a reply and moved on. Spartacus kept close behind him, his gaze aimed at the ground.

They reached the camp without incident. Rather than walking in the avenues that regularly split up the tents, Carbo opted to walk in the narrow gaps between them. It meant having continually to step over guy ropes, but there was far less chance of anyone noticing them. As he soon realised, it was also a good way of eavesdropping on conversations.

'How much further is Thurii anyway?'

'Not more than fifty miles, my officer says.'

From another tent, 'Hades below, who farted? It stinks worse than a rotting corpse.'

A snort of laughter. 'You shouldn't have fed us all those greens for dinner!'

Carbo smiled, looking forward to renewing his banter with Navio and Arnax.

'Where the fuck is Spartacus?' asked a deep voice from outside the next tent. 'He's been gone how long now?'

Carbo felt a tap on his back from the Thracian. He stopped.

'Nearly three weeks.'

'Not coming back then, is he?'

'You don't know that,' argued the second voice. 'Who are we to know when he'll return? He's the leader of this army. He does what he thinks best.'

'Pah! He's either not coming back, or he's dead in a ditch somewhere. What was the prick thinking? Leaving us with only those filthy Gauls to lead us?'

'Egbeo and Pulcher are in charge too, you know. Many men also listen to Ariadne. She has Dionysus' ear, remember,' said a third man.

'For the moment, maybe. But you mark my words,' growled the deep voice. 'It won't be long before they're all murdered. You know what Castus and Gannicus are like. They're a pair of sewer rats. They won't lose any sleep over killing a woman and child.'

Carbo's mouth opened and closed. He turned to the Thracian, whose face was twisted in a combination of delight and rage. 'Wait,' mouthed Spartacus.

'Come on, things aren't that bad. We've nearly reached Thurii. There hasn't been a sign of any Roman forces for weeks. Spartacus will appear any day now, and all will be well again.'

'If he does, I'll eat my bloody sandals,' declared the first voice. 'And when the Gauls take charge, I'm not hanging about to see what happens.'

There was a rumble of assent from some of their comrades.

To Carbo's surprise, he felt Spartacus shove past him, around the corner of the tent. Gripping his knife hilt, he followed.

They found a group of six men sitting around a small fire upon which sat a bronze pot full of bubbling stew. The group were dressed in roughly spun cream, red or brown tunics. All of them had knives, but only two were wearing baldrics and sheathed gladii. A stack of weapons – spears, pila and swords – lay a few steps away, along with a heap of scuta.

Spartacus curled his lip at the ring of surprised faces. 'Greetings.'

'Who in damnation are you?' demanded a bald man with a strong chin.

His was the deep voice, thought Carbo.

'Smelt our dinner, did you?' asked a younger soldier with deep-set eyes and thick black hair. 'Well, you can't have any! Piss off and cook your own.'

His companions laughed. The sound was amiable enough, but there was an edge to it that Carbo didn't like. It wouldn't take much for the situation to get ugly. Squaring his shoulders, he moved to stand beside Spartacus.

'Who's the one mouthing off about Spartacus?' barked the Thracian.

'That'd be me.' The bald man got slowly to his feet. 'Got a problem with what I said?'

'As a matter of fact, I do.'

At this, all but the young soldier who'd spoken stood up. Any trace of friendliness had left their faces. Meaningful hands were laid on the hilts of knives and swords.

'I'd advise you to walk away now,' snarled the bald man, stepping forward. 'Before you get badly hurt.'

'Or killed,' added one of his fellows with a toothy leer.

'Is that a threat?' growled Spartacus.

'Take it how you will.' The bald man moved even closer.

Good. Spartacus darted forward, grabbed the bald man by the front of his tunic and shoved him backwards. He landed on his arse in the fire. With a bawl of pain, he leaped up, clutching his rear end. Several of his companions – most notably the young man who was still seated – sniggered.

Carbo laughed out loud, but then the rest of the soldiers drew their weapons. Shit, he thought, pulling out his own knife. It would have been better to walk away.

'Think very carefully before you attack your leader,' cried the Thracian.

The bald man stopped yelling. A trace of fear entered his eyes. 'Eh? You're not Spartacus!'

'Am I not? Do I need to be wearing my mail and carrying my sica for you to know me?' Spartacus stepped forward, raising a fist. 'Who wants the glory of saying that he took a Roman eagle in battle and, by doing so, shamed an entire legion?' he roared.

All around them, men's heads turned.

It was the same cry that Spartacus had used to encourage his army the day that they had fought Gellius, remembered Carbo with delight.

The bald man's anger had been replaced by pure dread. 'N-no, sir. I recognise you now.'

His companions shared incredulous stares with one another before quickly shoving their weapons away. 'We're sorry, sir. We didn't realise,' mumbled one. There was a rapid chorus of agreement, and Carbo relaxed a little.

Spartacus' flinty eyes bored into the soldiers one by one.

'Gods above, Zeuxis, you're a bloody idiot! We'll all be executed now, because of your big mouth,' said a thickset soldier with cropped hair.

The balding man's face crumpled. 'Please forgive me, sir. I didn't know who you were.'

'A moment ago, you were complaining about how long I'd been away. Dead in a ditch, you said.'

'I didn't really think that, sir, I—'

'Don't lie to me, fool. I heard what you said.'

'You had been gone for an age, sir. I know I wasn't alone in worrying about what would happen to the army. To all of us. Without you, sir, we would have filth like Castus and Gannicus trying to take charge. That's what everyone's saying.' Zeuxis glanced at his companions for support, but none would meet his eye. Resigned and unsurprised, he turned back to Spartacus. 'Thank the gods that you have returned, though!'

'Is what he said true?'

No one answered.

They're too damn scared, thought Carbo, amazed at Spartacus' ability to instil awe with his sheer confidence.

'You!' Spartacus barked at the young soldier with deep-set eyes.

'Yes, sir?'

'Is your comrade right?'

'There is something to what he says, sir,' came the awkward reply. 'But it's only talk. You know what men are like.'

'You didn't agree with Zeuxis, however.'

'No, sir.'

'Why didn't you try to attack me as well?'

'I don't pick fights for no reason, sir.'

'Hmmm. You seem to be the most steady one here. What's your name?'

'Marcion, sir.'

Spartacus made a snap decision. 'So, Marcion, do you vouch for these men?'

A sharp tang of fear tinged the already tense atmosphere. Everyone had caught the underlying meaning in their leader's words.

'Yes, sir. I do. They are all good soldiers. They've fought bravely in every battle I've seen. Zeuxis might have a big mouth, but he killed a Roman officer in Picenum, and Arphocras there' – he indicated a man with a bushy beard – 'helped to capture a standard the day we fought Gellius.'

Spartacus glared at Zeuxis, who was rubbing gingerly at his burned arse. 'Is that right?'

'Yes, sir, it is!' He pointed at the pile of weapons. 'I can show you his sword.'

'There's no need. I believe you.'

Zeuxis fell silent. He watched Spartacus fearfully. So did his companions.

'The reason I went away was not as you thought, to scout out our route. I went to Rome.' He smiled at their surprise.

'Why, sir?' asked Marcion.

'To find out what the Romans have planned for us, and to assassinate the new general who will lead their army.'

More shock on their faces.

'Did you succeed, sir?' Zeuxis ventured.

'Partially. I learned that the legions will not wait until the spring to march against us. Two of us weren't enough to kill Crassus, but we put the fear of Hades into him, that's for sure.' He waved a dismissive hand. 'I'll slay the whoreson the next time I meet him.'

Now the soldiers looked awed.

'Would you like to hack down another Roman officer, Zeuxis? Are the rest of you ready to fight another battle against the legions? Because that's what we're going to have to do – sooner or later.'

'If you're leading us, sir, I'll fight anyone – even the Minotaur!' cried Zeuxis.

'What of you, Marcion?' asked Spartacus.

'Count me in, sir.'

'Me too!' shouted Arphocras.

Their companions roared their agreement. Around them, men began chanting, 'SPAR-TA-CUS! SPAR-TA-CUS!'

Carbo was amazed at how the situation had been reversed. A group of unhappy soldiers, many of them ready to desert, had become fervent believers in Spartacus.

A smile of approval flickered across the Thracian's lips, and he raised his hands for silence. 'You are brave men, all of you. And although you're a pain in the arse sometimes' – here, he eyed the embarrassed Zeuxis – 'I wouldn't ever be without you!'

The air filled with yells of delight.

'Everything that you suffer, every hardship and tribulation, I also endure.' Spartacus turned to regard the larger crowd of onlookers. 'I may have gone away, but I was always going to come back. Always! As the Great Rider is my witness, I will *never* leave you, my brave soldiers. NEVER!'

This time, Carbo joined in. 'SPAR-TA-CUS! SPAR-TA-CUS! SPAR-TA-CUS!'

'I will see you again soon,' Spartacus said to Zeuxis. 'You might have had time to chew on your sandals by that stage.'

Zeuxis' flush grew even deeper; his companions fell about laughing.

Spartacus clapped Zeuxis on the arm. Then he turned to Carbo with a wicked grin. 'It's time to sort out Castus and Gannicus.' *And see my child!*

With the soldiers' cheers ringing in their ears, they walked off.

This time, it was down the main avenue between the tents.

The camp filled with happy cries as men saw that their leader had returned. Spartacus waved and smiled, and kept walking. Inside, he was delighted that so few faces seemed disappointed by his reappearance. They were seeing only a tiny fraction of the army, but it boded well for the rest. Castus and Gannicus' poison hadn't spread that far. It wasn't long until they reached Ariadne's tent. Atheas and Taxacis were on guard outside. Recognising Spartacus, they sprang forward, fierce grins splitting their faces.

Spartacus raised a hand to his lips. 'Quiet,' he whispered.

The Scythians glanced at each other in surprise, but they obeyed.

'Want . . . to see . . . your son?' muttered Atheas.

'My son?' *Thank the gods – it's a boy!* His resolve wavered for a moment, but he held it in place with an iron will. The Gauls had to be dealt with at once, before they heard he was back.

'Yes. Maron.'

'She named him after my brother,' said Spartacus softly. 'That is a good name. Is he well?'

'He . . . fine.' Atheas beamed. 'He . . . like you.'

A tight smile. 'I'll see him later.'

Carbo was stunned. 'Later?'

Spartacus ignored him. Then, to Atheas, 'Do you have a couple of spare swords?'

The Scythian nodded.

'Get them.' Spartacus tapped a foot against the ground as Atheas hurried off. He looked furious. Carbo didn't dare say a word.

Atheas returned with two plain but serviceable gladii, each of which was attached to a leather baldric. He handed one to each of them.

Spartacus slung his over his right shoulder. 'Take me to Castus and Gannicus.'

Atheas led off, but he was clearly concerned. 'Why?'

'We were attacked two nights ago. It wasn't Romans. They had to be men from our camp. Who would have the best reasons for wanting me dead?'

'Castus. Gannicus. The bastards!' snarled Taxacis. 'We . . . kill them?'

Spartacus showed his teeth. 'Sadly, we need the cocksuckers. Ten legions are being raised. They could be here within three to four months. That might not be enough time to raise and train replacements for the soldiers who would follow the Gauls if they left.'

Carbo's nerves were wire taut now. *What can four of us do?* 'How are you going to play this?'

'I want to see their faces when they see that I'm alive. That will tell us if they're guilty or not. We'll scare the shit out of the dogs. Show them that they can be got at too.'

'They'll have dozens of warriors.'

'What of it?' spat Spartacus. 'They have to see that I'm not scared of them, not even a little bit, and to understand that if they order my death, they will die first. We'd manage that before they cut us down, eh?'

'Yes!' cried the Scythians fiercely.

Carbo gritted his teeth against his fear. It almost worked. 'I'm with you.'

'I knew you would be,' Spartacus declared. He threw Carbo a wink. 'As long as the gods are with us, it won't come to that. Lead on, Atheas.'

Wondering how in Hades Spartacus would prevent them being massacred, Carbo followed his leader.

The Gauls' tents weren't far away. They were surrounded by those of their closest supporters, which meant that the small group soon began to attract attention. Those soldiers who didn't recognise Spartacus knew the Scythians or Carbo by sight. Men stared hostilely and pointed. A few insults were thrown, but no one obstructed their passage. Yet.

A gob of phlegm landed by Carbo's feet, and his guts churned. Normally, he would have challenged such an insult, but not now.

'Keep moving,' muttered Spartacus.

Atheas' pace picked up.

They found Castus and Gannicus before a pavilion that must have once belonged to a Roman general. A large number of gilt standards had been stabbed into the ground by it, including five silver eagles. Castus was sitting on a log with a half-naked woman kneeling between his open knees. As her head moved up and down, he groaned softly. Gannicus lay on his back nearby, swallowing a stream of wine that fell from a jug held by a dull-eyed, semi-dressed woman. More than a score of armed soldiers lounged about, chatting idly, drinking or fondling yet more fearful-looking girls. A few noticed as the group approached, but they were far too late to prevent what happened next.

'Cover Gannicus,' Spartacus hissed at the Scythians. 'When you see me act, pour the whole jug over the bastard.'

With evil expressions, Atheas and Taxacis stole off.

'Carbo, you stay with me.' He strode right up to the woman who was pleasuring Castus.

Carbo stared at the Gaul with disgust. *He fucks in public, like an animal.*

Castus' eyes were still closed with pleasure when Spartacus gave the woman a hefty kick in the arse. She fell forward and made a horrible choking sound. With a roar of pain, Castus shoved her away. She lurched to one side, gagging.

Spartacus' gladius flashed into his hand.

Fifteen paces away, Atheas grabbed the jug from Gannicus' woman and emptied it over his head. There was an indignant roar, but when the Gaul saw who was crouched over him, he didn't resist. He lay there, shouting. 'You mad barbarian bastards! I'll have you strangled with your own guts for this!'

'You!' Castus had sprung up, his face the picture of shock.

Now there was no doubt in Spartacus' mind. White-hot rage splintered his vision for an instant.

Castus' eyes darted towards the sword that lay at his feet.

'Go on, limp prick!' roared Spartacus. 'Pick it up.'

'My men will cut you to pieces!'

'They can try, but you'll never see what happens, because you'll be dead before your fingers close on the hilt.' Spartacus glared at the Gaul, daring him to move.

Castus licked his lips, and didn't budge.

Carbo had never heard such anger in his leader's voice. Castus had heard it too. He knew if he reacted, he would die. Then the Scythians would kill Gannicus, and the surrounding warriors would fall upon them. Carbo gripped his own gladius with white knuckles. *Great Jupiter, let me die well.*

Spartacus' rage eased a fraction. 'Can you see me, Gannicus, or are your eyes still stinging?'

The Gaul lifted his head. 'I can see you,' he growled.

'Are you as surprised to see me as your friend here?'

'I suppose. We didn't know when you'd come back. There's been no word.'

'You're a bad liar, Gannicus. That and the disbelief on Castus' face when he saw me are all the evidence I need. You both thought I was dead, eh?'

'I don't know what you mean,' blustered Castus, awkwardly tugging up his trousers.

'Shut your filthy mouth, you,' snapped Spartacus. 'Understand that the only reason you're both not choking to death on your own blood is that it's still in all of our interests to stay together.'

'What are you talking about?' demanded Gannicus.

'Ten damn legions is what I'm talking about! Ten legions which will march south before winter. That's what I found out in Rome. Do you fancy fighting them without my men?'

His words were met with a shocked silence.

'I didn't think so. Maybe from now on you could spend more time finding new recruits and training them up instead of behaving as if you're at an orgy.'

Again neither Gaul replied.

Spartacus stared at both men, flinty-eyed. *They heard what I said. That's enough. There's no point mentioning Sicily yet.* 'One more thing. If either of you ever tries to harm me or my family again, I will not rest until you've been carved into a thousand pieces of meat. Do you understand?'

Gannicus nodded. Castus was too slow for Spartacus' liking, so he jabbed his sword at the ruddy-haired Gaul, forcing him to jump backwards. 'Do you fucking UNDERSTAND?'

'Yes,' Castus muttered.

'Excellent.' With a contemptuous look, Spartacus stepped away. 'Atheas! Taxacis. We're leaving.'

The Scythians moved away from Gannicus, who sat up, his face purple with rage.

A number of the Gauls' men began to move towards them. Carbo tensed.

'If I don't return soon, Egbeo and Pulcher have orders to mobilise every soldier in the camp before coming here to look for me. You can choose whether that happens or not,' said Spartacus loudly. 'It doesn't matter to me.'

Castus aimed an uncertain glance at Gannicus. 'He's lying.'

'How would you know?' retorted Gannicus. 'Stay where you are,' he ordered, and the warriors halted.

The four walked backwards until they were some thirty paces from the Gauls. 'Good work,' said Spartacus. He would have to watch his back from now on, but he doubted that there would be any more attempts on his life – from the Gauls at least. How long Castus and Gannicus would stay with the army was by no means certain, but for now they had learned their lesson. He could focus on searching out new recruits and finding pirates who could transport them to Sicily.

Both Scythians had broad grins plastered on their faces. So did Carbo. 'A convincing lie just there.'

Spartacus winked. 'Time to see my son.' *My son!*

Chapter XII

Leaving Carbo outside with the Scythians, Spartacus ducked inside the tent. His eyes adjusted fast to the dim light, and he was pleased with what he saw. Someone – Egbeo or Pulcher, he supposed – had taken care to decorate it well. There were thick rugs on the floor, a number of large bronze lamps, two ebony chests and a rosewood table and chairs. However, his attention moved rapidly to the unmade bedding along one wall, and the hand-carved wooden cot that stood nearby. He craned his neck, but couldn't see into it. Ariadne was by the crib, her back towards him. She was quietly singing.

Spartacus padded further inside, but he didn't interrupt. The tranquil scene was so at odds with the one he'd just left, with what had happened since he'd left for Rome, that he needed a moment to return to normality. To return to his *family*. For in the time that he had been absent, that is what they had become.

An aching joy began to replace the fury he'd felt towards the Gauls. Ariadne was well, and so too was his son. Maron. *You will never be forgotten, my brother.*

Ariadne's song came to an end. She bent over the cot and planted a soft kiss on the baby's head before she turned to Spartacus. Her face was cold. 'Thank you for not making any noise,' she said in a flat tone.

'You heard me come in.'

'Yes. I heard you arrive a while ago too – and then leave without seeing your wife and your newborn son. To talk with Castus and Gannicus.' She had to make an effort to lower her voice. 'How could you?'

He took a step towards her. 'Ariadne, I—'

'Don't,' she interrupted, boiling with fury. 'Don't even speak to me! Take a look at Maron. You owe him that much at least.'

Clenching his jaw, Spartacus moved to the cot and peered in. The sight that met his eyes instantly made his anger disappear. A little black-haired shape, lying on its front, swaddled in a blanket. Side-on, a tiny, scrunched-up face with a button nose. His heart swelled with love and pride. 'He's so small.'

'Maron is big for a boy, the midwife says. He's put on a lot of weight since he was born too.'

Spartacus nodded. He knew next to nothing about babies. He stared at his son, wanting to touch him but wary of waking him or doing the wrong thing.

Ariadne read his mind. 'For now, just rub his head or his back. You can pick him up once he's had his nap.'

Reassured, Spartacus reached into the cot and stroked the soft skin of Maron's cheek. A huge grin split his face at the touch; he gently repeated it. 'Welcome to the world, my son,' he whispered. 'It is good to meet you at last.'

Maron twitched, startling him. He lifted his arm.

'It's all right, you haven't woken him.'

Spartacus put his hand back into the cot. 'He's got your hair.'

'And your eyes. Although the midwife says that they might still change colour.'

'I don't mind. The main thing is that he's here safely, and that you are well.'

'You've seen that that's the case. Do you need to leave again?'

'No, of course not.' Her lips twitched, and he saw that while she was talking, she was still furious. 'Maron is a fine name. I couldn't have thought of a better one myself. No doubt my brother is watching from the warrior's paradise. He'll be very proud. My father will also.'

'It's nothing.'

'No, it means a lot, Ariadne. To me as well as to the dead. Thank you.' She didn't answer.

Spartacus had no desire for their argument to continue. Here at least, with his family, he wanted respite from conflict. 'I *did* want to come in and see you both the moment I arrived. How can you doubt that?'

Her eyes searched his accusingly. 'You've chosen your army over your family before. That I have forced myself to accept – almost – but to go and speak first with those *pigs* Castus and Gannicus? What kind of man are you?'

He was stung – and angered – by her comment. 'You don't understand!'

'No, of course I don't. I'm only a woman, eh?' Maron stirred, and she frowned. 'Step away, or we'll wake him. He needs sleep. He had a restless night.'

Spartacus' instant concern overrode his anger. 'Is he ill?'

She gave him a withering look. 'No. He's just got a bit of colic.'

'Colic? Like a horse gets?'

'Yes, but not as serious. All babies get it from time to time. The midwife made up some fennel water this morning, and that has helped a lot.'

'I took some of that once when I had bad gut cramp. It made me fart like my damn stallion!' She didn't smile at his joke. They stood in silence for a moment, and then he tried again. 'I wanted to see you both, but I had to deal with something first.'

'What could be more important than seeing your son?' she hissed. 'Did you want to boast to the Gauls about what you'd done, or found out?'

His irritation overflowed. 'Be quiet, woman, and let me speak!'

Ariadne's lips thinned, but she held her peace.

'I'll tell you what happened in Rome later. It's important, but it's not the reason that I didn't come in here first.'

'You're not making any sense.'

'Two nights ago, we were attacked in our camp by a group of men. If Carbo hadn't heard them coming, we would both have been killed.'

Ariadne heard the truth in his words. Terrible images filled her mind. Remorse tore at her for being so presumptuous. 'How did you get away?'

'By running for our lives.' Wryly, he indicated the rips in his tunic and the scratches on his arms and legs. 'I've barely eaten or drunk since it happened. Not that I care. What mattered was getting back here, first to make sure that you hadn't already been murdered, and second, to confront Castus and Gannicus.'

'They were behind this? How do you know that the killers weren't Roman?'

'One of them spoke. Carbo said that he wasn't a native Latin speaker. Besides, we had got out of Rome without difficulty. No one had followed us.'

'So if it wasn't Romans,' she said, frowning, 'it had to be someone who knew where you'd gone.'

'That's right. And there might be plenty of men in the army who aren't fond of me, but Castus and Gannicus had to be the most likely candidates to want me dead.'

Thinking of the Gauls' visit to her, Ariadne shuddered. Perhaps she had been more lucky than she'd realised. 'Have you killed them?'

'No.'

'Why the hell not?' she demanded. 'It's no less than they deserve! Maron and I would have been next.'

'Quite likely.' He was starting to enjoy her anger a little. It showed that she still cared about him. 'But murdering them would be counterproductive.' He filled her in on Crassus' plans, and on what they'd heard from the messenger on the road.

'Ten legions,' said Ariadne in a monotone. She felt numb. 'They'll be here in three or four months, you say.'

'Now you see why I didn't get rid of the Gauls. If they left, we'd barely outnumber the Romans, and that's not odds any general would want to start a battle with.'

'I know. So what did you do to Castus and Gannicus?'

'We surprised them. The savages got the shock of their lives to see me appear. The look on Castus' face told me all I wanted to know. He and Gannicus sent those men.'

'The treacherous dogs!' Ariadne's eyes flashed dangerously, and Spartacus was reminded of a wild beast defending its young. 'Now that they know about the ten legions, will they stay?'

'Who knows? Let's hope so. Until we can recruit and train more men at least.' *It's going to be a race against time to do that while trying to move the army and organise transport to Sicily.*

She still wasn't happy. 'How do you know that they won't make another attempt?'

'I don't. But they know damn well what will happen if they try. Prometheus' pain will be as nothing to what they endure.'

'I'd like to watch them scream,' she spat. 'I'd even wield the knife.'

'Quite the lioness, aren't you?' He touched her cheek, and was astonished by her reaction.

Her coldness melted, and tears formed in her eyes. 'Thank the gods for Carbo,' she whispered. 'Thank them for concealing you as you ran, and for bringing you back safely.'

Spartacus opened his arms, and she stepped into his embrace. He held her very tight.

'I've missed you so much.' Ariadne thought of the road lined with crosses, and did her best to shove the brutal image away. 'I thought you might never return.'

'It wasn't that bad,' he lied, glad at that moment that she could not see his face. 'Not like fighting a battle. And I'm back now, with you and Maron.'

She looked up at him, pulling a smile. 'So it was worth going?'

'Definitely. I told you what I heard about the legions that are being raised. And we nearly killed Crassus, the politician who's been put in charge of the Roman armies.' He scowled. 'If only I'd had Atheas and Taxacis with me, or a dozen of the gladiators. We would have sliced him up with ease.'

Ariadne was intrigued. 'Tell me.'

It all poured out and she shook her head in a mixture of amazement and exasperation. 'And you say what happened wasn't dangerous? You lead a charmed life, Spartacus.'

His frivolous mood vanished. 'I know, and I thank the Rider for it every day. Tomorrow I will offer him a ram, or better still, a bull.'

'And then? What do we do next?'

'There was an official messenger on the road the afternoon before we were attacked. He was taking orders to Messana, on Sicily. There have been two large-scale slave rebellions on that island in the last sixty years.'

Ariadne smiled at his enthusiasm, but she was confused.

'We're going to seize some grain ships and use them to transport the army over to Sicily. When the slaves on the island hear of our arrival, they will flock to my banner. The two legions over there probably haven't had to fight in years. We'll have time to gather an army twice the size of the one that's camped here before Rome reacts properly. With a host like that behind me, the war can start in earnest.'

Ariadne refused to get excited. 'How will you get enough men over to Sicily to take the grain ships?'

'By paying a pirate captain his own weight in silver and gold.'

'You've got an answer to everything.'

'For the moment, yes. Convinced?'

Even with Maron occupying all of her time, Ariadne had been racked by worry over their future. But this plan seemed feasible. She offered up a silent prayer. *Dionysus, I ask you to help us again, as you have so many times before.* 'It sounds a lot better than sitting around waiting for the legions to arrive.'

'That was my thought too. First I'll need to find out where the best anchorages are, and in which ports the officials turn a blind eye to pirate vessels.' A grimace, then a confident smile. 'The gods will help us.'

Ariadne nodded. 'Whom will you send?'

'Carbo.'

'He's a good man.'

'One of the best. He saved my damn life, you know. If he hadn't heard—'

She raised a finger to his lips. 'Don't, please. I live with the knowledge every day that I might never see you again. Today, I want to rejoice in the fact that you've returned to me, and to Maron. That you're alive. Whole.' She took away her hand and lifting her face to his, kissed him.

Spartacus had one last coherent thought before passion overtook him.

Thank you, Great Rider, for guiding me back to my army, my wife and my son.

Six weeks pass . . .

In his baking command tent, Crassus was preparing for his appearance of the day. Sweating slaves stood by, doing their best to ignore the buzzing flies as they held out the accoutrements of his office. The red tunic of a general. The polished, muscled bronze cuirass. The helmet with the scarlet horsehair crest. The gilt-plated belt with the studded pteryges that protected his groin and the red sash that circled his waist. The ivory-handled gladius with its ornate scabbard and bejewelled baldric. The calf-high, open-toed boots.

Gods, I'm glad that I don't have to wear this all day. Crassus beckoned to the slaves, eager to get on with his duty, which was to show himself to his troops. To raise their spirits. To tell them how brave they were. To let them know that they were engaged in a task sent by the gods: to rid Italy, and the Republic, of the blight that was Spartacus and his slave rabble. And of course, he thought slyly, to make him more popular than Pompey Magnus.

He shrugged on the tunic, trying to ignore the way that it stuck at once to his clammy back.

Pompey! The young upstart. Crassus hated that his rival had more of a public name for martial prowess than he had. In his mind, it was totally unjustified. Had he not been the man who saved the day for Sulla at the Colline Gate? But for him, Marius would have been dictator. All Pompey had done in the civil war was to raise three legions that had won a couple of trifling victories for Sulla. If the man was such an amazing bloody tactician, why had he taken so long to quell Sertorius' rebellion in Iberia? It still wasn't over. *I would have dealt with it long since. As Jupiter is my witness, I will mop up Spartacus' unrest in similar fashion.*

A slave helped him into his breastplate. Another slave crouched beside him to fasten the sash around his middle.

It was late afternoon, and the sun was tracing a bloody path towards the horizon. The army had left Rome two weeks before, seven days later than he'd wished. Despite this, they had travelled over two hundred sun-drenched, cloudless miles in that time. Thurii, the rebels' reported base, was now less than a third of that distance away. As his skin prickled with the heat, Crassus tried to be grateful for their remarkable progress, and for the fact that the dreadful daytime heat had begun to abate. It was difficult, however. It was still as hot as an oven in his tent, and riding a horse for nearly eight hours daily was exhausting work. He was glad not to be one of the ordinary soldiers, who'd marched twenty miles since dawn – in full armour. Half of them were currently erecting a temporary marching camp while their exhausted but grateful comrades stood watch.

When that was done, all but the veterans had two hours of drill to look forward to before they could rest or eat. But it's what they signed up for, he thought ruthlessly. They had done it every afternoon since they had left Rome, and so they would every damn day until the campaign ended. He would not relax the pressure on his new soldiers, not even for a moment. Not until Spartacus was dead.

Crassus lifted one foot and then the other, allowing his slaves to pull on his boots. More beads of sweat trickled down his back. *I can't wait for autumn to come.* No doubt the prolonged hot spell had the farmers thanking Saturnus, Ops, Ceres and Lactans for their munificence, but Crassus didn't give a shit about the harvest. What he wanted was for the unseasonably warm weather to end. He was sick of his officers whingeing about men who had dropped by the wayside each day. Casualties from heat exhaustion and lack of water were not the same as deaths through combat!

Yet Crassus knew that he couldn't ignore such losses. And so he had had Caepio organise a number of special units whose specific duty it was to travel up and down sections of the hugely long column that was his army – all twenty-odd miles of it – providing assistance and water to those who needed it. That way, hundreds of men who would otherwise have died would continue to march south, towards their target. Spartacus.

The flea-ridden, Thracian bastard. Crassus' memory of how close Spartacus had come to killing him was ever present. If it hadn't been for the information provided by his spy, the attempt might have succeeded. Saenius had done well in recruiting the man. With luck, they would hear from the spy again. Crassus had every confidence in his ability to end the Thracian's reign of terror with his ten legions. *When it comes to it,* he thought confidently, *they won't stand up against Roman courage. Roman virtus. Roman discipline.* But he wasn't averse to subterfuge if it brought the matter to a swifter conclusion.

'Liner.'

At once a tightly fitting piece of felt was proffered. Crassus eyed it askance before pulling it on. It would make him sweat worse than a smith at his anvil, but he wouldn't get bruised by the unforgiving inner surface of his helmet.

'I haven't got all day,' he snapped, clicking his fingers.

His silver-plated helmet was handed over, and Crassus took a moment to admire it. It had cost him a fortune, but it had been worth every last as. It was a piece of art, topped with hair from the finest stallion in Italy, and sporting enamelled cheek pieces. The brow was decorated with a magnificent motif of Mars receiving offerings from ranks of officers and legionaries. Crassus donned it proudly. It was fitting, he thought, for a victorious general.

'Sword.'

A slave hurried forward with his gladius and slipped the baldric over his shoulder.

Crassus used the full-length bronze mirror that stood nearby to make sure that his scabbard sat just so on his left hip. Lastly, he wiped his face clean of sweat with a cloth. Content with his appearance, he made for the door.

The sentries outside saluted as he emerged.

Crassus was pleased to see Caepio already waiting at the head of a half-century of veterans, some of the cohort that had been designated to protect him. Their helmets and mail shone in the sun. Even the bosses on their shields had been polished. To one side, his groom held ready a fresh horse.

'Attention!' bawled the old centurion.

In unison, the soldiers snapped upright.

Crassus allowed the trace of a smile to curve his lips. Few of his troops looked this good but, under Caepio's direction, things were improving every day. 'Centurion.'

'Ready to make the rounds, sir?'

'Indeed.' He eyed the centurion with approval. From the start, Caepio had wholeheartedly thrown in his lot with Crassus. Despite his age, his energy was boundless. He recruited tirelessly, helped to train the new men and provided practical advice to whoever needed it, whenever it was asked for. Crassus now appreciated him greatly. Soldiers such as Caepio were a rare commodity indeed. He strolled over to his horse, and used the groom's linked hands as a step up to its back. 'I thought we might begin at the western rampart, and move out to the defensive screen afterwards. Try and see as many of the troops as possible.'

'Very good, sir.' Caepio barked an order. Twenty of his men and an optio trotted to stand four wide, five deep in front of their commander. 'Towards the western gate. Forward march!' cried Caepio. The soldiers tramped off. Crassus nudged his horse in the ribs; Caepio walked alongside him, and the rest of the soldiers took up the rear.

Crassus' army was far too large to set up camp as one unit. From the outset, he had ordered his legions to pair off, meaning that five temporary encampments were built every afternoon, all of which accommodated close to ten thousand men. Each was shaped exactly the same, consisting of a massive rectangle with rounded corners, the walls of which were made up of a mixture of brushwood and packed earth that had been dug up by the legionaries around the perimeter. The resultant ditch served as part of the camp's defences. Midway along the four sides of each camp, a gap in the rampart had been angled so that both sides of it overran one another, creating a narrow, passage-like ingress that was easily blocked overnight, and which could be well defended in the event of an attack. Two straight avenues connected the entrances, which cut the vast encampments into quarters. The camps' headquarters, and the commanders' tents, were situated at the roads' intersection. Around these, every cohort, century and contubernium had an allocated position, which was marked out by the engineers each day.

There were small groups of soldiers present in the still-empty areas around Crassus' quarters: one legionary from every contubernium, and scores of mule drivers. Under the supervision of shouting junior officers, they were unloading their tents from hundreds of ill-tempered, tail-flicking mules. The stink of manure and the attendant clouds of flies were enough to make Crassus ride past with curled lip.

The path ahead, jammed with more mules and messengers hurrying to and fro, cleared miraculously as the officer at the front shouted his presence. On each side, red-faced, sweating soldiers pulled themselves to attention; *optiones* and *tesserarii* saluted; slaves looked at the ground. Crassus acknowledged a few of the officers and men with curt waves of his hand.

To protect the soldiers from missile attack, the tent lines ended some hundred paces before the western rampart, which had already been built to the height of a tall man. Sharpened wooden stakes decorated the outer face of the fortifications, forming a protective palisade. Along the top of the rampart, soldiers were busy tamping down the earth with their trenching tools. Branches were being laid down to form a walkway and, off to each side, Crassus could see the watchtower that would adorn each corner being constructed. They filed through the entrance to the outside. A faint breeze hit his flushed cheeks, and he turned his head from side to side, trying to get some relief: he was cooking in his armour. It made no real difference, and his temper frayed a little further.

He urged his horse off to the left, where a party of legionaries were completing the defensive ditch. Caepio shouted at the men in front, who did a hasty about-turn and marched at double time to get in front of their commander.

Crassus' presence was soon noted. Until he halted, however, or asked a question of an officer, no one dared to stop what he was doing. Surreptitious glances were cast at him aplenty, and everywhere he looked, the work rate shot up. Occasionally, he found it amusing to linger while the legionaries kept up the new, unsustainable speed of their labour. Still wearing their mail shirts, swords and daggers, they heaved and panted, never daring to slow down.

Spotting a portion of the trench that had collapsed, he rode closer to investigate. A burly centurion was in charge, cursing his men as they repaired the damage. Crassus reined in to watch. Caepio and his escort stamped to a halt too. Engrossed with his duty, the officer didn't notice that they were there.

'Faster, you lazy sons of whores! If you don't want my vine cane rammed up each of your sweaty arses, you'd better have this section finished before I can count to five hundred. One. Two. Three.' He leered as the soldiers, drenched in sweat, covered in a layer of dust, began to dig with renewed energy. 'That's a bit more like it. Four. Five. Six.' Looking up, he recognised Crassus and threw off a hasty salute 'Sir!' Then, at his men, 'Stop!'

Most of his legionaries obeyed. Still fearful, some didn't register, and kept digging. With the ease of long practice, the centurion brought his vine cane down across the back of the nearest offenders' legs. *Thwack. Thwack. Thwack.* 'STOP, you maggots! Your commanding officer, the illustrious Marcus Licinius Crassus, has deigned to visit you!'

Startled, the offending soldiers downed their tools.

'Attention!' roared the centurion. Standing waist deep in the earth, his men did as they were told. He glanced at Crassus. 'We are honoured by your presence, sir. Isn't that right, lads?'

'YES, SIR!'

'Commendable work rate, centurion. Are your men as keen to fight Spartacus as they are to dig dirt?'

'They're even keener, sir!'

'I shall keep you to your word. With men such as yours, victory will be ours!'

A cracked roar of agreement left the soldiers' parched throats.

Crassus gave a tiny nod of approval. 'I have every confidence that at the first opportunity, you and your comrades will smash the slaves apart.'

'Course we will, sir!' cried a short man with a gap-toothed grin. 'For you and for Rome!'

The centurion glared at the soldier's boldness, but Crassus smiled. 'Good, soldier. That's what I like to hear.'

'Thank you, sir.' The centurion saluted with gusto. 'Every one of us feels the same way.'

'CRA-SSUS!' shouted a voice. The chant echoed up and down the ditch.

Crassus accepted the acclamation with a nod. 'If your work is done ahead of time, every man is to receive an extra ration of *acetum* this evening. As you were.'

Broad grins broke out everywhere. There was a rush to pick up trenching tools.

Crassus rode on. He traversed the entire length of the camp's western perimeter, stopping here and there to interrogate officers, appraise their soldiers' work, and to deliver short, rousing speeches. He grew more encouraged as he went. The legionaries' zeal was palpable, not just here, but during the day when they were marching, and in the evenings, when they sat outside their tents, gossiping and drinking. He heard it in the tone of the bawdy songs they sang, and saw it in their sunburned faces. His men wanted a fight. Like him, they wanted to defeat Spartacus. Despite the fact that he felt as if he'd been in the *caldarium* all day, Crassus' good mood returned. Victory would be his.

He had turned his horse's head towards the open ground beyond the camp when something caught his attention. Crassus blinked in surprise. He looked again. An icy fury took him, and he glanced up and down the trench. 'Who's in charge here?'

There was no immediate answer, and Crassus' temper exploded. 'I SAID, WHO THE FUCK IS IN CHARGE HERE?'

'T-that would be me, sir,' replied a youngish centurion whose brown hair was spiked with sweat.

Crassus rode his horse right up to the officer, nearly knocking him over. 'What is the meaning of this?' He jabbed an arm to his right.

'The meaning of what, sir?'

'Look at that piece of shit there.' He pointed at a legionary.

Alarmed, the man froze. Instinctively, his companions moved a step away from him.

'I won't call him a soldier, because he clearly isn't,' growled Crassus. 'Had you not noticed that he had set down his sword?'

The centurion stared. The colour left his face as he saw the gladius lying on the earth behind the ditch. 'No, sir.'

'And you call yourself an officer?' spat Crassus. He sat up straight on his horse's back so that everyone could see him better. 'Hear me, legionaries! Since time immemorial, Roman soldiers have worked to erect their camps while fully armed,' he shouted. 'They have done this so that should the need arise, they can fight at a moment's notice. Men who disobey this simple order place their lives, and those of their comrades, at risk.' He paused to let his words travel. 'This dereliction of duty cannot, and will not, be tolerated in *my* army!' He glared at the legionary, whose face had gone grey with fear. 'Caepio!'

'Sir!' The veteran centurion was by his right foot.

'Take that man out before his comrades, and execute him.'

For the first time, Crassus saw real respect in Caepio's eyes. *Good.*

Gripping the hilt of his sword, the centurion stalked to the ditch and stood over the offending soldier. 'Out!' he bawled.

The man climbed out of the trench, stumbling as he did so. He pulled himself upright and threw a beseeching glance at Crassus. 'I'm sorry, sir! I've never done such a thing before. I—'

Crassus' lips thinned in disapproval.

Caepio was watching. 'Shut your mouth, filth! Your general isn't interested.' He backhanded the soldier across the face. 'Kneel!'

Sobbing, the man did as he was told.

Caepio's gladius was already in his hand. 'Chin up!'

Crassus took a quick look around. Every man within sight was riveted to what was going on, which was precisely what he had intended.

Swallowing, the soldier lifted his gaze to the sky, exposing his throat in the process.

'Make your last request of the gods, dung rat,' ordered Caepio, drawing back his right arm.

The man's eyes closed, and his lips moved in silent prayer.

With incredible speed, Caepio's blade flashed down. It entered via the hollow at the base of the soldier's neck, slicing through the soft flesh with savage ease. Death was instantaneous. The gladius cut every major blood vessel over the heart into shreds, coming to rest in the victim's backbone.

A horrible choking noise left the man's lips, and he went as limp as a child's doll.

Caepio tugged free his blade, and a scarlet tide of blood jetted up from the lipped wound. The centurion lifted his right foot and booted the corpse backwards so that it fell into the ditch, spraying the nearest soldiers in liquid gore.

'Remember, you sheep-humping bastards, that any man caught in future without a weapon will receive the same punishment,' Caepio roared, wiping his blade on the bottom of his tunic.

'Or worse,' added Crassus with a hint of spite.

A silence fell that no one dared to break – except a raven high overhead. Its derisive call seemed to mock the assembled soldiers.

'You,' said Crassus, pinning the young centurion with his eyes. 'What's your name?'

'Lucius Varinius, sir.'

'Not a relation of the disgraced praetor, surely?' asked Crassus with glee.

'He was a distant cousin, sir,' came the stiff reply.

'I see. There are two fools in the same family. That's not surprising, I suppose. Give your vine cane to Caepio.'

Miserably, Varinius did as he was told.

'Break it!' ordered Crassus.

Caepio snapped the wooden cane over his knee and dropped the broken pieces to the ground.

'You are demoted to the ranks with immediate effect,' barked Crassus. 'Consider yourself lucky to be alive. Expect to stand in the front line of every battle. There, perhaps, you might redeem some of your honour.'

'Yes, sir. Thank you, sir,' Varinius mumbled.

'Let this be a lesson to all of you.' Crassus cast one more contemptuous look at the watching legionaries before he turned his horse and rode away, Caepio marching by his side.

'That won't happen ever again, sir,' said the centurion approvingly.

'You think so?' asked Crassus, fishing.

'That put the fear of Hades into every man who saw it, sir. Each of them will tell his mates, and they'll tell theirs. The news will travel through the army quicker than shit through a man with cholera. Which, if you don't mind me saying so, sir, is a damn good thing.'

'I don't mind you saying that at all, centurion,' replied Crassus.

Chapter XIII

Near the town of Croton, on the Ionian Sea

Carbo eyed the headland that jutted out into the sea about a mile away. Above the town's tumbledown stone walls, he could just make out the impressive pillars of the sanctuary to Hera Licinia, the Greek goddess. Croton might be a ghost town compared to its heyday half a millennium before, but its remaining inhabitants were still civilised, he thought. The men in the cove he was spying on couldn't have been more different.

After seven fruitless weeks of trawling up and down the coast, he had found some pirates.

Carbo didn't know whether to feel relieved or alarmed: they looked even more cutthroat than the gladiators in the ludus. Black-, brown- and fair-skinned, they were for the most part clad in ragged tunics or simple loincloths. The number of weapons each man carried more than made up for their lack of clothing. There was hardly an individual that didn't have a knife, or two, as well as a sword, on his belt. Spears were stacked up near their tents. There were catapults on the decks of the two shallow-draughted, single-masted vessels that were drawn up on the beach. Carbo felt grateful for the presence – a couple of hundred paces back – of the century of soldiers that Spartacus had insisted he take with him.

The small bay to his front was protected from the worst of the weather by a large sandbar that ran outwards from a rocky promontory to his right. That had to be why the pirates had chosen it as their mooring point. There were perhaps eighty of them – forty to a boat, thought Carbo – sprawled about, sleeping, cooking food over fires, or wrestling with one another. They looked to have been busy. About thirty young people of both sexes sat wretchedly on the sand, ropes tied around their necks. A number of the women were being raped by some of the pirates, while others watched and made comments.

Carbo considered his options. There was no benefit to going in alone, or with just a few men. They'd end up dead, or captured as slaves. All he could think of was to march in peacefully, and to ask for the renegades' leader. He slid backwards, down the landward side of the large dune that had served as concealment from the beach. It was fortunate that the pirates on sentry duty were too busy watching the violation of their captives to have spotted him.

A short while later, Carbo and his men – some of his own cohort – came tramping over the dune and down towards the beach. They made no effort to be quiet. Panic reigned as they were seen. Men ran for their weapons, and the captives were kicked to their feet and hurried to the boats. That didn't worry Carbo as much as the sight of the catapults being manned. The light artillery pieces would have an accurate range of two hundred paces.

He raised his hands in the air, and began shouting in Latin and Greek, 'We come in peace. PEACE!'

As they advanced on to the flat ground, the mayhem did not lessen. About half the pirates arrayed themselves in a rough phalanx before their boats, while the rest were frantically helping to push the vessels into the water. The catapults were aimed straight at Carbo and his men.

He cursed. This was what he had thought might happen. In the pirates' minds, safety lay at sea. If they succeeded, he would lose all chance of making a deal with them.

There was a loud twang, and his stomach lurched. 'Shields up!'

A heartbeat's delay, and then the first stones from the catapults – chunks half the size of a man's head – landed with soft *thumps* in the sand, about thirty paces in front of their formation.

'Jupiter's balls!' Very soon, he was going to start losing men. And for nothing. 'Halt!'

His soldiers gladly obeyed.

'Stay where you are,' ordered Carbo. He dropped his shield and unslung his baldric, letting his sword drop to the sand.

'What are you doing?' asked his optio, a block-headed gladiator.

'Showing them that I mean no harm.' Carbo took a step towards the pirates. He did well not to flinch as the next stones landed. They were wide this time, but a lot nearer. 'If I'm killed, return to the army and tell Spartacus what happened.'

'You're crazy!'

'Maybe I am,' replied Carbo, his heart thumping. *But I'm not going back empty-handed. Not after Spartacus has placed such trust in me.* He lifted both hands, palms out, and walked forward. 'I COME IN PEACE!' He repeated himself in Greek and Latin, over and over.

Another volley of stones came flying over, and he heard them rattle off his men's upturned shields. There was a shout of pain as someone was hit. Carbo began to grow angry. 'You stupid bastards. Can't you see that we're not attacking you?' he muttered, continuing to advance. 'PEACE! PEACE!'

A moment later, to his great relief, he saw a short man in the phalanx bellowing orders at the crew working the catapults. No more stones were loosed, and Carbo walked a little closer. He heard curses being shouted at him in a number of languages. Weapons were still being brandished, but no one threw a spear or charged him. Yet. Wary of going too near, he stopped about fifty paces from the pirates, careful to keep his hands in the air.

He waited.

The short man emerged from the midst of his comrades. He was dark-skinned, but not black enough to be a Nubian. His beady eyes were set in a calculating and cruel face. Gold earrings flashed in his ears, and his tunic was of a richer cut than his fellows. He took a dozen steps towards Carbo. 'Who in damnation are you?' he demanded in bad Latin.

'I am one of Spartacus' soldiers,' replied Carbo as loudly as he could. He was pleased when a murmur of recognition rippled through the pirates.

There was a suspicious scowl from the short man. 'Spartacus? The gladiator who is fighting Rome?'

'The same. Do you always greet visitors in the same manner?'

'Usually we just butcher them.' He grinned, and his men snickered. 'But I'm in a good mood today, so I'll let you and your men piss off instead.'

'No, chief! Let's kill him,' said a large man, brandishing a rusty sword. There was a rumble of agreement from the rest.

The captain winked at Carbo. 'That's not a bad idea. Give me a good reason why I shouldn't do exactly that.'

Carbo resisted the urge to order his men to the attack. 'I have a proposition for you, from Spartacus himself.'

The man's eyes narrowed. 'Is that so?'

'It is. My name is Carbo. What do they call you?'

'Heracleo.'

Given half a chance, Heracleo would turn on him like a stray dog, but Carbo still felt encouraged. 'Can you locate ships bigger than these?' He indicated the two shallow-bottomed boats, which were now afloat.

There was a laugh. 'Of course I can. I've got a *lembus* at another anchorage.' He saw Carbo's confusion and laughed again. 'You'd know that as a liburnian. Like everything they admire, the Romans copied it.'

Apart from triremes, Carbo's knowledge of ship types was vague. 'How many men can that carry?'

'Sixty oarsmen, and about fifty slaves. Passengers.' He corrected himself with an evil leer.

'I need bigger vessels than that.'

'There are other captains knocking about the area in biremes. There's even a trireme or two. Why do you need them?'

'We want to get to Sicily.'

There was a long, slow whistle. 'The whole army?'

'No. Just a couple of thousand men.'

'Why so few? I've heard that Spartacus' army is massive.'

'None of your damn business.'

'It's my bloody business if you're on my ship,' retorted Heracleo.

The last thing his leader wanted any pirate to know was that he was considering retreat. Carbo had his lie ready. 'Spartacus wants to start a rebellion on Sicily.'

'Ahhh. To divert the Romans' attention?'

'Something like that,' said Carbo stiffly, as if annoyed.

'That's smart. I've heard that he's a canny one, your Thracian. You'd want to cross at the straits, I take it?'

'That's right.'

'How soon?'

'Whenever you can get the ships there.'

A cunning glance. 'He's in a hurry. What's he willing to pay?'

'Two hundred and fifty denarii per man. Say five hundred thousand in total.'

There was a collective gasp from the pirates. Each of their slaves was worth between two hundred and four hundred denarii, but they only had thirty. Slaving was profitable work, yet the securing of captives was unpredictable and irregular. This would be a prize haul.

'One and a quarter million,' replied Heracleo without even blinking.

'That's outrageous,' cried Carbo with all the bluster he could manage.

'Getting four or five ships that are large enough to carry your men won't be easy, you know. I'll have to cut the other captains in. Then there's the Roman navy to worry about.'

'I don't give a shit. It's far too much!'

Heracleo's grin was predatory. 'Spartacus needs me more than I need his money. I can tell. Take my price or leave it – it's up to you.'

Scowling, Carbo didn't say anything for several moments. Heracleo's greed was no surprise. Spartacus had told him he could pay up to a two and a half million denarii, but he had to play the part, to look annoyed.

Heracleo yawned, but a good number of his men seemed keen to carve Carbo up.

'We could pay nine hundred thousand, but no more than that.'

'It's what I said, or nothing, you ugly son of a whore!'

Carbo flushed. He hadn't been insulted about his pox scars for a long time. His gaze went flat. 'If you didn't have so many men with you, I'd cut you a new arsehole.'

Heracleo's face hardened. 'You cheeky bastard!' He opened his mouth, but Carbo interrupted.

'You drive a hard bargain. One and a quarter million it is.'

Heracleo's demeanour changed in a flash. His eyes glittered with avarice. 'You have the money?'

Carbo threw back his head and laughed. 'For the last year and more, we've been pillaging whole towns from here to the Alps!'

'Of course, of course.' Heracleo managed to sound obsequious as well as annoyed.

'How soon can you have the ships at the beach near Scylla?'

Mention of the mythical beast who guarded the straits made Heracleo purse his lips. 'A month. Six weeks.'

'Can't you do it sooner?'

A frown. 'I will do my best. Before that, however, a down payment will be necessary. I was thinking—'

'Twenty-five thousand denarii today. A hundred and twenty-five thousand when you arrive with the ships, and the balance when the last of our men set foot on Sicily,' interjected Carbo harshly. 'That's *my* final offer. Take it, or leave it.'

Heracleo smiled. 'You can pay me now?'

Carbo turned his head. 'Optio! Bring a chest over!'

Heracleo spoke a few words in a guttural argot, and his men cheered.

As half a dozen of his soldiers trotted over, Carbo eyed the grinning pirates sidelong. Not one of them could be trusted, yet with the gods' help, they were now the most important allies Spartacus had ever had. He sent up an urgent prayer to Neptune, the god of the sea, and Fortuna, the goddess of luck, that Heracleo kept his side of the bargain.

If this plan failed, they had ten legions to face.

That was without taking the Gauls and the spy into account. Carbo scowled. Sometimes it felt as if they had as many enemies within as without. He hoped that Crassus had not got wind of what he'd been up to. It seemed unlikely. Once it had been decided that he would leave, Carbo had packed his gear and departed. On Spartacus' orders, he had told only Navio where he was going.

From the hills that surrounded the ruins of Forum Annii, Spartacus and a party of his scouts – among them Marcion and his comrades – were looking down on to the Via Annia, the main road that led from Capua to Rhegium, the town at the southernmost point of Italy. After what he and Carbo had discovered in Rome, the sight of enemy soldiers was unremarkable, yet it was shocking nonetheless. This host dwarfed the others that they had seen, and it had arrived sooner than Spartacus had expected. Having had word the previous day, they had been waiting for it since dawn. He observed it with a jaundiced eye. His service with the auxiliaries meant that he knew intimately the formation taken by Roman armies on the march.

A couple of hours after the enemy scouts had come stealing through the woods on either side of the road, the vanguard had come into sight, one legion picked by lot to lead the column that day. After that had come the surveyors, a unit comprised of one man from every contubernium in the army, whose job it was to help lay out the camp. Next were the engineers, who removed any obstacles in the legions' path, and then the senior officers' baggage. The general in charge and his bodyguard of infantry and cavalry had been easy to spot. A succession of messengers rode from this position up and down the verges, carrying orders to various parts of the host. The commander had been followed by the remainder of the horse. Scores of mules carrying the dismantled artillery preceded the senior officers and their escort. After came the legions, each one signified by a large group of standard-bearers at its front. The ranks of marching legionaries filled the road entirely. Each legion was strung out over a mile or so, but they seemed to go on for far longer. Spartacus' own forces took up a similar amount of ground, but he and his troops never got to watch them from such a vantage point. It was an awe-inspiring and, even in the best of men, fear-inducing sight.

'Crassus is here,' said Spartacus softly. Gladly. It had been more than two months since he'd been in Rome. At last his waiting was over.

'You're sure, sir?' asked Marcion.

'I'd wager my life on it. We've seen, what, five legions so far, and they're still coming. There's no way that Crassus would let one of his subordinates lead that many soldiers against us.'

'What's your plan, sir?'

All eyes swivelled to Spartacus.

'We've done what we came for. Every grain store within twenty miles has been emptied. If we loaded any more on to our mules, they'd collapse.'

His men chuckled. They liked the idea of so much food.

'There's one more thing to find out before we head south, though. I want to test the mettle of Crassus' soldiers.' He saw their questioning, slightly nervous looks. Marcion was alone in seeming excited. 'Most of them are new recruits. I need to see how good their discipline is, so we know what we're up against.'

'We're up against ten legions, sir,' growled an unhappy voice from the back. Marcion scowled. As usual, it was Zeuxis.

'And if they're shoddy soldiers like those of Lentulus and Gellius, we have nothing to be concerned about. But if they're not, then we'll need to treat them with a sight more respect.' He threw them a warning glance.

'I've told you before: Rome is not an enemy to be taken lightly. Just because you've beaten its troops on a number of occasions doesn't mean that you will always do so. Those legionaries you can see might be a very different proposition to meet face to face.' They didn't like that, but Spartacus didn't care. The brutal reality of what they could expect to see for the rest of their lives lay on the valley floor below. If it wasn't this army, it would be another one.

There was far more, but Spartacus didn't say it. To his immense frustration, his forces – including the soldiers who answered to the increasingly hostile Castus and Gannicus – now only outnumbered those of Crassus by perhaps fifteen thousand men. If the new legions proved to be cowards, and he picked the right battlefield, that could be enough. Yet while Spartacus didn't like to admit it, there was a chance that Crassus' soldiers *would* stand and fight. If they did, he needed more troops than he currently had.

The days of his huge numerical superiority over Roman armies were but a memory; the deluge of runaway slaves joining them that had been the daily norm since their first remarkable victory had all but dried up. The news of Crassus' ten legions had to be part of the reason. Or maybe it was because every herdsman and farm worker in the south with any courage had already joined him? Only the gods knew, Spartacus thought bitterly.

His mind was made up. He would go head to head with Crassus now if they were somehow cornered, but otherwise he would seek out a skirmish and then move south, towards Sicily. There, for a while at least, they would have fewer enemy forces to deal with. There would be more recruits and supplies. More options.

He winked at Marcion. 'Don't worry, lad, we'll still have a fight. A chance to bloody Crassus' nose good and properly.'

Ignoring Zeuxis' sour expression, Marcion grinned. With Spartacus to lead them, what could go wrong?

Two days later . . .

Since their confrontation, Spartacus had met with Castus and Gannicus only twice. The encounters had been less than friendly, but there had been no open conflict, and no more threats to leave. While the Gauls and their followers had continued to march with the other soldiers, they had begun to do their own thing. Raids on estates and villages. Attacks on a small town. Refusing to train daily. To all intents and purposes, they had already split off from the main army. Yet while they were still physically present, Spartacus' hunch was that if the situation demanded it, they would fight alongside him.

On this occasion, the pair arrived outside his tent still dressed for battle, wearing mail shirts, crested bronze helmets and Gaulish patterned trousers. Both had long since given up their native longswords in favour of gladii, finding the stabbing blades easier and more efficient to use in a shield wall.

Hearing Atheas' challenge, Spartacus came out to meet them. He was pleased to see that they had no retinue. They weren't here to quarrel. 'Will you have wine?'

'No,' growled Castus.

'Gannicus?'

'Say what you have to say and have done.'

'Fair enough. I know that you took part in the fight earlier.'

'Of course we did. We're no cowards,' retorted Castus.

'You're both brave men, I know,' Spartacus acknowledged in a peaceable tone. 'All the same, it wasn't easy today. Those legionaries were keen to fight, and they didn't give way easily.'

'They were better than the soldiers we've faced before,' admitted Gannicus grudgingly.

Castus scowled, but he didn't argue, which told its own story.

'Imagine if all ten legions fought like that,' said Spartacus.

They glowered at him.

'We'll fight them anyway,' snapped Castus. 'And if we lose, at least we'll die like men.'

'You both know that I'll also take them on if I have to.'

Resentful nods.

'There is an alternative, though. To take the army over to Sicily.'

They looked at him as if he'd gone mad. Rallying his patience, Spartacus explained his plan.

'Has Carbo returned?' asked Gannicus. 'Did he find a captain willing to help?'

'He's not back yet.'

'So this is based on hot air,' cried Castus. 'Who's to say that the little bastard hasn't failed? We could march down there to find that we're cornered like rats in a trap.'

'Autumn is practically here too,' warned Gannicus. 'There'll be fuck all farms down there to plunder.'

'Carbo won't let us down,' asserted Spartacus. Inside, he was less certain, but his faith in the Great Rider, whom he had been praying to daily, was strong. He winked. 'When we arrive, there'll be pirate ships waiting to take us across.'

Gannicus smiled sourly, but Castus was still not happy. 'I don't like it. It feels wrong.'

'What should we do then?' demanded Spartacus. 'Fight a battle on ground we haven't chosen? On Sicily, there'd be an opportunity to continue the war on an indefinite basis! Or have you got another bright idea?'

Castus flushed with a combination of anger and embarrassment, and Spartacus hoped that he hadn't pushed the hot-headed Gaul too far. 'We'll still have the chance to fight Crassus, you know. He isn't going to let us just march down to Rhegium. The whoreson will be on our tails the whole way. If Carbo hasn't managed to make a deal with any pirates, we'll have a battle on our hands within days.'

'It's worth the risk, Castus. I don't fancy staying behind to face ten legions while the majority of the army buggers off,' said Gannicus. 'Sicily is big enough for us to do our own thing.'

'All right,' said Castus from between gritted teeth. 'But this is the last sodding time we follow one of your suggestions. I'm leaving the moment that my feet touch Sicilian soil.'

'Me too,' added Gannicus with passion.

'We're not there yet. More than one party of enemy scouts has been seen watching us. Crassus knows where we are. If he can harry us on the way south, he will. Whoever is in charge of the rearguard will need to be ready to fend off Roman attacks every day, and if things go wrong, we'll all have to fight. Let's put our differences aside one last time, at least until we've left the mainland behind. Up to then, we remain one army.' It was pushing things further than necessary, but Spartacus had to be sure. He was pleased and a little relieved when, after a moment, they both nodded.

'We'll leave tomorrow.'

*

Since the first contact with Spartacus' troops, Crassus had been in ebullient mood. The clash had been inconclusive, but that did not matter a jot. What was important was the fact that, unlike the vast majority of their fellows who had faced the slaves, Crassus' legionaries had not run away. They had stood their ground against sustained assaults, sending out a firm message to the enemy. *Things are different now, Spartacus. I am in charge.*

The day after the skirmish, Crassus had been even more pleased by another first. Instead of seeking battle again, the slaves had withdrawn – *retreated* – down the Via Annia. He'd heard of Spartacus' plan first from his spy, but hadn't believed it. When the truth of it became apparent, he'd had it announced to every cohort in the army. He could still hear the cheering now. Without delay, he and eight legions had set out after Spartacus. Mummius' two legions, both of which contained many veterans of Lentulus' and Gellius' defeated forces, had been sent inland, to shadow the enemy host. Mummius was under strict orders not to engage with the slaves. His mission was to discourage them from trying to break away to their previous haunts in the south-east.

A week had passed without event. Crassus issued orders; the legions broke camp, marched and erected another encampment. On the eighth day, surrounded by his bodyguard and with Caepio keeping pace along-side him, Crassus was some two miles from the front of the column. He had spent the morning deep in thought. Spartacus appeared intent on reaching the point of Italy's 'toe'. Could he really have delusions of escaping to Sicily? he wondered scornfully. That's what his spy had thought, although the fool hadn't known how it would be done. Perhaps Spartacus thinks he can hold us off at the straits while his men try to build ships! That would never happen. His forces were following the Thracian's too closely.

Soon, thought Crassus exultantly, the door would have closed on the slaves. Beyond Consentia, a town some thirty miles south of Thurii, they would enter a geographical bottleneck, all but doing his job for him. Once a blockade had been built across the peninsula, the legions would starve Spartacus and his men out, or force them into doomed attacks against their fortifications. Crassus already had pictures in his head of the siege of Numantia, which had been successfully prosecuted by Scipio Africanus sixty years before, in Iberia. The incredible feat of engineering was still celebrated. He would do the same. The campaign would end there, within sight of Sicily.

With luck, I could be back in Rome in time for Saturnalia. How the public will love me!

Crassus became aware of a cavalryman clattering along the verge towards him. 'Message for you from my decurion, sir,' cried the rider as he drew near. 'We've been scouting along the trails and valleys to the east.'

'Speak.'

The cavalryman wheeled his horse so that he could ride parallel to Crassus. 'We've just encountered some of Mummius' men, sir.'

Crassus frowned. 'Messengers, like you?'

A heartbeat's hesitation. 'No, sir. They weren't messengers.'

'Are you trying to confuse or annoy me, man? Because you're doing both.'

'I'm sorry, sir, that's not my intention.' The cavalryman swallowed. 'It appears that they clashed with some of Spartacus' forces.'

'When?' asked Crassus, his nostrils flaring. *Mummius will pay for this!*

'Yesterday, sir.'

'And the men you met were the wounded sent back by Mummius, is that it?'

'No, sir. Apparently, they were driven back by Spartacus' troops.'

Crassus shot a disbelieving glance at Caepio, whose face bore an unhappy scowl. His eyes returned accusingly to the cavalryman. 'Say that again.'

'They were driven from the field, sir. Routed, is what some of them said.'

'Routed,' repeated Caepio in evident disbelief.

'Gods above, what part of my orders did Mummius not understand? Under no circumstances was he to engage with the enemy!' shouted Crassus.

The cavalryman did not dare answer. He locked his gaze on the backs of the soldiers in front.

'Where is Mummius? Is the fool even alive still?'

'His men didn't know, sir,' muttered the cavalryman. 'We haven't seen him either.'

Crassus fought to control his anger. 'How many of the cowards have you met?'

'It's difficult to say, sir. They were straggling in in small groups. Eighty, perhaps a hundred?'

'That's all?'

'There were more following, but my decurion wanted you to know about it, sir.'

'He did well. So did you. Return to your unit and tell your officer that he is to send every last one of Mummius' men down to the road. There they are to find Centurion Caepio, who will direct them thereafter.'

Looking immensely relieved not to be punished, the cavalryman repeated Crassus' orders word for word before saluting and riding off.

'What do you want me to do with the yellow-livered rats, sir?' growled Caepio.

'Take a cohort from the front legion and use it to round them up. Isolate the first five hundred who reach you. Make sure that all of them keep up with the rest of the column. I'll deal with the mangy dogs when we've reached the site for our camp.'

'Very good, sir.' Caepio called for a horse. Mounting with an ease that belied his age, he rode off without a backward glance.

Left alone with his fury, Crassus began to plan his course of action. He prayed that Mummius *had* survived, not because he gave a whit for the man, but because he wanted to punish him. It was rare indeed for such a senior officer to be stripped of his rank, but that wouldn't stop Crassus. The thought of going further and having Mummius executed was appealing, but with regret, he decided against it. The man might be an idiot, but he came from a good lineage. Seventy years earlier, his grandfather had sacked the Greek city of Corinth while serving as a consul. The family was still well connected. Crassus had been given supreme command of the campaign to subdue Spartacus, but his position wasn't unassailable. Alienating elements within the Senate before he had succeeded was not a good idea.

It would be enough to humiliate Mummius by demoting him in front of his own men and sending him in disgrace to Rome. His men, however, would have to pay for their cowardice. Their punishment would show every legionary in the army that such behaviour would never be tolerated.

Crassus' lips thinned with satisfaction.

By the time the day's camps had been built, Mummius' soldiers had been in the sun for several hours. They had been denied both food and water. The five hundred men who had been first to arrive back — a virtually untouched cohort – had been made to stand facing the main entrance to Crassus' encampment. Their muscles were shaking from the effort of standing to attention for so long, but not a single soldier had dared to complain. Any weapons they hadn't discarded had been confiscated, and their mail shirts lay in a great silver pile alongside. A cohort of veterans with drawn swords had been deployed around them, and a score of centurions, including Caepio, patrolled up and down inside this perimeter, raining blows on anyone who relaxed even a fraction. The remainder of the disgraced legionaries, almost six thousand men, were arrayed in cohort-sized blocs to their right. Mummius stood in front, bareheaded and without a weapon.

Crassus had ordered that a hundred individuals from each legion should witness the punishment that was to be meted out. The selected soldiers marched in when the day's camps had been finished. They placed themselves opposite the main body of Mummius' troops, forming the third side of a large square.

Informed that the scene had been set, Crassus let the assembled legionaries bake in the heat for close to an hour. He wanted everyone present – not just the legionaries who had run – to be tired, sunburned and uncomfortable when he arrived. Finally, riding his best horse, a spirited grey stallion, and accompanied by his senior officers, he made his way to the platform that had been built by the engineers on the square's last side, parallel to the camp's wall. In front of it lay a large pile of wooden clubs, the ends of which had been studded with nails. As Crassus led the way up the steps, trumpeters blew a short, sharp fanfare.

Crassus began to speak the moment that the musicians had finished. He pitched his voice to carry. 'You all know why you are here! Some men, that is Mummius and the "tremblers", are to be punished severely. Their comrades can also expect to be disciplined. The rest of you are present to learn that the cowardice shown by these so-called "soldiers" cannot and will not be tolerated. EVER. You are to act as witnesses, so that every man in the army hears about what happened here today.' He let his words sink in, saw with satisfaction the condemned ponder their fates.

'Lucius Mummius Achaicus, present yourself!'

Mummius marched smartly forward and came to a stop in front of the platform. He saluted, but avoided Crassus' eye. 'Sir!'

'I sent you to shadow the enemy army. You were to avoid confrontation with Spartacus' troops, but when the chance presented itself, you did so anyway, in the process disobeying my commands. Is that not correct?'

'It is, sir,' answered Mummius in a low voice. 'Some of his troops had fallen behind the main body of—'

'Silence! Not only did you flout my orders, but you fell into Spartacus' trap. When the battle began, your men proved to be cowards of the first degree. They ran from the enemy in their thousands, leaving their weapons and standards behind. The first soldiers to appear consisted of an entirely unharmed cohort. Did they fight at all, I wonder, or did they just run when the slaves advanced as they did before when they fought with Gellius and Lentulus?' Crassus' tone was withering.

Mummius didn't say a word.

'Most of the cohorts that returned afterwards had suffered heavy losses. That doesn't excuse them fleeing the battlefield, but it shows at least that they are not complete cowards,' Crassus declared. 'I will come to them later. First I must deal with you. Lucius Mummius Achaicus, legate. Or should I say, former legate.'

Mummius' head lifted. His face was stricken, but not unsurprised.

'I strip you of your rank and your command with immediate effect,' Crassus cried. 'Only the memory of your glorious forefathers, who were far greater men than you, prevented me from punishing you further. You are ordered to return to Rome with all haste, where you are to present yourself to the Senate and explain your actions. The senators can do with you as they see fit.' He glared at Mummius. 'Are my orders clear this time?'

'Yes, sir.'

'I hope so. Get out of my sight!'

Head down, Mummius trudged back to his position.

'Every man apart from the tremblers is to be fined six months' pay. They are to be issued with new weapons to replace the ones that were thrown away or lost.' Crassus noted the relieved looks of those in the front ranks. 'But first, I would have you pledge that you will never again discard your sword or javelins. You will swear this upon pain of death. Anyone who refuses will be executed.' He eyed the legionaries again. 'Are there any men who do not wish to take the oath?'

Not a man stirred.

Crassus smiled. 'Repeat after me then: I, a soldier of Rome . . .'

When the assembled men had finished swearing, Crassus turned to the soldiers directly before him. 'In case you didn't know, you whoresons, the term "trembler" is a Spartan phrase. It was coined to describe the worst of men, the soldiers who didn't come back with their shields or on them, but without them entirely. Not only did you do that, but you were the first to run. The first to leave your comrades to the mercy of the enemy. You are all cowards. DAMN COWARDS!' He glared at them, daring anyone to meet his eye. No one would. 'There is just one punishment suitable for such men. Decimation!'

The word hung in the hot air.

'That's right, you maggots!' roared Crassus. 'Decimation is what you deserve.'

Shock filled the faces of those who were watching; utter terror twisted the faces of the condemned soldiers.

'You are to march before me in groups of fifty. You will draw lots, and then one man in every ten is to be beaten to death by his companions. Fifty of you in total will die, and the rest of you will be forced to pitch your tents outside the walls of the camp until I say otherwise. For the same period, you will be issued barley to eat, as the horses and mules are. Every one of you will be docked a year's pay. You can also expect to fight in the front ranks in any subsequent battles.' Crassus' eyes flickered left and right. 'Caepio, where are you?'

'Right here, sir.' The old centurion strode forward from the tremblers' ranks.

'You are to supervise. Any man not taking part in this punishment with sufficient enthusiasm is to suffer the same fate as those who are being decimated. Clear?'

'Yes, sir.'

'Begin at once.'

Caepio swivelled about. 'You heard the general! Fifty men, step forward in groups of ten!'

With dragging heels, the first couple of ranks began walking towards him. Other centurions shoved them into files of ten. Caepio produced a bag, which he shook vigorously. 'This contains nine white pebbles and one black. Each of you is to take one. Obviously, the one who gets the black stone is to die.' He held open the bag. 'First!'

Encouraged by a centurion wielding a vine cane, a soldier stepped up to Caepio. Plunging his hand into the bag, he pulled out a stone. It was white. His face sagged with relief.

'Next!' yelled Caepio.

The second pebble was white.

So were the third, fourth and fifth ones.

But the sixth was black. The man who drew it let out a cry of anguish.

'Stay where you are!' roared Caepio. The shaking soldier obeyed, and Caepio gestured at the pile of clubs. 'The rest are to pick up a weapon and get back here.' When the nine had returned, he bellowed, 'Form a circle.'

As soon as the legionaries had done as they were told, Caepio shoved the chosen man into the rough ring's centre. 'Get on with it!'

No one moved except the condemned, who fell to his knees and began praying in a loud voice.

'Roman citizens are not supposed to be crucified, but that won't stop me ordering it for every last one of you fools!' screamed Crassus, the veins in his neck bulging. 'Kill him! NOW!'

For a heartbeat no one reacted, but then a big legionary took a step forward. And another step. He was joined by three others, and in a rush, by the five remaining men. They closed in on their comrade, who was now begging for mercy. No one replied, and no one would meet his eye.

The big legionary acted first. As he brought down his club, the condemned man raised his right arm in defence. *Thump.* The heavy blow snapped his arm bones like a twig, and the nails in the club's head ripped scarlet lines all through his scalp. Screaming, he fell on to his back. 'Help me, Jupiter, please! Help me!'

Like a pack of wolves falling upon their prey, the nine soldiers surrounded him. Their clubs rose and fell in a terrible rhythm. Spatters of blood flew up, covering their arms and faces. The screaming quickly died to a low moaning sound, and that too was silenced fast. Yet the legionaries kept pounding away. It was only when Caepio called them off that they stood back, chests heaving. A combination of horror and demented rage contorted their faces. It wasn't surprising, thought Crassus. Their comrade resembled a badly butchered piece of meat. His limbs lay at unnatural angles, and his features were unrecognisable, a bloody mess of torn flesh, fractured bone and exposed teeth. Crassus fancied he could see brain matter on several of the clubs, which was curiously satisfying. 'Leave his body where it lies,' he ordered. 'Next!'

The dazed soldiers were marched away and the next group of ten forced to come forward. Each picked his pebble from Caepio's bag. When it was time to take a club and do the unthinkable, no one protested. The mould had been broken by the initial decimation, and everyone knew that if they resisted, a cross awaited them. Soon a second bloodied corpse lay beside the first. Then it was a third and a fourth. As the number of dead grew, Crassus had the bodies heaped on one another, like carrion.

And so it went on, for more than an hour.

When the last man had been beaten to death, silence fell over the assembled troops. Crassus' gaze moved over the legionaries, assessing their mood. He saw no resentment or even anger, just resignation, disgust and fear. 'Let this be a lesson to you and to your comrades.' He pointed at the pile of broken flesh and bone, and the pool of blood that was spreading around it. 'Spread the word. This is the end that awaits anyone who runs from the enemy!'

Chapter XIV

By now, Spartacus was sick of the view of the great island. Sicily filled the western horizon; the most prominent feature being the headland that was formed by the coming together of the isle's northern and eastern coasts. Near it was Charybdis, the famous whirlpool that would suck ships and their crews down to a terrible, watery death. The island was near enough to make out some of the large houses on the high ground above the shore. Beyond them mountains rose steeply up, vanishing in a blue-purple haze when they met the sky. They reminded him of Thrace. A sour taste rose in his throat. It was only a mile to Sicily's hinterland, but after more than two months of waiting, that distance felt as far as the moon. Even the merchant ships that sailed within a few hundred paces of the shore were wholly unreachable.

At first, the time had gone by easily. Thanks to the defensive screen of infantry that he'd thrown up across the peninsula, and the cavalry that kept the main road clear, Crassus' legions had made no real effort to break through to his main force. Instead they had busied themselves building ramparts and ditches that sealed Spartacus' troops into the isthmus that curved out towards Sicily. He hadn't liked this one bit, but there was the consolation of knowing that Carbo had completed his mission successfully. The announcement that a number of pirate vessels would soon arrive had been an enormous boost to morale. Once his two thousand men had sailed over the strait and seized the grain ships, the evacuation of his army could begin. With the gods' blessing, Crassus wouldn't suspect a thing about it until it was too late.

The knowledge that a battle wasn't imminent had eased Spartacus' tension a fraction. Life had continued much as it had at Thurii the previous year. There had been stints of drilling his troops, or listening to reports from the officers who were monitoring the Roman forces. Hours in the company of his quartermasters, making sure that the rations were divided equally and with the smiths, ensuring that every house and farm in the area was stripped of everything useful. Some of his men were still not that well armed. Forging weapons had to continue every day. He'd had nothing to do with Castus and Gannicus, who had camped with their men some distance from the main force. In essence, the army had already split up. It didn't matter. Crassus was unaware of the schism, and once they had reached Sicily, it would become immaterial. Spartacus tried to block the troublesome pair from his mind. He had wasted enough time on them. He had concentrated instead on his evenings, the favourite part of his days, which were spent with Ariadne and Maron, who was growing fast.

There had also been opportunities to walk the coastline, searching for the best place to embark when the pirate ships arrived. Spartacus had done this alone the first time, managing to give the Scythians the slip. He grinned. The roasting that Ariadne had given them on his return had ensured that had never happened again. While Castus and Gannicus appeared to be honouring their truce, he wouldn't put it past them to make another attempt on his life. And actually he liked the tattooed Scythians' company. They felt like old friends, even though he'd known them for less than two years. The pair were discreet, shadowing him from a distance, thereby allowing him the pretence of being on his own. As he walked, his mind had turned over every possibility a score of times. If things went on Sicily as he wished, he would be able to defend the island from Roman attack rather than just wait until they sent an expeditionary force against him.

Yet as the days had turned into weeks, it had become harder and harder not to let his thoughts become troubled. Autumn had come and gone. Winter had arrived, and with it, colder weather. The berries and nuts from the bushes that covered the mountain slopes had vanished. The area's farms had long since been stripped of all their grain. Spartacus wondered if the pirate captain had played Carbo false, taken the money and sailed away, never to return. It seemed unlikely. Only a fool or a madman would turn down fifty times that amount of coin for what was a simple task. That belief was what seemed to be keeping his troops' spirits up. His eyes turned to the south, searching the waves for a sail. For the thousandth time, he saw nothing. A scatter of gulls scudded overhead in the chill air, their sharp calls seeming to mock him. His mood darkened. If Heracleo was coming, where in the Great Rider's name was he? How long did it take to find a few cursed vessels and sail around Italy's tip?

He wondered again about climbing the high ground to the sacred cave opposite Charybdis, there to make another offering to Scylla, the monster with twelve feet and six heads that guarded the straits. No. Twice was enough. If the gods thought he was desperate, they could become even more capricious than they already were.

His stomach rumbled, reminding Spartacus that he hadn't eaten since dawn. He had ordered rations to be reduced, but sixty thousand men still ate a vast amount of bread every day. Unless Heracleo appeared within the next couple of weeks, their grain would run out. Then they would have to break through Crassus' fortifications. That wasn't a prospect that he wanted to be forced into.

He turned to study the land to his rear. Like much of the region's coast, there was only a narrow area of flat ground bordering the sea. In some places it was as much as half a mile or a mile wide, but in others, it was little more than a strip of sand. The majority of the toe was formed by steep, rolling hills, the beech-covered tops of which were often shrouded in lowering grey clouds. With the Scythians in tow, he had traversed the highest peaks, his mission to inspect the legions at work. The Romans' blockade had been constructed at one of the narrowest parts of the toe, some ten miles to the north. Thanks to the vertiginous terrain, there had been little need for Crassus' soldiers to erect any defences at all, other than on the coastline. Dangerously steep wooded slopes, jagged peaks and fast-flowing rivers meant that the interior was only suitable for the deer, wild sheep and wolves whose territory it was. On a mountaintop ridge Spartacus had located one spot suitable to move north – but so had Crassus, who had spared no effort in the construction of the defences there. They were truly impressive. Slaves had laboured to build an inverted 'V'-shaped earthen barrier that was topped by stone and twice the height of a man. Sharpened stakes bristled from the wall's outer surface, and a deep ditch running in front of it had been lined with spiked pits. Catapults lined the ramparts, and large numbers of legionaries were on duty night and day. Only one approach had been left, a narrow path that would force any attackers into the point of the 'V', where they could be pummelled from both sides.

Watching from a distance, Spartacus had been quietly impressed. If they had to take it, the loss of life among his soldiers would be huge. It would be at less cost than a frontal assault on the flat ground, however. Seven legions were massed on the western side of the toe, near his army, and two guarded the eastern coast. There was no point marching to that point, hoping to overwhelm the enemy defences. Crassus' scouts, of whom there were many in the area, would pass on the news. Wherever he led his men, thought Spartacus grimly, the Romans would be waiting. Except on the ridge. A single legion held that narrow section.

Trying to shift his thoughts from the bloody images that sprang to mind, he returned his gaze to the sea. Some distance out, a dolphin leaped out of the water. It was followed by another, and another. Soon Spartacus had counted eight. He grinned at their mischievous play, their clear pleasure at swimming together. *They are truly free.*

At first, the sail that came into sight beyond the dolphins didn't register.

When it did, Spartacus' heart leaped. Could the gods have answered his prayers?

Taxacis' guttural voice broke the silence. 'A ship!'

'I see it,' said Spartacus, keeping his voice calm.

'Is it . . . merchant?' asked Atheas.

'We'll have to wait and see,' replied Spartacus. He settled down on his haunches. Perhaps it was because of the dolphins, but he had a good feeling in his belly.

They waited for a long time. No one spoke, but the silence between them was companionable. There was plenty to watch. Drawn by the same shoal of fish as the dolphins, hundreds of gulls swooped and dived over the waves. Successful birds rose in triumph with a fish in their beaks, and screeched indignantly at any of their fellows that tried to steal their catch. Eventually, the vessel drew near enough for its shape to be determined. Spartacus eyed the long, predatory shape with undisguised glee. 'If that's a merchantman, my name's Marcus Licinius Crassus!'

Atheas squinted at him. 'No. You . . . still ugly . . . as ever.'

Taxacis chortled.

'It's not big enough to be a trireme,' mused Spartacus. 'It must be a bireme.'

The ship sailed closer to the shore. With increasing excitement, they waited until it was parallel with their position. As Spartacus had thought, there were two sets of oars, one above the other. It had a sharp prow and a typical rounded stern. A large rectangular sail billowed from a central mast. At a rough estimate, there were thirty to forty oarsmen a side. Other figures lined the sides. What drew Spartacus' attention more than the crew, however, were the weapons on view.

'Those are catapults on the deck!' he cried, jumping up and down. 'Here! Here!' he roared.

The Scythians copied him, and a moment later, it was clear that they had been seen. A shouted command and the ship hove to. The oars were shipped, and an anchor thrown out. Several men scrambled into the little boat that was tied astern.

Spartacus glanced at Atheas, who was already fingering his sword. 'Let's play it friendly. We don't want to scare them off. You too, Taxacis.'

Taxacis nodded, but Atheas adopted a false hurt expression, which made him look even fiercer. 'I . . . always friendly!'

For the first time in weeks, Spartacus laughed.

The rowing boat didn't take long to reach the beach. As soon as it was in the shallows, three of the four heavily armed men within jumped out. Led by a short, dark-skinned figure, they waded ashore. They stopped a short distance away.

'Well met,' said Spartacus, his manner amiable.

'Well met,' replied the dark-skinned man suspiciously. 'Who are you?'

'I could ask the same of you, my friend.'

'You don't have three catapults trained on you,' retorted the pirate.

He didn't bother checking. 'Since you spoke first, I will answer. I am Spartacus the Thracian. You may have heard of me.'

The pirate's composure slipped a little. 'How can you prove this?' he demanded. 'Half the brigands in Italy probably claim the same thing.'

'I have no need to demonstrate who I am. In the next bay sits an army sixty thousand strong. Ask any soldier in it who their leader is.'

The pirate's manner changed at once. 'It is an honour to meet you. I am Heracleo. Your messenger – Carbo, was it? – may have spoken of me. We met near Croton some time since.'

'He did. You were to bring as many ships as you could. You brought but one,' said Spartacus, showing none of his concern.

'It was more difficult than I expected to recruit ships. The market at Delos is busier than ever, and all that most captains are concerned with is finding slaves to sell there. The reality of that is easier to believe in than my tale. But do not fear, everything is in order.' Heracleo flashed a greasy smile. 'Two captains of my acquaintance operate in this area. I sent word to them, arranging a meeting to the north of here. A couple of days, and I'll return with at least one trireme and another bireme. Maybe more, if the word has gone out as I've hoped.'

Spartacus' eyes held Heracleo's for several moments, but the pirate did not look away. *The dog is telling the truth, or he's a damn good liar*, he thought. 'I had hoped for more vessels, but three should suffice. How many soldiers can each ship transport at a time?'

'For a short crossing like this?' Heracleo waved dismissively at Sicily. 'The biremes can carry fifty, perhaps even sixty each. The trireme will take nearly a hundred.'

Spartacus did a quick mental calculation. 'About a dozen trips should see my men on the other side then.'

'Indeed, indeed,' agreed Heracleo. A greedy look entered his eyes. 'And the price—'

'It remains the same,' interrupted Spartacus.

'I was to be paid a hundred and twenty-five thousand denarii when I arrived.'

'When you arrived with *ships*. I see only one.'

Heracleo licked his lips. 'The other captains might need some evidence of your . . . goodwill.'

Spartacus didn't trust the pirate, but the fact that Heracleo had turned up was a good indicator that he might honour his side of the bargain. It would be politic to keep him sweet. Like it or not, he had far more to lose than Heracleo. 'You've been honourable thus far. As a friendly gesture, I'd be willing to give you twenty thousand denarii more. What captain wouldn't be persuaded to help when you hand him some of that?'

Heracleo sucked in a breath, considering. Then he was all smiles. 'Thank you. How soon could—'

'Wait here. I'll have a party of my men bring the money at once.' Heracleo rubbed his hands together and Spartacus gave him a warning look. 'Play me false, and I'll hunt you down, even if it takes me the rest of my days. Do you understand?'

'I will return. You have my word on it.' Heracleo stuck out his hand.

Pleased, Spartacus accepted the grip. 'Two days until you return, you say?'

'Two, maybe three. No more than that.'

'Good. We'll be waiting for you here.'

Leaving Maron in the care of the midwife, Ariadne set off through the camp, the wicker basket containing her snake under one arm. Inside, she had carefully placed a small amphora of wine, a little sheaf of wheat and a bunch of grapes. Half a dozen soldiers – protection given her by Spartacus – dogged her footsteps, but they knew well enough to hang back. She didn't know exactly where to go, but as long as she found solitude, it didn't matter. Living in the midst of an enormous army felt like dwelling in a city. Ariadne didn't like it, nor had she grown used to it. The villages in Thrace that she had grown up with contained no more than a few thousand inhabitants. Even Kabyle, the only city, had not been large. There she had prayed to her god in the temple, but had also been able to access wild places. Places where she could almost feel the otherworld, where Dionysus' voice wasn't drowned out by the sound of people.

More than anything, Ariadne longed for guidance. It had been too long since she felt the certainty of the god's will in her actions. Spartacus' purpose seemed as implacable as ever, yet that didn't mean he wasn't also making mistakes. Since his return from Rome, they had resolved their differences, but there was a faint distance between them that hadn't been there before. Spartacus sought out her opinion less than he had; she asked fewer questions about what he was doing.

For her, the root of it was the resentment that she still felt towards him for choosing his army over her and Maron. Ariadne had always tried to deny the feeling, but like the weeds that spring up between flagstones, it kept returning. She wanted direction not just on the best course to choose for the army, but the best one for her. Should she try to resolve her differences with Spartacus or would it be easier to do the unthinkable and walk away?

Ariadne stumbled as her sandal caught against a stone. She looked up, noticing with surprise that she had left the camp behind her and was standing at the foot of the rocky slope that led up to Scylla's cave. An image of the monster popped into her mind, and she shuddered. She had seen the mouth of the cavern from the beach below. It was all too easy to imagine each of Scylla's long necks darting out to seize unsuspecting fishermen, sailors or dolphins. Only a fool would look inside and see whether the legend was true. Ariadne was about to go somewhere else, but she stopped. She hadn't been watching where she was walking. This was where her feet had led her. Who was she to turn away? Dionysus might have guided her here.

Steeling her nerves, she began to climb.

'Where are you going?' The nervous voice of one of her guards.

'Where does it look like?'

'It's not safe up there. Please, come down.'

A mischievous mood seized Ariadne. 'Are you frightened?'

'N-no, of course not.'

She scanned their faces. Not one was happy; most seemed scared. 'Stay here if you will.'

'But Spartacus said that you were not to be left alone.'

'I know what he said.' Ariadne began climbing again. Hampered by her basket, she moved slowly.

The guard tried again. 'He would not want you to visit the cave.'

'I am my own mistress,' retorted Ariadne, without looking back. 'I do what I choose. No one is stopping you from accompanying me.'

She ignored the argument that began behind her. After a while, she glanced around. Just one of her guards, the man who'd protested, was following her. The rest were huddled at the bottom of the slope like a group of frightened sheep. She wasn't surprised. Superstition ruled the minds of most men. If she, a priestess of Dionysus, was scared, then ordinary soldiers would be plain terrified of walking into the cave of a legendary monster. She set her jaw, forced herself to breathe, her legs to keep moving. With every step, she felt more confident that she was *supposed* to do this.

The view of the straits and of Sicily grew even more impressive as she climbed. Sunlight glittered off the water, turning it into a giant mirror, which meant that she missed the bireme setting out from the beach where Spartacus had been. Her eyes searched the south, but the haze prevented her from any sight of the famous volcano, Mount Aetna, whose eruptions were attributed to a fearsome giant who lived deep underneath it. Soon, she told herself, she would have the opportunity to see it with her own eyes.

Before Ariadne knew it, she had reached the top of the headland, which was covered in scrubby vegetation. A narrow trail beckoned. She wasn't surprised when the lone soldier came to a halt. 'I won't be long,' she said over her shoulder.

He gave her a nervous nod.

The man was probably as worried about what Spartacus would do to him afterwards as whether Scylla might eat him, she thought with a hint of amusement. There was no need for her husband to know, though. If she didn't tell him, her guards surely wouldn't.

The path meandered as it passed through the vegetation. Here and there, she could make out the print of a sandal in the dirt. She took heart. People had been here before, perhaps to make offerings in return for safe passage on the waters below. Her idea was confirmed as she reached the cliff top and saw a makeshift altar of stones. Miniature amphorae, votive lamps, coins and small cakes were arranged in front of it. Just a few steps beyond, a dizzying precipice overlooked the deep blue sea.

Ariadne was careful not to go too near. A gust of wind might carry her over the edge. There was a perilously narrow trail down to the cave itself, but she wasn't about to start trying to climb down to it. That would be a step too far. Tempting the gods, as if it she hadn't tempted them enough in the recent past. No, this was the right place to seek guidance.

Laying her basket on the ground, she knelt before the shrine. First, to placate the creature whose territory this was. Great Scylla, she prayed, I ask for your forgiveness in even approaching your home. I do so with reverence, and with great respect. Next, she opened her basket. At once, the snake raised its head. She spoke reassuringly to it, and it allowed her to lift out the amphora, wheat and grapes. Ariadne was so eager to present her gifts that she neglected to fasten the basket shut. 'Scylla, I offer you wine in acknowledgement of your power and your right to prey on those who pass by this point.' Removing the stopper, she poured a stream of wine on to the ground. The ruby liquid soaked into the earth, leaving only a stain behind. 'Accept this libation as a mark of my veneration. I also pray that you are not angered by my speaking to a god here.' Lowering the amphora, Ariadne closed her eyes and waited. Her ears filled with the whistle of the wind, the occasional screech of a gull and, from far below, the crash of the waves against the rocks at the cliff's base.

A little time passed, and there was no response. No monster had appeared to devour her; the ground had not opened up beneath her feet. The wine had been accepted, Ariadne decided. Hopefully, that also meant that Scylla did not object to her asking Dionysus for help. She opened her eyes again. Taking the sheaf in one hand and the grapes in the other, she gazed up at the sky. 'Dionysus, I am always your humble servant, even when it does not appear so. Of late, I have not spent enough time honouring you. Having given birth to a child is no excuse. I beg for your understanding and your forgiveness. I bring you tokens of my devotion, objects that I know you find pleasing.' With great care, she laid the wheat and grapes on the ground before her.

Another respectful silence; again no response.

Trusting this meant that Dionysus was in a generous mood, Ariadne picked up the amphora for the second time. 'I bring you some of the finest vintage wine. Accept this as a token of my commitment to you.'

She closed her eyes, and waited for a sign. Anything that would help her decide what to do. Should she go to Sicily with Spartacus? As if that plan will ever work, she thought bitterly. She had been wary of the idea of recruiting pirates from the beginning, but as time dragged on without any sign of a ship, Ariadne's doubts had solidified. To leave this place, they would have to break through Crassus' fortifications. And what then? Again she saw the road lined with crucifixes. Was that the end that awaited Spartacus? She prayed that it was not, but the haunting image would not leave her. Would it not be better to leave now, she wondered, before the same or worse happened to her and Maron? There would be no Roman mercy for Spartacus' woman or child. Yet to run would be to betray her husband. Guilt racked her.

Too late she heard the rush of movement behind her; too late she tried to rise.

A heavy blow across the back of her head sent Ariadne sprawling forward. She landed hard, knocking her forehead off a stone at the altar's base. Stars burst across her vision, and she struggled to draw in a breath. Someone grabbed her by the hair and wrenched her upright. Even as she opened her mouth to cry for help, a hand was clamped across her mouth.

'Try to scream, *bitch*, and I'll toss you over the edge,' hissed a voice. 'Do you understand?'

Terrified, furious, Ariadne nodded. *Who in Hades is it?*

'No one would hear anyway. Your guard is a dead man.' The hand was removed, and she was pulled over to lie on her back. She stared up at Castus' leering face with utter revulsion. 'Seeking the help of your god is all very well, but doing it on your own? I thought you'd know better than that by now.' He reached down and squeezed her breasts. 'Nice. They're bigger than they were.'

Ariadne's guts roiled with fear. *He's going to rape me and then throw me off the cliff anyway.*

'I didn't expect to see you here.' He cuffed her across the head. 'Answer me, whore!'

'I was seeking guidance from my god. W-what brought you to this place?' she mumbled, playing for time.

'I wanted to placate Scylla. If we're to sail across that stretch of open water' – he waved a hand at the straits – 'we'll need all the help we can get.'

He was terrified, Ariadne realised. It wasn't that surprising. Like most of the army, Castus would never have set foot in a boat. 'Did you receive an answer?'

A curt laugh. 'Of course not.' He shrugged off the baldric that suspended his sword and laid it to one side. Using both hands, he ripped her dress to the waist. 'But who cares? Even if I drown, I'll go down to Neptune knowing that I fucked Spartacus' woman.'

Ariadne tried to push him off. He laughed and slapped her hands away. She kicked frantically, but Castus was more than twice her weight. She watched in horror as he bent to nuzzle her breasts with his mouth. Savage memories of what her father's abuse, of what Phortis the Capuan had done to her, came rushing back. Now it was about to happen again. *Think! Think!* Her head twisted. On one side, all she could see was the outline of

Sicily, which she would never reach. On the other, the offerings left before the altar. Nothing she could reach would stop Castus. His sword was several steps away.

He reached down and his hand groped for her groin. She could feel his hardness pressing against her thigh. Waves of nausea mixed with the pain from her head. Ariadne wanted to die. She wished he had just tossed her over the edge.

'Spartacus' wife?' he panted. 'Who'd have thought I'd get to screw her, eh?'

It was if a lightning bolt had hit her. *Spartacus' wife. That is who I am. I cannot run away from that.* The thought gave Ariadne new energy to live. To survive.

Castus paused to lick at her breasts again. He looked up at her, his face full of lust. His fetid breath washed over her. Ariadne wanted to vomit, but she forced herself to hold his gaze. Anything to delay what was about to happen. 'You've wanted me for a long time?'

'Gods, yes! What man wouldn't?' he panted, tugging down his trousers. 'Ready for a decent-sized cock, not the sausage you've been used to? You've probably wanted me all along.' He shoved forward with his hips, trying to enter her.

Ariadne couldn't look at him any longer. She rolled her head to the left. Gods, let it be over quickly. A flicker of movement caught her eye. Her heart almost stopped. Her snake! It had got out of the basket, and had slithered on to a large stone at the altar's foot. If only she could reach it!

Fortune intervened. Grunting with irritation, Castus released her left arm. He spat on his fingers and moved them down to rub at her crotch. 'You'll be as wet as a whore during Saturnalia when I'm finished with you,' he growled, nudging forward once more.

Ariadne moved her freed hand out towards the snake. Never had she wanted it to do as she wished so much. Never had she needed it more.

Its head moved; its forked tongue flickered out towards her outstretched fingers.

Castus' prick touched her labia, and she flinched. He laughed.

With a few twists of its body, the snake slid forward on to her palm. *Yes!* There was a risk of it biting her if she moved fast, but Ariadne was beyond caring. Her arm flashed up; alarmed, the serpent arched its neck and opened its mouth in threat. Ariadne aimed it at Castus' neck.

The Gaul reacted with preternatural speed. It was the speed born of desperation, of years spent fighting as a gladiator, and it saved him from being bitten. He reared away from Ariadne, his mouth open in an 'O' of horror. As he fell to the ground, she rolled away and scrambled up. A muttered word to her snake, and it calmed a fraction. Spinning around, she found Castus already on his feet. Grim satisfaction filled her. The cliff edge was only a couple of steps behind him.

Holding the snake out before her, she advanced. 'Ready to die, you filth?'

Castus' face twisted with fear. He had nowhere to go. 'That thing might bite me, but I'll take you with me, you whore! We'll both dine with Neptune tonight!' He made a grab at her arm, but she swept the snake at his face and he had to dodge back out of the way. One of his sandals skidded; his foot shot out into nothingness and it took all of his effort not to fall backwards.

Ariadne was beginning to enjoy herself. 'How do you like it, you bastard? Which way would you rather die – from poison or by tumbling on to the rocks?' She rammed the snake at him again. Angry now, it tried to sink its teeth into his arm. By some miracle, he moved out of its way. Ariadne didn't mind. There was no way he could get out of this. 'You choose!'

Castus didn't answer. He just prepared himself for her next attack.

Ariadne would never say it, but he was a brave man. It was time to end it, though. 'Do this for Dionysus,' she whispered to the snake. Unsettled, it writhed within her grasp. 'Patience. Your prey is ready.' She looked up, expecting to see a trace of fear in Castus' face. What she saw was very different; he was trying to hide it, but there was triumph in his gaze. His eyes flickered; Ariadne sensed movement behind her. Instinct made her dodge to her right, towards the altar. As she struggled not to lose her balance, there was a muffled curse and Ariadne saw a thickset man carrying a sword – one of Castus' followers – hurtle into the space where she'd been. With a despairing cry, he shot over the cliff edge and disappeared from sight.

By the time she had righted herself, Castus had darted past her to safety. He swept up his weapon. Panic filled Ariadne, and she prepared to take him on with only the snake. To her surprise, however, he backed away. 'You're a crazy bitch!'

Taking a step towards him, she let out a cracked laugh. 'That's right, you piece of shit, I am mad! I am also one of Dionysus' chosen ones!' Right on cue, the snake opened its mouth, revealing its lethal fangs.

Castus' face went grey. Muttering a prayer, he shuffled backwards on to the path. Then he turned and was gone.

With a thumping heart, Ariadne waited, but he did not reappear. She calmed the snake, placed it back in the basket and fastened the lid. With her torn dress rearranged as best she could, she poured the rest of the wine on the ground, thanking her god with even greater fervency than before. Long moments passed, but nothing came to her. No vision, no words of wisdom. Ariadne felt no anger, just an overwhelming gratitude to be alive. More than anything, she wanted to see Spartacus.

His name triggered a memory. Castus had called her 'Spartacus' wife'. Ariadne smiled.

Dionysus *had* sent her a message after all. Two messages, in fact.

First, she was going nowhere. Standing by Spartacus was what counted – whatever the consequences. Second, Castus was not to be harmed. By rights, he should have just died. The fact that he had not told her that the gods still favoured him. It was not for her, or Spartacus, to intervene further.

To Ariadne's relief, the soldier who had followed her was not dead, as Castus had said. He'd been knocked half-senseless by a blow from behind, but he came to when she ministered to him. Having decided that Spartacus was to be kept in the dark, she swore the man to secrecy. His injury was to have come from a fall. He was only too glad to agree to her demand. His leader's fearsome temper was well known; the soldier who failed in his duty to guard Ariadne could not expect to live long.

The guards at the bottom were mightily relieved when the pair returned. They showed no sign of having seen Castus, who must have skulked down the far side of the headland. Ariadne ignored the sidelong looks aimed at her torn dress and dust-covered hair. They probably assumed that she had been taken by ritual mania, the trance-like state beloved of Dionysus' female adherents.

Reaching her tent, she found Maron asleep in his cot, with the old midwife dozing alongside. Ariadne quietly changed her clothes and combed out her hair. She washed her face and applied a little ground chalk to her face. It would conceal the swelling bruise on her forehead. After the horror of what had happened, it felt odd being back in normality. She drank a little wine to steady her nerves. No one could know about Castus, especially Spartacus.

Soon after, she was startled to see her husband appear in the entrance. 'They've arrived!' he cried.

Maron stirred, and Ariadne's instincts took over. 'Shhhh.'

'Sorry.' He reached her side, grinning. Happy that Maron was still asleep, she met his gaze. He wouldn't notice anything. He was visibly delighted.

'You're not talking about the Romans?' she whispered.

He gave her a surprised look. 'No! I've talked with the pirate captain whom Carbo met. He'll be back in a couple of days with two, if not three other ships. A dozen journeys will see the men on the other side. If all goes well, we could have the grain ships here inside a week.'

Ariadne gaped at him. This – a way out of their situation – she hadn't expected. 'A week,' she said slowly.

'It's wonderful, eh? Crassus hasn't got any ships. The prune-faced whoreson won't have a clue what's going on until we've gone! By the time he reacts, we'll have control of Sicily.' He kissed her on the lips. 'The first thing I'll do on the island is to set up a system of watchtowers along the coastline. The Romans won't be able to land without us being there to throw them back into the sea.'

Ariadne's worries dissolved before the burning belief in his eyes. This too *had* to be a message from the gods, she thought. From Dionysus, whose snake had saved her life. The pirates *would* return. They *would* escape to Sicily. Her heart leaped with joy, and she pulled his face down to hers. 'I always knew you could do it,' she said.

A day later . . .

Hearing raised voices, Crassus raised his head. A frown creased his brow. He'd given his guards specific orders that he was not to be disturbed. By all the gods, could the fools understand nothing? he wondered angrily.

'I don't give a damn! I have to talk to Crassus!' boomed a familiar voice.

'Get out of my way, you fool, or I'll have you digging trenches for the rest of your miserable life!'

'Is that you, Caepio?' Crassus put down the scroll on military tactics that he'd been composing and stood up. He found the whole process of writing a terrible bore, but this campaign was a golden opportunity for him to record his thoughts. They would be publicised and aggrandised afterwards, he could make sure of that. It wouldn't be long before every man in Italy knew of the expert methods with which he had defeated Spartacus.

The flap to his private quarters was drawn back and the veteran centurion stepped into the richly decorated room. He came to attention and saluted, meeting Crassus' icy stare stolidly, which angered but didn't surprise Crassus. 'This had better be good.'

'I think it is, sir,' came the measured reply.

'Let me guess. You've captured Spartacus.'

Caepio's lined face cracked into a semblance of a smile. 'It's not that good, sir.'

'How long are you going to keep me waiting? Spit it out!'

'One of our patrols happened upon a pirate ship anchored off a cove some miles to the north, sir. The crew were on the beach, replenishing its provisions, water and the like. The centurion in charge ordered an attack. Our men captured not just the pirates onshore, but the vessel as well.'

'That's very good, Caepio,' grated Crassus from between clenched teeth. 'Pirates are the scourge of the Mediterranean. The loss in merchant shipping each year is bleeding Rome white. But why would I care about that right now? We have bigger fish to fry than one leaky ship full of louse-ridden scum!'

'A search of the vessel revealed bags of coin, sir,' said Caepio with great patience. 'In total, it was more than ten thousand denarii. The centurion asked the captain where he'd come by such an amount. The whoreson wasn't forthcoming, so the centurion had his lads build a nice fire. When his feet were shoved into it, the pirate sang like a canary.' He paused, eyeing Crassus for any signs of interest.

Damn him, thought Crassus, his curiosity aroused. He adopted his most offhand look. 'Didn't the spy mention something of this?'

'He did, sir.' Caepio was far too shrewd to mention how at the time his general had dismissed the man's story as fantasy.

'Go on,' ordered Crassus brusquely.

'He was approached some time ago by one of Spartacus' men. A young Roman, he said. Made me think of the traitor at the munus whom I told you about. The one who was with Spartacus when he attacked you in Rome, sir.'

'I remember.' Crassus' interest was growing by the moment. 'Go on.'

'The pirate was offered more than a million denarii to carry two thousand of Spartacus' troops over to Sicily. He had to gather as many large ships together as he could, and sail them to meet the slaves.'

This time, Crassus couldn't conceal his shock. His spy hadn't been lying after all. 'By Jupiter, are you serious?'

'Yes, sir. There aren't too many men who can lie when the flesh is melting from their bones.'

'I don't suppose there are,' admitted Crassus. *Sicily — that's clever. He must know about the slave rebellions there.* 'Why so few soldiers, though? There are two legions on the island. What in hell's name was he planning?'

'I wondered if he had the idea of seizing some vessels, sir. Spartacus is a daring bastard; we know that. If he's heard what disarray the place is in over there, he might have thought it possible.'

Crassus pursed his lips in concentration. Gaius Verres, the governor of Sicily, was notoriously corrupt. 'Even if Spartacus doesn't know, he'd still try something that crazy. What's he got to lose? So what was the sewer rat of a pirate doing in the cove?'

'Waiting for two captains whom he knew, sir. Another day, and they would have arrived. Sailed off, and we'd have been none the wiser. Now, it will never happen. The other pirates won't understand why their friend never turned up, nor will they know about Spartacus' offer.'

'Excellent work, Caepio, excellent!' Crassus bestowed a dazzling smile upon the centurion. His day had just got *much* better. 'And the captain? I take it that he died under interrogation?'

'Indeed, sir. The centurion had his men crucify his entire crew, burn the ship and seize the prisoners as slaves. The money has been brought back to be put at your disposal. I hope that is satisfactory.'

'Most satisfactory,' Crassus purred. 'See to it that the centurion and his soldiers are each given a suitable cash reward.'

Caepio gave an approving nod. 'Very good, sir. Once again, I apologise for disturbing you.'

His bad mood forgotten, Crassus waved a forgiving hand.

'Was there anything else, sir?'

'Yes. Do we have any idea how much food the slaves have?'

'Last I heard from our man in their camp' – here Caepio winked – 'was that they had about a month's worth of grain left. That was about two weeks ago.'

'Damn his eyes, I told him to report more often than that!'

'It's very dangerous now, sir. Everywhere that we've built fortifications, Spartacus' men are like fleas on a dog. They're on watch day and night.'

Crassus bridled, but he knew Caepio was right. 'If the fool was correct, the slaves have fourteen days' provisions remaining. That's more good news. Even if they comb through every farm building, they won't find enough to last much longer.'

'That's right, sir. The land here is poor. It's better for cultivating olives than grain. There will be little in the way of stores on most farms.'

'We had best prepare for them to attempt a breakout soon then, eh?'

Spartacus, your days are numbered.

Chapter XV

Carbo had been ecstatic when Spartacus had told him of Heracleo's arrival. His trust in the pirate had been repaid, and his leader would think well of him for succeeding in his mission. They would escape from Crassus' legions! He had talked for hours with Navio, Publipor and Arnax about it. Navio had been to Sicily, and knew the lie of the land. 'Spartacus has made a good choice,' he had declared the first night. 'The latifundia there are immense. Most have hundreds of slaves. Some have far more. Tough bastards, the lot of them: you know what agricultural slaves are like. When the word gets out that we've arrived, they'll flock to us in their thousands.'

Publipor had winked. 'More men for you to train.'

'Good. The more soldiers we have, the more legionaries we can kill,' Navio had snarled.

Carbo had flinched, but said nothing: he knew his friend's insatiable appetite for the blood of his own kind was born from the anguish of losing both father and brother to Pompey's troops. As far as Navio was concerned, his war would end only when the Senate burned down and Spartacus had destroyed the Republic. It was an impossible dream, thought Carbo, but it made Navio the perfect soldier. He, on the other hand, was fighting because he was loyal to Spartacus. He would fight whomever the Thracian did and follow him anywhere, because he believed in him. Loved him.

That was why, by dawn on the fourth day after Heracleo's departure, Carbo's spirits had plummeted. There had been no storms, no intemperate weather to send the bireme off course. No Roman vessels to scare it away or to stop it from anchoring offshore. Heracleo must have reconsidered, thought Carbo miserably. He would not be coming back. Later that morning, he wasn't surprised to be summoned to Spartacus' tent. No doubt their leader wanted to grill him again about what had been arranged, or even to punish him.

Atheas and Taxacis greeted him in a friendly manner but the Thracian's face was as black as thunder.

'You called for me?' Carbo asked.

'I did.'

Carbo shifted from foot to foot. 'Is it about Heracleo?'

'In a manner of speaking, yes.'

'I'm sorry,' blurted Carbo. 'I never should have trusted him. It's all my fault.'

Spartacus reached down to pick up a leather bag. He tossed it at Carbo. 'A Roman catapult shot that over the ramparts earlier. Take a look inside.'

Seeing the red stain on the bag's bottom, Carbo's stomach wrenched. Gingerly, he peered in and was stunned to recognise Heracleo's waxen features, still twisted in an expression of terror. Revolted, angered and a little relieved, Carbo dropped the bag.

'I wanted to be sure. You think it's Heracleo too.'

'I do,' said Carbo. 'The Romans caught him then?'

'Evidently,' replied Spartacus in a dry tone.

Carbo wanted to scream at the sky. 'How? They have no ships worth talking about!'

'My guess is that Heracleo put in for water and was unlucky enough to be surprised on the beach by a Roman patrol. Maybe they questioned him; maybe they found his money. Either way, they discovered what he was up to. Why else would he have been killed and had his head thrown over the wall? I can't think of a better way for Crassus to say, "Fuck you, Spartacus." Can you?'

'No,' he muttered.

'A real shame that we didn't manage to kill him in Rome, eh?' Spartacus' right hand bunched into a fist for a moment. 'But what's done is done. We have to deal with the present, and the fact that we have no way of crossing to Sicily. There must be men of every profession under the sun in my army – except shipbuilders! Apparently, some fools tried to build rafts yesterday, but after a score of them drowned, the rest soon gave up.

It only leaves one option as far as I can see. Unless you've got any bright ideas?'

Carbo shook his head.

'Cheer up, man! It wasn't down to you,' cried Spartacus, his eyes flashing. 'And you don't think a stinking wall is going to hold us in, do you? We'll just smash the fucking thing to pieces. Focus your anger on that.'

Carbo's misery lifted somewhat. 'When do we attack?'

'Tomorrow or the day after. There's no point hanging around. The grain won't last much more than a week, maybe two at the outside. Rhegium has more within its walls, but we have no way of getting in there.'

'It's all thanks to you.' Gannicus came striding up, the Scythians dogging his footsteps. 'No wonder the grain's nearly gone. We've done nothing but waste our time here.'

'You've heard the news then,' said Spartacus.

'Just a rumour.' Gannicus eyed the bag at Carbo's feet. 'That's the evidence, is it?'

'Yes. It's the pirate captain who agreed to find us the ships.'

'How in damnation did he get captured?'

'No idea. It's immaterial now anyway,' Spartacus replied. 'We need to talk about getting out of here.'

'Damn right we do!' cried Gannicus.

'Where's Castus?'

'He wouldn't come.'

'Why the hell not?'

'He was furious. Said he wouldn't trust himself if he saw you.'

Spartacus' eyes narrowed. 'It would be more in character for the lowlife to come storming up here with a drawn sword.'

Gannicus said nothing and Spartacus didn't probe further. 'I take it that you'll both be doing your own thing from now on?'

'Without a doubt!'

'Will you help to break through the Roman defences?'

'That depends. What are you planning?'

'The ridge is the only place to do it. Anywhere else, and we'd have to fight nine legions on the other side.'

Gannicus tugged on his moustache, thinking.

You bastard, thought Carbo. You and Castus can just hang back while Spartacus' men take all the casualties.

'I'll bring one cohort of my best men,' said Gannicus after a moment. 'That's it.'

'My thanks.' Spartacus knew he was wasting his breath, but he had to ask. 'And Castus?'

'He won't help.'

'Was he scared of saying that to my face?'

Gannicus shrugged. 'I don't know. He's in a funny mood today.'

'A funny mood? Him and me both!' growled Spartacus. 'He had better be armed and ready the next time we meet. If he's got any wits, though, he'll stay well clear of me.'

'I'll tell him,' replied Gannicus with a sneer.

'You know the ridge where the Roman defences are?'

A nod.

'Have your men there no later than midnight. The rest are to follow at dawn. By the time they reach the top, it will all be over one way or another.'

'What's your plan?'

'We climb up there once it gets dark. Make a full-scale frontal assault through the centre—'

'Have you seen the defences?'

'Of course I have!' snapped Spartacus.

'Desperate measures for desperate times.'

'You'd be well advised to follow the same plan, or you'll find yourself in Hades quicker than you think.'

'D'you think you're the only tactician in this army?'

Spartacus' anger overflowed. He no longer cared whether Gannicus worked with him or not. 'Maybe not, but I'm certainly the best! You and Castus wouldn't know how to surround an army of blind men.'

'Hades take you! You can do this on your own, and when you cock it up, we'll be there to finish the job for you.' Gannicus spun on his heel and walked off.

'So ends the pretence,' said Spartacus quietly. Although his casualties the next day would be heavier, it was a relief. He was better off without the murderous, quarrelsome pair. It was a pity about their followers, but it couldn't be helped. *With the help of the Great Rider, I will replace them once we get out of here.*

The next day would be hell, thought Carbo, his guts twisting. It was easy to imagine the bloodshed when trying to scale a wall manned by thousands of legionaries armed with javelins and catapults.

'Are you ready for this?'

Carbo met Spartacus' gaze. 'Yes,' he said calmly. Given the choice between a chance of survival and the certainty of death, he would take the former.

'Good. Thirty-five cohorts will march up with me tonight.'

'What about Ariadne and Maron?'

'You're to stay here, with your unit.'

'I don't understand.'

'As before: I want you to protect them.'

Carbo felt a mixture of relief and guilt. 'But I—'

'This is as important as being in the first rank when we attack,' said Spartacus in a low voice. 'Please.'

Carbo swallowed hard. How could he say no? 'Very well.'

'Once we we've broken through, and it's safe, I'll send a messenger. The rest of the army can make it up there under Egbeo's command. We'll meet on the far side of the Roman wall.'

'Very well.' Carbo was pleased how firm his voice sounded.

'We march at sundown, from the eastern edge of the camp. Tell Navio to be ready.' Spartacus turned his back.

Carbo was about to go when he remembered Heracleo's head. 'Can I take this?' he asked, lifting the bag. 'The poor bastard deserves for this part of him to be buried at least.'

'Do as you wish.'

Carbo walked away with his grisly trophy.

Ariadne awoke as Spartacus re-entered the tent. Worn out by a sleepless night looking after Maron, she had been asleep for much of the morning and had missed Spartacus' conversation with Carbo and Gannicus. His grim expression hit her like a bucket of cold water in the face. 'What's wrong?'

'The pirates won't be coming.' He filled her in quietly. Emotionlessly.

Ariadne felt sick. She wondered again if she should have left and instantly hated herself for it. 'So we're trapped?'

'Trapped?' His laugh was fierce. 'No more than a wild boar that's been caught in an old, worn hunter's net.'

Ariadne had not seen the Roman fortifications on the ridge, but she had heard about them. 'Many men will die.'

'They will,' growled Spartacus, 'but by the Rider, that won't stop us forcing our way through. Nothing and no one will. And as for Castus and Gannicus – fuck them!'

'They're not going to help?'

He shook his head angrily.

Ariadne's pulse quickened. 'Were they here?'

'Gannicus was. Castus didn't have the balls to come and tell me what he was going to do.'

He was too damn scared that I'd told you what happened, thought Ariadne with relief. She knew Spartacus well. If he'd found out, nothing would have held him back from killing Castus. She would have liked nothing more than to have seen the Gaul bleeding to death outside their tent, but their position was precarious enough without trying the gods' goodwill further. For whatever reason, Castus was not to be punished at this time.

Ariadne took in a deep breath. 'Where will we go?'

'North.'

She gave him a blank look.

'I was thinking of Samnium, east of Capua. The people there hold no love for Rome. The farms are rich too. There will be plenty of grain to be had.'

'Crassus will follow us.'

'He will, but the whoreson can't march as fast as we can. By the time he catches up, we'll have thousands of new recruits.' He flashed a confident grin and kissed her. 'I'd best start spreading the word. There's a lot to arrange by nightfall.'

Hiding her concern as best she could, Ariadne nodded. She had made her decision to stand by Spartacus and she would stick to it. Great Dionysus, she prayed, watch over us all. After the way the snake had saved her,

Ariadne's belief was still fervent. She felt her resolve stiffen. Heracleo's death was nothing more than a setback. They *would* win tomorrow, and escape Crassus' blockade.

Zeuxis was first to notice Marcion swaggering up to their tent with Arphocras at his heels. 'Hey! You fuckers are supposed to be cooking! It's nearly dinner time, and you haven't even started.'

There was an angry rumble of agreement from the others. Marcion eyed his comrades as he approached. They were slouched around the fire, picking their nails with their daggers or pretending to scrub rust spots from their mail shirts. He wasn't surprised. Since their hopes of sailing to Sicily had vanished, his tent mates' morale had been suffering, like everyone else in the army. Their mood had soured even further since the order had come around, not two hours since, that their cohort was to take part in an attack on the Roman defences at the ridge. With stress rising to new highs, routine, especially that to do with meals, was not to be disturbed. *Hopefully, this will cheer them up.*

'Where in Hades have you been?' demanded Zeuxis.

Marcion lowered the sack from his right shoulder with a contented sigh. 'That's better.'

'Quite the joker, aren't you?' sneered Zeuxis. 'I'll soon wipe the smile off your face if our dinner isn't ready on time. I bet the other lads will help me too, eh?'

'Damn right!' growled Gaius. 'A man has to eat well before battle. Woe betide the cook who doesn't provide a decent—' He turned the word *last* into a muffled cough. '—meal for his contubernium.' An unhappy silence followed his words. Flushing, Gaius made the sign against evil.

'Aye, well,' muttered Zeuxis after a moment. 'There might only be fucking porridge to eat, but we want it hot, and we want it now. Get on with it!'

Arphocras, who had unslung his sack, swung it on to his back again with one smooth movement. He turned as if to go. 'Very happy to jump to the conclusion that we've been skiving, aren't you?' He glanced at Marcion. 'I reckon we should keep this grub for ourselves. What do you think?'

'I think you're right. It'll last us at least a week.'

'Hold your horses,' said Zeuxis, suddenly keen. 'What have you got there?'

'Nothing much,' replied Marcion in an offhand tone. All eyes were on him, however, as he reached into his bag. With a flourish, he pulled out a whole ham. 'Just this.'

Amazed gasps rose from around the fire. There were jealous looks from the soldiers outside other tents. Gaius gave an appreciative whistle. 'Where in the gods' names did you get that?'

Marcion didn't answer. He just looked at Arphocras, who produced a large round of cheese. He clutched it to his body so that others could not see what he was holding. 'No point upsetting our neighbours even more,' he said with a chuckle.

'What else have you got?' asked Zeuxis greedily, his bad temper forgotten.

'A pot of *garum* and another of olives,' answered Arphocras. 'And Marcion has an amphora of wine.'

'You're a pair of magicians,' said Gaius, beaming from ear to ear.

'Damn right,' agreed Zeuxis with a rare smile. He whipped out his knife. 'Are you going to let us starve to death looking at your haul?'

Zeuxis hadn't thanked them, but the lift in his comrades' mood was so marked that Marcion didn't care. He took out the wine and then laid the ham on the sack. 'Get stuck in.'

There was a rush forward. Soon the only sounds were those of chewing and loud appreciation. Marcion's belly grumbled, reminding him that it had been many hours since he'd eaten. He didn't mind. There was enough food for all. Life was still good, he thought. Tomorrow was another day.

Conversation vanished as the eight soldiers devoured Marcion and Gaius' haul. It wasn't long before most of it was gone. Satisfied belches and farts filled the air, and the soldiers' faces grew more contented than they had in a long time.

Zeuxis gave Marcion and Arphocras a friendly nod. 'My thanks for that. You can prepare dinner again tomorrow if you like!'

'Don't think that I don't know that it's your bloody turn to cook tomorrow, Zeuxis!' retorted Marcion to hoots of amusement.

'All right, put us out of our misery,' demanded Gaius. 'Where did you get it?'

Marcion glanced around the fire and was gratified by the intense interest in his comrades' faces. 'We were heading back here to cook, when I spotted a patrol returning to their tents. They seemed particularly happy, so we hung about for a bit to see why. It became obvious that they had come upon a farm that hadn't been raided before, and ransacked it. Naturally enough, their officer took much of it for himself. He had his men put it in his tent while he went off to report whatever he'd seen.'

'He must have left a guard, surely?' asked Zeuxis in a disbelieving tone.

'He did,' replied Marcion with a grin. 'Two of them. At the *front* of his tent.'

His comrades exchanged delighted looks.

'Arphocras kept watch while I slit a hole in the *back* and took all that I could carry.'

'Hades below, it's as well that you weren't caught,' said Zeuxis, whistling in appreciation. 'You'd have been whipped within a hair of your life!'

'The things Arphocras and I do for you miserable whoresons, eh?' said Marcion. 'Nothing's too good for you!'

As their laughter rose into the night sky, it was almost possible to forget that the following dawn, they would be facing death once more. Almost, but not quite.

By sunset the next day, Spartacus had suffered his first defeat. Of the thirty-five cohorts that he had led up to the ridge, only five thousand shattered survivors remained. More than twice that number had been left bleeding, screaming and dying in the lethal traps that were the Roman defences.

Spartacus realised he had badly underestimated his enemy's ability to build fortifications and to defend them with obstinate determination. Having rallied the last of his men into a semblance of order, he led them away from the carnage, from the churned up, glutinous, red mud and the ground covered in mutilated corpses and discarded weapons. The air was thick with the reek of blood, piss and shit, and it left a sour taste in his mouth. So too did the Roman taunts that followed them through the trees. A last stone was fired from a ballista, thumping into the earth some distance to their rear, its purpose not to kill but to hammer home the depth of their defeat. The slaves had lost more than two-thirds of their force, but no more than a hundred legionaries had been slain.

Spartacus hawked and spat a defiant lump of phlegm in the stone's direction. What in the Rider's name had gone wrong? The march up to the ridge had passed without major incident, and the day itself had started well enough. His men had been full of high spirits, laughing and joking, and boasting to one another about how many legionaries they would each kill. Looking at them, he had been full of pride, sure that they were capable of taking on any enemy. The reality of the fight at the bottleneck had been very different. In retrospect, the Roman defences reminded him of the way fishermen caught vast numbers of tuna, placing complex systems of nets across their migration routes. That thought stopped him in his tracks. A trap. It had been a trap. Crassus had known he was coming, told no doubt by the same damn spy who had managed to thwart his assassination attempt on the general.

He cursed. Why hadn't he anticipated that his cover might have been blown? The answer was simple. All he'd seen was a way out, a road north, away from Crassus' ten legions. He had let his desire for that prize dull him to the dangers of the Roman defences. His troops had gone along with his wishes. Despite taking horrific numbers of casualties during the first attack, they had not argued when he had ordered them to advance for a second time. There had been less shouting, less enthusiasm, but they had bravely walked into another withering hail of enemy projectiles. Spartacus had seen the effect of such concentrated missile attack when he had fought as a Roman auxiliary, but he had never been on the receiving end. It was impossible to blame his soldiers for breaking and running. Only a madman or a god would continue to march forward when his fellows are being cut down in their hundreds. He hadn't run, but he had eventually pulled back. There had been no option. A handful of men had stood with him; if he hadn't retreated, they would have all been slain, and that would have served no one but Crassus.

Spartacus' mind was full of shocking images. A soldier struck in the head by a bolt from a catapult, whose skull had burst apart like an overripe fruit. The men for ten paces in every direction had been sheeted in his blood and nervous tissue. A javelin that had taken a soldier just above the top of his mail shirt, running deep into his chest cavity. Spraying pink froth from his mouth and keening like a stuck pig, the man had knocked two comrades to the ground before someone had put him out of his misery. Spartacus could still hear the *clatter, clatter, clatter* sound of slingshot bullets striking shields and the screams of the soldiers who'd suffered a shattered cheek or jawbone. Could still see the startled expression on the face of the man whose eyeball and following that, his brain, had been ruptured by a piece of lead no bigger than a bird's egg. Oddly, he'd recognised the unfortunate as one of the tent party he'd overheard on his return from Rome. Spartacus was damned if he could remember the man's name.

The Romans had ranged their catapults in well, using markers on the ground to show them where to aim. Spartacus had been surprised by the number of enemy artillery pieces. Hundreds of slaves must have toiled like oxen at the plough to transport the heavy weapons up from the coast. Their presence proved that Crassus wasn't just a canny politician. He was a shrewd general as well. That knowledge made Spartacus even more wary of trying to break through the Roman defences on the flat ground by the sea. His troops might batter their way through, but he doubted if they could then stand up to nine legions. Not without the help of Castus' and Gannicus' men at least.

Spartacus ground his jaws with frustration. It would have been better to burn his bridges with the Gauls not when he had, but at the very last moment. He considered his options. It was doubtful that the pair would be open to a new approach. Why even bother trying? he thought savagely, remembering the attempt on his life. Old anger surged through him once more. *Fuck them both! I'll do it on my own.*

Where? he wondered. His gut answered at once. The ridge. It had to be the ridge. But if they failed again, Crassus would have won the war. His fury began to glow white-hot. He was damned if that was going to happen. There was little point waiting either. With every day that went by, his troops' morale would plummet even further, and the chance of escaping would vanish. Men were already deserting – Carbo had seen them with his own eyes. They'd be better off without such cowards, thought Spartacus angrily. Yet he had to act fast, or his numbers would shrink further. And that was before fucking Pompey arrived from Iberia. He hadn't wanted to believe the taunts being thrown at them as they withdrew, but the legionaries' voices had sounded so delighted that he suspected they were. The Senate must have grown impatient with Crassus. Pompey was the flashy general who had crushed Sertorius' rebellion. Before that, he had had a prominent role in Sulla's war to seize control of the Republic. Would his bad luck never end? Pompey was an able tactician and his legions were battle-hardened. According to Navio, he had at least six of them too. His mood darkened further at the thought of seeing sixteen legions take to the field against his men.

Back at the camp, he went to speak with Ariadne. She gasped with horror as he entered the tent. Surprised, Spartacus glanced at his arms and mail, which were spattered with blood. He guessed that his face bore the same gory evidence. 'It's all right. I'm not hurt.'

She rushed to him. 'Men have been saying that you were thrown back from the Roman wall. That thousands of our soldiers have been killed. Is it true?'

Nodding grimly, he filled her in.

Was this the beginning of the end? wondered Ariadne. 'What are you going to do?'

'I'm going to walk from tent to tent, campfire to campfire. Speak with the men. Make them understand that tomorrow we cannot fail.'

'You're going to attack again so soon?'

'Damn right I am. I have to.' He saw her confusion. 'The Romans knew we were coming. The spy must have told them. Attacking again tomorrow and preventing anyone from going near the enemy defences are about the best ways to prevent another slaughter like the one today. There are other reasons I have to act now too. Some men are leaving already. A few more days, and the grain will begin to run out. Imagine what will happen to morale then.' He touched her cheek, and was glad that she did not recoil from the encrusted gore on his fingers.

'What about the spy?'

He shrugged. 'A needle in a large haystack. We keep our eyes and ears open. Tell only those who need to know about important decisions.'

'It's so frustrating. I wish there was more you could do.'

Another shrug. 'I have a notion to send Crassus a message.'

Her eyebrows rose. 'Saying what?'

'Asking him to take me into his *fides*.'

She looked at him as if he were insane. 'That's the same thing as surrendering! Why would you ask Crassus to become your patron?'

'First, it would force him to acknowledge me as his equal. Second, he could become my ally against Pompey. He must be livid at the idea of that glory hunter coming to steal his thunder. Imagine the strength of his army if my soldiers were added to it!'

'Crassus would never agree to something like that.' Ariadne's laugh was a little shrill. 'He wouldn't let your men leave, free to settle where they chose. To him, they're just slaves!'

'I know, but it would show him — in the most uncertain terms — that I do not regard him as my superior. He'd also hate that I've heard how pissed off he is about Pompey being invited to the party. Infuriating him like that can only be a good thing, surely?'

'I'd rather stick a knife between the whoreson's ribs!'

Spartacus grinned. He had always loved her feistiness.

'Whom will you send?'

'A prisoner.'

'A pity that we can't send a man who could kill Crassus.'

'He'd never get close enough.'

'What about Carbo? He's a Roman. He could pretend to have deserted; that he had information useful to Crassus.'

He gave her a reproachful look. 'You might as well ask him to commit suicide! Even if I was prepared to ask Carbo, which I'm not, he has another job, which is far more important.'

Ariadne was about to ask when she remembered squeezing the truth of that from Atheas during the battle with Lentulus. Shame scourged her, that she should have asked Spartacus to send Carbo, the most loyal of men, to his death when his mission was to protect her and Maron if things went awry. She was angry next, for reminding herself of such dread possibilities. 'You should eat something,' she said, changing the subject. 'Get yourself clean.'

'Later.'

'You look exhausted. Why don't you lie down? Even an hour's sleep would help.'

His smile was grim. 'I can rest when I'm dead.'

Ariadne's fears resurged. She pulled him close. 'Don't say things like that,' she whispered. 'That isn't going to happen.'

He squeezed her tight. 'Not yet it isn't! The Rider was by my side today. He'll be with me tomorrow too, when I have my vengeance.'

Ariadne found the fury in his eyes chilling. It almost made her forget her concern for his safety. 'I will ask Dionysus for his help.'

The smile became savage. 'My thanks. We will need it.'

Spartacus was more weary than he could ever remember being. His muscles ached, his joints cracked with every movement, and he had a headache worse than any hangover. He had spent half the night moving through the camp, praising, cajoling, injecting new energy into his men. He had drunk wine with some, argued with others and even arm-wrestled a few. He had shouted, railed and threatened. He had warned the soldiers of the fate they could expect if they failed to break the Roman blockade. Spartacus had promised them that he would, as always, lead from the front. Nothing – absolutely nothing – would stop him from carving a path through for his army. They had cheered him then until they were hoarse, even the bloodied, battered soldiers who had been on the ridge that day. He had gone to his bed satisfied that there was no more to be done. Ariadne had been awake, but Spartacus was in no mood to talk. A couple of hours' rest, and he'd been up again. It was at least three hours' march to the Roman wall, and he wanted his troops in place before dawn. There was a lot to do before their attack. He had kissed Ariadne farewell and spoken with Egbeo and Carbo – ordering them to take up the rear with his wife and son. Then he had gone to meet his senior officers.

At least five hours had passed since. Normally, Spartacus would have cursed fog. It made finding one's way treacherous, marching even harder and battle well nigh impossible. But the grey blanket that had fallen over the steep slopes as the army had made its way to the ridge had been a blessing. It had dulled the sound of their advance, and had provided good cover for his men to approach the Roman ditch with their loads of wood.

The fog had also shrouded the scene, meaning that his soldiers had only seen groups of their dead comrades lying stiff and cold, rather than the full, terrible extent of the battlefield. To try and alleviate the horror further, Spartacus had ordered that no one was to look anywhere but forward as they marched.

He had chosen five points along the wall as his focus for their assault. At each point, the trench was to be filled if possible to a width of a hundred paces, in order to allow a full cohort the space to attack. Inevitably, the noise of their approach had alerted the enemy sentries. Close to the foot of the wall, Spartacus had heard the hisses of alarm, the call for an officer and the shouted challenges. To protect against missile attack, he'd ordered two ranks of soldiers to stand before the ditch, their shields raised one on top of the other in a protective wall. The men whose job it was to approach with wood exposed themselves at the last moment, when they threw their loads into the trench.

His tactic had worked: when the Roman officers had ordered several volleys of javelins, only a handful of Spartacus' soldiers had been injured, and none killed. Encouraged by this, he had ordered the mules to be brought forward. As he'd suspected, the ditches hadn't even been half filled by the timber. The beasts' braying had again set the confused enemy to scurrying about on the rampart. Another ragged volley of javelins had rattled off the front ranks' shields, but that had been all until a couple of stones were fired from the catapults atop the wall. One of those had killed two men and a mule, but because of the fog the Romans had not seen this. The enemy officers had sensibly decided to save their ammunition, which had allowed the process of dragging the mules forward and killing them to continue. The beasts' bodies had levelled the ground in three of the assault points, but in the last two, a significant difference in the level of the earth had remained.

Spartacus didn't hesitate. The fog was beginning to thin out. Dawn wasn't that far off. He ordered the soldiers with shields to withdraw, and for the prisoners to be brought forward to the two ditches which still needed filling. They could have used the bodies of his men who had fallen the previous day, but that would have been terrible for morale. Besides, he had a better plan.

Men hurried off to do his bidding. Spartacus watched them go. He had never been keen on taking captives. They needed to be guarded, fed and watched constantly. From time to time, however, some were taken. This had been the case about a week prior, when a Roman patrol that had been sent over the wall to scout out his forces had strayed into an ambush set by Pulcher. More than a hundred legionaries had surrendered. On a whim, Spartacus had ordered their lives to be spared. He was glad of that decision now.

It wasn't long before the first file of twenty came into sight, emerging from the fog like a line of ghosts. A dozen soldiers shadowed their every move. The prisoners' wrists were bound behind their backs, and a long rope held by one of Spartacus' officers secured each by the neck. Many of the Romans had cuts and bruises on their faces, arms and legs from the falls that they had sustained on the nightmarish climb to the ridge. To a man, they looked absolutely terrified. They had no idea why they were here, but it couldn't be good. Spartacus didn't bother speaking to them. In his mind, they were as expendable as the mules.

'Line them up in front of the ditch.'

Realising their fate, the legionaries began to beg for their lives.

Spartacus' men ignored their pleas. Using their fists and the points of their swords, they drove the prisoners forward.

A sudden gust of wind moved the fog slightly, allowing the Romans to see their comrades. Roars of anguish rose up, but before the legionaries could react further, the cloud settled again. Curses rained down on Spartacus and his men, but there was nothing that the defenders could do. Spartacus' lips peeled upwards. As well as angering the men on the wall, the executions would drive shards of fear into their hearts. 'Kill them!'

The ground had already been soaked by the mules' blood. Now it was bathed anew. With savage dedication, Spartacus' men set about slaying the captives, who were wailing with fear. A few muttered prayers to their gods, and a couple spat curses over their shoulders at their executioners. It made no difference. With terrible soughing sounds, gladii sliced through the flesh in their backs to emerge, crimson-tipped, from their chests and bellies. A couple of thrusts were enough to inflict mortal wounds. Spartacus' men shoved their victims off their blades and set upon the last prisoners. The Romans toppled in twos and threes into the ditch, where they twitched and moaned as they bled out. It was over fast.

'Bring the next lot!' ordered Spartacus.

'Spartacus, you whoreson!' yelled a voice from the ramparts. 'By the gods, you'll suffer a thousand deaths for this.'

Shouts of agreement rang out all along the parapet.

'Go fuck your mother! If you even had one,' roared Spartacus. 'At least we're giving them a swift end.'

His soldiers whooped and cheered.

'That's something you won't have, or my name's not Gnaeus Servilius Caepio!'

An alarm bell began to toll in Spartacus' mind. 'What are you doing here, old man?'

'Not much. Polishing my sword. Making sure that the legion I guided up here last night is ready to repel your attack.'

Spartacus' heart thumped in his chest. Had the spy somehow got word to Crassus, or was Caepio just trying to put the fear of the gods into his troops? He glanced at the nearest men and was angered to see the first traces of panic in their eyes. 'You're lying, Caepio! I know you are.'

'Am I? Why don't you climb up here and see what awaits you then?' retorted the centurion.

'We'll do that. After the ditches have been levelled,' Spartacus announced loudly. The next group of prisoners shuffled into view. 'Kill them! Quickly!' He moved to the second ditch, making sure that it was also being filled, and gauging the mood of his soldiers there. He was angered to see that Caepio's words had also affected them. The idea he had considered was required. He ordered one from the last group of prisoners to be spared. The final captive, quaking with fear, was forced by the Scythians to walk with Spartacus as he returned to the first of his cohorts. They were waiting some two hundred paces from the wall – the outer limit of accurate catapult range. They stood silently, three cohorts wide, with their centurions in the front ranks. Behind them, the densely packed soldiers extended for more than a mile. He would have had them spread out further, but the beech trees prevented it.

The distance hadn't been enough to mask Caepio's voice, Spartacus noted sourly. The front cohorts had clearly heard what he'd said too. There was no chanting of his name, no clashing of weapons off shields. Those who were holding ladders looked less than enthusiastic. Few soldiers would meet his eye. The officers he could see were scowling, or reprimanding their men.

Steely resolve took hold of him. It was time to stiffen his troops' morale with a savage demonstration of what they could all expect. If he didn't, their attack was doomed before it even began. He drew his sica and began walking along the face of the cohorts. Atheas and Taxacis followed, shoving the prisoner before them. 'What's my name?' Spartacus shouted.

'Spar-ta-cus!' cried a voice he recognised.

He gave Marcion a tight nod. 'That's right. I want to hear it again!'

'SPAR-TA-CUS!' Many more men joined in this time.

He strode on, stabbing his sword into the grey, clammy air. 'Again!'

'SPAR-TA-CUS! SPAR-TA-CUS!'

'That's more like it.' He bestowed a wintry smile on the nearest soldiers.

Up and down he went, until all three cohorts had seen him. He returned to the centre of the line. 'Bring the cross! Now!'

Men gaped at him, and the prisoner's face went grey with fear.

Orders rang out; led by an officer, half a dozen soldiers, Marcion and Zeuxis among them, broke away from their positions and scurried off to the side. They soon returned. Marcion and a pair of his companions were carrying two lengths of roughly carved timber that had been prepared the night before. The longer piece had had an iron hook hammered into one end. The others were carrying mallets, a set of wooden steps, lengths of rope and bags of nails.

'Put it up thirty paces out there,' commanded Spartacus. 'Get a move on!'

His men hurried to a spot opposite him. Fastening several ropes to the longer of the two pieces of wood, they pulled it upright. The steps were moved in close, and two soldiers began hammering the timber into the ground. *Thump. Thump. Thump.*

The legionary's mouth worked in silent terror.

Soon the vertical post had been pounded in to the depth of a man's forearm.

Spartacus gestured at the prisoner. 'Strip him naked. Then take him out and crucify him.'

'I'm a citizen! Please! You can't do this to me!' screeched the Roman as his tunic and undergarment were ripped off.

'Bullshit! You're identical to every man here!' roared Spartacus, spittle flying from his lips. 'You eat and drink, breathe, sleep and shit the same as us. This punishment is no different to what your kind would do to us.' He scanned his men's faces. 'Do you hear me? *This* is what you can expect if we don't break out today.'

Yelling at the top of his voice, the legionary was hauled out to the vertical post and forced down on to what would be the crosspiece. A soldier knelt on each of his arms, holding him so that his wrists and hands were exposed. The officer in charge glanced at Spartacus.

'Get on with it!'

A barked order, and Zeuxis touched a long iron nail to the point where the bones of the legionary's right arm met those of the wrist. The prisoner began gibbering in fear, praying to the every god in the pantheon. Zeuxis raised his mallet high, and without hesitation, brought it down with all his strength. 'This is for Gaius,' he hissed. A shriek of indescribable pain shredded the air, but the mallet came down again and again. Marcion looked away, but Zeuxis didn't stop until the nail was flush with the legionary's flesh. The captive's screams reached a new pitch as the same process was repeated with his left wrist.

Spartacus studied his men, and was pleased to see how shocked and revolted they looked. The message had to sink in. If it didn't, they were all damned. Angry shouts carried from the wall. The Romans' blood would be up, but that couldn't be helped.

Lapping a rope around the hook at the top of the vertical post, his soldiers fastened it around both ends of the crosspiece and then hauled the crucified legionary up until his feet came off the ground. He roared in agony as his arms took the strain of his body weight. The steps were moved in front of him, and a number of nails were pounded in over his shoulders, fixing the crosspiece to the vertical length of timber.

Without ado, his left leg was seized and his foot nailed to the cross. He kicked frantically with his free leg, striking Zeuxis in the face. Cursing, he heaved the man's right foot sideways on to the timber and hammered in another nail through his heel. It was too much for the legionary. 'Mother! Please, Mother,' he babbled. 'Mother, help me!' Piss began leaking from his shrunken member, spattering Zeuxis. He leaped back in disgust as his fellows roared with laughter. Even Marcion's lips twitched.

Zeuxis grabbed the mallet again and stepped up to the cross. 'Can I break his legs, sir?'

'No. Leave him,' ordered Spartacus. 'I want the bastard alive for every man to see as he marches by.'

With a disappointed look, Zeuxis stepped away. Marcion wondered if it would have been better to let him take his revenge. No one deserved to die in such pain, not even a Roman. But the decision wasn't down to him. He was just a foot soldier.

'Back to our place in the line,' hissed their officer. They hurried to obey.

Spartacus turned his back on the crucified legionary and began pacing along the front of the cohorts again. 'Watch his suffering, you maggots, and learn! It could take two or three days for the dog's pain to end, perhaps even longer. Is that the death you want? Do you want to end your life begging the Romans to break your legs so that you can die quicker?'

No one had the balls to speak.

Spartacus shoved his face into that of the nearest soldier. Their helmets knocked off each other. 'Answer me, or by the Rider, I'll do the same to you!'

'NO, SIR!'

Spartacus stepped back. 'That's one man who knows what he wants at least. What about the rest of you? Is that the end you want?'

'NO, SIR!' they yelled.

He walked for fifty paces, eyeballing every soldier that he passed. 'Are you fucking sure?'

'YES!' they roared.

On he went, defying any man to answer him back, to look in any way uncertain. 'Sure? Sure?'

'YES!'

'SPAR-TA-CUS!' yelled Marcion. He glared at Zeuxis, who joined in. This time, the chant was taken up with gusto.

Finally. Spartacus stepped up and clashed his sica off a man's shield boss. 'Louder!'

The soldier's companions quickly copied him. So too did the men behind, and to either side. *Clash. Clash. Clash.* 'SPAR-TA-CUS! SPAR-TA-CUS!'

Soon the racket was deafening.

Spartacus let them shout for some time. He wanted every soldier in the army to hear the noise, to feel the blood rush in his ears, the battle rage begin to stir. When he saw the confidence appearing in men's faces, he knew it was time. A signal, and the waiting trumpeters sounded their instruments, a strident call to arms that no one could mistake.

The fanfare was met by an equally forceful set of blasts from behind the wall.

Spartacus hastened back to his position with the Scythians, who slotted in to his left and right. Atheas took a ladder from someone. A shield was handed to Spartacus; grounding it, he rested it against his body. He glanced to either side. Atheas and Taxacis gave him their usual feral grins; the men beyond looked tense but ready. 'On my command, advance at the walk! Open order!' His words went echoing both ways down the line. Spartacus took hold of the brass centurion's whistle that hung from a thong around his neck and stuck it between his lips.

Peeeeeeep! Spartacus emptied his lungs.

The shrill sound repeated itself through the cohorts.

'ADVANCE!' Spartacus walked forward with an even tread. On either side, his soldiers matched his pace. His gaze travelled along the enemy ramparts. The catapults would start shooting at any moment. So too would the ballistae. In the Romans' eyes, the more bolts and stones that could be launched before he and his men arrived, the better.

Sure enough, he heard the familiar noise of thick gut strings being ratcheted back, and the thump as stones were loaded into place. Next, the indistinct sound of officers' voices, followed by a shouted order. 'Close order! Raise shields!' bellowed Spartacus. 'Keep moving.'

All around him, men moved shoulder to shoulder. If they were in the front rank, they lifted their scuta up, so that the curved shields protected them from eye level to their ankles. Those behind heaved theirs up to protect their heads. Only those who were carrying ladders remained unprotected, needing both their hands to carry their awkward burdens.

They drew near to the crucified legionary, whose legs were now soiled with urine and faeces. His eyes were closed, and he was moaning softly, 'Motherrr . . .' He kept shifting position, letting his bloodied arms take the strain, and when that was too much, trying to stand on his nailed feet. Poor bastard, thought Spartacus. He's served his purpose. He was going to slide his sica into the man's belly as he passed, end his suffering. But he didn't.

His troops had to witness the savagery of such a death. Spartacus threw up a heartfelt prayer. *I ask for any end but that.* Grimly, he moved on.

The Romans let them approach for another ten paces. Then, with a rush, the air between Spartacus' soldiers and the wall filled with missiles. Stones the size of a man's head. Metal-tipped arrows the length of a man's forearm. Slingshot bullets smaller than a hen's egg. *Whoosh. Whirr. Whizz.* They covered the distance in a frightening blur of movement.

Great Rider, let Caepio be lying about the legion. Let my casualties be few, Spartacus prayed. We *have* to succeed here.

With loud crashes, the stones landed. Their effect was devastating. Whatever they hit, be it man or scutum, was struck as if by the fist of a god. Shields were smashed in two, ribs splintered into fragments, and limbs and skulls crushed. The rocks' force was so great that often the soldier behind was also killed, his final moment a screaming terror as his comrade's head burst apart before his eyes. The bolts were no less lethal, slicing through shields, mail and flesh with ease. Gutting the first man, they drove on, wounding others grievously or just lodging in another scutum, forcing the bearer to discard it.

The only consolation during the barrage was that the slingshot bullets were far less dangerous than the other missiles. For the most part, they clattered and banged off the soldiers' shields like massive hailstones off a roof during a summer storm. On occasion, they shot through the little gaps between scuta, making men yelp in pain as their mail shirts took the brunt of the strike. More unlucky individuals were hit in the face, suffering fractured cheekbones or, if the clay hit their foreheads, a mortal blow.

'Close the gaps! Move on!' yelled Spartacus. He blew his whistle again. If they faltered at all, men would lose heart.

Stepping over the wounded and dying, they walked on. It was a hundred paces to the wall, he judged. The trees had thinned out, exposing them entirely to the enemy barrage. The legionaries manning the catapults were working at blinding speed. Scores more bolts and stones came humming towards them. Soon the javelins would come scudding in too. It was now, or never, he thought.

'Cohort to my left, cross at the first space over the ditch. Cohort to my right, take the third. My cohort takes the middle one. CHARGE!' Trusting that the officers leading the following units would remember to advance towards the final two crossing points, Spartacus began to run. As always, he counted his steps. It helped to keep him focused, to ignore the sounds of men going down screaming, the curses of their comrades as they tripped over the unexpected obstacle, the prayers of soldiers trying to conquer their fear.

Eighty. A shower of javelins arced over them in a graceful pattern. Reaching their zenith, they sped downwards, their barbed points promising injury or death to those who were unprotected. Spartacus raised his shield so that his head was protected, and prayed that a catapult stone didn't take him in the belly instead. Seventy. His stomach was a balled, painful knot, and there was a tang of fear in the salty sweat that ran down his face and into his open, gasping mouth. With an almighty bang, a pilum hit his scutum. The barbed head punched through, missing Spartacus' helmet by a finger's breadth. He dropped the useless shield with a curse. Fifty steps. *Run. Run. The Great Rider's shield is before me, protecting me from harm.*

Forty paces to the wall. There were gaps in the line to either side of him now, but Spartacus did not order them closed. Everything was moving far too fast. What mattered was reaching the base of the Roman wall, and getting out of the withering hail of missiles. They'd have a moment's respite before more stones were dropped on their heads, but that would be enough time to encourage his men to swarm up their ladders.

They reached the filled-in ditch. Because of the prisoners who had been dumped in last, it looked as if it contained only corpses. Except, as Spartacus realised, they weren't all dead yet. Here and there amid the careless sprawl of bloodied men, an arm or a leg moved, a voice called out for a comrade, or for someone to end the pain. Even if he had been inclined to provide the killing stroke, there was no time. In two heartbeats, he had pounded over the soft 'ground' and was tearing across the forest floor again.

Twenty paces. They had passed under the lower limit of the catapults' arc of fire. The Roman slingers had redoubled their efforts. So many of Spartacus' men had dropped their shields that their work was now easy. It was the same for the legionaries still with pila. Despite this, Spartacus' front rank, which had been eighty men wide, was ragged but unbroken. 'Ladders at the ready!' he yelled, increasing his speed to a sprint. He sensed the Scythians matching his pace. Encouraged, the soldiers to either side swarmed forward, screaming insults at the defenders atop the wall. Ten paces. Five, and then Spartacus slammed into the fortification's wooden stakes. 'Ladder!'

Atheas was already by his right shoulder, shoving the ladder's foot into the ground, leaning it against the wall, supporting it, gesturing at him to start climbing.

Spartacus eyed the remaining scuta held by his men. Things would be far worse on the rampart without them, but there was no way they could safely ascend carrying such a weight. 'Leave your shields!' he shouted. 'Grab one from the first Roman you kill. Up! Up! Up!' More and more ladders came smacking in against the barrier. Spartacus gritted his teeth and began to climb. This was the most dangerous part. He peered grimly up at the pointed stakes that formed the lip of the rampart. It was difficult to climb with one hand – the other held his sica – and easy to miss his footing on the rungs. Even more perilous were the defenders who awaited him. He was two-thirds up the ladder when a legionary appeared above, gripping a forked length of stick. With fierce concentration, he placed it against the top of Spartacus' ladder and began to push.

Shit! Adrenalin surged through Spartacus' veins and he shot up several more rungs. His ascending body weight made it much harder for the Roman to push the ladder outwards. Cursing, the legionary braced his feet and put all of his strength into it. Spartacus felt himself begin to move backwards. He climbed another rung and stabbed forward with his sica. His blade skidded off the Roman's mail, causing no injury. For an instant, however, it distracted the soldier from what he was doing.

Spartacus came up another rung. A quick glance to the right revealed no defenders close enough to skewer him in the armpit. Up went the sica. Down it came, striking the legionary in the neck. The curved blade nearly clove him in two. His torso split apart, exposing neatly bisected muscles, the white of ribs and the purple-blue of pumping organs. Spartacus was showered in blood as he came leaping on to the walkway. The Roman's body fell backwards off the wall, spraying sheets of crimson over the soldiers below.

Spartacus' heart leaped. There weren't more than five thousand of them. Caepio had been lying; the spy had not been able to get the word through to Crassus. After the previous day's fighting, his enemy had assumed that the slaves had had enough. *How wrong he was.* Spotting a scutum leaning against the palisade, he scooped it up. He had just enough time to spin and raise it as a legionary thundered in from his right. With a heavy *thump*, the two shield bosses met.

Spartacus shoved his blade at the Roman's eyes, but his opponent saw it coming. Sparks flew as the sica hit the iron rim of his shield. The legionary lunged forward with his gladius, and Spartacus twisted desperately out of the way, smacking his back off the rampart. There was almost no room to manoeuvre. All the advantage was with the Roman, whose blows hammered in, away from the void. With every strike of his own, Spartacus risked hurling himself into space.

He clenched his jaw. If they didn't gain a foothold on the wall, their attack would fail. Placing his left shoulder behind the scutum, he advanced a step. *Clash, clash.* Their swords battered off their shield fronts. Spartacus punched forward with his scutum and then his sica. One, two. One, two. He pushed the legionary back a step. And two more. They traded blows again before the Roman's heel caught on a pilum that had been left lying on the walkway. He stumbled, and Spartacus was on him like a hawk on its prey, barging him backwards so that he fell on his arse, squawking with surprise. The last thing he ever saw was the Thracian's blade scything in towards his open mouth. The legionary choked to death on a gobful of iron and blood.

Air moved past Spartacus' head. Instinct made him pull back, which just saved him from being struck in the neck by a pilum. Instead it scudded harmlessly by, over the palisade. He glanced down. The soldiers below were launching volleys at the rampart, regardless of the fact that they could hit their own men. Exultation gripped him. That meant the enemy officers thought the fight on the walkway was being lost. He leaned out over the front of the wall. He could see at least five ladders. 'Come on!' he roared at his men. 'It is I, Spartacus! We have the whoresons on the run!'

Eager shouts met his words.

He spun back to the walkway to find a grinning Taxacis at his side. Behind him, Atheas' head was emerging into view. 'Which . . . way?' asked Taxacis. 'Left . . . or right?'

To his left was a large bunch of enemy soldiers, and in their midst, the scarlet transverse crest of a centurion. It was Caepio. *We won't get through there quickly enough.* Spartacus pointed to his right and the nearest set of steps. 'There!' Six legionaries blocked the walkway, but before them, there was a gap perhaps ten paces wide where more and more of their men were spilling over the palisade. He darted forward. The Scythians were right behind him. 'Get to the stairs!' he shouted at his soldiers. 'Kill those bastard Romans! MOVE!'

They hurried to obey.

Spartacus shoved in behind them. The outcome of the attack still hung in the balance, but at last he had a good feeling in his belly.

Chapter XVI

Despite Crassus' wealth, he was a man of moderate taste. It was a small weakness to like a comfortable bed. The mattress in his quarters was purportedly of good quality – gods, it was thick enough – but he hated it with a vengeance. At first, when they had left Rome, it had seemed fine. Now, though, it felt lumpier than a straw tick used by the poorest of the poor. It was the reason that he was already up, a good hour before dawn. A scowl twisted his handsome face. The damn thing would have to do for the moment. There was no chance of locating a better one around here. As far as he'd seen, no one lived in Bruttium but primitives and latrones. And Spartacus.

Crassus put the mattress from his mind, but felt no less irritated. He was sick of everything about this shithole. It felt laughable now, but he had been glad to enter Bruttium. He had enjoyed the sea breezes and the escape from the filthy heat that they had endured in Campania and Lucania. No one could deny that the wild, mountainous countryside was magnificent or that the views of Sicily were incredible. Yet as autumn had passed into winter, these pleasures had soon soured. Weeks of lowering grey cloud, damp cold air and frequent rain had worn him down.

Crassus longed to finish the campaign not just because he wanted to crush Spartacus, but so that he could go home. In the capital, he could bask in the winter sun and the adulation of the Roman public, who would rightfully revere him. He could finish the account of his campaign and the superb generalship that had given him victory over the slaves. He would be the talk of the bath houses and the markets, cheered wherever he went. Crassus glanced at the letter he had begun composing, and the momentary improvement in his mood vanished. Would he have time to end the affair before that golden-tongued, arrogant little shit Pompey arrived? When he'd first heard the news that the Roman assembly had recalled his biggest rival from Iberia, Crassus hadn't believed it. The effrontery of it! *Fucking plebeians.*

Yet the senators, unhappy as they must have been at the thought of such a prominent general returning to Italy with his legions at his back, had approved the order. *That wouldn't have happened if I had been there,* Crassus thought furiously. *Like all sycophants, however, his supporters in the Senate wouldn't have been organised or vocal enough to prevent the decree from being carried. They're a shower of pompous, self-serving whoresons! Couldn't they and the rest just leave a man to do a job properly?* He had only been in command of the Republic's armies for a few months.

In the biggest clash since, his troops had proved their mettle by standing up to the slaves. Yes, there had been the inglorious rout of Mummius' legions, but he had dealt with that in the most vigorous fashion possible. The practice of decimation had not been used for more than a hundred years, and its effect had been dramatically successful. Subsequent to that, he had cornered Spartacus in the toe and denied him the chance of escape to Sicily! Best of all, his soldiers had yesterday thrown back the slaves' attempt to break through his fortifications on the ridge. Caepio had reported enemy losses of more than ten thousand men, which was a sizeable chunk of Spartacus' forces. The end was surely nigh.

Not that the Thracian would admit it! Remembering the filthy legionary who had been brought to him the night before, Crassus felt his face purple. He hadn't wanted to believe the soldier's story, but he had definitely been a prisoner of the enemy.

'How dare he? How dare he ask for such a thing? Fides, for a savage such as he?' Crassus ranted at the bronze mirror which stood to one side of his desk. 'The fucking cheek of it!'

Calm yourself, he thought. *This is just what the whoreson wanted. The request had been designed to goad him – and it had worked admirably.* Crassus took a deep breath, remembering how through a supreme effort, he had not ordered the immediate execution of the unfortunate legionary who had carried the message. *Let it go, as you did the soldier.* After a moment, he felt more composed.

A tiny, devilish part of him couldn't help wondering what it might be like to lead a combined force of over one hundred thousand men against Pompey, to seize control of Italy once and for all. The Republic was weak, and so too were most senators. As in the days of Sulla, a strong leader was needed. Crassus knew that he was the right man for the job. He had been born for it. Regrettably, this was not the time. The Roman people would never stand by and let an army of slaves help to take control of their destiny. Crassus' lips twisted. He could never trust a man like Spartacus – a Thracian, a former gladiator? – anyway. It was beneath his dignity even to think of replying. The stony silence would tell Spartacus all that he wanted to say.

Crassus returned his attention to the campaign, and his frustration mounted. Pompey, it came back to fucking Pompey, and whether he could engineer total victory before the prick arrived with his legions. To end the rebellion, he would need to force a pitched battle with Spartacus' army within days. Tactically, though, it would be foolish to do anything other than wait. His men were secure behind their defences; javelins and ammunition for the catapults had been stockpiled by the wall. The legions had plenty of grain and meat; fresh supplies arrived daily down the Via Annii. This while Spartacus' followers were slowly starving on the bare ground that led down to Cape Caenys, the southernmost point of Italy. All he had to do was sit tight until Spartacus and his men had rallied their courage enough to essay another attempt at breaking the blockade. Weakened by hunger, demoralised by their previous failure, the slaves would be slaughtered. The matter could be ended in one fell stroke.

What, however, if that battle didn't take place for another month or more? The messengers recalling Pompey had been sent ten days before. They would have already reached him. With a curse, Crassus stabbed his stylus on to the desk so hard that the tip broke. Pompey could appear at the head of his army inside the next six to eight weeks.

There was nothing for it, he decided. He would have to move first. Force the slaves into open battle. Yet doing that wouldn't be easy. Spartacus was a wily general, not a man prone to making mistakes. At last, a slow smile spread across Crassus' face. A night attack might do it. The Thracian's major strength was his cavalry. Crassus had fewer horsemen and, although he hated to admit it, they were of inferior quality to those of the enemy.

A cohort of legionaries, whose sole mission was to panic and injure Spartacus' horses, might succeed. It would be good to use the same trick on the Thracian as the dog had used on Glaber's troops, thought Crassus with glee. He knew the men to use too. Some of Mummius' disgraced soldiers would leap at the chance to redeem their honour. They wouldn't have to shinny down a cliff on vine ropes, just make their way unseen to where the enemy's horses were tethered. If they succeeded, the prospect of a pitched battle would be something to anticipate. After their recent losses, the slaves would be wary; spurred on by the threat of decimation, his legionaries were eager to fight. Without the advantage of their cavalry, victory would be there for the taking. Crassus could picture the scene already. Pompey would arrive too late.

The glory would all be his.

His gaze returned to his letter. Was it even worth finishing? He was on the verge of consigning it to his brazier, to erase even the idea of what he had been asking for. Then his more prudent side took control. The message had to be sent. By the time it had reached Rome and been acted upon, he would have crushed Spartacus as a man stamps on a scorpion. Crassus placed the letter back on the desk, smoothed it down and found another stylus before reading what he'd written.

'To the Senate of Rome. I, Marcus Licinius Crassus, commander of the Republic's armies, send loyal greetings.' His lip curled. Given half a chance, he'd put the names of more than half of the senators on a proscription list. Instead, he had to pretend that he respected their decision to recall Pompey. He read on:

Word has reached me that the illustrious general Gnaeus Pompeius Magnus is to return with his legions to Italy, his mission to assist me with the prompt quelling of Spartacus' uprising. As ever, I submit to the Senate's wishes. I shall be honoured to serve the Republic along-side another of its faithful servants.

Crassus mouthed a curse. He loathed every word on the parchment – yet he had to keep up the pretence. *I will have the last laugh.*

He dipped the stylus point into the glass pot that sat by his right hand, gently shook off the excess ink and prepared to write. His lips twitched with sardonic amusement. Pompey would hate what he was about to ask as much as he hated the idea of Pompey returning to Italy.

> While recent days have seen Spartacus suffer a major setback at the hands of my troops, the outrages committed by his followers have continued for too long. His uprising must be crushed with all haste and with no effort spared. I therefore ask that the Senate recall not just Gnaeus Pompeius Magnus, but also Marcus Terentius Varro Lucullus, the governor of Macedonia. His recent successes against the Thracian Bessi have marked him out as a general of note. His skills and his experienced legions would add immeasurable strength to my forces, but also to those of Pompey. Spartacus and the vermin who follow him will have nowhere to turn, no sewer in which they can hide. Faced by the dedicated leadership of three of the Republic's most able servants, this shameful uprising will soon be nothing but a distant, unpleasant memory. Rome's besmirched honour – and the reputation that was the envy of the Mediterranean – will have been restored.
>
> I ask the gods that you see fit to agree to my request. Rest assured that as I humbly await your response, the campaign against Spartacus is being prosecuted with all the vigour and courage that Rome's finest soldiers can bring to the conflict.
>
> With filial piety, I remain your servant, Marcus Licinius Crassus

He reread the letter carefully, and was pleased with his efforts. His words contained just the right mix of humility, cajolery and flattery to win over most senators. They would no more be able to resist the idea of Lucullus also returning than a man with dysentery could stop himself from shitting. When Pompey found out, he would be incandescent. But he would be unable to do a thing about it.

Not that it mattered, thought Crassus in triumph as he rolled up the parchment and sealed it with wax. Before either Pompey and Lucullus had come upon the scene, he would have ended the rebellion. With a little bit of luck, he would be able to invite both of his fellow generals to his victory feast, the highlight of which would be to display the Thracian's head on a silver platter.

A discreet cough brought him back to the present. Crassus turned his head. One of his guards stood in the doorway.

'A centurion is here to see you, sir. He's come from the ridge.'

A finger of unease tickled Crassus' spine. 'What does he want?'

'He didn't say, sir. Just that Caepio sent him,' replied the soldier awkwardly. He wouldn't have dared to ask such a senior officer his business, but he couldn't say that to Crassus.

'Send him in.' It's probably Caepio asking again for blankets, he thought irritably. The veteran had already mentioned that his soldiers on the ridge were suffering from exposure. Crassus had meant to do something about it, but it had slipped his mind. Damn Caepio for being impatient! A night or two in the cold would do the men good. It'd sharpen them up.

A middle-aged centurion with a sharply pointed nose and close-cut beard entered. He approached the desk and came to attention. 'Sir!'

'At ease.' Crassus noted the spatters of mud that covered the officer's legs and the pteryges protecting his groin. This wasn't about blankets, he thought in surprise. The man had come in a hurry. 'You've come from Caepio? From the ridge?'

'Yes, sir.'

'Well?' snapped Crassus. 'Why are you here?'

'There's been another attack, sir.'

Scorn twisted Crassus' face. 'What, a morale-building exercise for Spartacus' men after yesterday's humiliation? One of our patrols ambushed, is it, or have the ditches been filled with burning branches again?'

'It's worse than that, sir.' The centurion's eyes flickered towards him, and then darted away.

'Explain yourself, centurion,' said Crassus in a wintry tone. 'Quickly.'

'It started before dawn, sir. At first we thought it was just a probing attack, something to keep us on our toes, but it soon became apparent that it was a full-scale assault.'

There had been no word from the spy about this, mused Crassus. 'So soon? They must be even shorter of grain than I thought. It was fortunate that I ordered more ammunition to be carried up there after yesterday's skirmish, eh?'

An unhappy grimace. 'Yes, sir.'

'What is it, man? The ditches were cleared by last night, weren't they?'

'They were, sir, but Spartacus' men filled them in a number of places.'

'They'd need to chop down the entire forest to have enough wood. What did they use?'

'Mules, sir. They didn't have enough, though, so they led out about a hundred of our lads whom they'd taken prisoner. The poor bastards were executed in cold blood and then their bodies were thrown on top of the beasts, like so much carrion. It was as bad as the Esquiline Hill, sir,' he said, referring to the place outside Rome where the corpses of slaves and criminals were disposed of alongside household rubbish and the carcases of animals.

'That is monstrous, but Caepio didn't send you here to tell me that. Did their attack come immediately afterwards?'

'I wish it had, sir, but that savage Spartacus wanted to make an even bigger statement. He'd held one of our boys back in order to crucify him in front of his own men. The fuckers loved that.'

'Are there no lows that these *slaves* will hold back from?' Crassus was furious now. 'So they attacked after that?'

'Indeed, sir. They came on hard and fast.'

'The artillerymen must have wreaked havoc.' Crassus was pleased by the centurion's nod of agreement. 'Did the scum break and run as they did yesterday?'

Another dart of the eyes. 'Not exactly, sir.'

'*Not exactly*,' repeated Crassus.

The centurion straightened his shoulders. 'Between the artillery, the slingers and the men's javelins, they must have lost hundreds of men. It seemed to make no difference, sir. They were like wild beasts, or demons of the underworld.'

Crassus' nostrils pinched white with fury. 'What are you telling me, centurion? Has the wall been breached?'

'It hadn't when I left, sir, but things weren't looking good. Caepio sent me to inform you, and to ask for reinforcements.' The centurion hesitated, but didn't have the courage to remind Crassus that it was he who had elected not to send any fresh soldiers up to the ridge after the previous day's encounter. 'He said to say that he would hold on as long as he could, sir.'

Crassus' jaw clenched and unclenched. He clutched his fury to him as he would a lover, using it to fuel his loathing of Spartacus. He had under-estimated the Thracian's determination. It had been a reasonable decision not to send fresh troops to the ridge, he told himself. There had been no word from the spy. Besides, what enemy would mount such a daring attack so soon after a heavy defeat? Spartacus would, and did, his inner critic shot back. And now he had no chance of responding. Any reinforcements sent up the mountain would arrive too late. The battle would have been won or lost, the wall held or breached. Crassus knew in his gut that it would be the latter. Caepio, his best officer, would probably be among the dead. Even worse, his chances of ending the campaign before Pompey arrived had just vanished into thin air. The letter asking for Lucullus' recall would have to be sent to Rome with all speed. Damn Spartacus to Hades and back!

Crassus rubbed his temples, trying to decide what to do. Carry on, he decided. 'Have two of the legates assemble their legions and march them to the ridge. There may still be slaves trying to get across the wall.'

'Yes, sir.' The centurion didn't argue, which told Crassus that he also thought Spartacus had escaped. 'Which ones, sir?'

'I don't fucking care! The remaining legates are to have their men strike camp. We march as soon as possible.'

'Where are we heading, sir?'

'Where do you think?' shouted Crassus. 'After fucking Spartacus of course!'

When the Romans had been driven back from a large enough section of the wall, Spartacus had had several thousand of his troops continue engaging them. Some of his soldiers had been ordered to set fire to the ballistae while the rest had begun tearing a hole in the fortifications. It wasn't long before a gap wide enough for ten men to pass through abreast had been made.

Spartacus had immediately sent a messenger to Egbeo, ordering him to bring his cohort forward. The moment that had been done, and he had seen Ariadne and Maron were safe, he'd sent word for the rest of the army to advance. It had been an orderly enough procedure, oddly accompanied by the sound of fighting to either side, where the outnumbered Romans were retreating further.

It had been a wise decision to have the remainder of his men trail the footsteps of those who would lead the attack. In little more than two hours, the vast majority of his forces had crossed the wall. Even Castus and Gannicus had made it, skulking by without so much as a nod or wave. When word reached him that Roman reinforcements were making their way up to the ridge, only half the cavalry remained without the enemy fortifications. Cursing, Spartacus had ordered the mounts that could not be brought through in time to be set free. Riders were worth more to him than horses, more of which might be captured as they marched. The myriad of camp followers – tradesmen, whores, itinerant priests and hucksters of every hue who had trailed after his troops for months – were absent. Spartacus had ordered them, on pain of death, to stay behind. Their fate did not concern him. It was time to move fast.

Leaving five thousand men under the command of Pulcher and Navio to hold the passage to their rear, Spartacus had ordered his army to move out. They had taken the mountaintop road that snaked its way along Bruttium's spine to join the Via Annia some fifty miles to the north. At first, it had been understandable that Castus and Gannicus had done the same thing. There were legions on both coastal plains but none at this altitude. After three days, however, Spartacus' patience had worn thin.

He had wandered the camp each night, assessing his soldiers' spirits, and had seen plenty of Gauls talking to men by their fires. They had sloped off at his approach, but there was little doubt that they returned when he'd gone. Much as he tried, he couldn't be everywhere at once. Castus and Gannicus' motives were obvious. Morale had been boosted by their audacious escape, but memories of the pirates' failure to appear and of the defeat suffered at the wall were still raw. Men were also unhappy because they were hungrier than ever. Until they renewed their stores of grain, Spartacus had ordered that everyone was to receive one-third of his normal daily ration.

'Those Gaulish bastards are like vultures picking over a corpse,' he ranted to Ariadne. 'They want to win over as many soldiers as possible before they split off.'

'You can't stop them.'

'Oh yes, I fucking can! I'll take a cohort over to their tents and kill the pair of them! It's what I should have done a long time ago.'

Ariadne's temper flared. 'Do you think their followers would take that lying down? You'd set the entire army at each other's throats. Crassus would piss his pants when he heard that you had done his job for him.' Spartacus glowered at her, but she was determined to say her piece. 'Do you really want to keep men who are so easily persuaded to leave?'

'I suppose not,' he admitted.

'What do you care if Castus' and Gannicus' followers talk to the faint-hearts then?' He didn't answer, which encouraged her. 'We know now that Crassus' soldiers are wary of attacking us, but we didn't at first. It's been no harm having the Gauls at hand while the legions were only a few miles behind us.'

'So I'm supposed to do nothing while they spread their poison?'

'Did I say that? You need to be seen by as many of the troops as possible. Men love to see their commander appear among them. Your words help to give them courage. You know that as well as I do.'

Brooding, Spartacus stared into the fire. He knew that Ariadne was right, but that didn't douse the fury he felt towards the Gauls. After all he'd done for them, this was how they repaid him? He longed to crucify both men, to smash their legs and arms in multiple places, to stand over them as they cried for their mothers and pleaded to die. Like the legionary on the ridge. But he wouldn't do it. Any short-term satisfaction he gained from such an action would surely be lost by the benefit gained by Crassus.

As if that whoreson needed any more advantage handed to him, he thought grimly. The cost of breaking out of the toe had been high. Nearly a thousand men had been killed, perhaps twice that number wounded. These were in addition to the eleven thousand lives lost during the first, failed assault. About half of the cavalry's horses and a similar number of mules had been left behind. Of the sixty thousand or so soldiers who had hoped to sail to Sicily, about forty-six thousand able-bodied men remained. And that was before Castus and Gannicus were taken into account. They wouldn't stick around for much longer. As soon as they reached the fertile lands of Campania and Samnium, Spartacus reckoned, they would leave.

There would be no fixed battles from now on if he could help it. Crassus' soldiers now outnumbered his. The odds would lengthen once Pompey arrived. Spartacus knew the Roman war machine well, and one lesson stood out from all the others that he had learned during his time in its service. To have any chance of victory against the legions, it was imperative to have superior numbers of troops. Parity of forces was not enough. If his people, the warlike Thracians, had not been able to beat Rome that way, neither could those who had once been slaves. Spartacus grimaced. He hated having to think like this, but it was the brutal truth. Few men thought or acted as he, a trained warrior, did. Navio did; so too did those some of his soldiers who'd been born free, and who had fought for their living.

To expect the rest of his army to do so when faced with such an implacable enemy would be to court disaster. He had to work to his men's strengths, and that did not include standing toe to toe with equal numbers of legionaries. Once again, they would have to act like latrones. Hide out in the wilderness, among the forested peaks that formed Italy's backbone. From there he would send out word that hard men – agricultural slaves and herdsmen – were wanted. There, with the help of the Great Rider, he could rebuild his army. Until the time came to face Crassus once more.

Spartacus knew in his gut that that would happen one day. Crassus and he had become mortal enemies. Their struggle would go on until one of them was dead. He tried to stay focused on that outcome, but it was hard not to dwell on the fact that if Crassus defeated and killed him, the rebellion would be over, whereas if he did the same to Crassus, the war against Rome would merely enter another phase. Not for the first time, Spartacus compared the Republic to the Hydra. Each of that creature's multiple heads breathed poisonous fumes, and if one was cut off, two grew in its place. It was like that with every damn legion that his men had destroyed. Yet the Hydra had not been invincible: only one of its heads had been immortal. Its end had come when the hero Hercules had cauterised the stumps of each head he'd chopped off, preventing them from regrowing and allowing him to find the head he really needed to remove. What was Rome's invincible head? Spartacus wondered. And how could he sever it? *Before the Great Rider, I swear that I will never stop searching for it as long as I live.*

Spartacus had barely seen either Carbo or Navio since the breakout. They were uninjured, but more than that he did not know. Wanting some companionship as much as to hear their thoughts, he made his way to their tent later that night. There was no sign of either Roman. It wasn't that late, thought Spartacus. Had they already gone to bed?

'Carbo? Navio?'

'Who is it?' Carbo's voice came from a short distance away. He sounded irritated.

'It is I, Spartacus.'

A moment's delay, and the flap on a nearby tent was thrown back. Carbo poked his head out.

'What are you up to?' Spartacus asked.

Carbo's face clouded over. 'It's Publipor. He took a flesh wound on the ridge. At first, it didn't look like much, but then it turned septic. The poor bastard has gone downhill fast since. The surgeon offered to take off his arm, but he's too weak to survive the operation. I don't think he'll last more than another day or two.'

Another good man lost. Spartacus ducked past Carbo and entered the tent. The stench of rotting flesh and urine inside was overpowering. He choked back a cough and approached the pile of blankets upon which Publipor lay, clad in only an undergarment. Navio, who was sitting alongside, looked up with a rueful smile. 'He'd be glad to see you, sir.'

Carbo was right, thought Spartacus grimly. Publipor's pallor was terrible. His eyes were sunken, his forehead drenched in sweat, his ribs clapped to his backbone. The injury to his sword arm had been wrapped in bandages that did little to stop a green-brown liquid from oozing on to his bedding. 'Is he conscious?'

'From time to time,' replied Navio. 'Often he's not lucid, though.'

Spartacus crouched down and took Publipor's good hand. 'I'm sorry to see you in this state.'

Publipor's eyelids twitched and then opened. His rheumy eyes swivelled around the tent, falling eventually on Spartacus. A strange expression twisted his gaunt face. 'You!'

'Yes,' said Spartacus gently. 'Can I get you anything?'

A hiss of pain. 'How about my family?'

Spartacus glanced at Carbo, who mouthed the word 'fever'. 'That's not within my power. But I can get you some wine if you like. A piece of ham.' He winked. 'Even a woman if you're up to it?'

'Go to Hades.'

Spartacus waved Navio and Carbo back. 'You're feverish, Publipor. I'll have the surgeon make up something that will help.' He turned to go.

'The fever didn't make me say that, you cocksucker.'

Spartacus' lips thinned. 'I see. Why would you insult me then?'

'Because you're responsible for the deaths of my family.' His voice cracked. 'My wife. My beautiful children.'

'I thought they died of cholera,' said Carbo in confusion.

'No.' A weak cough as he sat up. 'They were murdered at Forum Annii.'

Spartacus frowned. 'If that's where you're from, why didn't you say so before?'

It was as if Publipor hadn't heard. 'May the gods forgive me, I was away hunting in the mountains. I got back when the slaughter was over.' Tears dribbled down his unshaven cheeks. 'I returned to find them in my master's house, all dead. Butchered!'

'Publipor, I am deeply sorry for what happened to your family,' said Spartacus. 'I did my best to prevent atrocities from happening, you have to believe that.'

'Clearly, you didn't do enough!' Spittle flew from Publipor's mouth. 'My children were aged three, five and eight. They were innocent! Defenceless!'

'That's terrible,' Spartacus acknowledged, but then his face hardened. 'So you joined my army to get your revenge, is that it?'

A half-smile. 'Something like that.'

'Did you have ought to do with the Gauls' attempt on my life?'

'That? No. I knew nothing of it. I had a different master.'

Suspicion tickled Spartacus' spine. He saw the same doubt in Carbo and Navio's faces. 'Who would that be?'

'Marcus Licinius Crassus.'

White-hot fury lanced through Spartacus. In a heartbeat, his dagger was at Publipor's chin. 'Tell me everything.'

'You can't scare me. I'm dying.'

Spartacus' chuckle was evil. 'How would you like five men to haul on a rope that's been tied to your bad wrist?'

Publipor swallowed.

'Just tell me what happened, and I'll give you a swift death.'

A tiny nod. 'Months after the massacre, I was still living in the ruins of Forum Annii. I had no reason to go anywhere else. One day, a man came snooping about. He began asking me questions, and when I'd told him my story, he offered me money and the chance of revenge on you. He explained that his master was Crassus, who wanted an inside man in your army. All I had to do was become one of your soldiers, and to find out whatever I could.'

'You were being hunted by Roman cavalry when we found you!' cried Carbo.

'That was staged. My companions were both to be killed to make it look more authentic. It was a mistake that Kineas survived.' A grimace. 'He nearly gave the game away too.'

Spartacus' memory snaked back to the fight in the woods, and the way that Kineas had tried so hard to speak before he died. It all made sense now. 'You were the one who told Crassus that I was in Rome.'

A proud nod. 'I spoke to a rich farmer near the camp. He sent word to the capital.'

'What else did you do?'

'I told Crassus when you were going to march to the toe, and about the pirates. He didn't believe me about them, though. The best thing I did was to let him know that you were going to attack the ridge.'

'You dirty rat,' Spartacus snarled. 'Thousands of your comrades died there.'

'They were never my comrades! They were murdering bastards of the worst kind. I wish that every last one had been killed. And you as well!' Publipor's mouth opened to throw more insults, but the sound never came. He gasped a little, and looked down at Spartacus' dagger, which was buried to the hilt in his chest.

'That's more than you deserve, you traitorous piece of shit.' Spartacus savagely twisted the blade to and fro before pulling it free. His eyes already glazing over, Publipor slumped backwards on to his bed and lay still. A hot tide of blood began saturating the blankets.

Spartacus regarded him without emotion. He wished that he'd never gone hunting that day. Never set eyes on Publipor. Never taken him into his trust. But it was too late for that. Too late for so many things. 'At least we know who the spy was,' he said in a dry tone.

'I should have seen through his story,' said Carbo angrily.

'How? It was entirely feasible. There could be a score of others like him in the army, with different motives, but the same desire to do me harm.

That's why I trust only a handful of men, such as you two.' Spartacus stood up and walked outside.

'What shall we do with him?' called Carbo.

'Leave him out for the wolves. He shouldn't have any better treatment than any of those who died at the ridge.'

The fractured army spent two weeks on the march, passing from Bruttium to Lucania. Spartacus was aiming for Campania, one of the most fertile regions of Italy and the birthplace of the rebellion. Keen to get a head start on Crassus, he had driven his men harder than ever before; unencumbered by baggage or supplies, and free of their previous raggle-taggle of followers, they were able to cover twenty-five miles per day. Spartacus had taken charge of a shaggy white stallion, one of the largest horses belonging to any his cavalrymen. Riding up and down the column made it far easier to encourage his men. Realising what he was doing, Castus' and Gannicus' soldiers had matched the furious pace. The tactic worked. Soon his scouts were reporting that the legions were more than thirty miles behind them, and marching at a slower speed.

Spartacus took heart from this, and allowed his men a much-needed day off. Before moving to Samnium, he hoped to lure new recruits to his cause. He began the process by sending raiding parties to the biggest latifundia, their mission not just to find grain and supplies, but to win over the slaves they encountered there. Upwards of 250 men joined from the first two estates; after a few weeks Spartacus was sure that number would turn to thousands. Navio would soon whip them into shape. All they had to do was avoid confrontation with Crassus' legions until the recruits had been trained, and in the mountains of Samnium, that would not prove too difficult. Spring had arrived and, with it, better weather. In the coming days, the countryside would start yielding its own bounty of plants, nuts and berries. They wouldn't have to rely exclusively on raiding homesteads and farms.

When word came one morning that Castus and Gannicus were leaving, Spartacus was oddly surprised. As a man learns to live with his lice, he had grown used to the Gauls and their followers shadowing his army. It was hard not to be pleased, however, like a man who exchanges his infested tunic for a new one. Keen to see their departure for himself, he took Carbo, the Scythians and a century of soldiers. Even at this late stage, there was no point laying himself open to attack. Ariadne insisted on coming with him. She was carrying the basket containing her snake, so Spartacus did not object. The god might have spoken to her.

He found the troublesome pair marshalling their troops outside the camp. It was difficult to tell how many there were, but Spartacus guessed that it was somewhere in the region of ten thousand. Five eagles and nearly thirty Roman standards provided the proud focal point for the men, the badges of their achievements thus far. Spartacus wasn't worried about losing the Roman emblems; he was grateful instead that there were few horsemen among them.

'Come to make sure we're leaving?' shouted Castus.

'I thought you'd decided to stay,' retorted Spartacus. 'It's been a while since *my* men broke through the blockade.'

Castus' lips twisted. 'Our soldiers would have done it as easily as yours. Seeing as you wanted to take the glory – again – we didn't see any point in arguing over it.' He winked at Gannicus, who smirked.

Spartacus felt his anger swell. It had been a shrewd move by the Gauls. His troops had taken all the casualties while theirs had remained unscathed. He let out a slow breath. *Just let them leave.* 'Where will you go?'

'Who knows?' answered Gannicus with a shrug. 'Wherever the pickings are richest.'

'Wherever the best-looking women are to be found,' added Castus.

A cheer from their men.

Animals. Spartacus didn't probe further. Even if they knew, the Gauls wouldn't tell him. 'Watch your step. As the weaker group, Crassus will target you first.'

'Screw you,' roared Castus. 'We have nearly thirteen thousand men here!'

It was a larger number than Spartacus had expected, but he was careful not to show his displeasure. 'You've got about the same number of troops as in two and a half legions, but almost no horse. Sadly, Crassus has four times that number of men, and plenty of cavalry. In my mind, that's not wonderful odds.' He was gratified by the unhappy expressions that appeared on some of the faces opposite.

Castus' mouth worked furiously, but Gannicus got in first. 'We're no fools, Spartacus. Crassus won't find us easy to find, or to defeat.'

They glared at one another for a moment.

'If you hadn't proved to be so treacherous, I'd wish you well. As it is, I'll be glad to see the back of you.'

'The feeling is mutual,' jeered Castus. 'I'll see you in Hades sometime.'

Before Spartacus could answer, Ariadne had swept forward, her snake prominent in her right hand. Castus paled. Although he was nowhere near, he moved back a pace.

'Thus far, you have escaped paying for your crimes, Castus,' said Ariadne loudly. 'The gods deemed that it should be so. Do not think that you will enjoy their protection for ever.'

'Crimes? Piss off, woman! Peddle your lies elsewhere!' cried Castus, but his voice was a tone higher than normal.

'I predict that you will have a violent end.'

'Ha! Nothing wrong with that!' roared Castus.

Some of his men shouted in agreement. Gannicus even laughed. 'That's what every warrior wants.'

'It will be soon, however,' intoned Ariadne. 'In a matter of days. And it will come at the hands of the Romans.'

Gannicus scowled, but Castus' confidence oozed out of him like piss out of a pricked bladder. 'You're lying!'

Ariadne raised her snake high. The gesture was met by a hushed, reverential *Ahhhhh*. 'This is Dionysus' sacred creature, and I am one of his priestesses! I do not lie about such things. Best hope that someone is left to bury your body, Castus! Otherwise your tormented soul will be cursed to wander the earth for ever.'

'That kind of superstitious claptrap doesn't scare me, you stupid bitch!'

Ariadne was delighted. Castus' bluster couldn't conceal the fact that he was severely rattled. Most of the men within earshot looked unhappy, including Gannicus.

'Unless you want to head for Hades right now, watch your mouth, cocksucker,' roared Spartacus. Sure that Castus wouldn't take up his challenge, he took a few steps forwards.

'Shit for brains! You're outnumbered a hundred to one!' snapped Castus.

'That wouldn't stop me killing you, and taking great pleasure as I did so,' hissed Spartacus. Ariadne touched his arm, but he shook it off. 'Just say the word and we can get down to it.'

Castus held Spartacus' eye for a moment before his gaze dropped away. 'Time to move,' he growled.

Coward! thought Spartacus. You know I'd kill you. His risk-taking side wished that the Gaul had taken his challenge, but the rest of him knew it would have led to pointless bloodshed, and possibly his own death. A stupid way to die.

'If you've stopped quarrelling,' said Gannicus sourly, 'are you ready?'

'Yes, yes!' Castus shouted a command to his officers and stalked off.

Gannicus didn't immediately follow. He glanced at Spartacus and gave him a respectful nod, as if to say, 'In other circumstances, things might have been different.' Then he too walked away.

Spartacus' shoulders relaxed a fraction. 'May they kill thousands of legionaries, wherever they go. And may Crassus never catch them,' he said quietly. He looked at Ariadne. 'How many days will it be before he dies?'

'I'm not sure.'

'But you said—'

'I know what I said,' she retorted. 'That doesn't mean I saw it. It's true that he'll die in a matter of days anyway. One day. A hundred days, a thousand, what does it matter? I didn't state the number.'

'Did the god really send you a message?'

She glared at him. Her anger at Castus had overflowed at last. Spartacus happened to be in the way. 'Sometimes it's useful to make men think that the gods have decided their path. As when you told the soldiers that you were marching to the Alps, and I said it was Dionysus' will.'

'You made that up?'

'Of course I did. Don't tell me that you didn't have some inkling that I might have. Most likely you didn't ask because it suited you to think that your mission had divine backing.'

He looked taken aback, and then angry. 'And your interpretation of my dream with the snake? Did you invent that too?'

'No,' she said, sorry now that her temper had got the better of her. 'I would never lie about something so serious.'

His eyes probed hers. Spartacus was relieved to see no sign of deceit. He probably would have acted in the same way, but thinking that his mission had divine approval *had* helped to fuel his convictions. He hoped that her falsehood hadn't angered the gods. That possibility was one more thing he didn't need weighing down on his shoulders.

A doubt nagged at him. 'Have you seen ought about my future lately?'

An image of Egbeo on the cross flashed before Ariadne's eyes. She'd had the nightmare enough times – thankfully, though, not in recent weeks – to place some store in it. Spartacus hadn't been in it, but that didn't mean he would be safe *if* the horror came to pass. Should she tell him? Her gut answered at once. No. It took all of Ariadne's self-control to meet his gaze. 'Sadly, not a thing,' she lied.

His trusting grin relieved her. 'Good. I'm not sure I want to know what the gods hold in store for me. Better to make my own way in life rather than always be looking over my shoulder to see what might happen.'

'You do that anyway!'

A lopsided grin twisted his face. 'I suppose I do. And you love me for it, don't you?' He pulled her to him, and she did not resist. He was right, she thought, relishing the feel of his body against hers. Despite his faults, she loved him. It was why she would stand by him, come what might.

Chapter XVII

A week later . . .
Northern Lucania, near the town of Paestum

Followed by a gaggle of his senior officers and an escort of legionaries, Crassus had come to survey the battlefield. The site was about five miles inland, on a plain below a range of hills that ran eastwards to join the Apennines. The earth was littered with thousands of bodies: bloodied, mangled, mutilated. There was a disquieting order to the dead. Crassus paced slowly to what had been the front of the enemy position. There lay the victims of the artillery volleys. Thousands of acorn-shaped pieces of lead or baked clay dotted the ground here too, the work of his slingers, who could rain down a withering hail of fire from about three hundred paces out. The slingshot bullets had caused few casualties at this distance. Not so the artillery, which had wreaked a terrible slaughter. It was a revolting sight, Crassus reflected, taking care not to get the splattered gore on his red leather boots. There was no dignified way of describing men whose innards had been ripped out by a bolt the length of one's forearm, or whose flesh had been crushed to a crimson, oozing pulp by a large chunk of rock.

'Interesting, eh?' He gestured at an enemy soldier who had been decapitated. The body lay like a puppet with cut strings, a half-circle of scarlet staining the earth around the stump of its neck. There was no sign of its head.

'What is, sir?' asked Lucius Quinctius, the officer in charge of his cavalry.

Today, Quinctius was in Crassus' good books. Rather than rebuke him, therefore, he smiled. 'Normally, an injury like that would put undisciplined savages to flight. Not today.'

'It was unusual, sir. A measure of their determination.'

'Indeed. And you know about determination, Quinctius. You showed real skill in tricking Spartacus earlier today. If your horsemen hadn't succeeded in making him think that you wanted a fight, matters here could have taken an entirely different course. It was annoying enough yesterday when he arrived just as I was about to crush these slaves.'

'You do me great honour, sir,' said Quinctius proudly. 'Taking Spartacus off on a wild goose chase while you got to grips with this lot was the least that I could do.' He didn't mention what had happened to Mummius or his men. If anything, the memory of their fate had been the greatest spur to his efforts.

'Which way did he go?' asked Crassus. There had been no word from the spy for days now. The fool had either run away, or was dead. It was annoying, but of little consequence. The man had served his purpose.

'North, sir.' Quinctius' smile was wolfish. 'They haven't gone that far either. I had some of my men follow their trail.'

'I'm glad to hear it.' *With luck, I will still have defeated him before Pompey gets here.*

'This group had clearly split off from Spartacus' main force, sir. I wonder why he tried to intervene on their behalf twice?' asked Quintus Marcius Rufus.

Inbred fool. Crassus threw him a patronising frown. 'It's not that odd at all. Imagine that you took a quarter of my strength away, the result of which was that my enemies outnumbered me. In such a situation I'd do my best to win you back, even if I thought you were a useless whoreson.'

A couple of the others hid their smiles, but Rufus flushed as red as his hair. He knew better than to say more. Crassus didn't care that what had happened the day before wasn't his fault. The main reason that the enemy had escaped was because Spartacus had mounted a surprise attack and driven the legions away from his former followers. However, Crassus wasn't going to admit to that. Nor was he about to let Rufus forget his 'mistake' in a hurry. The redhead just had to suck on the bitter marrow of it until his general's attention moved on.

Fortunately for Rufus, Crassus was more interested in today's triumph and the carnage it had left. They walked on, disturbing the crows which were hopping from one corpse to another, pecking out the men's eyeballs. Despite the strong sea breeze, a low moaning sound carried through the air – the sound of those still alive, but too weak to move. Some of the officers studied the fallen with revulsion, but Crassus strode ahead, oblivious. 'After the catapults and ballistae come the pila,' he mused.

His men's javelins had accounted for fewer of the slaves' losses than the artillery. It was easy to see where the first volley had landed. There the ground was covered in peppered shields, but not that many bodies. The second volley of pila had showered down thirty paces on, a rain more lethal than any clouds could emit. A good number of the slaves had not possessed mail shirts; after the fashion of their own kind, many had gone into battle wearing nothing but a pair of trousers. Some were stark naked, carrying only their weapons. As a consequence, the human toll here had been far heavier. Even the smallest slingshot bullet could stave in a man's skull if it hit the right spot.

Crassus paused by a dead slave who had been struck by no less than three javelins. He pointed to the pilum that had run through the victim's thigh and pinned him to the earth. 'This must have hit first.'

'Poor bastard, he would have known what was coming afterward,' muttered Quinctius, looking up at the sky. 'No signs of any of them fleeing, though, sir,' he added. 'They continued to advance in good order.'

'I'll give them that much,' admitted Crassus. 'Outnumbered, without artillery or horse of their own, they didn't back away from this fight. Even when it came to hand-to-hand combat.'

They moved on, to where the main fighting had taken place. Soon there was barely space to see the ground for the corpses. More scavengers, both animal and human, were at work here. Vultures flapped down awkwardly in ones and twos, their target the men whose bellies or arses were on view. Ripping open these soft areas with their strong beaks, they fought over the purple loops of intestine that came spilling out into the spring air. Peasants of all ages skulked among the dead, rifling for purses or jewellery, even amputating fingers for the rings thereon. They were careful to keep well clear of the large, well-armed party.

Crassus was not interested in the living. He was here to glory in what his legionaries had done. He took immense satisfaction that almost none of the bodies were Roman. So far, there had been perhaps a dozen. The victory here had not just been decisive, he thought triumphantly, it had been total! An outstanding example of how the legions could win a battle. Proof of the effectiveness of discipline, and the deadliness of scutum and gladius.

As far as the eye could see lay men who had lost legs or arms; or who had taken a blade in the guts; or who had suffered wounds to their lower legs or ankles, easy targets on men without shields, and been finished off with thrusts to the belly or chest. The ones who had died most easily, Crassus reflected, were those who had had a gladius rammed into their throat in the textbook manoeuvre taught to all new recruits. Open-mouthed, blank-eyed, they lay; the gaping wounds under their chins a mark of his legionaries' good training. Crassus could hear the centurions repeating over and over: 'Ram the scutum boss at your opponent's face. When he pulls back, stick the fucker in the neck. Twist the blade to make sure, then tug it out. Job done. Man down.'

Finally, he began to see Roman casualties. It was inevitable, he supposed. Thousands of soldiers cannot stand face to face with their enemies, hammering blows at one another, without suffering some losses. Yet his men had not broken and run as so many of their comrades had done in the two years prior. Crassus knew this from the evidence before him, but also because he had watched the entire battle from a vantage point on the slopes of Mount Camalatrum, the first of the peaks that rolled off to the east. It had been an incredible sight, watching the hordes of slaves sweeping forward at his regimented cohorts. Their ranks had been swept by bolts and stones from his artillery, and then by slingshot bullets and javelins, but their charge had not checked. The *crash* when they had struck his men's lines had reverberated through the air like a thunderclap. Yet the slaves had not broken through. Instead, they had washed off the shield wall like waves off a rock. 'How many legionaries did we lose?'

'Just over three hundred killed, sir,' answered Rufus quickly.

'Injured?'

'Two hundred men and fifteen officers will never fight again, sir. About twice that number suffered minor injuries.'

'And the number of enemy dead?' Crassus had been told the figure already, but he had to hear it again.

'At a rough count, sir, something over twelve thousand, sir,' said Rufus with great satisfaction.

'So the enemy lost about forty men for each of ours, or my mathematics isn't what it was.'

'That'd be about right, sir.'

He glanced around, smiling. 'We can live with casualties like that, eh? Especially when five eagles and more than two dozen standards have been recaptured in the process!'

His officers muttered in agreement.

I can lose a damn sight more men than that, thought Crassus ruthlessly, just as long as I do it before the others get here. There had been no recent word of Lucullus' progress towards Italy from Thrace, but the man would certainly arrive within the next two months. And unless the gods had done him a huge favour, Pompey's legions would reach them within a matter of weeks. *Curse him!* Time was of the utmost. Spartacus had to be brought to bay, and fast.

'Were many prisoners taken?'

'Three or four score, sir,' said Rufus. 'Perhaps three times that number got away.'

'Let them go.'

Rufus goggled. 'Sir?'

'You heard me! They are to be released.'

'I don't understand, sir. They're vermin, who deserve nothing but a cross. Some of them might try to rejoin Spartacus.'

'That's precisely what I want them to do, fool. A few slaves less or more in the rabble we fight is nothing to me. I want Spartacus to hear of this defeat as soon as possible.'

'A shrewd move, sir,' said Quinctius smoothly; behind him, Rufus coloured again.

Crassus' gaze turned to the north. He wasn't a man for continually asking things of the gods, but at times, it felt right. *Great Jupiter, All Powerful Mars, I ask you to help me find Spartacus. Soon.*

Spartacus stood outside his tent with a blanket around his shoulders. It was his favourite time of the day – just after dawn. To the east, the sky was marked a vivid pink colour by the rising sun. Tiny trickles of smoke rose from the fires that had not gone out overnight. It was late enough to be light, but early enough that most men were still asleep. In the distance, a mule brayed softly at one of its companions. Apart from that, the huge camp was quiet.

Spartacus' thoughts had only one place to go. Crassus and his legions. He did not like retreating from the enemy, not without a battle. Retreat? That was what men who'd been beaten did. Yet again, he wished that his assassination attempt on Crassus had succeeded. The man was turning out to be a half-decent tactician. Three days before, Spartacus had been delighted when his arrival had thwarted Crassus' intended ambush of Castus and Gannicus' forces. Yet his opponent's response the following day had stolen all his pleasure.

A daring feint made by Crassus' horse – a series of stinging attacks followed by measured withdrawals – had fooled first Spartacus' cavalry commanders and then he himself into thinking that Crassus wanted to fight both them and the Gauls simultaneously. They had pursued the Roman horsemen with haste for some miles. It had been nothing but a ruse, engineered so that Crassus' full strength could be deployed against Castus and Gannicus. By the time Spartacus had realised, it had been far too late to think about turning his army around. Choose the ground you fight on; do not let it be chosen for you, went the old maxim, and he stuck to that with religious fervency. He hawked and spat. Forty-odd thousand legionaries against thirteen thousand slaves? Such an unequal contest would only ever have one result.

His presumption had been proved correct the previous evening, when a few dozen survivors had straggled into his camp. They had been brought straight to him, bloodied and battered; he'd heard the sorry story from their cracked lips. The Gauls and their men had died well enough, he thought bitterly. They had fought right to the end. 'What fucking use is that, though?' he muttered to himself. 'They're all dead. If the fools had stayed with me, they would still be alive.' *And my army wouldn't have been reduced in size by a quarter.*

By now, his entire army would have heard of the crushing Roman victory. The shocking news would have passed from tent to tent faster than the plague, and would have a profound effect on his men's morale. The same would be true of Crassus' legionaries, but in reverse. They would now be raring to confront his soldiers, and with good reason. While the odds weren't as badly stacked against him and his men as they had been for the Gauls, Spartacus was still chary of an open battle against Crassus. If it had to happen, the ground had to be right. Otherwise he might as well lay down his arms.

There were other problems to consider too. Crassus' close proximity and Spartacus' need to keep his army on the move meant that few slaves were coming to join them. Then there was Pompey. How soon would he bring his legions into the equation? Say a month at the earliest, he thought darkly, three months at the outside. Not long. Scarcely enough time to recruit and train ten thousand men, let alone five times that number. With an army sixteen legions strong, the Romans would hunt them down with ease. *It won't matter where we go. They will find us.*

'Can't sleep?'

He looked up in surprise. 'Carbo. I'm just enjoying the quiet. What are you doing here?'

'I had a poor night's rest, decided to go hunting. I wondered if you'd come?'

A weary smile. 'Another time, maybe.'

Carbo glanced at Spartacus, and then looked away. 'I can't stop thinking about what will happen when Pompey arrives.'

This is the real reason he's here. 'Things will get a lot worse, that's what will happen.'

'Maybe we should fight Crassus now, before Pompey arrives?' Carbo ventured.

'We might have to,' came the grim reply. 'But we need a battlefield that would suit us, and I haven't seen too many of those in the last couple of days. Somewhere narrow is vital, where Crassus wouldn't be able to use his superior numbers to flank us. Or a good spot for an ambush. That would do.'

Carbo did not know how to say what he'd been brooding about all night, so he just came out with it. Spartacus might think he was mad, but he had to try. 'Have you considered Brundisium?'

'The town in the south-east?'

'That's the one. From what I know, it's not that well defended. There's no need for it to be. We could easily take it.'

Spartacus frowned. 'Why would we do that? Crassus would hem us in there, as he did in the toe.'

'It's the biggest port in Italy. I don't know how many ships would be tied up on the quay at any one time, but it'll be a lot. Certainly enough vessels to carry a few thousand men, but there could be more. From Brundisium, it's not far to Illyria, or even Greece.'

Spartacus' mind began to race. The Alps were too far, and his men had balked there before, but this, this was news he hadn't expected. He chewed on it for a moment. 'How far is it to Brundisium?'

'I'm not sure exactly. Two hundred miles, maybe a bit less? It's straight down the Via Appia, which is only half a day's march from here. We could make it in ten days.'

Ariadne's voice broke in. 'Make where in ten days?'

Spartacus lifted a finger to his lips and beckoned her closer. Quickly, he explained.

Her face lit up. 'You think we could do it?'

'I don't see why not.'

'What about Crassus?' she asked warily. 'His cavalry are shadowing us as if their lives depended on it.'

'He knows our every move,' Spartacus admitted. 'The prick will be after us like a hound on a hare if he suspects what we're up to.' His eyes glittered. 'We'd have to act fast. Take the town in the first attack.'

'I could ride ahead with Navio, see if I can bribe a guard on one of the gates,' offered Carbo. 'If that didn't work, we might be able to lower ropes over the wall at night for an assault party.'

'You're a good man, Carbo.'

Ariadne murmured her agreement, and Carbo flushed with pride. He eyed his leader, his heart thumping. What would Spartacus decide?

'Very well. We'll head south-east.' Ariadne let out a little cry of happiness and Spartacus held up a warning finger. 'But if the right site offers itself on the way, I'm going to make a stand. This idea might come to nothing, and Pompey's legions will get here soon. Defeating Crassus before they join up would nicely reduce the numbers facing us. It would also give us more breathing space to reach Brundisium and possibly get the entire army out – not just part of it.' He clapped Carbo on the shoulder. 'My thanks.'

Carbo grinned. It was risky, but there was a way out of their predicament after all.

Two days later, Spartacus had begun to believe that his future was finally brightening. They had reached the Via Appia without incident, camping the first night in a valley that was split into two by a fast-flowing river. The following afternoon, he'd been brought news that the Roman horse dogging their trail were drawing closer and closer to his rearguard. Spartacus had seized the chance to take on the enemy again. Sending his cavalry into the wooded hills that ran along their right side, he had made his way to the army's tail. An hour or so later, he'd heard a single trumpet sound from the treeline some distance behind the Roman horsemen. It had been the signal for the rearmost cohorts to turn about face and present arms.

As the enemy cavalry had reined in, pondering their best course of action, his riders had charged from cover. The ambush had been a resounding success. Mad for revenge because of what had happened to Castus and Gannicus and their men, Spartacus' soldiers had fought like demons. The Romans had been driven from the field with heavy casualties. Among the injured had been one of their commanders, who'd been lucky to escape with his life. Crassus would have discovered that the scorpion was still well able to sting, thought Spartacus with great satisfaction. He hadn't seen an enemy scout or horseman since. The legions were still following, but at a safer distance.

He grinned. There was no way that Crassus could yet know of his intention to make for Brundisium. Carbo and Navio had set out on horse-back at dusk two days previously, leading a pair of spare mounts each. Because their extra horses would attract unwanted attention – normally, only official messengers or cavalry travelled in this way – they would travel while it was dark, and conceal themselves during the day. With a little luck, Spartacus would have some news within two weeks.

In the meantime, he could march his army south – not at breakneck speed, for that would raise Crassus' suspicions, but at a more leisurely pace of twelve to fifteen miles daily. This in turn meant that in the eventuality of a battle, his soldiers would be more rested than if they were marching hard. Spartacus' men had no idea of his intent. He had told Egbeo, Pulcher and a few of his other senior officers, but the rest thought that they were in search of more supplies. He didn't want a reaction similar to the one when he had suggested that they cross the Alps. For his plan to have any chance of working, the army had to do exactly as he wished.

If a confrontation with Crassus had been avoided by the time Carbo returned, he would tell his men then. There would be no mention of their previous glories, just a heavy emphasis on the sixteen legions that they would soon have to face. If that didn't persuade the dogs to leave Italy, thought Spartacus, nothing would.

If, however, an opportunity presented itself to fight Crassus, there would be no mention of Brundisium until afterwards. As at the Alps, however, a recent victory might make it harder to win over his soldiers. Spartacus estimated that the majority would see sense. Being penned into the toe by the legions for two months had given a clear indication of what could happen to them. It wasn't as if he was planning to end his fight against Rome either – far from it. The war could continue in Illyria, and then Thrace. His homeland.

Since seeing his troops' reaction to their first defeat on the ridge, he had begun to long for Thrace and his own kind. That major setback – their first – had been enough to knock the confidence out of most. Yes, they had flocked to him in their tens of thousands previously – not of late, he thought bitterly – yes, they had just won another clash against the Romans, but they had not been born to war as he and his kind had. He still felt great loyalty towards them, but Thracian tribes were more used to fighting Rome. Although many had been subjugated, the flames of their hatred towards the foreign invaders still burned. Spartacus wanted to fan those flames into a conflagration once more. His people's fierce independence would be an obstacle to uniting them, but would it be any worse than having to manage men such as Castus and Gannicus?

The prospect now seemed better than facing ever larger armies here. If he left, Rome would still want vengeance, but Spartacus doubted that they would send sixteen legions after him. A few maybe, but those he could deal with.

Another two days passed in similar fashion. Spartacus' army marched south-east without hindrance; the Romans did not attempt to move any closer to his forces, which Spartacus assumed meant that Crassus hadn't realised that he might break for Brundisium. Yet the changing terrain would soon force Spartacus' hand one way or another. The Via Appia was angling out from the shadow of the Apennines, threading a route through the countryside that would soon take it close to the east coast. Away from the mountains' protection, his intention would be obvious to anyone but an imbecile. Frustratingly, it would be at least a week until Carbo and Navio got back. Spartacus didn't like it, but he was going to have to make the decision to continue travelling south-east or to double back on his trail before the pair returned.

To help him decide, Spartacus rode his stallion to the army's vanguard, the better to spy out the land. Atheas and Taxacis trotted on either side of him, keeping pace without even breaking sweat. The tattooed pair could ride – what Scythian couldn't? – but the shortage of horses since the fight at the ridge precluded them having any.

The farms here were not as large as the latifundia of Campania and Lucania, but impressive nonetheless. Artificial terraces spilled down the lower slopes of the mountains, affording level ground for countless thousands of olive trees. More of them marched right up to the road, their characteristic grey-green foliage concealing the ground behind. Spartacus was glad that he had scouts patrolling in advance of the army, for it would have been easy to set an ambush among the dense network of trees.

Grapes and grain were also cultivated in abundance, but the neat rows of vines and the open fields of slow-growing wheat provided no cover for enemy troops. There were few villages in the area; the majority of people lived on farms. Spartacus had his soldiers checking houses and buildings for supplies, and most importantly, for food. All flocks of sheep and goats and herds of cattle found were to be rounded up and driven to join the army. Even the poultry were to be taken. Nothing was to be left behind; any resistance could be met with lethal force.

Spartacus felt no remorse for the farmers whose livelihoods he was devastating and whose lives he threatened with famine. He didn't worry either about the stubborn individuals who refused to abandon their properties, and who died as their wives and daughters were being gang raped. Before, he had made some effort to minimise the atrocities, but not now. Rome was out to destroy him, so he would do it and its people as much harm as possible. Besides, what his men did was but a small taste of bitter medicine for a few of those whose fathers, sons or brothers had done the same in Thrace. It was a form of retribution.

By the time the sun had reached its zenith in the sky, it had grown pleasantly warm. Larks fluttered high overhead, their lilting song providing a welcome break from the sound of hooves striking off the road's stone paving and the heavier tread of thousands of hobnailed sandals. Men bawled out verse after verse of filthy songs about the carnal proclivities of a young man on the island of Lesbos, or the habits of a sexually rapacious merchant's wife. Half listening, Spartacus was considering whether he would save the piece of cheese in his pack or eat it now when through the haze that shimmered over the road, he spotted a pair of riders. A dust cloud trailed behind them, evidence that they were riding hard.

The cavalry officer he was riding with saw them at the same time. 'Who in Hades could that be, sir?'

'Good question.' The news of their approach had taken all traffic off the Via Appia. Only an occasional slave came walking along it now, their mission to join them. But slaves didn't generally ride. The horsemen wouldn't be Roman envoys either. The bastards hadn't tried to negotiate with him before. Why would they start now? 'I'd say it's Carbo and Navio,' he said with a scowl.

Hearing the anger in Spartacus' voice, the officer did not reply.

Spartacus' tension grew as the parties drew nearer. It was all he could do not to gallop out to meet the pair, but that would have looked panicky. Who else could it be? His mind tossed around every possible answer to their early return. Unless the pair's horses had grown wings, they hadn't had time to ride to Brundisium and back. Could they have been ambushed by latrones, and lost their spare mounts?

Finally, Spartacus urged his horse forward, away from the front ranks of riders. He wanted to hear their report in privacy. Only the Scythians loped beside him. Close up, there was no mistaking Carbo and Navio's dejected expressions, or the sweat lathering their mounts' flanks. Spartacus' belly gave a painful clench, but he smiled in greeting anyway. 'Gods above, those horses you have must be related to Pegasus! Either that, or it's not nearly as far to Brundisium as you thought.'

Carbo and Navio exchanged a quick glance. 'We didn't get as far as Brundisium,' said Carbo.

'Oh. Why not?' Although he longed to shout, Spartacus kept his tone light.

'Two nights ago, we hid the horses in an olive grove and went to a nearby roadside inn for some wine,' said Navio, shooting a guilty glance at Spartacus. 'I know you'd told us to avoid public places, but we were both dying of thirst.'

'You both seem to make a damn habit of disobeying my orders,' snapped Spartacus. 'What you're going to say had better be good.'

'It's not good, sir, it's fucking awful,' said Navio.

Spartacus became very still. 'Go on.'

'There was an official messenger staying in the inn. The prick was telling anyone who'd listen that he'd been sent to find Crassus at all costs.' Carbo hesitated.

'Why?'

'Lucullus has been recalled from Thrace,' said Carbo quietly. 'He's already marched his legions over the mountains and into Epirus. A fleet of ships was sent there to meet him.'

Time felt as if it had stopped. Spartacus was acutely aware of his horse shifting beneath him, of the sun beating down on his face, of the larks trilling above. Of all the reasons for their return, he had not expected this hammer blow. 'How many soldiers?'

'It depends whether Lucullus brings his entire army or not. He has six legions, two of which have already landed. The messenger seemed to think that he would leave one behind to garrison parts of Thrace.'

Five extra legions to fight. *Five.* 'When will the rest arrive?'

'He wasn't sure. Apparently, two of the legions are much closer than the rest. They'll sail within the next week to ten days. The last will embark within a month or so.'

Spartacus wanted to curse every god in the pantheon. This was the cruellest joke that had been played on him yet. What had he done to deserve this? Gritting his teeth, he held his fury in. It was pointless to insult the gods, even if they had sent him this misfortune. With luck, he could win back their favour yet, and it wasn't as if he didn't need all the help he could get. 'Did you kill the messenger?'

'We were going to,' said Navio, 'but it seemed pointless. He mentioned being one of four. They had been sent out separately, to make sure that Crassus received the news.'

'And if by some small chance we'd been caught doing it, you wouldn't have found out,' added Carbo.

Screw the consequences. I would have killed the messenger anyway. Spartacus took a deep breath and let it out again. That was just his fury speaking. He stared east, towards the sea, imagining that he could see the glitter of the sun off the waves, and a fleet of ships bobbing at anchor. Shoving away the fantasy, he returned his gaze to Carbo and Navio. 'Crassus could well have already heard the news. If not, he'll receive it today, or tomorrow at the latest.'

They nodded miserably.

'There's no point continuing towards Brundisium. Knowing what he does, Crassus would march after us at double pace. Once he'd caught up, the prick would seek battle on open ground. Even if we somehow manage to evade him on the road to the coast, he would hound us all the way. We could arrive with him at our backs, to be greeted by two or even four of Lucullus' legions. Being caught between the hammer and the anvil is not a good place to be.'

Carbo and Navio glanced at one another. This was what they had talked about, argued about, since they'd set out. 'What can we do?' ventured Carbo.

'There's only one damn option left,' grated Spartacus. 'Turn around and head for the mountains again. We *have* to find a suitable place to fight Crassus, and fast. With him defeated, we can try for Brundisium again, and smash Lucullus on the way there.'

Apart from the defeat on the ridge, thought Carbo, Spartacus had always led them to victory. Despite the fearful odds that were stacking up against them, why should that change now?

'And Pompey?' asked Navio.

'We'll just have to keep our ears to the ground for him. In our favour, it's likely that Crassus will want to fight us without Pompey's help. If I know one thing about the fucker, it's that he's arrogant. He'll want the glory for himself. Yes, he will unite with the other generals eventually – he'll have to. But if we can stay two steps ahead of them, we'll be fine.' He searched their faces for signs of dissent. He didn't see it. There was a hint of fear in Carbo's eyes, which Spartacus had expected, but the young Roman gave him a resolute nod. Navio looked as keen as ever, which didn't surprise him either. All he wanted was vengeance for his dead family. It was a quest that could never end until Navio, or every Roman who lived under the Republic's rule, was dead. Spartacus wondered which would come sooner.

He wondered the same thing about himself.

Chapter XVIII

The upper Silarus valley, north of Paestum

Spartacus' senior officers began assembling outside his tent when the sky was still full of stars. Hearing their low murmurs, the Thracian stirred from his position by the cot, but he didn't move further. It was hard to turn away from his sleeping son. Tousle-headed, beautiful, with a thumb stuck in his mouth, Maron was the picture of innocence. Long may he remain like that, thought Spartacus. Before life changes him. Makes him hard. He kissed the first two fingers of his right hand and trailed them across Maron's forehead. *Sleep well, my son. I will see you later.*

He was already fully dressed. Tunic, padded jerkin, mail shirt, studded sandals. Baldric over his shoulder, sica in its scabbard by his left side. A leather belt with a sheathed dagger on it. He reached down to the stool by his bedding and picked up his Phrygian helmet.

'Were you going to leave without saying goodbye?'

He looked at her in surprise. 'I thought you were asleep.'

Ariadne let out a dismissive snort. 'I've spent the night praying. Staring at the ceiling. Or you.' In fact, she had slept for a time, but her head had been filled with the crucified men again. She wasn't going to mention that now, or ever. It was just her imagination running riot. *Let it be no more than that, Dionysus.*

'At me?' He sounded amused.

'Why wouldn't I? You're a handsome man.' She reached up to trace the line of his jaw with a finger. 'I've thought that from the first time we met. When you saved me from Kotys' men.'

'That seems a lifetime ago.' There was a touch of wistfulness in his voice. 'But I can remember your face as if it were yesterday. You were quite the beauty. And still are,' he added, smiling.

'Don't leave like this,' she said, trying to keep the emotion from her voice.

'I'll come back in when I've finished talking with the officers.'

She nodded, grateful that the semi-darkness concealed the tears welling in her eyes.

Helmet under one arm and carrying his shield, Spartacus walked outside. His stomach knotted in a familiar reaction. It felt similar to the times he'd emerged from the tunnel into the gladiatorial arena. Instead of a single opponent, he found Pulcher, Egbeo, Navio and Carbo waiting for him. All four were dressed for a fight. Plumes of exhaled air rose above them into the cool air, and they stamped from foot to foot in an effort to stay warm. Rather than banks of seating full of baying spectators, the black outline of a huge massif loomed to their rear.

After nearly a week of marching north and west and aware that Crassus was closing in, Spartacus had been grateful to find this valley. It was bounded on both sides by mountains. To the east, the sheer-faced plateau behind him, and to the west, a line of similarly high, but more undulating peaks. At the valley's bottom was a river, the Silarus, which meandered westwards to Campania's coastal plain. The land here was fertile. Farmhouses were dotted throughout the olive groves and fields. On this side of the river, there was a significant amount of open space given over purely to the cultivation of wheat. It was what had attracted Spartacus' eye as he'd spied out the terrain from the top of the massif two days earlier. There wasn't too much flat ground – he estimated it was about two miles wide. That was enough for his troops to deploy without giving Crassus' legions the space to envelop them. It would constrain the effectiveness of his cavalry, but that couldn't be helped. Time was not on their side, so this battlefield would have to suffice.

They hadn't been here for long – twelve hours? – before the Roman scouts had found them. It had only taken another night and day for the legions to appear. They had come from the opposite direction to Spartacus' army: up the valley from the west, a snaking column that had taken five hours to arrive fully. It was clear from the outset that Crassus was keen for a fight. Instead of using the Silarus as a natural barrier, first his cavalry and then his legionaries had forded the watercourse. They had set up camp on the bank, at the edge of the open ground that led up towards Spartacus' men's tents. The provocative move had blocked off all avenues of retreat, except to the east, and short of attacking on the spot, had issued the most direct challenge possible.

Spartacus murmured a quiet greeting to his officers, who gave him tense nods in reply. He had already decided that Egbeo would command the left flank and Pulcher the right. Navio would be with him, in the centre. Carbo would stay with Ariadne and Maron, his job as before. 'Have the sentries seen anything overnight?' He had ordered pickets to be set up far beyond their own lines in case Crassus tried any tricks.

'There hasn't been a thing until just now, sir,' said Pulcher.

Spartacus' gaze fixed on the smith's face. 'What have they seen?'

'It's been too dark to see, sir. But they heard the sound of digging.'

'Where?'

'On the ground before both ends of Crassus' camp, sir.'

'The bastards must be digging trenches, to prevent our cavalry from charging.'

'That was what I thought, sir,' replied Pulcher with a scowl.

'In that case, there's only one thing to do.'

They stared at him without speaking.

'Attack now. Disrupt the soldiers who are digging. With the Rider's help, they'll have to abandon the trenches without finishing them. Egbeo, you can take charge of the left flank, eh?'

The Thracian's craggy face split into a smile. 'Be my pleasure!'

'Pulcher, you take the right.'

'Of course.'

'How many men will we take?' asked Egbeo.

'Six cohorts each should be enough. Any more, and they might not hear your orders. Take a few trumpeters each to be on the safe side. Push the Romans back, out of their trenches. When you've done that, withdraw. The rest of the army will be ready by then. Before you go, remember to instruct your officers to ready their men. Lastly, send the cavalry commanders to me. Well, what are you waiting for?'

With broad grins, the pair hurried away.

'Where do you want us, sir?' asked Navio.

343

'You're to stand with me, in the very centre.'

Navio grinned. 'I'd be honoured.'

Spartacus' eyes moved to Carbo. 'My most loyal of men.'

Carbo's stomach lurched. He suspected what Spartacus was going to say.

'I want you to stay behind, to protect Ariadne and Maron. Today will be harder fought and more desperate than any of the battles we have fought. If things go wrong—'

'Leave someone else!' interrupted Carbo. 'I won't do it! Not this time!' Beside him, Navio stiffened in surprise.

Spartacus' eyes narrowed. 'I could order you to do so.'

'But you won't,' replied Carbo furiously.

'Why in Hades won't I?'

'Because Crassus is the man who ruined my family. He's the reason that my parents ended up in Varus' house. He's to blame for their deaths! This is the first chance since Rome that I will have had to kill him. It might be the only opportunity I'll ever get, and you're not going to take it away from me.' Carbo glared at Spartacus, afraid yet unwilling to back down.

Navio's worried eyes shot from one to the other.

'Well, well,' said Spartacus. 'The young cock stands his ground at last!'

Carbo set his jaw and prepared for Spartacus' rebuke, punishment, or even dismissal.

'Very well, you can fight. Who am I to stand in the way of a man's need for vengeance? I would ask that instead of positioning yourself with Egbeo and your cohort, you stand with me and Navio in the centre. Will you do that?'

Carbo's throat closed with sudden emotion. 'I–I'd be honoured.'

A brief smile. 'Good. Best get to rousing the men, eh? I want the whole army ready to fight in within two hours.'

'Yes, sir!' Stunned at the ease with which Spartacus had given way, Carbo beat a hasty retreat. As well as obeying his orders, telling Arnax what to do if things went against them was paramount. Navio followed, threading his way between the dense lines of tents.

Spartacus watched them go. He glanced at the eastern sky, which was lightening fast. Daybreak had arrived. He caught first Atheas' and then Taxacis' eye. 'With Carbo out of the picture, I had a mind to ask you,

Taxacis, to protect Ariadne with Atheas if things went badly. I would feel better knowing that you were both by her side, but I think you would attract too much attention.'

Taxacis' lips peeled upwards, and he pointed at the tattoos on his cheeks and arms. 'These . . . get noticed.'

'Which would not be the best thing for Ariadne or the baby. The less attention, the better. I will ask someone else.' Aventianus, the slave with the scar on his cheek, Spartacus thought. He seemed a decent sort, and trustworthy.

'I not . . . want miss fight anyway,' muttered Taxacis.

'Good! First, though, find a man called Aventianus – he's in Navio's cohort, I think – and bring him here.' Putting down his helmet and sword, Spartacus ducked back into the tent.

'What have you planned?' Ariadne asked in a whisper. She was up, and fully dressed.

'You look beautiful.' Even in the poor light, he could see her blush. 'It's true!'

Ariadne's emotions were surging between utter terror that she might never see him again, and pride in what he was about to do. 'Hush. Tell me your plan.'

Spartacus told her about the Roman trenches. 'My hope is that we can push the bastards back. If Egbeo and Pulcher can achieve that, the cavalry will still be of use. While the main part of the army is getting ready, they can be darting in and out like clouds of mosquitoes, annoying the legionaries, preventing them from forming up properly. Panicking them a little.'

'Then you'll advance?'

He nodded. 'Our first charge will be the one that counts. It nearly always is. With the Rider's help, we'll break through. The cavalry will be working their flanks, and I hope to roll the bastards up until their backs are against the river. That's when they'll break, and the slaughter will start.' He smiled at her. 'I'll be back before dark.'

Ariadne forced herself to return the smile, but she wanted to break down and cry. She had never thought to find a man she could love, but then she had met Spartacus. Now, after all they had been through, this might be the end. Her pain was exquisite, but she made herself speak. 'What happens if you don't come back?'

His eyes met hers without wavering. 'Know that I will have died fighting. All my wounds will be on my front.'

A sob escaped her lips at last. She moved forward, into the welcome circle of his arms. 'I don't want you to go.'

'I have to, Ariadne, you know that. This is the most important battle of my life. My men need me.'

Your men, it's always your fucking men! Ariadne wanted to rage. What about me and Maron? She didn't say a word, however. There was no point.

There was silence between them for a long time. They stood, savouring the warmth of the other's flesh, the rhythm of each other's breathing.

Great Rider, Spartacus prayed. I ask that you watch over Ariadne and my son, especially if I should fall today. Dionysus, look after this woman, your loyal priestess, and her baby, who will learn to follow your ways.

Ariadne was offering up similar, fervent prayers. All too soon, she felt Spartacus' grip fall away. Stricken, she pulled his face down to hers and kissed him. 'Come back to me.'

He smiled, more gently than she could ever remember. 'If I can, I will. I swear it. Atheas and a man called Aventianus will watch over you here. If the battle goes badly, they are to take you and Maron to safety. There are bags of coin under my spare clothes, enough to last you for many years if you're careful.'

She nodded, unable to speak.

He walked to the cot and scooped up Maron, who stirred and then woke. He scrunched up his eyes and stretched. Enfolding him in his arms, Spartacus rocked his son to and fro for several moments. Maron soon settled. 'Grow up to be strong and healthy. Honour your mother, and my memory. Remember that Rome is your enemy,' Spartacus whispered. 'Know that I will always be watching over you.'

He handed Maron to Ariadne. Tears trickled from her closed eyelids as he embraced them both. Ariadne did not open her eyes as Spartacus let go, because she could not bear to see him leave. Instead, she buried her face in the crook of Maron's neck, letting his baby smell wash over her.

'Goodbye, wife.' He spoke from some distance away.

Panic ripped through Ariadne. In the dreadful eventuality that he did not return, she did not want his last memory to be of her avoiding his gaze. Nor that hers would be of letting him walk away without a last look at his face. She lifted her head, dabbed away the tears. 'Goodbye. I will see you after it's over.'

He smiled. 'You will.'

And then he was gone.

Ariadne's tears began to flow in earnest. Gone was the composed priestess that most people knew. In its place was a woman who had just sent her husband into battle, perhaps for the last time. Although Maron was in her arms, she had never felt more alone.

The sun had emerged from behind the massif to their rear and was bathing the valley by the time Spartacus' troops were ready. He had assembled them in two strong lines, more than thirty cohorts wide rather than the typical Roman triplex acies pattern that Crassus' legionaries were adopting five hundred odd paces opposite. His attack, a gamble, required the maximum force his men could muster. He had therefore placed his best soldiers, the ones who possessed mail shirts and Roman shields and weapons, in the centre with him. It was where the fighting would be hardest, bloodiest, deadliest.

Beyond these eight cohorts slightly more than half of the men were as well armed. Of the rest, few had helmets. Some had shields; others had mail. Their weapons were swords, spears and even axes. He hoped that what they lacked in equipment, they would make up in bravery. Egbeo and Pulcher would exhort the best from them, he was sure of that. On the flanks, his cavalry waited, hundreds of riders on shaggy mountain ponies. They didn't look that fearsome, but Spartacus had seen what they'd done to the Romans on numerous occasions.

Normally, he'd have been cursing the fact that less than half of his original force of horsemen remained. Today it didn't matter, because there wasn't room on either side for more riders to manoeuvre. His cavalry's role would be vital; he had given the officers in charge detailed instructions on what to do. He wanted them to act like Hannibal's famed Numidian horsemen, whose tactic of attacking and withdrawing had so often led enemies to break ranks, thereby exposing themselves to danger. If his cavalry could replicate that even to a small extent, Egbeo and Pulcher would capitalise on the advantage to its fullest, which in turn would increase the likelihood of the Roman flanks folding. And if that happened, Crassus' legions would break.

As he'd supervised the men, Spartacus had kept half an eye on the struggle around the enemy trenches and half an eye on what Crassus' soldiers were doing. Thus far, the legions were making no move to advance. Like him, Crassus was merely marshalling his forces in case the battle proper began. Spartacus began to give the clashes on the flanks his full attention. The two bouts were some distance away, making it difficult to see what was happening. It was clear, however, that neither Egbeo nor Pulcher had succeeded in driving the Romans back far, if at all. The figures of fighting men ebbed to and fro, accompanied by the usual clatter of weapons, shouts and screams. 'What the hell's going on down there?'

'The Romans have brought up their catapults, sir,' said Navio. 'Listen.'

Spartacus pricked his ears. After a moment, he heard the familiar twangs that signalled the release of bolts and stones. The noise was coming from both Egbeo's and Pulcher's positions. He hoped that Crassus didn't have too many of the deadly machines. Suddenly, his attention was drawn by a large formation of troops marching towards the enemy's left flank. His eyes swivelled, seeing a similar force moving in the direction of the right flank. Crassus was reinforcing the men in the trenches, not ordering them to withdraw. His decision had just been made for him. 'We advance. Now.'

'The whole army?' asked Carbo nervously.

'Yes.' He pointed down the slope. 'Look at those cohorts. We've got to move now, or Egbeo and Pulcher's troops will get massacred.' He glanced at them both. 'Ready for this?'

They both gave him a grim nod.

'Egbeo and Pulcher will be up to their eyeballs with what's going on. Someone else needs to lead their men down there. Navio, I want you to take charge of the left flank.'

Navio saluted. He exchanged a quick glance with Carbo and then trotted off at the double.

Spartacus called for a messenger. 'The most senior centurion on the right flank is to take command there. The order to advance will come very soon.' The man saluted and sprinted away. 'Bring me my stallion!' cried Spartacus.

A soldier who'd been waiting off to one side hurried forward, leading the horse.

Beckoning, Spartacus walked out some thirty paces from his troops.

Gods, but he looks magnificent, thought Carbo. Spartacus' Phrygian helmet glittered in the sun, drawing everyone's attention. His mail shirt had been burnished until it shone like silver, and on his left hip sat his sica, the blade that had led them to victory so many times before.

Spartacus cupped a hand to his lips. 'You see this magnificent beast?'

There were puzzled nods of agreement. 'We see him,' shouted a voice. 'And we all wish that we had one too!'

This raised a few laughs.

'In Thrace, a white horse is regarded as a mount fit for a king. They are to be honoured, and treated with respect. It is why I picked this stallion to ride. He has served me well, but today I will use him for another purpose. He is to be a sacrifice to the gods! To ask them for victory at any cost.'

The shock among his troops was palpable. This was a powerful rite indeed. Men whispered to one another, and the word began to spread.

Spartacus smiled. This had been his intent. 'Instead of riding into battle, I would fight beside you, my brothers, in the shield wall. I would take every blow that you do. I will bleed with you, and kill Romans beside you. I will stay to the bitter end with you, though my shield be shattered and my blade broken!'

The oath made Carbo shiver, and stirred his passion as never before. The men around him were comrades, whom he would die for, as they would for him. He glanced to either side, seeing the same emotion on others' faces.

Drawing his dagger, Spartacus stepped up to the horse. Recognising him, it whinnied and nibbled at his arm. 'Gently, brave one. I thank you for your faithful service. I ask one more thing of you. This will be your finest moment, and give you a rapid journey to the Great Rider's side. There you will be received with great honour.' To the soldier, he whispered, 'Pull out his head.'

With Spartacus rubbing his shoulder, the stallion let the soldier extend his neck forward.

Great Rider, this is for you. In return, I ask for victory.

Spartacus brought up the knife under the horse's chin. In one swift movement, he brought it back towards him. The wickedly sharp blade slashed a gaping hole in the stallion's flesh, severing both its jugular veins and setting free a tidal wave of blood. It staggered, blowing red froth from the hole in its windpipe. Spartacus leaned into it with all his strength, stroking its shoulder with his free hand. 'Steady, brave heart, steady. The Rider awaits you.'

The horse's knees buckled, and it dropped to the ground like a stone. More blood flowed, creating a huge pool of crimson around its forequarters. One of its back legs shot out to the side. It kicked madly several times and was still. Spartacus reached down and worked the knife deeper into the stallion's neck. This time, he cut an artery. Bright red blood sprayed over his hand. He continued to whisper calm reassurances. The broad chest went in and out, in and out, slower and slower. At last it stopped.

Spartacus let his hand rest on the stallion for a moment, honouring its life and its death. Then, dipping his hand in the blood, he smeared a liberal coating on to his cheeks and forehead. Wiping his blade clean, he sheathed it. When he turned to regard his troops, he saw that all eyes were on him. In the cohorts further away, men had moved out of position so that they could witness what was going on. 'My soldiers! The offering to the gods has been made. My stallion died well, and without protest. The sacrifice has been accepted!'

They roared their approval at that. *Clash, clash, clash* went their weapons off their shields.

Sica in hand now, Spartacus took a few steps forward. 'Today, we shall have . . . VICTORY – OR DEATH!'

A heartbeat's delay.

'VICTORY – OR DEATH!' roared Carbo. Taxacis' voice echoed his. 'VICTORY – OR DEATH! VICTORY – OR DEATH!'

Letting his men's chant wash over him, Spartacus resumed his place in the line, between Carbo and Taxacis. Without ado, he signalled at the trumpeters, and at the riders who would carry the order to advance to the cavalry on the wings.

The instruments' strident notes had no difficulty carrying through the noise. Still shouting, the soldiers were urged forward by their officers. They walked at first. It was a good five hundred paces to the Roman lines. There was no point in tiring themselves out. They would need all the energy they had to win the fight that was to come.

Carbo could taste bile in the back of his throat. Grant us victory, and give me one chance to kill Crassus, he begged. I don't care if I die after that. Prayer over, he glanced at Taxacis, who was to his far right. The Scythian gave him a fierce grin. Carbo returned the smile. He couldn't ask to be in a better place. Spartacus to his right. Beyond him, Taxacis. Both were deadly fighters. On his left was a broad-chested man with a strong chin. Carbo vaguely recognised him, but he wasn't sure why. He was just proud to be included in their number, and for the first time in his life, he felt truly at home.

'Keep walking,' shouted Spartacus. 'Hold the line!'

As they drew parallel with the dead stallion, more than one soldier copied their leader by daubing his face with its blood. Carbo didn't – the Rider wasn't his god – but he understood why men were doing it. In a situation such as this, anything that might help one to survive was useful. One hundred paces went by. The Romans were advancing to meet them. Carbo watched Spartacus, who was scanning the enemy lines. He did the same, eventually spotting a scarlet-cloaked man riding back and forth behind the central cohorts. 'There's Crassus! The cocksucker!'

'That's him,' agreed Spartacus with a scowl. 'We're right where we want to be: directly opposite his position.'

Tramp, tramp, tramp. Carbo counted his footsteps. Another hundred paces, and he could differentiate the Roman officers from the ordinary soldiers. He had never seen so many transverse-crested helmets in the front rank. It was a measure reserved for the most desperate of situations. Crassus was also gambling everything on this throw of the dice. Sweat slicked down Carbo's back, made gripping his pilum more difficult. He'd be lucky to be alive by nightfall.

'That's it, lads,' shouted Spartacus. 'Stay together!'

'SPAR-TA-CUS!' roared the man to Carbo's left. He hammered his pilum off the metal rim of his scutum with each syllable. 'SPAR-TA-CUS!'

Inevitably, the shout was taken up all around them. Carbo roared at the top of his voice, but the din was so loud that he couldn't hear himself. It felt as if he was miming in a stage play, except that instead of an audience, he had a wall of legionaries approaching him. Apart from occasional blasts from their trumpeters, Crassus' men came on in silence. It was a typical Roman tactic, designed to send fear into their enemies' hearts. It wasn't working yet, thought Carbo, his heart thumping, because the crescendo from their soldiers was so overwhelming.

On they marched, trampling the young wheat back into the earth. Because they were still descending the slope, Carbo had a good view of the ground to his left and right. On the periphery, he could see their cavalry moving forward like a dark stain across the landscape. With any luck, the Roman trenches wouldn't extend far enough out to prevent them from sweeping around the enemy flanks. Carbo couldn't see Navio's position, but he sent up a prayer for his friend, and for them all. Bring us victory, great Jupiter, great Mars. Let me reach Crassus. One more chance, that's all I ask.

Two hundred paces until the enemy lines. Carbo had grown used to the routines of battle, and his eyes flickered warily to the air above the legionaries. Were there enough artillery pieces to target them as well, or were they taken up with the struggle on the flanks? He didn't hold any ill will towards the men there, but he hoped that it was the latter.

It was wishful thinking.

Perhaps two heartbeats later, a volley of darts came scudding in. Carbo felt his bowels loosen. He'd seen the carnage that the missiles could do. Around him, more than one man cried out in fear. Their advance slowed, and then stopped.

'Close order! All ranks except the front, shields up!' bellowed Spartacus.

They'd been drilled to do this a thousand times before. With a loud clattering noise, the scuta of those behind Carbo came up, forming a giant cover, the famed Roman *testudo*. He and the men of the front rank closed their shields together, forming an almost solid wall to the front. It was good protection against lighter missiles such as javelins, but, as everyone knew, it could not stop larger ones, such as the darts that were humming down towards them with frightening speed.

'STEADY!' shouted Spartacus. 'STEADY, BOYS!'

Other officers shouted similar reassurances.

Carbo didn't look up. If he was going to be transfixed by a barbed dart, he wanted it to happen without him knowing. His heart was thumping off his ribs like a wild thing. The soldier to his left was muttering the same prayer over and over. A man nearby began to vomit. Carbo started counting his breaths. One. Two. Three. Gods above, slow down. He forced himself to exhale as slowly as he could.

Crash. Crash. Crash. Crash. Crash. With a noise like thunderbolts, the missiles arrived. Carbo closed his eyes. Sent skywards by a torsion catapult that had to be cocked by two legionaries winding a handle, the darts had huge penetrative power. They punched through scuta like a hot knife through cheese, maiming and killing the unfortunate men beneath. Arm bones were shattered, skulls smashed open, chests ripped apart. Howls of agony marked the spots where soldiers had only been injured. The dead just collapsed to the ground.

Carbo blinked. He was still alive, and whole. So too were Spartacus and the man to his left. They exchanged a relieved look.

'Lower shields. Forward, at the double!' shouted Spartacus.

Carbo needed no encouragement. The quicker they closed with the Romans, the fewer volleys would land among them. The risk of death from a blade seemed far more appealing than having his brain pulped to mush or his chest split asunder by a dart. Cocking back his left arm, he trotted forward. Soon there would be an exchange of javelins. Then a final charge.

A hundred and fifty paces. Still the Romans made no sound. Carbo didn't like it one bit.

Another volley, this one of stones, came sweeping over the enemy lines. He was hypnotised by their trajectory. Part of him wanted to sprint forward, to miss the deadly rain if he could. Another part wanted to drop his shield and pilum and run away. But he couldn't. Spartacus was by his side, relying on him. And Crassus, the cause of his parents' deaths, was skulking behind a wall of legionaries. He focused his attention on the lines nearing him. All he could see was their eyes, peering over their shield rims, and their javelins, which were already aimed at the sky, ready for the order to release. Carbo was suddenly aware that he needed to piss. More than anything, he needed to piss. He swallowed hard, forcing the urge away.

Thump. Crash. Bang. The stones landed, splintering shields into kindling, crushing men's ribs and stopping their hearts.

Carbo shot a glance at Spartacus, who seemed oblivious. He rallied his courage. Here was the closest thing to a god that he'd ever seen. Was the man scared of nothing?

'Ready javelins!' Spartacus drew back his left arm. 'On my order!'

Carbo squinted at the enemy lines, which were about ninety paces away. Too far for an accurate throw. He could see the Roman officers watching them, waiting until they drew closer. *Bastards.*

Spartacus was doing the same. His lips moved as he counted down the distance. Eighty. Seventy. Sixty. The legionaries' pila flew up into the air.

Damn it, thought Carbo, give the order!

'Aim short! LOOSE!'

Carbo heaved his javelin into a low, curving arc. He tried to follow its progress, but it was joined by scores of others. He watched in fascination as they sped towards the Romans.

'Shields up!' roared Spartacus for the second time.

The javelins caused far less consternation than the artillery barrage. They crashed down, turning many shields into useless lumps of wood, but injuring and killing fewer men. Behind him, Carbo heard a couple of soldiers wagering with one another about who would get hit first. He felt an elbow in the ribs from his neighbour.

'Crazy the things that men can laugh about, eh?'

Carbo's dry lips cracked as he smiled.

'Zeuxis is the name. Yours?'

'Carbo. Do I recognise you?'

A sour grin. 'Maybe. You were with Spartacus when he shoved me arse first into a fire.'

Carbo's chuckle was drowned by Spartacus' shout. 'Anyone with a second javelin, LOOSE!'

Half as many pila as had gone up the first time took to the air. In the same instant, a far greater number of Roman javelins were launched.

'Raise shields, draw swords! FORWARD, AT THE DOUBLE!'

Ducking his head in a futile attempt to make himself smaller, Carbo broke into a run. His world had narrowed. All he could see was the Romans directly opposite him. Crassus, even the line of standards that waved above their lines, had vanished. He was aware of Zeuxis on his left, Spartacus on his right, his shield in one hand and his gladius in the other. That was it.

Little more than thirty paces separated the two sides.

The legionaries had drawn their swords now. Finally, an almighty roar left their throats, and they ran forward.

Carbo and every man around him responded with an ear-splitting yell. He heard Spartacus shout something unintelligible in Thracian. A quick glance sideways. Awe filled him. He'd never seen his leader look so angry. The veins in Spartacus' neck were bulging. His face was bright red, and his eyes were flat and dead. The eyes of a killer. Carbo had never been more glad to be on the same side as this man.

Gaze back to the front. Twenty-five paces. Carbo felt the scream crack in his throat, but that didn't shut him up. He must sound like a madman, but that was a good thing. The aim before they struck was to cause as much fear in their enemies as possible.

The two sides closed in on one another with frightening speed. Twenty paces. Fifteen.

Carbo focused on the designs emblazoned on the shields nearing him. The majority were a red colour with a swirling yellow line decorating each quarter, but the most striking one had lightning bolts radiating from the shield boss. The eyes above its rim were calculating, the helmet battered. A veteran, thought Carbo, his fear bubbling up. And they were heading straight for each other.

The last steps were covered in a blur. Carbo did his best to make sure that as he hit, his left shoulder was shoved forward. Of course his opponent did the same. Their shields crashed off other with an almighty bang. Both men staggered back a pace; both regained their poise and lunged forward with their swords. Carbo ducked down behind his scutum first, which allowed the legionary to follow through with his thrust, while Carbo's right arm shot uselessly into the air. Aware that he'd exposed his armpit, Carbo desperately pulled his blade back down. As he tried to peep over his shield rim, his enemy stabbed at him again. Cursing, Carbo hid again. He battered forward with his scutum, wanting to catch the other off balance. It was a faint hope. The legionary's shield was like a brick wall.

Carbo didn't give up on his attack. He punched his shield at the other's, following through with a thrust of his sword. It was what Paccius had taught him. One, two. One, two. The legionary's response was to do exactly the same thing. Carbo realised that his enemy was stronger and more skilled than he was. It seemed as if the legionary knew it too. His eyes glittered as he redoubled his assault.

Carbo's need to urinate returned with a vengeance. Is this how I'm going to die? he wondered. Covered in my own piss? He changed tactic, stabbing his gladius down at his opponent's feet. His effort failed. The legionary blocked the blow by angling out the lower edge of his scutum; he followed through with a lunge of his sword that nearly took out Carbo's left eye. There was a screech of metal as the iron blade skidded off the brow of his helmet. Stars flashed across Carbo's vision. Dimly, he heard the legionary roar in triumph. This is it, he thought. Now the bastard will knock me over and finish me off.

What he heard next was an odd, choking sound.

With difficulty, Carbo focused on the legionary again. To his amazement, he saw Spartacus' sica sliding out of the man's throat. Blood spattered him in the face; the metallic taste of it hit his tongue. Carbo's head turned.

'Come on, lad! Get your wits about you,' growled Spartacus.

Carbo nodded, still a little confused.

'Eyes front!' Spartacus shouted.

Carbo obeyed. The gaps in the enemy ranks had already been filled by those behind. His next opponent was four steps away and closing fast. Carbo let him come, forcing the man to step over his comrade's body. As the legionary was in mid-stride, Carbo drove into him with all his force. The soldier rocked back on his heels, and Carbo's sword shattered his left cheekbone, slicing through his nasal chambers to exit at the angle of the opposite jaw. A keening noise tore at Carbo's hearing, and he shook his head in an effort to stop it. Then he realised that it was the legionary screaming. He'd never heard someone make so much noise. With a grunt, he tugged his blade free. The man dropped, still shrieking like a spitted boar.

Carbo wounded the soldier who followed, slicing one of his feet down to the bone. Bawling in pain, the man drew back, unable to fight. The press was too tight for anyone to get by, so Carbo used the respite to help Zeuxis dispatch his opponent. Two legionaries shoved through the gap left as that man fell. One moved sideways to get at Carbo; the other went for Zeuxis. This fight was as protracted as Carbo's first struggle, but driven by adrenalin and the knowledge that Spartacus had saved his life, he gave a better account of himself. It was a measure of his opponent's skill that it took so long for Carbo to put him down. The legionary sank to his knees, the wound in his throat open wider than his gaping mouth. Blood jetted from both openings, covering the ground between them in another tide of crimson.

No one filled the empty space before Carbo. He didn't understand until the shrill *peeeeeeep* of whistles hit his eardrums. The Roman line retreated a step, and then another. He tensed, preparing to advance.

'Fall back!' roared Spartacus. He thumped the side of Carbo's shield with his own. 'Ten paces, no more.'

As he dumbly obeyed, Carbo felt the sweat drenching him. The felt liner beneath his helmet was saturated. There were rivulets running down his forehead and continuing, stinging, into his eyes. He wiped a bloody hand across his face.

'You've done well, lads. Time for a breather!' shouted Spartacus. 'Help the wounded to move back, away from the front ranks. If you've got any water, have a drink. Share it with your comrades. Do the obvious. Those with damaged weapons or equipment, try to find replacements from the dead and injured. Clear the ground around your feet so that you don't trip up when the fighting starts again. Check the rest of your gear. Make sure that the straps on your sandals aren't loose.' He broke out of formation and began to move along the ranks to the left, muttering encouragement to the soldiers.

No more than twenty paces away, the Romans were doing the same thing. Carbo felt odd standing so close to men whom he'd been trying to kill just a moment earlier, and with whom he would shortly resume hostilities. Best to make the most of it. He stabbed his gladius into the earth before him and let his scutum rest against it. Relieving himself of that weight felt so good. Next he tugged up the bottom of his mail shirt and freed himself from his undergarment. At once his urine arched out in a yellow stream. Carbo thought it would never stop. He had never known such relief. From the jokes and sighs of satisfaction he could hear, plenty of other men felt the same way. Finishing, he became very aware of his overwhelming thirst.

'Here.'

Zeuxis had shoved a small clay vessel with a strap around its neck in his face. Carbo put it to his lips and took a mouthful. The water was warm and stale, but it tasted better than anything he'd ever drunk. 'Thanks,' he said, handing it back.

Zeuxis grunted. He took a long pull himself and passed it to the soldier on his left. He leaned back towards Carbo. 'Never thought I'd stand this close to Spartacus in battle, I can tell you.'

'He's some warrior, eh?'

'It's like watching a god take to the field.' The awe in Zeuxis' voice was palpable.

'I'd be a dead man if it wasn't for him.' Carbo undid his chinstrap and took off his helmet. He let it drop.

'I saw some of that fight. Sorry I couldn't help. I was a bit caught up.'

'It's all right.' Carbo pulled off his liner and wrung it out. Streams of water ran between his fingers. A light breeze tickled his soaking hair. It felt wonderful, but he jammed the felt back on his head and put on his helmet again, tying the strap securely. 'You been in the army long?'

'I joined before the battle against Lentulus. Marcion here' – he jerked his head at the man to his left – 'came along at the same time. So did most of our contubernium. And you?'

'I was in the ludus with Spartacus.'

Zeuxis' mouth fell open. 'Really?'

Carbo nodded.

'So you took part in the attack on Glaber's camp? And the fight at the villa when Cossinius was caught naked?'

Carbo grinned. 'I was there.'

'Hear this, Marcion!' He muttered a few words to his comrade, who gave Carbo a look of awe. 'Those were the days, eh?' said Zeuxis. 'When we won every fight.'

Carbo gave him a grim smile. 'With the gods' help, this could be another one.'

Zeuxis' eyes flickered away from his. 'Let's hope so.'

Spartacus came hurrying back to his position. 'READY, LADS?'

'YES!' Carbo shouted, his voice one of hundreds. Tugging his gladius free, and picking up his shield, he scanned the enemy lines. The legionaries were moving closer together, and he could hear their officers roaring at them to prepare to advance.

'Let's hit them hard, eh?' said Spartacus to Carbo.

'Of course!' His heart began to race again.

'The left flank looks to be holding its own from what I can see, but I've got no idea how things are on the right, or what the cavalry have achieved. To be sure of victory, we *have* to break through here.'

The pressure mounted. 'I'll do my best.'

'I know you will.' Spartacus flashed him a smile, and Carbo's devotion to him grew yet stronger.

'READY? CHARGE!' roared Spartacus.

They pounded forward at the Romans, who shouted a challenge and broke into a run of their own. Carbo was more prepared for the fight this time. His eyes narrowed as he noticed the man closing in on him had a limp. He was already injured: a weakness to exploit. As their shields cracked against each other and they both began to push, Carbo hacked down at his opponent's sandals. There was a loud cry as the tip of his blade connected with the toes on the man's left foot. It was only a small wound, but it was painful enough to make the legionary lower his guard a fraction. Carbo raised his gladius and shoved it forward, around the other's scutum. There was a heartbeat's delay and then it had punched through the iron rings of the man's mail shirt. It sank deep into his belly, and his mouth opened in an 'O' of pure shock. Carbo twisted the blade as he'd been taught, and wrenched it free.

'Jupiterrrrr, that hurts!' screamed the legionary. He dropped his shield and clutched a hand to the bloody hole in his mail.

Carbo smashed his scutum forward, knocking his opponent into the soldier immediately behind.

'FORWARD!' shouted Spartacus.

Blood pounding in his ears, Carbo advanced two steps. Then another. Despite the protests of the man to his rear, the injured legionary staggered backwards. Carbo's eyes shot from side to side. Zeuxis was at his left shoulder; Spartacus was to his right and beyond him was Taxacis. Further out, their comrades also appeared to be moving forward. His heart leaped. He took another step.

'FORWARD!' roared Spartacus again.

Pace by pace, they walked towards the Romans, who continued to retreat. It went on for about twenty steps, and Carbo began to hope that their enemies would break. They didn't. His attention was drawn to a couple of centurions in the front rank near him. They were screaming blue murder, threatening their men with the most terrible punishments if they did anything but hold the line. Their tactic was working. The legionaries slowed down and came to a halt.

'When we hit the whoresons, I want every centurion killed! Hacked into a hundred pieces! Do you hear me?'

The nearest soldiers bellowed in assent.

'If we can do that, they'll fucking run,' Carbo heard Spartacus mutter. Then, 'CHARGE!'

They ran forward. This time, the Romans did not come to meet them. Carbo took some solace from that. The enemy officers didn't trust their men to advance. That meant they were worried.

Carbo saw that the man to face him would be a centurion, and his breath caught in his chest. The previous bouts he'd fought would be as nothing compared to this. Centurions were veterans of at least twenty years' service, brave men who led by example, who stuck at nothing to win a fight. He struggled against the first tinge of panic, knowing that if he gave in to it, he was sure to die. The centurion was staring right at him and roaring insults at the top of his voice. Blocking out the sound as best he could, Carbo tried to spot any detail that would help him win. He saw nothing except the scarlet-dyed horsehairs on his opponent's helmet crest and the merciless eyes beneath its tinned brow. Death was waiting.

Three paces out, it came to Carbo. The centurion was a short man. In turn, that meant that he was a lot heavier than him. Praying that his idea would work, he ducked as low as he could behind the rim of his scutum. Pulling his left arm close in against his body, he slowed down a fraction before throwing his entire body weight forward with his shield. He struck the centurion with such force that the Roman was shoved several steps backwards. Carbo lifted his head, readying himself to land the killer blow. He got the shock of his life. Incredibly, the centurion had maintained his balance, and was waiting for his chance. Carbo had just enough time to register the other's blade as it swept forward at his face.

I'm dead.

There was a loud crash.

Carbo blinked. The gladius was gone. He looked again. The centurion had been knocked on to the flat of his back by Spartacus, who had driven sideways into him with his scutum. Stooping over the officer, the Thracian ran him through the throat. Dismayed cries rose from the legionaries who'd seen what had happened, and they fell back a step or two. Spartacus quickly resumed his position, throwing Carbo a grin. 'Push the whoresons back!' he yelled.

Carbo took a step forward with the rest. He glanced at his sword arm, which was trembling like a leaf. Snap out of it! he told himself. You're still alive. The battle's not over. Steeling himself for more carnage, he looked up. The centurion had been replaced by a furious-looking legionary.

Perhaps five paces separated them. 'I'm going to rip your head off and shit down your neck!' the Roman screamed.

Behind the ranks of enemy soldiers, Carbo caught sight of a red cloak. It was Crassus, dismounting from his horse. Standard-bearers swirled around him, including one bearing a silver eagle. Carbo couldn't believe his eyes. He's concerned enough to make a stand right here. 'Spartacus! This is our chance!'

A moment later, there was a shout of acknowledgement. 'CHARGE! CHARGE!'

Carbo's gaze returned to the legionary. Cold rage now filled him. All he wanted to do was reach Crassus. 'I'm coming for you, you fucking maggot!'

There was a surge behind him as he advanced. It was the men in the ranks behind, Carbo realised with exhilaration. He made short shrift of the legionary, dispatching him with a couple of vicious stabs to the face. The man after him was a barrel-chested individual who spat obscenities with each thrust of his gladius. Carbo had little difficulty in dodging the powerful but inaccurate blows, but soon the press grew so great that he was driven right up against the legionary. Neither was able to use his sword.

'Slave filth!' screamed the soldier. 'You're dead! Dead!'

'Fuck you!' Carbo let go of his gladius, which, jammed between them, didn't even fall to the ground. With a struggle, he reached around to his left side and tugged out his dagger. Drawing up his arm with great care, he whipped it up, above the crush. Panic flared in the legionary's eyes, more curses filled the air, but he could not prevent Carbo from hammering the blade down into his neck. Carbo stabbed him several more times for good measure. Gouts of blood splattered his forearm, his face, the front of his shield. He didn't care. 'Crassus, I'm coming for you!' he shouted, spittle flying.

But he couldn't move – forward or back. In fact, the pressure from both sides was starting to become uncomfortable. The cursing legionary had slumped forward; he was now being held upright by Carbo's scutum. Blood ran in streams from the wound in his neck, covering Carbo's left hand and arm. There was nothing he could do about it. He was glad that the Romans in the second rank weren't trying to get at him. They had to be as tightly compressed as he and his comrades were.

'Gods above, what do we do now?' roared Zeuxis.

The red mist receded a little. Carbo glanced at Zeuxis, who had also killed the Roman in front of him. 'We're stuck!'

Zeuxis glowered. 'Bloody genius, aren't you?'

Fighting a crazy urge to smile, Carbo looked to his right. Unsurprisingly, Spartacus had slain his man. He was helping Taxacis to slaughter his opponent. Carbo waited until it was done. 'What do we do now?'

Spartacus' head turned. His face and helmet were covered in blood, and his eyes had a mad gleam to them. Carbo had difficulty holding his gaze.

'We'll have to withdraw a few steps. The sheep-fucking Romans won't do so, that's for sure. This kind of stalemate suits them. Crassus will be trying to wear us out.'

Carbo was suddenly aware that his muscles were screaming for a rest.

'Fall back!' cried Spartacus. 'Fall back ten steps. Only ten! Pass the word along!'

Carbo leaned over to Zeuxis. 'Tell your mate to spread the word. We're to pull back ten steps, no more.'

Zeuxis nodded and did as he was asked. Spartacus was doing the same to Carbo's right. Soon the air was filled with the shouted command. As the men in the ranks behind realised, they began to shuffle backwards. Feeling the pressure on his chest reduce, Carbo sucked in a deep breath. He gripped his gladius again and took a couple of steps away from the big legionary. The man's corpse slumped to its knees. A heartbeat's delay and it toppled on to its face. Carbo tensed, preparing himself for an enemy charge, but it didn't happen.

Keeping in line with Zeuxis and Spartacus, he walked back six, seven, eight more paces.

'HALT!' roared the Thracian.

His command was obeyed.

Carbo saw Spartacus eyeballing the Romans, but they did nothing. They had to be grateful for the breather too, he thought.

'Pull back another ten steps!'

Carbo glanced at Spartacus in alarm. 'Why?' he hissed.

'I need to see what's going on at the flanks. This is the only damn way I can do it.'

The word went out again. Counting carefully, they withdrew. Still the

Romans did nothing. Carbo's eyes travelled up and down their line. All he saw were men heaving bodies out of the way, spitting or drinking from water bags. Some legionaries shouted insults, but most were ignoring them. It was a small relief.

Spartacus strode out into the gap between the armies. His head swivelled from side to side for a few moments. A javelin was hurled at him, and another, but he ignored them, standing on tiptoe to get a better view. Then a third pilum came scudding in and he had to dodge out the way in order to avoid being struck.

'They've recognised him,' muttered Carbo. He could see enemy javelins being handed forward for the men at the front to throw. The taste of fear was acid in his mouth. Spartacus' extraordinary charisma was what held the centre together. If he went down, they were finished.

'What in Hades is he doing?' growled Zeuxis.

Carbo explained.

'A bit fucking risky, isn't it?'

'Maybe, but there's no other way.' Even as he defended Spartacus' actions, Carbo wanted to scream at him to return to safety.

He soon got his wish. Turning his back on the Roman lines, Spartacus sauntered back to their position. Two javelins followed him, one landing right by his feet. He didn't even look at it. A smile played across his face. 'Is that the best they can do?' he shouted, turning to make an obscene gesture at the Romans.

Whoops and cheers rose around Carbo, and a sea of hands went up in the air, mimicking Spartacus' sign.

Doing the same, Carbo grinned. He couldn't help it. 'Fuck you all!' he bellowed.

Spartacus shoved in beside him.

Carbo turned, his face alight. Spartacus' words hit him like a hammer blow.

'It's not going well with Pulcher on the right. The Romans must have brought up every spare catapult they have. The whoresons are hammering our ranks behind where the fighting is going on. The men there are starting to waver.'

Carbo's next insult turned to ashes in his mouth. If the rearmost soldiers turned and fled, the ones at the front wouldn't be far behind them. And if that happened, the enemy's left flank could wheel around to hit the centre – their position. An abyss had just opened at their feet. 'And the left?'

'It's all right, thanks to Navio. I can't see the damn cavalry anywhere, though. On either side. I'm concerned that the ditches were too deep for them. That they haven't been able to sweep around to the enemy's rear. We'd have heard something, seen something by now if they had.'

Carbo's hopes plummeted. He searched Spartacus' face for a hopeful sign. 'What can we do?'

A savage, unforgiving smile. 'I'd wager that we've got the time for one more roll of the dice before the left flank gives way. Will you come?'

Carbo knew in that moment that his death was near. He fought the urge to vomit. 'I'm with you.'

Spartacus' eyes softened. 'I never thought to say this, but I'm proud to stand and fight beside a Roman.'

Carbo had to fight back tears. Unable to speak, he just nodded.

Spartacus threw back his head. 'My soldiers, listen to me!'

Somehow, amid the din from the fighting to either side, the nearest men's heads turned.

'I ask you for one more effort. One more charge! I can see Crassus there, opposite us. Do you see the bastard, in his red cloak, behind his legionaries?'

Silence for a moment as men's eyes searched for their enemy, and then an angry roar went up.

'Let's kill Crassus right now. End the battle at a stroke. Are you with me?'

'YES!'

'ARE YOU WITH ME?' Spartacus began hammering his sica off his shield.

'YESSSS!' Carbo screamed with everyone else.

'THEN CHARGE!' Spartacus shot forward so fast that he caught Carbo and the man on the other side by surprise. He was five strides ahead before they had even started running. Carbo sprinted to catch up. To his left, he sensed Zeuxis. He knew in his gut that the rest were coming too. Every man who had heard that cry would answer it. Would give his life to be with Spartacus as he descended on the Romans in a dreadful, killing rage. The words 'Victory or death' had never been more true.

He drew alongside the Thracian. Heard him muttering.

'Great Rider, watch over me. Great Rider, protect me. Great Rider, help me to kill Crassus.'

The prayers made Carbo's spine tingle. He could feel the gods' presence. *Let them be on our side.*

Ten strides until the Roman lines. Carbo could see Crassus at the back. His heart jolted with hope. The legionaries opposite him were no more than six ranks deep. They could do it! Five steps. Imagining that he'd been stabbed in the guts, Carbo let out a piercing shriek. The man facing him flinched, which was what he'd wanted. He covered the last two paces in a blur, smashing into the soldier with all the pent-up hatred that he'd ever felt towards Crassus. He felt the impact as Zeuxis and Spartacus hit their opponents. Still yelling like a madman, Carbo rammed his gladius into the space between the two scuta before him. His blade struck, and then slid deep into something. A scream, and the legionary facing Spartacus dropped his sword. Surprised, Carbo's eyes shot to his own opponent who, with teeth bared, was trying to reach around and stab him in the belly. Too late, Carbo pulled his right arm back to retaliate.

When Zeuxis' gladius slid over to take the Roman in the throat, he could have cried with relief. 'Thanks.'

Zeuxis threw him a broad wink. 'Just do the same for me if you can.'

'I will.'

'ON! ON! ON!' roared Spartacus.

Having smashed the first enemy rank, they shoved into the next. Punching with their shields, thrusting with their swords, howling like wolves. Blood sprayed in the air, covered their faces, showered on to the muddy ground. Cries of triumph mixed with shrieks of pain and the gurgles of men drowning in their own blood. They pushed forward another hard-fought two steps. A few paces to his left, Carbo saw a legionary lose an arm to a sword cut; with a stunned expression, he raised the stump into the air, showering his comrades in crimson liquid. As if he'd only realised what had happened, an inarticulate wail left his throat. Those of Spartacus' soldiers who could see laughed and jeered. The man wasn't just useless, he was now a danger to his comrades. It didn't take long for a legionary to stab the unfortunate in the neck from behind and step over his body to fill the gap.

Carbo was vaguely aware that Spartacus was fighting another centurion, but his next opponent was a skilful legionary who pre-empted his every move. For long moments, they each battered their shield off the other's and thrust at one another's faces to no avail. Carbo's throat was so dry that he couldn't shout any more. His arms kept moving of their own volition – punch, thrust, punch, thrust – but he began to feel as if he were no longer within his body. Deep inside his head, a voice was screaming at him to come back to reality or he'd end up dead, but it was more than Carbo could do to obey.

To his surprise, the legionary's gaze shot to his left. A gasp of dismay, the briefest moment of hesitation. Carbo didn't know what had caused the distraction, but he took his chance, ramming his gladius into the soldier's open mouth so hard that the blade ran out of the back of his neck. Gouts of blood and pieces of broken tooth flew into the air. Making a terrible choking noise, the legionary dropped out of sight. Carbo glanced first to his left. Zeuxis was still there. Beyond him, so too was Marcion. A look to his right then. Creeping exultation filled him. The centurion was down, screaming. They had broken through another rank.

A stifled gasp by his side doused his joy like a lamp that is suddenly snuffed out. His head turned. Wincing, Spartacus met his gaze. Blood was running from a cut on his forehead into his eyes. 'The bastard got me, Carbo.'

'That's only a flesh wound!'

'Not that. In my sword arm.'

Time stood still. Carbo wanted to weep, but he had no tears. 'Can you fight?'

'For a while.'

A shout to his front dragged Carbo's attention back to the fight. This time, an optio was coming for him. *I'll kill you too, cocksucker!* Then he saw the fresh legionaries piling in behind the back ranks, and his heart sank. There were now at least eight rows of men between them and Crassus. Even if Spartacus had been uninjured, they might not have been able to reach him. As it was, they had no chance. He met the optio's shield with a fierce drive of his own. To Spartacus, 'We've got to pull back!'

'Never! We can still kill that son of a bitch Crassus!'

Carbo parried a gladius thrust by raising his scutum. In return, he lunged forward with his blade; withdrawing, he looked again. Crassus now looked as far away as the moon. It was asking the impossible even to try. He wasn't going to leave Spartacus, though. Never. A strange madness took him. 'All right then! CRASSUS! CRASSUS!' He saw the ornate helmet turn; saw the arrogant expression he'd seen in Rome. Hatred twisted his guts. 'We're coming for you, Crassus!' It gave Carbo the most intense satisfaction to see a flicker of fear pass across the general's face.

Punch. The optio's shield boss smacked into him. Carbo was driven back a step; he fought not to fall over.

'Think you can kill our general?' roared the optio. 'You've got to get through me first.'

Bellowing with rage, Carbo went on the attack. His speed caught the officer by surprise, and he managed to slice open the Roman's cheek, a minor but painful injury. Encouraged, Carbo pressed forward.

'You're crazy,' spat the optio. 'Don't you know when you're beaten?'

'Piss off!'

'Take a look around you, fool! You're almost alone.'

The back of Carbo's throat filled with acid. The optio pulled back a step, as if to invite him to check the veracity of his words. At first glance, all seemed well. Taxacis was still on Spartacus' far side. Carbo could see other soldiers beyond. Then his head turned to the left. Horror filled him. Zeuxis was still on his feet, but the deep gash on his neck told its own brutal story. Marcion was there, ducking to avoid the thrusts of a bearded legionary, but that was it. He twisted his neck further. *No, please, no.* Perhaps forty or fifty men were still behind them. The rest were backing away, some slowly, fighting the Romans who were charging forward, but the majority had turned to run. Shields and swords already littered the ground. Despair took Carbo. The dream was over.

'Convinced?' The optio swept forward, lunging with his gladius.

Carbo spun back, raised his guard too late.

With incredible speed, Spartacus' sica came scything around from the right. It took the optio in the neck, removing his head with ease. Carbo had never seen blood fountain so high in the air. It rose in a thick jet to eye height as the head, helmet and all, spun gracefully to one side. The optio's body took another step forward before it crumpled, twitching, to the ground. The nearest legionaries pulled back in instinctive horror, granting the pair momentary respite.

Even injured, he's still more skilful than me, thought Carbo in amazement.

'Help me take off my helmet.'

He didn't understand. 'Eh?'

'Do as I ask!'

Carbo shoved his gladius under his left armpit, then leaned over and fiddled with the chinstrap. After a moment, it came undone. Spartacus ripped off the helmet and flung it to the ground.

'Why did you do that?'

'Go. Leave. Get away. It's over.' There was a touch of grey to Spartacus' face now, but his voice was still commanding.

With sickening insight, Carbo understood. *He threw it away so he can't be recognised after he's been killed.* 'I'm staying right here!'

'Find Ariadne. Protect her and the baby. Get them away from here with Atheas, before the madness begins.'

'What about you?'

A harsh laugh. 'I'm going nowhere. The Rider is waiting for me.'

'And me!' Taxacis had never sounded fiercer.

Carbo's mind raced as it had never done. He knew the chaos that descended on battlefields when one side began to run away. That was when most casualties were suffered. Panicking men without weapons made the easiest targets. Apart from women and babies, that was. Even with Aventianus and the Scythian to hand, they would have little chance of survival. He stared at Spartacus, torn between his need to stay loyal and the desire to honour his leader's request. 'I—'

'Please. I ask you as a friend.' Spartacus' eyes held his like a vice.

Throat closed with emotion, Carbo nodded.

'Go, or it will be too late!' Spartacus pushed at him weakly with his shield.

Carbo obeyed, stumbling away like a drunk man. The tears that had not come before flowed at last, half blinded his vision. He wiped them away savagely, aware that if he wasn't careful, he would trip over a body. Around him, soldiers were shouting, crying, turning to flee. The sense of panic was thick enough to cut with a knife. At times like this, men lost all reason. If he went down, he'd be trampled into the bloody earth. Carbo didn't care about himself, but he had to save Ariadne and Maron. He'd given his word.

Gripping his sword and shield tightly, Carbo began to run. With every step, shame cut at him like butcher's knives. He had abandoned Spartacus, who had saved his life so many times. Left him to his death.

Carbo did not look back.

Chapter XIX

South of the Silarus valley

Maron whimpered. It was his new sound, thought Ariadne sadly. Pulling down the neck of her dress, she put him to the breast. Although she had precious little milk, it would keep him quiet for a while. She stared down at him, feeling a mixture of love and immeasurable sorrow. *You look so like Spartacus.*

It wasn't surprising that Maron was unsettled, she thought, gazing around their small forest camp, which contained only a rough shelter fashioned from branches and outside it, a stone ring fireplace. He hadn't known what was happening two days previously either, when the tide of battle had swung in Crassus' favour. He'd been fast asleep until the clash of weapons and the screaming had woken him. That was when Atheas had ordered her to grab him and to throw a few things in a pack. She'd never seen the Scythian so worried. 'Quickly! Quickly!' he had shouted as she'd fumbled a couple of blankets and a spare swaddling cloth into a satchel and handed him the basket containing her snake. Outside, they had found Aventianus standing guard, a gladius clutched in his fist. It was at that moment that Ariadne had stared down at the battle and seen how bad things were.

Their army's flanks had lost all semblance of order. Thousands of men had been streaming away from the Roman trenches, pursued by waves of legionaries. In the centre, she had made out a small bloc of soldiers still fighting – had Spartacus been among them? – but the overwhelming enemy numbers surrounding them offered but one outcome. The sight had frozen Ariadne to the spot with shock and grief. Only Atheas' arm around her shoulders had brought her alive again, and given her the strength to move.

It had soon become apparent how fortuitous the tent's position near the

370

back of the camp had been. The rocky massif to its rear had afforded no escape route, so most soldiers were fleeing through the tent lines some distance below them. A few, mad with panic, had climbed up to the same level, but the sight of Atheas' and Aventianus' naked blades had kept them at a respectful distance. Having to threaten their old comrades seemed insane, but it had since become their reality. Ariadne had thought to be safe once they'd reached the mountains, but scores of stragglers had continued to cross their path. On Carbo's advice, they were shunning all contact unless it was unavoidable. In his opinion – and Atheas agreed – no one could now be trusted unless he was known to them, or had proved himself. It was part of the reason why they were hiding like wild animals in the most remote spot that the Scythian could find. Five soldiers approved by Carbo had joined them subsequently. Ariadne felt a little safer for their presence. Extra men to hunt also meant more food. More than one of the new arrivals had mentioned the rumour they'd heard: that thousands of survivors were heading for the hills above Thurii, but she didn't want to consider following until her grief had subsided a little. Until she could bear the idea of leaving the battlefield – and Spartacus' body – behind for ever.

Maron made another grumbling noise as he snuffled at her breast.

'Is he sick?'

Ariadne looked up. She managed a half-smile. 'No, he's just tired, and upset. And hungry.'

'Like us all,' replied Carbo with a sigh.

'We should be grateful to be alive. If it wasn't for you and the others—'

'I didn't do much,' he said, waving a dismissive hand.

Ariadne remembered the pack of terrified men who'd come pounding towards them as they had reached the edge of the camp. They probably hadn't even known who she and her two companions were. The fact that they had been blocking the path eastward, the only direction not filled with Roman troops, had been enough for the deserters to threaten them. Shoving her and Maron to the rear, Atheas and Aventianus had prepared to sell their lives dearly. Ariadne had begun to pray for a quick death when, from nowhere, Carbo had appeared behind the gang. Drenched in blood, screaming like a lunatic, he had cut down two men with savage thrusts of his gladius. The rest had taken to their heels. 'You saved our lives, Carbo,' she said quietly.

His gaze slid away.

She touched his arm. 'It's true. I cannot thank you enough.'

'I left Spartacus behind,' he muttered. *And Arnax.* The boy had probably got away, he told himself yet again. The same couldn't be said of his leader.

'It's pointless torturing yourself. It wasn't for you to choose the way he died, any more than it was mine.'

Carbo was shocked out of his own grief for a moment.

'Spartacus was his own master. You must respect his decision to die fighting. As, somehow, must I.' Her gaze grew distant. Deep in her gut, Ariadne worried that her dream of the crucifixes would now come true. If it did, she prayed that Spartacus would not have suffered that degrading fate. That was why she had not seen him, she thought, trying – and failing – to wrest certainty from the dream.

'I do respect it,' he protested.

She saw that there was more. 'You think that you should have died with him.'

Carbo didn't answer, but the agony in his eyes said it all.

'What would have happened to me and Maron if you'd done that?'

'I don't know,' he replied uneasily.

'I think you do. Can you not remember the group of deserters that attacked us?'

No answer.

'Is that the end you would have wanted for me? For Spartacus' son?'

'Of course not!'

'Doing what you did – leaving him – means that Spartacus' memory will live on. Not just in men's hearts and minds, but in real flesh and blood.' She caressed Maron's head. 'Is that not a worthwhile deed?'

He stared at the baby, his face twitching with unreadable emotion. 'Yes,' he muttered. 'It is.'

'I cannot think of a finer legacy. A better way to ensure that Rome's victory was not total. Can you?' The words were to assuage her own savage grief as much as to help Carbo. To Ariadne's ears, they rang hollow. That might not be the case for ever, but for the moment she knew that if it weren't for Maron, she might have already given up.

Carbo's lips finally tugged into a smile. 'Crassus would hate to know that Spartacus' son was alive.'

'He would.' She touched Maron's smooth cheek, and he redoubled his efforts on her breast. 'That is why he must never know about him.'

Their conversation was disturbed by Aventianus. 'Pssst!' He pointed beyond the clearing. Hearing movement in the undergrowth, Carbo ushered Ariadne into the shelter. He ran to join Aventianus. They both drew their swords, hoping that it was one of the group.

When Atheas emerged, they both smiled with relief. Their expressions changed the instant they saw the man limping behind the Scythian. Covered in spatters of blood, without a helmet but still carrying his sword, it was Navio.

Carbo's heart leaped with joy. He darted to his friend's side. 'The gods be thanked. You made it!'

Navio rubbed at the dark rings beneath his eyes. 'I don't know how. I tried hard enough to die.'

'I found him . . . by the river,' said Atheas. 'Just lying . . . looking at nothing.' Muttering an excuse, he set about starting a fire.

'We saw you. Well, saw your position. You held the left flank for an age,' said Carbo.

'The men did well,' admitted Navio. 'It was the damn artillery that did for us. That, and the fact that the cavalry couldn't cross the ditches. They were too deep, too wide. Crassus was damn clever to think of that. He must have heard about Sulla doing it at Orchomenus fourteen years ago.' He let out a hacking cough. 'What happened to you?'

In a low voice, Carbo explained. When it came to the final moments before he'd fled, his voice cracked. 'He said that he was proud to fight beside a Roman. I'm sure he meant you too.'

A spark lit in Navio's dead eyes. 'Well, I was proud to serve a slave.'

'And I.'

They were quiet for a moment. Their leader's face filled their minds.

'I didn't run,' blurted Carbo. He was intensely grateful for Navio's accepting nod. 'He asked me to go, to see that Ariadne and the baby were safe.'

'Ariadne's here?' cried Navio.

'I am. And Maron. I've just put him down for a sleep.' She ducked out of the shelter and approached them, smiling faintly. 'I am glad that you survived, Navio.'

He gave her a respectful half-bow. 'Jupiter be praised that you and the baby are unharmed. Atheas first, and then Carbo . . . I had not thought to hear even more good news. Since waking after the battle, I've wondered why the gods let me live. Now I know.'

'Tell us your story,' urged Carbo.

Navio studied each of their faces, and then looked away. 'We had held our ground for some time, which was no mean feat considering how many troops Crassus threw at us and the fact that the cavalry couldn't help. Things got worse when the enemy artillery's volleys suddenly got heavier. Maybe it was as the left flank was giving way, I don't know. One thing was certain, though: the bastards didn't mind hitting their own men. The barrage went on and on. My troops withstood it for a time, but they finally cracked. I couldn't hold them.'

'In a situation like that, no one can,' said Carbo.

'That doesn't make it any easier,' said Navio with a heavy sigh. 'I managed to rally together about thirty soldiers, and we kept fighting. It didn't take long for most of us to be cut down.' His eyes went dark. 'I was left with a man either side of me. I felt like Horatius on the bridge, except there was no river to jump into. A rock must have hit me soon after that, and knocked me unconscious. When I woke up, I found that my helmet was split in two. There was a body half across me. It was dark. The battle was over. I could hear men screaming, begging to die. Checking that there were no Romans about, I managed to get up. I began searching for anyone who might have been trapped like me. All I found were those heading for Hades. I helped more than a few of them on their way. I wandered like that for a long time, hoping that I'd be discovered and killed. There was no point in living after what my soldiers had done. After we'd lost.' His eyes flickered to them. 'I feel differently now. But at the time—'

'I can imagine what you must have been going through,' said Ariadne with feeling. *If it weren't for Maron . . .*

'So can I,' said Carbo. 'What happened next?'

'The most crazy thing. I – I found Spartacus' helmet. It had to be his. No one else in the whole damn army had a Phrygian one like it.'

Beside Carbo, Ariadne went very still. 'Did you find his body?' he whispered.

'No. I searched and searched, but it was as black as the underworld. There wasn't even a moon. The bodies were heaped everywhere, so many of them. They all looked the same. I kept going until it began to grow light . . .' Navio's words ground to a halt.

'What you did was above the call of duty, for which I thank you,' said Ariadne gently. She glanced at Carbo. 'Could he be alive?'

His doubts renewed, Carbo thought hard. 'I doubt it. He wanted to go down fighting. Without a helmet, the Romans wouldn't have known who he was. They would have just killed him like any other of our soldiers.'

'But you can't be sure. You didn't see him fall.'

Carbo felt even worse. 'No.'

Navio also looked stricken. 'I would have continued my search, but there were groups of legionaries spreading out through the area. They were killing anyone still left alive. I had to crawl on my belly for an age to make sure that they hadn't seen me.'

Guilt redoubled in Carbo, clawing at his mind and heart. *He couldn't be alive. Could he?* 'We could go down and try to find him.'

Great Dionysus, please, thought Ariadne. *My pain is bad enough. I don't need this uncertainty.* She knew how awful the scene would be by now. The stench of rotting flesh, appreciable long before the battlefield itself. Bodies bloating, discolouring in the warm sun. Maggots crawling in wounds, mouths, open bellies. Peasants scouring the site for valuables. Carrion birds hanging overhead in clouds, and gorging on the expanse of flesh below. At night, wolves and even bears might lurk at the fringes, keen not to miss out on the unparalleled feast. Revulsion filled her. If he was dead, Spartacus' body would be prey as much as anyone else's. If he was injured and unable to move, however—

'It's far too dangerous,' said Navio. 'Crassus has left most of his army in place. From what I could see, they're patrolling the whole area.'

Ariadne closed her eyes. Was it worth risking Maron's safety by returning to the battlefield? What real chance was there that Spartacus had survived?

Navio's next words struck like a lightning bolt. 'They've taken about six thousand prisoners.'

'That many?' cried Carbo, staring at Navio in horror.

'Apparently so. I heard some patrolling legionaries talking when I was hiding among the bodies. On Crassus' orders, they are to be marched to Capua and crucified on the Via Appia, all the way to Rome.'

In that instant, every terrible detail of Ariadne's dream came back to her. It was true. Dionysus must have sent it. Thank the god she had never mentioned it to a soul.

That there would be crucifixions was unsurprising – it was a common enough fate for slaves who had committed a serious crime – but the sheer number was almost beyond belief. 'We have to act,' said Carbo.

Navio's eyebrows rose. 'What are you suggesting?'

'I don't know!' Carbo shot back. 'But imagine if Spartacus was on a cross? Or Egbeo? Taxacis?'

'We can't kill six thousand men.' Navio's tone was sympathetic.

'I won't do nothing!' cried Carbo.

In unison, they looked to Ariadne. 'You want my approval to go?' she asked.

'I don't want to leave you and Maron,' said Carbo.

'You won't be.'

Her meaning crashed down on Carbo. 'You're not coming with us!'

'Try and stop me. There might only be a tiny chance that Spartacus has survived, but that's enough for me.' Ariadne's concerns about her dream had changed. What if Egbeo had been trying to reveal that her husband was nearby? 'At the very least, I have to see the crosses for myself.'

'All of them?' asked Navio in disbelief.

'I don't know. Maybe.'

'This is insane,' muttered Carbo, but part of him felt the same way.

'It's more than a hundred and twenty miles from Capua to Rome. There will be regular pickets of soldiers. They might even be stationed on the road to make sure that no one interferes with the victims.'

'If there was the tiniest possibility that your father or brother were down there, what would you do?' she snapped.

Navio's mouth worked, and he looked at Carbo.

'If we do this, Ariadne,' said Carbo, 'it's going to be done our way. You, Maron and me and Navio will go. No one else. It's too dangerous. Atheas would attract attention, and so would a group of male slaves wandering the roads this soon after the battle. You'll have to leave your snake as well. Being Romans of a certain class, Navio and I will get by any roadblock. You'll just be a slave belonging to one of us. No one will care about the baby.' He glared at Ariadne, expecting her to argue, but she nodded meekly.

'We leave at once. It's seventy-five miles to Capua from the River Silarus, and Crassus has a head start on us of at least a day.'

The Via Appia, between Capua and Rome

Crassus had been in a jubilant mood for a number of days – ever since the battle in fact. He smiled broadly as the first nails were hammered in and the screaming began. This is what victory tastes like, he thought, nodding and waving to the crowd. He was sitting on his horse not far from Capua's walls, supervising a group of his soldiers as the process of crucifying the captured slaves began. Hundreds of the city's inhabitants had gathered to watch; in the moments prior, he had bade them welcome and ordered fistfuls of coins and loaves of bread thrown to them. They had cheered him then until their throats were hoarse. Now they jeered and hurled insults as the first victim was fixed to the crossbar and hauled on to the upright portion of his cross. Soon Caepio indicated that the procedure was complete.

'Such a fate awaits every enemy of Rome,' declared Crassus.

More cries of approval.

'This miserable specimen is but one of the six thousand pieces of shit who will end their days in agony. They will die thirsty, sunburned and covered in their own filth, all the way from here to Rome. Every slave who sees them will put any thought of treachery from his mind.' Crassus paused, enjoying the acclaim that washed over him. 'Some of you may have heard that thousands of the slaves escaped. That they fled into the mountains, and to the north. Rest assured that the rats will have no bolthole to call safe. As I speak, no fewer than six of my legions are scouring the lands to the east and south of here. Any slaves found without an owner to speak for them will be killed on sight.' Another rousing cheer. He was grateful that no one asked where Spartacus was. He'd been spotted near Crassus' position for much of the battle, but no one could remember seeing

377

him after the slaves had broken. He had ordered his soldiers to look for the Thracian among the fallen, but searching for one man amidst ten thousand corpses was no easy feat. Given the Thracian's predilection for leading from the front, it seemed unlikely that he had survived. However, despite his best efforts, Crassus had no proof. This irked him immensely.

'The rabble that went north will get soon a nasty surprise. Pompey and his soldiers have reached Italy, and no doubt they will give the scum short shrift.' He was pleased that the crowd's response was a trace more muted than it had been for his announcements.

In his benevolence, Crassus even wished Pompey well with his tiny 'mission'. What would be remembered was *his* glorious effort in crushing Spartacus' main army, not the pathetic part played by his rival in mopping up a fraction of those who had survived. Lucullus' legions would have nothing to do at all. It *was* unfortunate that Pompey was closer to Rome than he was. He longed to ride to the capital at once, to ensure that his side of the story was heard first. Crassus could almost hear the adulation of the city's population and the fawning thanks of the senators. But his triumphal arrival would have to wait. Despite his claims that the rebellion was over, there was still some fighting going on. Some of the slaves had not given up. The back of their resistance had to be broken before he could entirely relax.

There would be undoubted advantages to marching on Rome *after* the completion of the six thousand crucifixions, when the spectacle was complete. Crassus could not think of a better way to impress the populations of Latium and Samnium. Everywhere he went, crowds would come to see him. The sight would cement his reputation. People would speak of the gruesome display for years to come: it would be the greatest number of crucifixions that the world had ever seen and would show the Republic that he was the man to lead it into the future. The consulship for next year beckoned.

'Ready for the next one, sir?' asked Caepio.

'Indeed. Get the bastards in the air as fast as you can.' Crassus waved a languid hand. 'The parties that have gone ahead are to start as well.'

'Very good, sir.' Caepio barked an order, and a messenger rode off to the north.

Crassus watched contentedly as the soldiers, a group of slaves in their midst, marched forty paces on. He had the feeling that Caepio disapproved of the number of crucifixions – the old sod probably thought it was a waste of men who could be used in the mines, or as labourers for a Roman army in the field – but he didn't care.

He knew best.

As he always had.

It had taken the trio six days to reach Capua, better time than Carbo had expected. Carrying Maron had proved to be exhausting for Ariadne, and their initial progress had been much slower than he'd wanted. His purchase of a mule from a farm on the second day had been a godsend. The beast had been able to carry not just the baby, but their gear and, underneath it, their swords. Previously, they had been risking everything by wearing the weapons under their cloaks. The remaining miles to Capua had been covered at a good pace, and they had been ignored by the groups of legionaries and military wagons travelling the road. They had stayed in wayside inns. Ariadne and Maron had slept in Carbo's room, letting anyone who noticed assume that she was his bed companion. In fact, he had lain by the door each night, a naked blade beside him.

It was the first time that Carbo had been this close to Capua since he'd fled the ludus with Spartacus, and it felt most odd. The last thing he wanted was to be recognised. Yet it would have looked strange to circumvent the city rather than go through it, so he had let Navio take the lead. He had followed, his gaze directed at the rutted surface of the road. Ariadne had taken up the rear with the mule.

In the event, they had crossed from Capua's southern gate to its northern without any difficulty. Now they were shuffling along with everyone else, in the queue to get out of the city. Carbo had had plenty of time to imagine what he would see when he emerged on to the Via Appia. The moment was at hand, and he felt sick. How many of the wretches would still be alive? How many would he recognise? Was it possible that they would find Spartacus?

Before long, they had passed under the large archway that led out of Capua. The practice of banning construction close to the walls had long since been discarded. Here was prime commercial territory, through which a captive audience – the passers-by – daily walked or rode in their hundreds.

As well as restaurants and watering holes, there were businesses of every type: carpenters and wheelwrights, fullers and potters. Butchers, bakers and vendors of wine and sweetmeats. Scribes, whoremasters and slave dealers. Carbo could have pointed out the position of each even if he'd been blindfolded. This was where he'd grown up. And so it was that he knew when the buildings would end.

When the crosses would begin.

They had already discussed what to do once the ordeal began. Walking slowly would not be difficult, or regarded as strange. The road would be busy, and everyone would be gawping at the crucified men. Studying the victims would not considered unusual either, as long as they didn't go too close, or linger unnecessarily. If any of the trio saw someone that they knew, they were to look away in case the unfortunate recognised them and called out. Nothing was to be said until they were safely beyond the man in question. Extra care was to be taken if there were soldiers about. All three knew now that they would travel to the gates of Rome itself just to be sure that Spartacus wasn't one of the six thousand soldiers captured by Crassus.

Although Carbo had steeled himself for the sight of the first cross, he still couldn't stop a little gasp from escaping his lips when it appeared. Navio stiffened, but he quickly shuffled on. Carbo was grateful not to recognise the brown-haired, stocky man who hung naked before him, his bloody feet nailed just a handsbreadth from the ground. Mercifully, the victim was already dead, but his face was twisted in a final rictus of suffering. The first flies of the season swarmed around him, attracted by the ripe odour. A group of people clustered around the cross, holding their noses and making crude jokes. A small boy poked at the corpse's penis with a stick and giggled.

'They scourged him,' said Navio in a conversational tone.

For the first time, Carbo noticed the red lines that extended around from the man's back. The streaks of shit that had run down the wooden post from the man's arse. He longed to drive the onlookers away, cuff the boy around the head, cut the poor bastard down and give him a decent burial, but of course he did nothing. He glanced at Ariadne, whose lips were moving in anguished, silent prayer. Her eyes flashed to his. 'Ignore me. I shall be all right,' she whispered.

Carbo gave her a tight nod. Thankfully, Maron was asleep.

The second body was forty paces down the Via Appia, on the opposite side. Carbo didn't know this victim either. The third man, another stranger, was on the same side as the first. In a savage indication of what was to come, his cross was also two score paces from the second. The moment that Carbo realised, his eyes moved to the front. The crucified men ran as far as the eye could see, every forty steps, on alternate sides of the road. His mind struggled to take in the horror. The grisly exhibition would continue the entire way to Rome.

The trio walked on, mesmerised by the bodies and the smell, and the revolting magnitude of Crassus' display. The crosses marched on, uncaring of the landscape. They were present on the straight stretches, the bends, on the slopes of the hills, even in the villages. They lined the road when it was bordered by vineyards and fields, where gangs of slaves worked under the close supervision of their vilici. They ran under the aqueduct that bridged the Via Appia, carrying water from the Apennines to Capua. Their presence had already become the norm. Farmers drove their carts along, scarcely looking at the bodies. Merchants were more interested in ensuring that their mules kept up a steady pace. The slaves who were on their way to market or repairing the road kept their gaze averted. Only the children on their way to their lessons or running errands seemed uniformly fascinated.

The horror deepened for the trio when they came upon the first living man, a once strapping figure who was being guarded by a pair of bored-looking legionaries. Carbo offered up a prayer of thanks. He didn't know the luckless creature – they had recognised none of the victims so far – but he clearly didn't have long for this world. They dared not approach, passing by with the most casual of glances.

Things grew even worse when Carbo noticed a body with a sword cut on his left arm. It would have prevented the man from holding himself up at all, and granted him a quick death. 'Could that be from the battle?'

'Maybe.' Navio sounded as tormented as Carbo felt. 'But he's the first wounded one I've seen.'

Carbo told himself that this meant Spartacus could not be on a cross. The injured would have died on the battlefield. He hoped that Ariadne thought the same.

Ariadne had heard about crucifixion, but she had never seen the practice with her own eyes. By the time the sun began to set, she had seen it hundreds of times over. The reality of it would live with her until her dying day. The tortured expressions on the faces of the dead. Their cracked lips. Their vacant, staring eyes, which seemed to blame her for their deaths. The wounds from the scourging inflicted on them as they had marched. Their gas-filled bulging bellies. Laced through the stink of their piss and shit, the overwhelming smell of decay. Everywhere, the flies. The scrawny dogs that hung about, clearly responsible for the gnaw marks on some of the bodies' legs. The passers-by, with their cruel comments. Every two miles, the soldiers on guard, so inured to the scene that they no longer even looked at the crucified men.

How could she have thought the reality would not be as bad as her nightmare?

Ariadne didn't want to journey all the way to Rome, past so much suffering. Yet she had to. They had seen a handful of prisoners who still lived. These few were enough to keep her doubt alive. Regardless of the horror, she would never be able to live with herself, or look Maron in the eye when he grew older, if she hadn't checked every last crucified man. Her husband deserved no less respect. So she walked on, in a daze of revulsion at what Crassus had done. They had heard that the general was some two days' march ahead of them, supervising the erection of many of the crosses himself. *The whoreson.*

'Help me, please.'

At first, Ariadne thought it was Carbo's voice. Then she heard it again, from her left. Shock filled her as she realised that the wretch on the nearest cross had spoken. *Gods above, no!* A quick glance up and down the road revealed that there was no one about. 'Navio, keep a look out. Carbo, get over here!' Even as he turned, Ariadne was darting to the man's side. 'Egbeo?'

The big Thracian's head lifted. He showed no sign of recognising her. 'Help. Water.'

Carbo fumbled the strap of his water carrier from around his neck. Uncapping it, he held it to Egbeo's mouth. The Thracian was so weak that most of the liquid dribbled back out of his mouth. Carbo persisted, but Egbeo didn't seem able to swallow. Eventually he gave up, and Egbeo's head slumped back down.

'He's nearly gone,' whispered Ariadne.

Carbo's face was full of helpless rage. 'Look.' He pointed at the nails transfixing Egbeo's wrists, which had been driven in flush with his flesh to make them impossible to remove. 'We can't even take the poor creature down to let him die a more natural death.'

A sharp whistle from Navio. 'Someone's coming!'

Ariadne reached out and touched Egbeo's face. 'The Rider is waiting for you. Go well. We shall always remember you.' She saw Carbo reach for his dagger. 'No! If you're seen doing that, we'll have every legionary within twenty miles after us. You can come back later, when it's dark.'

'He'll be dead by then.'

'He's almost dead now,' hissed Ariadne.

Carbo's fingers fell reluctantly to his side.

'Come on.' Without looking at Egbeo again, Ariadne hurried back to the mule, which was grazing the grass on the verge.

They moved off. Soon they encountered the small party that Navio had spotted. The travellers passed by with cordial greetings. At once the trio's eyes returned to Egbeo. His head seemed to have lifted, which made walking away even harder. Yet Carbo was right. By the time darkness fell, Egbeo would have passed into the otherworld. It felt cruel beyond belief leaving him to die alone, on a cross, but to have done otherwise would have risked all of their lives. Egbeo would have understood. Or so she hoped.

If Spartacus had known that so many of his soldiers would die in such a manner, would he have crossed the Alps? she wondered. The answer was still a resounding 'No'. He had known throughout what might happen. Wasn't that half the reason he had staged the munus with the Roman prisoners?

'Marcion!' cried Carbo. He tore to the far side of the road, where a black-haired man with deep-set eyes hung from a cross. Rank-smelling liquid ran from a terrible cut in his belly.

Checking that the travellers had gone around the next bend, Ariadne and Navio followed.

'He's still alive,' whispered Carbo. He reached out and brushed the hair that hung over Marcion's face. 'Can you hear me? It is I, Carbo, who stood near you during the battle.'

Ariadne paled. *Near Spartacus too, then.*

Marcion's breathing, which was loud and rasping, checked. After a moment, his eyelids flickered. A low moan left his mouth.

Carbo stroked his cheek as tenderly as he might a baby's. 'Two of your comrades are here. Spartacus' wife is here. Your pain will soon be over.'

Marcion's head came up slowly. His eyes took in Carbo, but there was no recognition. 'Kill me,' he croaked. 'Please.'

Ariadne saw Carbo's dagger rise. This time, she couldn't bring herself to order him to put it away.

'Elysium awaits,' whispered Carbo. 'Just answer me one question.'

Marcion's grunt might have been a 'Yes' or a 'No'.

'Did you see Spartacus fall?'

They all stared. Ariadne was very aware that behind her on the mule Maron was stirring. That the sun was illuminating every line of blood, every cut and bruise on Marcion's battered body. That her heart was pounding in her chest fit to burst.

'Marcion?' asked Carbo again.

There was no answer.

'He's too far gone,' muttered Navio.

Please, O Great Dionysus, prayed Ariadne. Great Rider, give him the strength to speak.

'Saved . . . life.'

'Spartacus saved your life?'

'Yes.' A shuddering breath; a sense of energy being rallied. 'Soon after, he took a bad cut to one of his legs. Even that didn't stop him, but then three legionaries attacked him. He went down under a flurry of blows. That was when I gave up. No reason to go on, was there?' Drained, his head sagged down again.

Ariadne felt faint. She was aware of Carbo and Navio's grief-stricken faces, of her own knife-edged sorrow dulling somewhat. Most of all, she felt an overpowering feeling of relief. After the battle, she had thought Spartacus was dead, only to have Navio place the doubt in her mind that he might be suffering on a cross like the near-dead wretch before her. That doubt had vanished. Spartacus had died on the field, as he would have wished. In the circumstances, it was the best she could have hoped for.

A glance up and down the road. Thank the gods, she thought. Not a soul in sight. Her eyes slid to Carbo. His face looked haunted. When she looked at his dagger meaningfully, though, he gave her a resolute nod. On impulse, Ariadne unstrapped Maron and carried him back to the cross. 'Do you see this man Marcion?' she whispered. 'He fought with your father until the end. Now he is going to meet him again. Let's ask Marcion to carry a message for us.'

Maron gurgled with happiness, unaware of the dreadful reality in front of him.

Tears welled in Ariadne's eyes as she went up on tiptoe to reach Marcion's ear. 'When you reach Elysium, tell Spartacus that he died well. That his soldiers loved him. That we loved him also, his wife and his son. That Atheas, Carbo and Navio are alive and as faithful as ever. Tell him too that he will never be forgotten as long as men draw breath in this world. That Crassus will have a dreadful death, the worst of ends a man can have, and will be remembered more for his failures than for what he did at the Silarus.'

Marcion's breathing settled. Ariadne wasn't sure, but she thought that there was a faint nod. She waited, but he didn't move again.

'I think he's gone.' Carbo's tone was wondering.

'He was waiting for us,' said Ariadne with utter conviction. 'Once he'd heard my message, he let go.' *Thank you, Dionysus, for that gift. I am in your debt, Great Rider.*

Carbo and Navio stared at one another, both taking comfort from the knowledge that Spartacus had died in combat. That he would soon receive word from Ariadne and Maron. That Crassus would not die as a contented old man.

It seemed justice of a kind.

'I don't want to see every crucifix,' Ariadne announced. 'We have discovered what we needed to, thank the gods.'

'There's no point in torturing ourselves further,' added Carbo. 'Or endangering you and Maron.'

'Where shall we go?' asked Navio.

'They say that many hundreds of men are heading for the mountains above Thurii,' answered Ariadne. *They will honour me not just as a priestess, but as the mother of Spartacus' son.*

'That sounds as good a place as any. It's easy terrain to hide in if you don't want to be found. Maybe Arnax will find us there too.' Carbo glanced at Navio.

'I can hardly let you go on your own. You haven't got the first idea about how to turn men into soldiers!' Navio indicated Maron. 'He'll need instruction from the best.'

Carbo was surprised to feel a smile tug its way on to his face. His grief for Spartacus was yet raw, but he still had many of the people who had become his family around him. It was a blessing that he could not ignore. 'It will be good to have you with us.'

'Life will be different,' said Ariadne, kissing Maron, 'but it will go on.'

Author's Note

It doesn't seem more than a few months ago that I sat down to write what I thought would be one book about Spartacus. Over a year later, I find myself at the end of a second novel, bereft of the presence of a man whom I've always admired but have come to regard even more highly. During this time, I've lived and breathed little else than things to do with Spartacus, even travelling to Italy to journey in his footsteps. Nearing the end of the second book and the final battle therein was something that I came to dread, because of the well-known outcome. Committing the scenes to paper (screen) was an emotional experience, yet one of the best periods of writing that I have experienced. I wrote the final 15,000-plus words in about five days, often working more than twelve hours a day. The words just flooded out of me and when I had finished, I felt more drained than I have ever been. I hope that the intensity of my experience is conveyed on the pages throughout the book, but especially in the final sections.

This volume takes up Spartacus' tale directly after the conclusion of the first novel. I have tried hard to stick to the known historical facts. Any notable changes are mentioned below and any errors that you might find are mine. Sadly, only about four thousand words about Spartacus have come down to us through the tides of time. As I've mentioned before, this is frustrating but does leave a novelist a great deal of leeway when constructing a story. It would have been good to have more historical material, but it wasn't to be.

Crixus and his men faced Gellius' legions on Mount Garganus, today's Promontorio del Gargano; I've shared what details we know of their final battle. I made up the details about the Romans amputating his and his men's hands. The gory munus celebrated by Spartacus and his soldiers is known to have occurred, although it was my idea to allow one man – Caepio, a fictional character – to survive. Obviously, Carbo and Navio's mission into Mutina is imagined; so too is the manner but not the outcome of the clash against Longinus. A man called Publipor did guide Spartacus and his men through the mountains of southern Italy in the early months of the rebellion, but my fictional version of him comes into the story later on. I do think it's entirely possible that the Romans tried to plant spies in the slave army; this could, as I have written, account for some of Spartacus' failures.

Unless one day an historical document is unearthed that gives us Spartacus' actual voice, we will never truly understand why he marched all the way to the Alps only to turn around and return south. It's no surprise that his reasoning has been the subject of much debate. The subject is covered very well in Professor Barry Strauss's excellent text, *The Spartacus War*. My incarnation of the man didn't want to give up his army; it's unlikely that he would have heard about Lucullus' successes in Thrace, but for me it gave him a better motive to remain in Italy.

It's not clear how Crassus managed to worm his way into command of the Republic's armies, but his wealth and influence would have helped enormously. He was famed for being the richest man in Rome, as well as one of its canniest politicians. It was my decision to describe the young Julius Caesar as one of Crassus' officers, but the suggestion is not unreasonable. He served as one of the twenty-four military tribunes in either 72 or 71 BC, and there is no mention of him going overseas, which means that he could well have been posted within Italy. Given the slave rebellion that was raging at the time, it's likely in that case that he could have served in Crassus' army. There is absolutely no evidence to suggest that Spartacus ever visited the capital, or attempted to assassinate Crassus. I liked the idea of him trying, however, and of imagining: 'What if he had succeeded?'

I'm tired of receiving emails about wagons not being allowed in Rome during daylight hours, so let me set the record straight. That law was not passed until more than forty years after the events related in this book. The speed with which Crassus raised his legions and marched south has been exaggerated, but not by much. The punishment meted out to a soldier who had laid down his sword as he dug a trench was not ordered by Crassus, but it did take place some generations before. The decimation I described was carried out by Crassus' specific command. Spartacus did try to recruit pirates to carry some of his men to Sicily; one of them was called Heracleo. I made up what befell Heracleo and his men; we don't know why they never honoured their side of the bargain. The manner in which Crassus and his men walled Spartacus' army into the 'toe' of the 'boot' is true; as is so common with ancient transient constructions that have not survived, its location is hotly debated. Having driven the area, I agree with Barry Strauss' suggestion that the Melìa Ridge, which runs east to west across the peninsula about fifty miles north of the modern-day city of Reggio di Calabria (ancient Rhegium), was the site of the Roman fortifications. Of course that's just my opinion!

The slaves' failed attack on the enemy defences happened. They suffered huge casualties, but then, spurred on by Spartacus' crucifixion of a Roman prisoner, they succeeded in breaking out. There is no evidence that captured legionaries were executed to fill the ditches, but the bodies of men and animals were used for this purpose. The bitter rivalry between Spartacus and Castus and Gannicus throughout is my invention, but it's not an idea without basis, because the pair did split off from the main army around this time. The exact manner of their fate and the location where they met it are not clear, but they were saved once by Spartacus' intervention as I described, only to go down fighting courageously soon after. Of the 12,300 men reputed to have been killed by Crassus' legionaries, just two had wounds in their backs. Spartacus is then reported to have headed for Brundisium, only to hear of Lucullus' arrival. The site for his final battle is also uncertain, but many have mooted it to be the valley of the River Sele (historically, the Silarus), near the modern town of Oliveto Citra. I have been there, and recommend anyone who's visiting the Naples area to go and take a look. It's quite atmospheric.

As far as I know, there is no evidence for the use of whistles by Roman officers to relay commands. Trumpets and other instruments were used for this purpose. However, whistles have been found in sites all over the Empire, including in the proximity of the legionary fortresses at Regensburg in Germany. It's not too much of a jump after that for me to have one in Spartacus' hands during a battle. A whistle could have been very useful in getting the attention of men who were only a few steps away.

On that momentous day in spring 71 BC, Crassus ordered his men to dig ditches; Spartacus' response was to have his soldiers go on the attack.

The battle developed slowly from these skirmishes. The dramatic image of Spartacus sacrificing his horse is recorded; so too is the bitterness of the combat that followed. Crassus is known to have stayed close to the fighting, and Spartacus to have led from the front, and to have aimed straight for his enemy's position. Although he personally killed two centurions, he failed in his attempt to kill Crassus. Injured, he fought on until he and the men around him were cut down. Significantly, his body was never found (this was why I had Spartacus remove his helmet near the end – so he could not be identified). As was so often the case in ancient times, the news of their leader's death made his army break and run. They were pursued from the field with savage zeal; perhaps as many as ten thousand were killed, and about two-thirds that number made captive. Many more escaped, however, and were pursued by Crassus' legionaries. All were reputed to have been taken prisoner, but we know that is untrue because resistance to Roman rule continued in the area around Thurii for more than a decade afterwards.

The six thousand men crucified on Crassus' orders lined the road from Capua to Rome as I've described. It was the joint greatest number of crucifixions ever to take place, and the horror of it can only be imagined. I recently went to Rome, where I visited the remains of the ancient Via Appia that are still to be seen in the southern outskirts of the city. There is one section that is nearly a mile in length, which is almost entirely intact. Standing on paving slabs with deep ruts from Roman carts, fields either side and with few people around, it was easy and unnerving to envisage the scene. I strongly urge anyone who visits Rome to make the time to see this spot. It's only a short bus ride from the Circus Maximus, and is an oasis of calm after the bustle of the city centre.

Crassus' satisfaction with his victory over Spartacus was short-lived. Pompey, his arch-rival, was quick to seize the limelight when his troops massacred a group of five thousand survivors of Spartacus' army whom they encountered in Etruria (modern-day Tuscany), sending a letter to the Senate to report that 'Crassus had defeated the slaves in open battle, but he, Pompey, had torn up the very roots of the war.' To add to Crassus' frustration and jealousy, Pompey was afforded a triumph for his exploits in Spain; so too was his co-commander; the same honour was also granted to Marcus Lucullus, who had returned from his war against Mithridates.

Four parades therefore took place in Rome in 71 BC, but Crassus' one was only an *ovatio*, because he had defeated slaves, not free men. He must have hated having to enter the city on foot or on a horse rather than in a chariot; to have worn a standard magistrate's toga instead of garments lined with gold thread; not to have had a sceptre. The sound of flutes would have grated on his ears rather than the clarion call of trumpets. Crassus should have worn a myrtle wreath rather than a laurel one, but at this he balked, requesting the Senate to make an exception in his case. This was granted, perhaps allowing Crassus to salvage some pride. Determined not to be outdone by Pompey, he paid for extensive celebrations in Rome and, after the manner of a returning victorious general, dedicated one-tenth of his wealth to Hercules. His rivalry with Pompey continued through the year that followed, however, when they served together as consuls. The bitterness was only put aside towards the end of their term of office, when after a request from another politician, they made a public gesture of reconciliation.

In the decade that followed, Crassus continued to strengthen his position through politics while Pompey did the same by undertaking more military campaigns on the Republic's behalf. Both were very successful in their fields. Their rivalry appears to have simmered beneath the surface, never disappearing entirely. The gradual rise to prominence of Caesar eventually led to the pair accommodating a third party, forming what was known as the second triumvirate. Together the three men ruled Rome until Crassus departed for the east in 55 BC, his intention to win a major victory over Parthia, a desert region to the east of Syria and Judaea. As many of you know, his decision was unwise. At the battle of Carrhae in the summer of 53 BC, Crassus, one of his sons and twenty thousand legionaries were killed. Anyone interested in the story of that campaign would do well to read *The Defeat of Rome* by Gareth C. Sampson, or a novel called *The Forgotten Legion*!

As I wrote in the first book, the list of references for Spartacus is shorter than normal, because of the aforementioned lack of material. Apart from my standard Roman history texts, the main sources I used were (as previously mentioned) *The Spartacus War* by Barry Strauss; *Spartacus and the Slave Wars: A Brief History with Documents* by Brent D. Shaw, which details every little scrap of ancient text about the man; *Spartacus and the Slave*

War 73–71 BC, an Osprey book by Nic Fields; *The Thracians* by Chris Webber, also published by Osprey, and the same author's textbook *The Gods of Battle*, which I recommend highly. The brilliant website RomanArmyTalk.com has to be mentioned too – it's a wonderful place to find out anything and everything about the Roman army, and its members are always quick to answer any queries. There's also a great site called UNRV.com, which deals with all things Roman, not just the army.

There are many, many people whom I have to thank as well. Rosie de Courcy, my editor; Charlie Viney, my agent; Nicola Taplin, Ruth Waldram, Amelia Harvell and Jen Doyle, Richard Ogle, Rob Waddington, Andrew Sauerwine, Jane Kirby, Monique Corless, Kasia Thompson, Dave Parrish, Richenda Todd and Steve Stone. In the USA, Keith Kahla, Jeanne-Marie Hudson and Jessica Preeg at St Martin's Press. Without you all, my job would be impossible. Thank you! As ever, I'm grateful to Claire Wheller, my first-class physio, and to Arthur O'Connor, my friend and critic. I appreciate the friendship and help of all the re-enactors I know too, from the legionaries of Legio XX in Deva to those of the Ermine Street Guard, Legio II Augusta and others further afield in Italy, Spain and the USA. To you, my readers, I raise a glass in huge appreciation of your support. If it wasn't for you, I wouldn't be writing. Your emails, Facebook comments and tweets brighten my days at my desk. Please pop by my website benkane. net any time, where your opinions are always welcome. You can also look for me on Facebook, or Twitter: @benkaneauthor. Lastly, I have to thank my wonderful wife Sair and my two lovely children, Ferdia and Pippa, whom I love so very much.

Glossary

acetum: sour wine, the universal beverage served to Roman soldiers. Also the word for vinegar, the most common disinfectant used by Roman doctors. Vinegar is excellent at killing bacteria, and its widespread use in Western medicine continued until late in the nineteenth century.

Alba Longa: an ancient city near modern-day Castel Gandolfo that preceded the founding of Rome and other Latin cities. It lost its primacy in the seventh century BC.

amphora (pl. *amphorae*): a large, two-handled clay vessel with a narrow neck used to store wine, olive oil and other produce.

Apulia: a region of south-east Italy roughly equating to modern-day Puglia.

aquilifer (pl. *aquiliferi*): the standard-bearer for the *aquila*, or eagle, of a legion.

Ariminum: modern-day Rimini.

as (pl. *asses*): a small bronze coin, originally worth two-fifths of a *sestertius*.

Asia Minor: a geographical term used to describe the westernmost part of the continent of Asia, equating to much of modern-day Turkey.

atrium: the large chamber immediately beyond the entrance hall in a Roman house. This was the social and devotional centre of the house. It had an opening in the roof and a pool, the *impluvium*, to catch the rainwater that entered.

auctoratus (pl. *auctorati*): a free Roman citizen who volunteered to become a gladiator.

aureus (pl. *aurei*): a small gold coin worth twenty-five *denarii*. Until the time of the early Empire, it was minted infrequently.

auxiliaries: Rome was happy to use allied soldiers of different types to increase its armies' effectiveness. For most of the first century BC, there

393

was no Roman citizen cavalry. It became the norm to recruit natural horsemen such as German, Gaulish and Spanish tribesmen.

ballista (pl. *ballistae*): a two-armed Roman catapult that looked like a crossbow on a stand, and which fired either bolts or stones with great accuracy and force.

Basilica Aemilia: a large covered market off the Forum in Rome.

Bithynia: a territory in north-west Asia Minor that was bequeathed to Rome by its king in 75/4 BC.

Brennus: the Gaulish chieftain who is reputed to have sacked Rome in 387 BC. (Also a character in my book *The Forgotten Legion!*)

Brundisium: modern-day Brindisi.

Bruttium: the modern-day Calabrian peninsula.

bucina (pl. *bucinae*): a military trumpet. The Romans used a number of types of instruments, among them the *tuba*, the *cornu* and the *bucina*. To simplify matters, I have used just one of them: the *bucina*.

caldarium: an intensely hot room in Roman bath complexes. Used like a modern-day sauna, most also had a hot plunge pool. The *caldarium* was heated by hot air which flowed from a furnace through pipes into hollow bricks in the walls and under the raised floor.

caligae: heavy leather sandals worn by the Roman soldier. Sturdily constructed in three layers – a sole, insole and upper – *caligae* resembled an open-toed boot. Dozens of metal studs on the sole gave the sandals good grip.

Campania: a fertile region of west central Italy.

Capua: modern-day Santa Maria di Capua Vetere, near Naples. Site of an excellent amphitheatre, built upon the one that Spartacus would have fought in.

Caudine Forks: the narrow valley in which a Roman army was trapped and defeated by the Samnites in 321 BC.

centurion (in Latin, *centurio*): the disciplined career officers who formed the backbone of the Roman army. In the first century BC, there were six centurions to a cohort, and sixty to a legion. See also entry for cohort.

Ceres: a goddess of growth.

Charon: the ferryman over the River Styx in Hades.

Charybdis: the whirlpool just off the eastern coast of Sicily that sat opposite the cave on the mainland in which the monster Scylla lived.

Cilician pirates: corsairs from a region in southern Asia Minor who, in the second and first centuries BC, caused severe problems to shipping in the eastern Mediterranean.

Cimbri: a Germanic tribe who in the second century BC migrated to southern Gaul, where they encountered the Romans, winning several large-scale victories in the process. They were annihilated by Marius in 102 BC.

Cinna, Lucius Cornelius, died 84 BC: little is known of the early life of this four-time consul. An ally of Marius, and an enemy of Sulla, he was killed in a mutiny by his own troops in 84 BC.

Cisalpine Gaul: the northern area of modern-day Italy, comprising the Po plain and its mountain borders from the Alps to the Apennines.

cohort: a unit of the Roman legion. There were ten cohorts in a legion in the 70s BC, with six centuries of eighty legionaries in every unit. Each century was under the command of a centurion.

consul: one of two annually elected chief magistrates, appointed by the people and ratified by the Senate. Effective rulers of Rome for a year, they were in charge of civil and military matters and led the Republic's armies into war. Each could countermand the other and both were supposed to heed the wishes of the Senate. No man was supposed to serve as consul more than once. But by the early decades of the first century BC, powerful nobles such as Marius and Sulla were holding on to the position for years on end. This dangerously weakened Rome's democracy.

contubernium (pl. contubernia): a group of eight legionaries who shared a tent or barracks room and who cooked and ate together.

corona civica: a prestigious award made of oak leaves, given for the saving of another citizen's life.

Crassus, Marcus Licinius (c.115–53 BC): an astute Roman politician and general who joined with Sulla and whose actions at the Colline Gate on Sulla's behalf helped to take Rome. Despite being known as the richest man in Rome, he lived modestly. He made much of his fortune by buying and seizing the properties of those affected by Sulla's proscriptions.

Curia: the building in Rome in which the Senate met.

Delos: a small Greek island. By the first century BC, it had become a free port and the largest slave market in the Mediterranean.

denarius (pl. *denarii*): the staple coin of the Roman Republic. Made from silver, it was worth four *sestertii*, or ten *asses* (later sixteen).

Dionysus: the twice-born son of Zeus and Semele, daughter of the founder of Thebes. Recognised as man and animal, young and old, male and effeminate, he was one of the most versatile and indefinable of all Greek gods. Essentially, he was the god of wine and intoxication but was also associated with ritual madness – *mania* – and an afterlife blessed by his joys. Named Bacchus by the Romans, his cults were secretive, violent and strange.

Dioscuri, Castor and Pollux. The twin sons of Zeus, they shared one immortal life between them, living half their lives on Mount Olympus and half in Sparta.

Elysium: a paradise inhabited by the distinguished or good after their death.

Enna: an ancient city in central Sicily.

Epirus: the ancient north-western area of Greece.

Falernian: a wine from the fertile area of north Campania, the Falernus ager.

fasces: see lictor.

fides: essentially, good faith. It was regarded as an important quality in Rome. The system whereby citizens sought the patronage of the rich and powerful had been around for centuries. In return for loyalty, the client could expect the guidance and protection of their patron.

Fortuna: the goddess of luck and good fortune. Like all deities, she was notoriously fickle.

Forum Annii: a farming settlement on the Via Annia to the east of Paestum, the location of which has been lost to history.

Gaul: modern-day France.

gladius (pl. *gladii*): little information remains about the 'Spanish' sword of the Republican army, the *gladius hispaniensis*, with its waisted blade. It is not clear when it was adopted by the Romans, but it was probably after encountering the weapon during the First Punic War, when it was used by Celtiberian troops. The shaped hilt was made of bone and protected by a pommel and guard of wood. The *gladius* was worn on the right, except by centurions and other senior officers, who wore it on the left.

Great Rider: almost nothing is known about Thracian religion. However, more than three thousand representations of one mysterious figure survive from Thrace. These depict a deity on horseback who is often accompanied by a dog or a lion. He is usually aiming his spear at a boar hiding behind an altar. Invariably, there is a tree nearby with a snake coiled around it; often there are women present too. Other carvings depict the 'hero' god returning from a successful hunt with his dogs or lions, or returning to the altar in triumph, a bowl held in his hand. No name for this heroic deity survives, but his importance to the Thracians cannot be understated. I have therefore given him a name I thought suited quite well.

gugga: In Plautus' comedy, *Poenulus*, one of the Roman characters refers to a Carthaginian trader as a 'gugga'. This insult can be translated as 'little rat'.

Hades: the underworld – hell. The god of the underworld was also called Hades.

haruspex (pl. haruspices): a soothsayer. A man trained to divine in many ways, from the inspection of animal entrails to the shapes of clouds and the way birds fly. In addition, many natural phenomena – thunder, lightning, wind – could be used to interpret the present, past and future.

Hera: wife of Zeus and one of the most significant Greek goddesses.

Hercules (or, more correctly, Heracles): the greatest of Greek heroes, who completed twelve monumentally difficult labours.

Hermes: the messenger god.

Horatius: called Horatio in modern times, an ancient Roman hero who held the Sublician bridge over the Tiber against an invading army until it could be cut down. He then swam to safety across the river.

Hydra: a mythical, many-headed beast with poisonous breath that lived in a lake in the Peloponnese region of Greece. It was slain by Hercules as one of his twelve labours.

Iberia: the Iberian peninsula. In the first century BC, it was divided into two Roman provinces, Hispania Citerior and Hispania Ulterior.

Illyria (or Illyricum): the Roman name for the lands that lay across the Adriatic Sea from Italy, including parts of modern-day Slovenia, Serbia, Croatia, Serbia, Bosnia and Montenegro.

imperium: supreme power, involving command in wars and the understanding and implementation of law (including capital punishment), which was granted to consuls, proconsuls, military tribunes, praetors, propraetors and other magistrates. This power was symbolised by the fasces carried by the lictores.

impluvium: see *atrium*.

Juno: sister and wife of Jupiter, she was the Roman goddess of marriage and women.

Jupiter: often referred to as *Optimus Maximus* – 'Greatest and Best'. Most powerful of the Roman gods, he was responsible for weather, especially storms.

Lactans: a god of crops.

lanista (pl. *lanistae*): a gladiator trainer, often the owner of a *ludus*, a gladiator school.

lararium: a shrine found in Roman homes, where the household gods were worshipped.

latifundium (pl. *latifundia*): a large estate, usually owned by Roman nobility, and which utilised large numbers of slaves as labour. *Latifundia* date back to the second century BC, when vast areas of land were confiscated from Italian peoples defeated by Rome, such as the Samnites.

Latin: in ancient times this was not just a language. The Latins were the inhabitants of Latium, an area close to Rome. By about 300 BC it had been vanquished by the Romans.

latro (pl. *latrones*): thief or brigand. The word also meant 'insurgent'.

legate: the officer in command of a legion, and a man of senatorial rank.

liburnian: a bireme adapted by the Romans from the lembus, an Illyrian vessel. It probably had between fifty and sixty oarsmen.

licium: linen loincloth worn by nobles. It is likely that all classes wore a variant of this.

lictor (pl. lictores): a magistrates' enforcer. Lictores were essentially the bodyguards for the consuls, praetors and other senior Roman magistrates. Such officials were accompanied at all times in public by set numbers of lictores (the number depended on their rank). Each lictor carried fasces, the symbol of justice: a bundle of rods enclosing an axe.

Lucania: modern-day Basilicata, a mountainous region of southern Italy.

ludus (pl. *ludi*): a gladiator school.

lyre: an ancient Greek musical instrument with varying numbers of strings.

Maedi (also spelt Maidi): a Thracian tribe from which Spartacus may have originated.

maenads: women inspired to *mania*, or ritual ecstasy, by Dionysus. Euripides reported that they ate raw meat, handled snakes and tore live animals apart.

Marius, Gaius (*c*.157–86 BC): another prominent Roman politician of the late second century and early first century BC. He served as consul a record seven times, and was a very successful general, but was outwitted by Sulla's march on Rome in 87 BC. Marius was also responsible for extensive remodelling of the Roman army. He was married to Julia, the aunt of Julius Caesar.

Mars: the Roman god of war.

Messana: modern-day Messina.

Minerva: the Roman goddess of war and also of wisdom.

Mithridates (also spelt Mithradates): the greatest and most famous king of Pontus in Asia Minor. In the first century BC, he was one of Rome's foremost enemies, fighting three wars against the Republic.

Mount Camalatrum: possibly the modern-day Mount Soprano.

Mount Garganus: the modern-day Promontorio del Gargano, the 'spur' above the heel of the Italian 'boot'.

mulsum: a drink made by mixing four parts wine with one part honey. It was commonly drunk before meals and with lighter courses during them.

munus (pl. *munera*): a gladiatorial combat, staged originally during celebrations honouring someone's death. Their popularity meant that by the late Roman Republic, rival politicians were regularly staging *munera* to win the public's favour and to upstage each other.

Mutina: modern-day Modena.

Neptune: in Latin, Neptunus. The god of water, he was linked with Poseidon, the Greek god of the sea.

Numantia: modern-day Garray near Soria in Spain.

Numidian: someone from Numidia, the area to the south and west of Carthage in North Africa.

Ops: a goddess of the harvest.

optio (pl. *optiones*): the officer who ranked immediately below a centurion; the second-in-command of a century.

Ostia: a city at the mouth of the River Tiber; for centuries, the main port for Rome. (In my opinion, the site is a 'must-see' for anyone interested in ancient Rome.)

Padus: the River Po.

Paestum: modern-day Pesto, a town south-east of Naples that was founded *circa* 600 BC.

Pegasus: the immortal horse who carries the thunder and lightning of Zeus.

phalera (pl. *phalerae*): a sculpted disc-like decoration for bravery which was worn on a chest harness over a Roman soldier's armour. *Phalerae* were commonly made of bronze, but could be made of more precious metals as well.

Phrygian helmets: these originated in Phrygia, a region in Asia Minor. They had a characteristic forward curving crest.

pilum (pl. *pila*): the Roman javelin. It consisted of a wooden shaft approximately 1.2 m (4 ft) long, joined to a thin iron shank approximately 0.6 m (2 ft) long, and was topped by a small pyramidal point. The range of the *pilum* was about 30 m (100 ft), although the effective range was probably about half this distance.

Pisae: modern-day Pisa.

Placentia: modern-day Piacenza.

Pompeius Magnus, Gnaeus (106–48 BC): Son of a leading politician, 'Pompey' fought at a young age in the Social War. He led three private legions to Sulla's aid in the civil war, helping Sulla to gain power. In 77 BC, he was sent to Iberia as proconsul, his mission to defeat the rebel Sertorius.

Pontifex Maximus: the leading member and spokesman of the four colleges of the Roman priesthood.

Pontus: the area of Asia Minor that included the south coast of the Black Sea.

praetors: senior magistrates who administered justice in Rome and in its overseas possessions such as Sardinia, Sicily and Spain. They could also hold military commands and initiate legislation. The main understudy to the consuls, the praetors convened the Senate in their absence.

proconsul: a magistrate who operated outside Rome in place of a consul (or in the case of a propraetor, a praetor). His position lay outside the normal annual magistracy and was usually used for military purposes, i.e. to conduct a war on Rome's behalf.

propraetor: see proconsul.

pteryges (also spelt *pteruges*): this was a twin layer of stiffened linen strips that protected the waist and groin of the wearer. It either came attached to a cuirass of the same material, or as a detachable piece of equipment to be used below a bronze breastplate. Although *pteryges* were designed by the Greeks, many nations used them, including the Romans and Carthaginians.

Pyrrhus: a king of Epirus who is best known for his bloody war against Rome on behalf of the Tarentines, a Greek people living in third century BC Italy. The term 'Pyrrhic victory' originates from his habit of winning battles but suffering heavy losses of his own.

Rhegium: modern-day Reggio di Calabria.

Samnites: the people of Samnium, a confederated area in the central southern Apennines. A warlike people, the Samnites fought three wars against Rome in the fourth and third centuries BC. They also backed Pyrrhus of Epirus and Hannibal against the Republic. Their fight against Sulla in the civil war was their last gasp. The large number of Samnite prisoners of war is thought to have given rise to the gladiator class.

Saturnus: a puzzling god, who may have been connected with the sowing of seed, or with an older Etruscan god. The word 'Saturday' derives from his name.

Saturnalia: in the first century BC this was a seven-day festival held in mid-December and one of the most important celebrations in the Roman calendar.

scutum (pl. *scuta*): an elongated oval Roman army shield, about 1.2 m (4 ft) tall and 0.75 m (2 ft 6 in) wide. It was made from three layers of wood, the pieces laid at right angles to each other; it was then covered

BEN KANE

with linen or canvas, and leather. The *scutum* was heavy, weighing between 6 and 10 kg (13–22 lbs).

Scylla: a mythical monster with twelve feet and six heads that dwelt in a cave opposite the whirlpool Charybdis, in the modern Straits of Messina.

Scythians: a fierce, nomadic people who lived to the north of the Black Sea. They were tattooed, warlike and superlative horsemen, who were widely feared, and whose women are reputed to have given rise to the legend of the Amazons. By the first century BC, however, their heyday was long gone.

Senate: a body of six hundred senators (historically, it had been three hundred, but Sulla doubled its number), who were prominent Roman noblemen. The Senate met in the Curia, and its function was to advise the magistrates – the consuls, praetors, quaestors etc. – on domestic and foreign policy, religion and finance. By the first century BC, its position was much weaker than it had ever been.

Sertorius, Quintus (*c.*126–73 BC): a prominent noble who allied himself to Cinna. He was given control of Spain in 83 BC, but proscribed a year or so later. His campaign against Rome was initially very successful, but his own defeats and those of his lieutenants in 76 BC cost him dearly, reducing his activities from then on to guerrilla warfare.

sestertius (pl. *sestertii*): a silver coin, it was worth two and a half *asses*; or a quarter of a *denarius*; or one hundredth of an *aureus*. By the time of the late Roman Republic, its use was becoming more common.

sica: a large curved sword used by Thracian cavalry in the first century BC. Sadly, little is known about the sica; it may have been similar to the *kopis*, a Greek weapon, or the traditional Thracian curved sword.

signifer (pl. *signiferi*): a standard-bearer and junior officer. This was a position of high esteem, with one for every century in a legion. Often the *signifer* wore scale armour and an animal pelt over his helmet, which sometimes had a hinged decorative face piece, while he carried a small, round shield rather than a *scutum*. His *signum*, or standard, consisted of a wooden pole bearing a raised hand, or a spear tip surrounded by palm leaves. Below this was a crossbar from which hung metal decorations, or a piece of coloured cloth. The standard's shaft was decorated with discs, half-moons, ships' prows and crowns, which were records of the unit's achievements and may have distinguished one century from another.

Silarus, River: modern-day River Sele.

Sulla Felix, Lucius Cornelius (*c.*138–78 BC): one of the most famous Roman generals and statesmen who ever lived. He was a ruthless man who made himself dictator, caused civil wars and ultimately helped to weaken the Republic, yet he also strengthened the position of the Senate, and retired from public life rather than remain in power.

tablinum: the office or reception area beyond the *atrium* in a Roman house. The *tablinum* usually opened on to an enclosed colonnaded garden.

tesserarius: one of the junior officers in a century, whose duties included commanding the guard. The name originates from the *tessera* tablet on which was written the password for the day.

Teutones: a Germanic tribe who in the second century BC migrated with the Cimbri to southern Gaul, where they encountered the Romans. In 102 BC, they suffered the same fate as the Cimbri.

Thrace: an area in the ancient world spanning parts of Bulgaria, Romania, northern Greece and south-western Turkey. It was inhabited by more than forty warlike tribes.

Thurii: modern-day Sibari.

tribune: a senior staff officer within a legion; also one of ten political positions in Rome, where they served as 'tribunes of the people', defending the rights of the plebeians.

triplex acies: the standard deployment of a legion for battle. Three lines were formed some distance apart, with four cohorts in the front line and three in the middle and rear lines.

trireme: the classic Roman warship, which was powered by a single sail and three banks of oars. Each oar was rowed by one man, who was freeborn, not a slave. Exceptionally manoeuvrable, and capable of up to eight knots under sail or for short bursts when rowed, the trireme also had a bronze ram at the prow. Triremes had very large crews in proportion to their size. This limited their range, so they were mainly used as troop transports and to protect coastlines.

triumph: the procession to the temple of Jupiter on the Capitoline Hill of a Roman general who had won a large-scale military victory.

Venus: the Roman goddess of motherhood and domesticity.

Vestal Virgins: the only female priesthood in Rome, who served Vesta, the goddess of the hearth. During their thirty years of service, they had to remain chaste. Their main ceremonial duties were the preparation of the grain mixed with salt used during public sacrifices, and the tending of the goddess's sacred flame.

Via Aemilia: a road in northern Italy that ran from Ariminum to Placentia, and then on to other towns.

Via Annia: a road in northern Italy; also an extension of the Via Appia, which ran from Capua to Rhegium.

Via Appia: the main road from Rome to Brundisium in the far south of Italy.

Via Labicana: a road leading south-east from Rome to Labici.

Vinalia Rustica: a Roman wine festival held on 19 August.

virtus: a much-respected Roman virtue, associated with courage, honour and manliness.

Vulcan (or Vulcanus): a Roman god of destructive fire, who was often worshipped to prevent – fire!